THE BUREAU OF UNKNOWN FATES

GAËLLE NOHANT

Translated by Maren Baudet-Lackner
and Sophie Buchan

Gaëlle Nohant is the author of *L'Ancre des rêves*, published in 2007 and winner of the Encre Marine prize, organised by France's Navy. Her second novel, *La Part des flammes*, was awarded the 2016 Prix du Livre de Poche and the Prix du Livre France Bleu – Page des Librairies. The *Légende d'un dormeur éveillé* also won the 2017 Prix des Librairies. Her latest novel is *The Bureau of Unknown Fates* which is currently being translated into ten languages and adapted to the screen.

THE BUREAU OF UNKNOWN FATES

GAËLLE NOHANT

Translated by Maren Baudet-Lackner
and Sophie Buchan

MANILLA PRESS

First published in the UK in 2026 by
MANILLA PRESS
An imprint of Bonnier Books UK
5th Floor, HYLO, 105 Bunhill Row,
London, EC1Y 8LZ

A CIP catalogue record for this book is
available from the British Library.

Hardback ISBN: 978-1-78658-370-3
Trade paperback ISBN: 978-1-78658-380-2

Also available as an ebook and an audiobook

1 3 5 7 9 10 8 6 4 2

Typeset by IDSUK (Data Connection) Ltd
Printed and bound by CPI Group (UK) Ltd, Croydon CR0 4YY

The authorised representative in the EEA is Bonnier Books
UK (Ireland) Limited.
Registered office address: Floor 3, Block 3, Miesian Plaza,
Dublin 2, D02 Y754, Ireland
compliance@bonnierbooks.ie
www.bonnierbooks.co.uk

To the witnesses
And all those who keep the memory of the departed alive

For my grandmother Tayou

Oh, the crying of things abandoned forever by their owners,
Becoming degraded in strange hands
like corpses not buried who have no one to do right by them.
He who has not seen the weeping of dead things,
he has not seen or heard in his life any sad things.

Rachel Auerbach, *The Weeping of Dead Things,*
The Ringelblum Archive

Translated from the Yiddish by
Sarah Traister Moskovitz

Irène

EVERY MORNING SHE DRIVES through the woods. As she navigates the gloom created by the trees and the early hour, Irène feels the forest imbue her with something ancient but timeless, something in a state of constant renewal – the dust of soil and ghosts. Guided by the yellow glow of the headlights, she slowly glides from the darkness into the light.

In the little town, freshly painted shutters open without a creak. Chimneys smoke in the foggy morning. Not a single imperfection has escaped her neighbours' watchful gaze. Irène sees the butcher opening his storefront shutters. When she waves, he frowns, and his eyes betray a hint of distrust. She's lived in this town for twenty-five years, but the people of Bad Arolsen still see her as an outsider. The Frenchwoman who's always quietly judging them. Yet another person come to rub salt in the wound when it's high time to let sleeping dogs lie.

She brakes hard to let a cyclist pass, then takes the long road which snakes through the trees. On the far side of the park, modern buildings house miles upon miles of archives and files. You could walk through them for hours without hearing the cries of agony they contain. Or the silences. For that you need a sharp ear and a steady hand.

You have to know what you're looking for and be prepared to come across things you didn't set out to find.

*

Irène still feels moved every time she walks past the inconspicuous plaque. The first time she climbed the building's steps, she made out the words INTERNATIONAL TRACING SERVICE without knowing what they meant.

She was just a girl back then. She'd left her native France to assert her independence, but she'd stayed in Germany for love, following her fiancé to this town surrounded by forests. She'd put a great deal of effort into being accepted here, but she never really had been. Still, this town had become the closest thing she had to a home. Even after love deserted her and she retreated to the outskirts of town, her child ferried between two homes, she never considered leaving. Because every time she climbs these steps, she knows she's exactly where she should be. Her mission here is so much bigger than she is. It demands her presence.

On her first day in post, it was the smell that struck her. A unique blend of damp, old paper, photocopier ink, and stale coffee. She didn't know it at the time, but she was breathing in the mystery housed within these walls, countless drawers, and files hastily snapped shut as she walked past.

Today a chorus of *Hello, Irènes* greets her as she crosses the lobby and takes the stairs. She belongs here. In this hive of activity, where the worker bees hail from all over the world. Their names come together in a mosaic of contrasts: Michaela, Henning, Margit, Arié, Kathleen, Kazimierz, Dorota, Constanze, Igor, Renzo, François, Diane, Gunther, Elzéar, Christian, and the list goes on. Each of them leaves their personal lives and problems at the door. To do this job, you have to be receptive, which means letting go of everything else.

Irène puts her things on her desk and opens her diary to today's date: 27 October 2016. When she pulls up the blinds, grey light glints off a photo of her son in a silver frame. It's the only personal object in her office, which is piled high with books and files. She alone understands the system behind the apparent mess. In the photo, Hanno is laughing. It was taken four years ago, on his sixteenth birthday. She'd been teasing him, her finger poised on the camera button. Afterwards they'd gone out to dinner in a brasserie in the town centre, where she'd let him have a little sparkling wine.

'Don't tell your father,' she'd said.

'Dad's been letting me drink beer for a while, you know,' he'd replied with a smile.

He was so handsome, with his curly hair and proud, dark eyes. Even then, he was already drifting away from her, towards his own life as a grown man.

When he leaves, what will I have left? Irène had thought, though she was ashamed of her feelings. Hadn't she also left her family behind? She hadn't let anyone tie her down. She refused to be a burden on Hanno.

He's at university in Göttingen now but he comes home at weekends, when he isn't with his father or his friends.

She's made her peace with the distance. Her loneliness is her problem, and she's made keeping it from him a point of pride.

She knocks on Charlotte Rousseau's door.

'Bonjour, Irène. I've been expecting you. Would you like some coffee?'

'Yes, please.'

'By the time we get used to the grey and the damp, we'll be snowed under,' Director Rousseau says with a frown as she places a capsule in the machine. 'Such an unpleasant part of the world.'

Rousseau is from Toulouse and struggles to embrace the weather here in Hesse. Her warm voice betrays the inflections of her south-western accent on certain words. Its melodic cadence seems to embody her wild native region, baked by the sun and whipped by strong autumn winds. Charlotte doesn't go back as much as she would like.

'Speaking of which, you're looking a little pale,' Charlotte says as she sips her espresso. 'I've got just the project to put some colour back in your cheeks.'

Irène can't help but smile. Since Charlotte Rousseau took the reins of the International Tracing Service, she's heard that phrase about three times a day. This small, energetic woman is determined to make up for everything her predecessors left undone, even if it means working her staff to the bone. As a result, several of Irène's colleagues have devised elaborate strategies to avoid the director in the corridors.

But not Irène. Rousseau's energy galvanises her. When Charlotte joined, Irène felt as though she'd been living in a dusty mausoleum, and suddenly the doors had been flung open. They bonded over shared memories of their native France.

'Tell me more,' Irène replies.

The director watches Irène drink her coffee.

'Yesterday evening I was thinking of the artefacts we have from the camps. They don't belong to us. We've been holding on to them like souvenirs from hell. I think it's time we returned them to their rightful owners.'

'But when you say rightful owners . . . The owners are dead. At least, most of them are.'

'But they may have children or grandchildren. Just think how meaningful these objects, returned from a place so far removed, could be to them now. Like words from beyond the grave. So I thought of you, and your team. Of course I'll make sure you have all the help you need.'

Irène hears herself say yes.

Even though she suspects the peace she's finally found might implode. She isn't sure she's ready. A combination of excitement and a vague sense of fear wash over her.

She accepts.

And that is how it all begins, one foggy autumn morning.

Eva

At the end of the corridor, there's a door that always leaves a lump in Irène's throat. She still thinks of it as Eva's door, though many people have occupied the office since she left. For so many years, Irène went there when she needed reassurance. When she needed an ally. Eva gave her those things, and a lot more besides. Eva helped make Irène who she is today.

'You don't know what we do here, do you?' Eva had asked, a touch of levity inflecting her deep voice.

Irène often thinks back to that day in September 1990. She was twenty-three years old with a new wedding ring on her finger and the youthful naivety to believe her charm alone could bend the world to her will. She felt like she'd already accomplished difficult, admirable things: she'd moved to a different country and married a foreign man. Now she doesn't quite know how to feel towards that younger version of herself. She's torn between embarrassment and tenderness. *You knew nothing at all. All of life's hardships lie ahead.*

Eva Volmann had conducted an interview of sorts. From the start she addressed Irène informally, using *du,* not *Sie* – an old sage teaching her disciple. Though she was slight, Eva exuded strength. It was difficult to guess her age or imagine her life outside of work. Her face was deeply lined but her bright, grey-green eyes burned intimidatingly. She wore her hair in a tight bun, the black streaked with silver. Her Polish lilt lent a musical quality to her hoarse voice.

Irène was embarrassed to admit she had acted on impulse alone when she saw the advert in the local paper. The International Tracing Service was looking for someone who wrote and spoke fluent French to work on a research project. She had no idea what this project was. But she'd been drawn to the word 'international'.

'Until 1948, the ITS was known as the Central Tracing Bureau,' Eva had explained.

The Allies had anticipated the need for a place like this. Even before the Second World War ended, they realised the cost of peace would exceed tens of millions of casualties, but also millions of displaced people. And millions who simply disappeared. When the last shot was fired, someone would need to locate all the displaced people and help them to return home. And when people couldn't be found, someone would need to find out what happened to them.

'When you've lost someone, you need information for closure. Without it, your heart is like an open grave. You understand?'

As she listened, Irène felt as though she were travelling back in time, to a sepia landscape where columns of bedraggled survivors roamed a world in ruins.

Strangely, she'd been worried about how her husband would react. Why was she afraid her new job would bother him? They'd never discussed Nazism or the war. Perhaps it was the way he brushed it off one day, though she couldn't remember what they'd been watching. A news report, perhaps, a commemoration? He shrugged and sighed. She turned off the television.

'When I first got here,' Eva had continued, 'Arolsen was an SS town.'

'I imagine everywhere was, back then.'

'No,' Eva said abruptly. 'During the war, the SS was the lifeblood of this town. In the streets and surrounding woods, you were more likely to see a man in black uniform than a civilian. Just imagine.'

Irène still didn't understand. So Eva explained that before the war, Arolsen had been a big town, dominated by the imposing baroque castle, its outbuildings and its thousand-year-old trees, which stood like sentinels. The Hereditary Prince of Waldeck and Pyrmont, Josias, became infatuated with Hitler. As proof of his devotion to this religion of pure Aryan blood, he stamped his family crest with the SS's runic bolts. In return, he enjoyed a lightning ascent through the ranks, quickly becoming a general. Arolsen regained its former prestige as a garrison town. The prince had grand ambitions. In the castle he established a military academy to train a regiment of elite SS officers, and a huge complex comprising administrative offices, barracks to house the Second Regiment of the SS Germania Division of the Waffen-SS, and storehouses for the supply corps. The people and their prince were so drunk on their new importance that they would spare no expense to please the SS. Elaborate military parades and weddings were celebrated with the grandest pomp. It was the first SS town, and it bled red and black. Josias had many responsibilities but prioritised his most demanding role: inspecting Buchenwald concentration camp, which fell under his authority as an SS general. He was one of the fifteen highest-ranking SS officers in all of Germany. Himmler was a close friend and his son's godfather.

'The majority of the townspeople went along with it all wholeheartedly. They had always been loyal to their prince. After the war, despite the sting of defeat, they continued to wear their allegiance, like hidden tattoos. Even though their fallen prince had been tried at Nuremberg and sent to Landsberg Prison. Even though they had to go to ground for days, humiliated and terrified of what the victors would do.'

The prince was exiled far from his castle. The only sounds in its echoing, empty rooms were the footsteps of American GIs. The foreigners leaned against statues as they smoked, with no consideration for customs or medieval coats of arms. They disturbed the solemn silence, marching in with boxes in their arms.

'The Americans initially set up the Central Tracing Bureau in the castle's outbuildings.'

'To spite the locals?'

'No, actually.' Eva smiled. 'Pure convenience. The town hadn't been bombed. There were so many empty buildings. More than enough space to house the documents that were arriving by the truckload from all over Germany. The town sat at the intersection of Germany's four occupied territories. It's so ironic when you think about it. Choosing this place to build the biggest archive on the victims of Nazi persecution!'

'I imagine the locals took a while to get their heads around it.'

'That's a very mild way of putting it. In the end they got used to us. We're one of the town's biggest employers.'

In the early years though, the Central Tracing Bureau, which later became the International Tracing Service, represented a concrete threat to the town.

'They loathed us. They were terrified of us.'

Eva gave a wide smile and Irène wondered what sort of life had left her teeth in such terrible condition.

'They weren't wrong, but all we care about is the victims, and of course the people who miss them.'

*

Irène still remembers feeling rather dizzy after that first meeting with Eva. Like a child at a party, blindfolded, then spun round and round. Her town had once been ruled by a Nazi prince. And now, in *1990*, they were still trying to find the people who had disappeared during the war. How could that be?

Eva showed her the stacks of mail which piled up in the office. Tens of thousands of imploring letters arrived every year, in every language, telling of long, fruitless searches. Some of the senders had moved heaven and earth in vain. Others would write, *I know nothing at all. There's nothing but a deep, dark hole before me.*

10

Or, *My mother took her secrets to the grave. Please don't leave me alone with this silence.*

Every letter was worth its weight not in gold but in hope. The words themselves held their breath.

'If you take the job, you'll be processing letters from French citizens,' Eva explained.

Irène considered the burden this would place on her shoulders. She wanted to run away.

'I'm not sure I'm up to that,' she said softly.

Eva looked right through her. 'Well, if you aren't, you can leave. You wouldn't be the first or the last. But it's too early to tell for now. Follow me.'

Eva led her through a maze of corridors and staircases where employees busied themselves with files. Some said hello, distractedly. Some stared.

'Almost two hundred and fifty of us work here full-time. Most people who started with me have now left. The new people are ... different,' Eva noted.

Irène couldn't help but hear the judgement in her voice.

As they walked, Irène felt intimidated by the austere buildings. They were too empty, too monumental, with their stacks of yellow paper piled right up to the ceiling, their walls of shelves, drawers with cryptic labels, and interminable corridors. The paper labyrinth rustled all around them.

They reached a hall with coffee makers and worn pleather benches. The many doors to adjoining rooms were labelled: CAMP RECORDS, WARTIME RECORDS, POSTWAR RECORDS, MISSING CHILDREN, HISTORICAL RECORDS, and so on. Eva explained that the ITS housed all sorts of archives.

Most importantly, documents from the camps. At least those that could be saved after Himmler ordered all evidence to be destroyed. A few faint remnants of Nazi bureaucracy had survived: lists, prisoner registration cards, and registers either hidden by deportees or that the murderers had no time to hide. The Allied forces reached Buchenwald, Mauthausen, and Dachau before the Nazis could complete their dirty work.

In the war's final months, the Allies had raced to search German institutions: hospitals, prisons, police stations, asylums, and cemeteries. Later, German companies agreed to share information on the forced labourers they'd exploited. Then there were questionnaires filled in by displaced persons, correspondences between Nazi officials, a list of mentally ill people who were murdered at Hartheim Castle, records of the number of lice found in the hair of Buchenwald detainees, and so much more. Since 1947, the Service's archives had expanded continuously, like a river fed by a host of tributaries. The first investigators had scoured Europe for documents for the archives, but sometimes the files had come to them in the most surprising ways. The fall of the Iron Curtain revealed even more secrets. Now, placed end to end, the archival spoils of war would stretch dozens of kilometres.

Irène felt small in the shadow of the paper monument. Eva's hoarse voice brought her back to the moment.

'Don't let the scale intimidate you. You'll get used to it. The main sections are the ones you see on those signs. The most important thing to remember is that everything here serves a single purpose: to find those who are still missing. That's what makes these archives so special. And the crown jewel is the Central Name Index. Come, let me show you.'

It contained more than seventeen million individual records. The man who had compiled the Index was a Hungarian pilot who had been shot down over Arolsen and never left. Nicknamed 'the Brain', he had overseen the Index for more than thirty years.

'It's organised both alphabetically and phonetically. That's what's so brilliant about it. When SS officers or fellow detainees took down new prisoners' names, they often misspelled them. Sometimes they even translated the names into German, to make things easier. Quite a few people were impossible to trace because the records featured creative spellings. Look, this card here languished for years, just because the clerk at Auschwitz didn't leave a space between the first and last names. *Leibakselrad* was actually *Leib Akselrad*.'

The Brain had led a team of polyglots, some of whom spoke a dozen languages. For months they worked tirelessly to create a master file that allowed for every possible variant, in every language, taking alternate pronunciations and diminutives into consideration too. Some names had around 150 different spellings.

As Irène scanned the lists, she experienced a mixture of melancholy and excitement. She could already tell she was going to enjoy this. Looking for people, finding them. The tingling in her fingertips was a sure sign. She wanted to be alone with the ocean of names – so many mysteries to unravel.

'All our enquiries begin here,' Eva said with a smile. 'But in order to be truly efficient, you need to get the lie of the land.'

'The lie of the land?'

Eva led her to a map so large it covered an entire wall. Hundreds of camps were marked with red dots. The key detailed the nature of each, the duration of its existence, and a tally of its victims. This map was a tool. A huge spider web depicting the vast swaths of Europe that had been under Nazi control.

'The fate of tens of millions of people was decided on this map. Some managed to flee, others were captured, went into hiding, resisted, or were killed. A few were saved in extremis. And then we come to the post-war period. Millions of people had been displaced. Shifting borders, occupation treaties, immigration quotas; the new Cold War landscape was emerging. You'll have to read up on all this, become an expert. The better you know the context, the more efficient you'll be. And every minute, every hour, is a lifetime to those waiting for answers. Life is fragile. We're all just hanging by a thread.'

After the tour, Eva and Irène continued chatting. Most of the staff had left. The gentle late afternoon summer heat enveloped the front steps and the surrounding park. Eva offered Irène a cigarette and they smoked as they strolled among the trees.

'If I haven't scared you off yet, you'll need to have a final interview with the director. The International Committee of the Red Cross has overseen the ITS since the mid-fifties, when the Allies decided they were tired of being in charge. They originally thought our work would quickly run its course, but they soon realised our mission was far from complete. So they handed supervision over to a "neutral" body. Well, neutral in Cold War terms anyway. And for twenty-five years, things didn't go too badly. We've had a few directors who were up to the task. But then Max Odermatt took over in 1979. We knew straightaway that we were entering a different era. You might as well know now: he demands total obedience from everyone and everything.'

The irony in Eva's voice lent it a biting quality as she took a drag on her cigarette.

'He implemented new rules which put off more than a few people. The first is that you must not talk to anyone about our work here. Not even your husband. Don't ask me why, only he knows. Maybe he always dreamt of becoming a CIA agent as a child. If you're the sort of person who has to tell your husband everything, this isn't the job for you. But that would be a shame, I have a good feeling about you.'

Irène actually liked the thought of hiding the nature of her work from her husband. It would be much simpler to say 'My employer requires absolute confidentiality' to avoid any sort of disagreement.

It was only when Eva rolled up her sleeves to feel the last rays of sunshine on her arms that Irène noticed the tattoo. She quickly averted her eyes, not wanting to upset her. But Eva caught her and answered the unspoken question. 'Auschwitz. They took everything from me but my life.'

Irène felt paralysed, unsure what to say. Maybe Eva didn't expect a response, since she simply took a final drag on her cigarette and tossed the butt. In all their years working together, they would never mention Eva's past again.

Irène can't forgive herself for this. For so long she told herself that Eva preferred her privacy. When she finally realised their silence was protecting her, not Eva, it was too late.

And now, every time Irène thinks of Eva, every time she misses her, it's too late.

Teodor

Irène surveys the boxes stored in big metal cabinets. She opens a few, then closes them again. Each of them has a label with a number and a short summary. Nearly three thousand objects are stored here, sheltered from the light. The staff wear gloves and handle them with utmost caution.

The objects are old and worn. Like the many foggy watch faces whose hands stopped one morning in 1942. Or perhaps on a rainy afternoon the following spring, or on a cold winter night in 1944. All they can tell us for certain is when they stopped ticking, the same way a heart stops beating. What the objects meant to their owners – control over their own time and lives – has lost all meaning.

Other boxes contain empty wallets. On the pages of a diary, a few words in a foreign language. Maybe they resound with the anguish someone felt that day, with their urgent need to stay alive. Irène could have them translated, but no one would really be able to tell her what they meant to the person who wrote them. To the person who was stripped as they entered the camp.

There are also plain wedding rings, which hadn't left the finger of the husband or wife since their wedding day.

Engraved signet rings. Overwrought, outdated costume jewellery. A pair of broken glasses.

These items have no monetary value. Anything that could be sold was stolen and never returned. These modest objects, which betray their owners' humble backgrounds, are what remains. Objects scorned by the murderers. When their owners were forced out of their homes and into the unknown, they carried with them these precious yet portable things. Identity papers, talismans, and sentimental objects. Reminders of the life they hoped to find intact after they were arrested, tortured, thrown into cells, and packed into trains.

The majority belong to Neuengamme and Dachau prisoners. Political prisoners, people labelled 'asocial' and 'homosexuals', and forced labourers. When they entered the camps, their belongings were sent to a warehouse.

It was rare for Jews to enjoy that privilege. Most of them were killed as soon as they arrived. Everything they owned was plundered and funnelled back into the Nazi war machine. Even their hair, their gold teeth, and the fat from their dead bodies.

The ITS inherited almost four thousand items in the early sixties. A thousand were returned at the time.

Here people say that the objects waiting to be reunited with their owners are in purgatory.

Irène feels these objects call to her. She has to choose one. Or be chosen.

She decides on a small puppet, whose faded fabric is fraying. It's a Pierrot in traditional costume – once all white but now mostly grey – complete with a stiff ruff and a black cap sewn directly to its head. It's the size of a man's hand and seems out of place among the watches and wedding rings. A relic of childhood.

Irène dons her white gloves like a second skin, then carefully lifts the doll from its box and lays it on her desk, which is bathed in milky light. As chance would have it, this box states the owner's name: Teodor Masurek. This is all he owned when he arrived at Neuengamme. Irène imagines the child sobbing as his fabric companion, who comforted him during the long, terrifying journey, is ripped from his hands. It's so small he could have hidden it in his pocket. She thinks of the stuffed rabbit her son dragged everywhere he went as a child. Of the smelly, worn ear he would suck to get to sleep. After the divorce, Hanno couldn't sleep when her ex-husband forgot to pack that rabbit.

Who were you, Teodor? Does anyone still remember you? There were so many ways of killing people in those camps. Some as efficient as possible. Others more inventive. The person who gave you this Pierrot is long dead. But might there still be someone who holds you dear? A younger brother, perhaps, a cousin?

Irène queries the Central Index. Since 2007, when the archives were opened to external researchers, most of their records have been digitised. She finds five hundred Masureks. Two from Belarus, the rest from Poland. But only one Teodor, born on 7 June 1929. When he was sent to Buchenwald in September 1942, he was thirteen. A kid. Under reason for admission the clerk wrote *Thief*.

Irène zooms in on the photo. He's thin with olive skin, sharp features, bright eyes, and tousled light-brown hair. He was five foot six. The scar beneath his chin was a useful identifying feature. He was from a Polish village called Izabelin. Irène finds it on Google Maps, about a dozen miles from Warsaw. The card states his mother's name, Elzbieta, but there is no mention of a father.

Could he have got hold of the puppet inside the camp? His card says he spent eighteen months there before he was moved to Neuengamme.

Another document indicates he was admitted to the Revier at Buchenwald with scarlet fever, a month before his transfer. The doctor wrote 'high fever' in the margin of a temperature chart that speaks for itself. The infirmary was death's antechamber. But Teodor was discharged a few days later. What state was he in by then? Was he transferred to a different camp because he was too weak to work?

When Irène rubs her eyes, an image takes shape in the darkness. Just before the feverish Teodor is loaded into a cattle car,   a Revier nurse in the striped outfit of a fellow prisoner hands him the puppet, recovered from the body of a child who didn't make it.

But these are just hypotheses. She needs to reconcile them with reality. She needs proof.

*

Irène goes out to the terrace overlooking the park for a cigarette. A text from Hanno lights up her screen. He's

20

staying with his friend Toby and his family, and won't see her until Sunday morning.

We're revising for exams. I work better with him. You don't mind, do you?

Tobias has been Hanno's best friend since kindergarten. They're roommates in Göttingen. Ten years earlier, when Irène was finally able to tell friends about her job, Toby's mother, Myriam Glaser, couldn't believe it. She confided that her maternal grandmother, Dora, once wrote to the International Tracing Service. Dora was Jewish and had fled to Palestine shortly after the invasion of Czechoslovakia.

'She didn't have high hopes,' explained Myriam. 'She got a reply three years later. Everyone was dead: her parents, her uncles and aunts, her cousins. Dora was the only survivor.'

After receiving the news, Dora's health deteriorated quickly. She died the following spring, holding out just long enough to see her granddaughter turn ten.

Irène didn't work for the ITS back then, but she knew it used to take years to process requests. When investigators finally got around to responding they would send just a brief summary of what they'd found. They weren't allowed to share copies of documents. Luckily, that rule had been lifted some time ago. So, one June morning, Irène took Myriam to the ITS to show her the traces her maternal family had left on Nazi bureaucracy. Myriam cried when she saw their names on a list of prisoners bound for Theresienstadt. Ever since, the two women have been firm friends.

Irène replies to Hanno:

And here I was hoping you'd cook me a nice dinner.
Give Myriam my love.

This is their little joke. Her son's culinary skills amount to ruining spaghetti, then ordering pizza.
He texts back quickly:

She's going to call. She says I'm too skinny. She wants to fatten me up.

Irène smiles. Myriam's specialities, especially her cholent, simmered for hours, have long been some of Hanno's favourite dishes.

Irène turns back to Teodor's file. She doesn't feel the same emotion with digital files as she does with paper archives, but they save a great deal of time and make it easier for all staff to access most documents. Before digitisation, only trained archivists had been allowed to access them.

Just a few pieces of paper sum up Teodor's life, but there are surprises nonetheless. Irène finds a letter his mother wrote to Buchenwald's commandant. Her farm was in a part of Poland which hadn't been annexed by the Reich – the General Government. It was a lawless area, a reservoir of forced labour, and a dumping ground for undesirables. The Nazis pillaged the territory and terrorised its inhabitants. Poland had refused to collaborate and was paying an astronomical price.

Elzbieta naively hoped a camp commander could be moved to pity. She wrote to him in German, in a style so deferential it was stilted. The words betrayed how much she feared the distant authority of this man who wore his SS runes and Totenkopf insignia with pride.

I would be exceedingly grateful if you would consider my humble request for clemency. I am a widow in the possession of a nine-hectare farm. As you can see from my medical certificate, I am currently disabled and cannot work. And my son Teodor is now in your concentration camp, because he made the mistake of keeping back some apples which were meant for your soldiers. He is still young and did not realise the weight of his actions. I swear on my life that he is a good boy. Before this indiscretion, he kindled in me nothing but pride. He is all I have. Without my boy I cannot tend to my farm. And at present, every farmer must do their best to maximise their harvest.

It's unlikely she wrote the letter herself. She would have asked for help from someone more knowledgeable, someone capable of translating her predicament into words that might cleave open the camp door. The argument is a pragmatic one: every farmer must maximise their harvest. For the German soldiers – the victors are always hungry.

The last line implores the commandant to return her son. Teodor means 'gift from God'. Hitler's men took what God had granted her. And all for a few apples.

Eleven months later, Teodor was transferred to Neuengamme. Still unwell, he embarked on a journey that would last days, crammed in a cattle car. What comfort had he found in the Pierrot? By that point he'd been detained for twenty months. A month later, he would turn fifteen. Irène remembers Hanno at that age. You could still see the boy beneath the emerging man. But deported children were forced into adult lives too soon, their bodies broken before they reached their full strength, their innocence shattered before its time.

In 1946, Elzbieta wrote to the Polish Red Cross to try to locate her son. After the war, after the devastation and fires, the retreat of the Nazis, and the arrival of the Russians. For years she kept her hope alive. In her heart and mind, he was still thirteen, the scar on his chin still fresh. She wouldn't have recognised Teodor if he'd walked through her door. He would have been a stranger, his hardened demeanour a shock. She would have had to forget everything she knew of him. Get to know him all over again.

Later, ITS received her request to locate Teodor Masurek. Investigators spent weeks going through the Neuengamme archives. The search ended in late May. His name appeared on a list of bodies that had been identified in a mass grave in Lübeck Bay. Elzbieta had a long road to travel to say goodbye.

*

As the Allied armies advanced in spring 1945, thousands of Neuengamme prisoners were packed into trains bound for Hanover, Bergen-Belsen and Sandbostel. Laden with human cargo, they were rerouted again and again as the tracks ahead were bombed. The Allied strikes killed hundreds of prisoners. Those who survived long enough to reach Lübeck were shut in the holds of four SS ocean liners docked in the bay. As the days passed, the bodies piled up. One morning, the SS moved the ships into open water and hoisted swastika flags. Then they left on motorboats, leaving their prisoners in floating coffins. The British saw Nazi colours, dropped bombs, and sank the ships. Of the seven thousand prisoners locked in those holds, five hundred managed to swim clear of the ships, but most of them drowned, too exhausted to swim, or were killed by the SS as they approached the docks.

Teodor was on the *Cap Arcona*. The records don't say if he managed to escape his floating prison, if he still had the strength to swim. They don't say if he was shot, or if his heart simply gave out from this final ordeal.

Yet another life cut short, crushed by the gears of the Nazi machine.

*

Irène still has time to call Janina Dabrowska, who works for the Red Cross in Warsaw and speaks fluent German. Though Irène has never met her in person, they've developed something akin to friendship over the course of their many telephone conversations.

It's unlikely Teodor's mother is still alive, but Irène asks Janina to run a search to see if there are any living relatives. As Irène relays the address of the farm, she looks at the puppet and feels the need to touch it. Her gloved fingers lift the greying costume without thinking. Her breathing speeds up.

A camp number is written on its fabric stomach.

She jots it down on a loose sheet of paper. This doesn't add up. She goes back to her computer to double-check Teodor's Buchenwald registration card. The number isn't his. So the young Pole inherited the puppet, but it had first belonged to someone else. Irène is troubled as she remembers her vision. A Good Samaritan must have taken pity on the boy and given him the doll. But who should it be returned to?

Irène firmly believes that if Teodor's mother is still alive, she should receive all that remains of her murdered son.

*

Two weeks later, Janina Dabrowska confirms that Elzbieta Masurek died in the fifties, in a Catholic hospice, and that she hasn't identified any relatives.

Teodor's trail has come to a dead end.

Now Irène has to find the person who gave him the Pierrot at Buchenwald.

Elsie

'WHAT'S THIS?' IRÈNE ASKS, with her eyes on a package covered in black tape which her colleague, Henning, has just placed on her desk.

'No idea, but it's for you.'

She doesn't understand and it irks her. She doesn't have any time to waste. She has to find the owner of the puppet – and three thousand other objects waiting in the stacks, not to mention her other responsibilities. She begins to feel like this herculean task might swallow up years of her life.

She and Henning have worked together in the Research and Clarification of Fates Department, also known as the Tracing Division for almost eight years now. It comprises several teams of researchers who turn back time as they hunt for clues to determine exactly what happened to the victims of the Nazi regime. The focus of Irène's team is to reunite family members.

Henning is meticulous, the kind of man who can spend weeks locating a former Yugoslav hamlet that has changed names several times since the forties. He's so patient she pictures him spending snowy weekends completing six-thousand-piece jigsaw puzzles without scratching his ginger beard in frustration even once. His wife is equally contained, making his twins seem particularly exuberant. Though they work together closely and see each other every day, Irène has no idea what motivated Henning to apply for the job. All she knows is what he's happy to share: cosy, picture-perfect vignettes of family life. Though they often discuss their active cases, which is now allowed and even encouraged, their conversations never venture into personal territory. The reticence displayed by her colleagues suited her well for years. After her tumultuous divorce, it was comforting not to have to deal with other people's vulnerability – or her own. She focused on her work and her son. But now she wishes the polished façade would crack. She's ready to risk it.

She's disappointed when he calmly waits for her to dismiss him.

'I can take care of it if you like,' he says in his usual placid tone, 'but it's addressed to you personally.'

She sighs. The package is indeed addressed to her, *c/o the International Tracing Service*. She opens it with a utility knife, but only after she's had a second cup of coffee. Inside she finds a letter written in German, in a tight and urgent hand.

Stuttgart, 7 November 2016

Dear Ms Martin,

My name is Volker Neumann, and I'm a lawyer by profession. Last year my daughter's history teacher told her class that the largest archive on Nazi persecution was housed in Bad Arolsen and that it helped people to find out what happened to relatives who were deported or killed during the Second World War. I suddenly remembered all this just a few days ago.

My maternal grandmother died at the start of summer this year. She was senile for the last few years of her life, and we had little contact. But sometimes my wife and I would take our children to visit her. She could watch them play for hours.

Following her death, my mother and I sorted her personal effects before we put her house up for sale. While clearing out the attic, I found a lovely jewellery box. I thought about giving it to my daughter, to remember her great-grandmother, but I noticed it was locked and that there was a sticky note on the lid. Do not open until after my death. *I didn't want to break the lock, so I looked around for a key, which I eventually found in her bedside table. Luckily, I was alone when I opened the box. I found the pendant I am sending you, and several pages in her handwriting.*

It's taken me a long time to write to you. I'm only doing it now because this item belonged to a woman who was murdered. It keeps me up at night, thinking about her, wondering if her loved ones know what happened to her. If I were in their shoes, I would want to know. So I finally made up my mind, even though it's difficult to accept that my beloved grandmother participated in such horrific events. If I hadn't read these pages with my own eyes, I never would have believed it.

Above all, sehr geehrte Frau, *please keep this information to yourself. I looked into you before writing. Thanks to you, the aunt of one of my friends tracked down the son she had by a French soldier. She told me that though you're not German, you're respectful and trustworthy. Do whatever you can to help this poor woman, but please don't expose my family to the pain and shame of it. I intend to bear the burden of this story alone.*

In 1943, my grandmother had just turned twenty. Elsie wanted to continue her studies, but her father was a farmer in Derental, Lower Saxony. He wanted her to work on the family farm, but the war had other ideas. She was conscripted to work as a guard at Ravensbrück. While in law school, I discovered she had been tried after the war and even gone to prison. When I asked my mother about it, she told me that Elsie and many other conscripts were also Hitler's victims in a way. That was all she ever said on the topic, and my grandmother never brought it up in my presence. In hindsight, I wonder why I wasn't more curious. It would have been easy for me to access the files from her trial. Maybe I was afraid.

After you've read Elsie's confession, you'll have every reason to think she's a monster. But you should know she was tormented till the very end, ravaged by anguish. She didn't die an easy death. On her deathbed she looked as though she had expended every last bit of strength battling an invisible enemy.

I'm not trying to justify what she did. But I can't help but wonder what I would have done in her shoes, if I had been sent to that awful place. How much leeway did she have? Can you hold on to your humanity in a place where inhumanity is the rule? Questions like these haunt me. I don't recognise the humble woman who cried when I passed my bar exam in these pages. It's as if there were always two Elsies, and they could never be reconciled. The woman trapped inside the jewellery box consumed her in the end, but I'd like to preserve the memory of the Elsie we loved for my family.

I'm entrusting you with this wish, however delusional it may seem, sehr geehrte Frau. *I still think of the Polish woman who was killed. I hope you can do her justice without bringing shame on my family.*

Irène lights a cigarette at her window. This man makes her out to be a stone deity, weighing mankind on the scales of justice without batting an eyelid. His letter condemns and justifies in a single breath. He can't even bring himself to say what it was that killed the prisoner. He keeps to the passive voice, imploring her not to destroy his family. It's a heartbreaking but familiar tune for Irène.

She has no interest in pursuing murderers, but traces left behind by their victims invariably shed light on dark times. Their dried blood still manages to stain the perpetrators' descendants. Volker Neumann wanted to free himself of the albatross round his neck. Since he had no choice but to rely on Irène, he wanted her to know that Elsie Weber had paid her debt. That her sentence had lasted longer than the time she served – until her dying breath.

The smoke from Irène's cigarette disperses in the damp air outside. Her sense of time and the shapes around her blur, taking her back to an Easter Sunday twenty years earlier. The family lunch where she and her husband announced her pregnancy. It turned into a disaster. She can still see her father-in-law's face twisted into a hateful expression. She hadn't meant to judge anyone, but she heard herself utter words she could never take back. Her husband's love began to crack that day, and she went back to being a foreigner in her own home.

The lawyer's words ring hollow in her ears: *she said you were respectful and trustworthy.* If only he knew what she did to her marriage. The chaos she provoked as she welcomed her son into the world.

Muffled noises from the neighbouring rooms disturb her thoughts. The hive is abuzz. Irène needs to tune it out to focus her train of thought.

She closes the door and begins reading Elsie Weber's confession, dated April 1975.

My dearest daughter,

By the time you read this letter, I'll be dead and buried. People will feel free to say the worst about me, and I'll no longer be around to explain myself. That's why I'm writing this, so you know.

When I look at you, I remember my youth. I wanted a good life, just like you do. I wanted to get away from my father's farm. I wanted to travel, to get an education. Some of my friends from the League of German Girls had the opportunity to go east to help further Germanisation efforts in Warthegau, and they sent us postcards. We dreamt of joining them, of being part of the adventure. We were young and idealistic! I pictured myself as a primary school teacher, helping little Sudetenland peasants to become true Germans. But my father wouldn't stand for it. I got my stubbornness from him. Back then, the Party provided opportunities for young women. But I was trapped at home tending cows in the mud. At night I'd dream about the farm burning down, flames licking the sky.

In autumn 1943 I was sent to serve the Reich in a concentration camp. I was relieved to be leaving, even though it was hardly the east – your grandfather's farm was only five hours' drive away. But we had smart uniforms and other benefits. I even earned twice as much as a factory worker. When I arrived, the camp conditions were perfectly decent. I rented a flat overlooking a lake with a few other young recruits. One girl cried every night. But I was tough and resilient. Every week we had shooting practice, though I never had to use the gun in my belt. To discipline prisoners, I had my whip and a dog who obeyed my every order.

The SS men were tall and handsome, and we all dreamed of marrying one. It was the first time I'd seen them up close. As you'd imagine, there were plenty of trysts, but members of the SS couldn't marry without the permission of the Reichsführer. Some of the girls were shameless, but very few got what they wanted in return.

After the war, I was tried by a British military court. They alleged I'd been cruel to the detainees. I was just following orders. We were trained to be strict. Ravensbrück was a women's camp, and conditions weren't as harsh as at the camps further east, but the inmates lacked discipline. Especially the political prisoners and gypsies. The head of the camp Gestapo had a network of female spies who identified thieves and saboteurs. The Polish and Jewish women were disgustingly dirty. The Frenchwomen drove us crazy, and the Red Army prisoners refused to contribute to the war effort. Some of them had even killed German soldiers. We had to be vigilant. Striking a prisoner or two for being lazy ensured the others would toe the line. The first time my supervisor made me beat an inmate unconscious I couldn't eat for days. But after a while you get used to it. I was proud to be doing such a difficult job to serve the Reich. Unfortunately, conditions at the camp worsened significantly in late 1944.

The Russians were advancing. In the east, camp after camp was being evacuated. Thousands of prisoners were arriving in appalling condition. We didn't know where to put them. We didn't have the resources. In autumn, a horde of women and children arrived from Warsaw. Our troops had toppled a Resistance uprising and razed the city. We crammed all of them into a big tent outside the camp, we didn't even manage to register them. The Polish women were filthy and constantly complaining.

Many of them were pregnant. Fights would break out day and night. We had to hit them to calm them down. As soon as the first rains came, the tent turned into a muddy pond. Women and children sat festering, surrounded by dead bodies. One day when I went in to restore a bit of order, I saw a Polish woman who had come to talk to the new arrivals. She told me she was looking for her sister. I ordered her to return to her block, or else she'd end up in the bunker. She had very pale blue eyes and hair so blonde it was almost white. She was skinny but still beautiful. Without her uniform, she could have passed as Aryan.

In January, I was assigned to Uckermark Youth Camp, which had been a reform centre for teenage girls until late 1944, when it was emptied to house our weakest inmates. Uckermark was just two kilometres from the main camp. By then, Ravensbrück had 45,000 prisoners. Orders came from Berlin that we had to make room. The commandant was preparing to evacuate; not a single prisoner could be allowed to fall into the hands of the enemy. A lieutenant from Auschwitz was tasked with dispatching those who couldn't travel.

That freezing winter has stayed in my bones. Whenever the temperature outside dips below zero and my boiler struggles, it comes back to haunt me. I think back to the inmates shivering in their cotton clothes. If they stamped their feet to keep warm during the long hours of roll call, or even put their hands in their pockets, we would whip them. The head guard would set her dog on them. Looking back, I'm ashamed. At night, temperatures could drop as low as minus thirty. We slept fully clothed as we waited for the bombs to drop. For the prisoners, the bombs brought with them the hope of liberation. For us, the dread and humiliation of defeat. Terror at what the Russians would do. You'll be reading this thinking, 'Himmel sei Dank! Thank goodness Hitler and his bloodbath are behind us!' But for us, it was the end of everything we'd believed in. I couldn't imagine outliving the Reich. That my life would continue, with its sadnesses and joys.

At the trial I was asked if I ever considered turning down the post at Uckermark. But why would I? I was just following orders from my superiors. They lied to the inmates. They told them they were going to be transferred to Mittwerda, a sanatorium where they could rest, excused from the rigours of roll call.

But Mittwerda wasn't real. It was just another word for death.

Irène calls Henning and asks for a moment of his time.

Ravensbrück was the largest all-female camp, and the training hub for female guards. In the final weeks of its existence, the staff burned mountains of papers. Prisoner lists and files, execution orders, and correspondence between the camp and the industrialists who ran dozens of subcamps. They were always demanding fresh labour since the workers the Nazis sent them wore out so quickly. The Allies found almost nothing. Apart from a few documents which the Russians kept until the Iron Curtain fell, or documents prisoners managed to conceal on their person. Mittwerda doesn't ring any bells for Irène. Perhaps it will for Henning.

'Are you enjoying your surprise gift?' he asks as he comes in, awkward as usual. It's as though he has no idea what to do with his spindly body, like a tree trunk topped with patches of red leaves.

'I'm confused,' she says, fishing the pendant from its bubble wrap. 'I wasn't expecting to read the memoirs of a woman who worked as a camp guard.'

'*She* wrote to you?' Henning raises his ginger eyebrows. 'Are we in the business of returning Nazi souvenirs now?'

'She appears to have stolen it. Her grandson sent it to me. His grandmother worked at Ravensbrück. Have you ever heard of Mittwerda?'

He creases his eyes in a faint smile while the suspense builds. He enjoys reminding her that he's been here longer. But his little game isn't entirely innocent. Perhaps he's slightly jealous she was chosen to lead the team.

'Did she mention it in her letter?'

'She said Mittwerda was a sham.'

'I admire her honesty.'

'Come again?'

When he first arrived at the ITS, Henning was assigned to the department which dealt with camp documents. One day, he was researching an Austrian prisoner who'd worked at the Siemens factory, which was conveniently located near Ravensbrück. He eventually found her name on a list of women who had been transferred to 'Mittwerda rest camp' in February 1945. The document indicated that she suffered from hysteria. The other prisoners on the list were afflicted by extreme weakness, madness, or other diseases, including tuberculosis, a leg infection, a high fever, weeping abscesses, or diphtheria. Others still had crutches or prosthetic limbs.

Someone else might have been heartened to hear these fragile women were being sent to a sanatorium. But, in Henning's world, the phrase 'rest camp' set off alarm bells. He already knew the realities that lay behind other Nazi euphemisms like 'decontamination room', 'evacuation', and 'special treatment'. So he kept looking until he found a transcript from the American interrogation of the Ravensbrück commandant. In the period leading up to his trial, he had reluctantly provided the names of subcamps and business partners. The Americans showed him a list of names for transfer to Mittwerda rest camp, a site he had failed to mention. The commander claimed to have no knowledge of it, but the stenographer noted his distress in the transcript. The interrogator pointed to his signature at the bottom of the document, and the commandant faltered briefly. It was all so long ago. But yes, it was coming back to him. The camp was in Silesia. The transfer couldn't be completed because when the day came, the region had already fallen into Soviet hands.

A stamp indicated that the transfer had, in fact, gone ahead. 'That's all very peculiar,' said the American interrogator, 'since there's no such place in Silesia. We've checked. So, let's try again. What really happened to all these women who were transferred to a camp that didn't exist in 1945?' The commander stuck to his story, even under pressure. The transfer must have been cancelled, he didn't know anything more. The Americans smelled blood, so they launched an investigation into the women on the list and found two survivors.

The women testified that female prisoners selected for Mittwerda 'rest camp' were in fact transferred to the Uckermark Youth Camp for extermination. Miraculously, these two women survived several attempts to murder them. They didn't know how their bodies had survived when pushed to the absolute limit. The youth camp was a silo for the old and sick. They were beaten, starved, and poisoned. They were made to stand for hours in the snow, barely clothed, or even naked, until night fell. Every day the head guard would select fifty to seventy women to be ferried by lorry to the gas chamber, a wooden building near the crematorium. One evening, a woman managed to jump from the lorry as it reached its destination. Once she was free, she made her way through the entire camp screaming that the prisoners were being gassed. The SS managed to catch her. But it was too late, everyone knew.

Henning calls up a note on the internal ITS server informing staff that Mittwerda is a codename for extermination. It's dated January 1975. And yet, he explains to Irène, for years his colleagues refused to issue death certificates for women on the list. Most likely because they were still falling for the Nazis' lies. So Henning took up the cause, sending dozens of letters and memos, even laying siege to the director's office, until he finally prevailed. He wrote personally to every descendant and included words of sympathy with the death certificates he sent. 'I regret to inform you of the death of your mother/sister/grandmother. Though this tragedy was perpetrated years ago, please accept my sincerest condolences.'

Henning stops there.

Now Irène has a better idea of the darkness Elsie is inviting her to explore.

Wita

IRÈNE IS SURE SHE OWNS Germaine Tillion's book about Ravensbrück. These days, her books enjoy pride of place. Before her divorce she hid her extensive library on Nazi persecution in her attic office. She had always told her husband that she managed an archive from the war, and he never expressed any desire to learn more. Though it made her life easier, his lack of curiosity also disappointed her. Perhaps Wilhelm felt that a woman's career was tangential, that the centre of her life was, by definition, domestic.

As for Irène, she had worried that the baby, once born, would monopolise what remained of her independence. It took her a long time to decide she even wanted to be a mother. Her work occupied more and more space in her life and mind, and she couldn't imagine giving it up. She read all sorts of documents on the war in secret, taking advantage of Wilhelm's business trips to drive to Kassel or Göttingen and stock up in the bookshops there. Sometimes she would stay overnight in a hotel and spend the evening strolling through the streets, enjoying biergarten terraces, and soaking up the atmosphere of the university towns. She rediscovered the freedom to do as she pleased, to act on her desires rather than suppress them to please someone else. She could catch the last screening of an Italian film at the cinema or read on the sunny steps outside a museum. More than once, she'd even met the insistent gaze of a stranger. In the evening, she'd fall asleep listening to the sounds of the city, still high on the joy of anonymity. The next day she would wake up to pangs of guilt, missing Wilhelm, and would speed on the drive home. She was surprised by her ability to love him while hiding parts of herself from him, like breaths of fresh air snatched in secret. But she didn't feel she was harming him in any way. This job, which was becoming a calling, helped her withstand a feeling she couldn't quite express, the shape of which she couldn't quite discern. Pressure building up just below the surface.

*

Irène's thoughts turn to Elsie Weber, who wanted to escape a fate decided for her. The Third Reich offered her that opportunity. Her new horizons may have been circumscribed by men and barbed wire, but she finally had some semblance of independence. She could exercise her own power over women she had been conditioned to treat as inferiors. Though some of them were better educated or from a higher class, they did not belong to the *Volksgemeinschaft*. In Elsie's eyes they were wild animals it was her duty to tame and subdue. When she saw that Polish woman looking for her sister, she was surprised a prisoner could conform so well to Aryan beauty standards. Thirty years after denazification, her world view was still defined by the bigotry she'd learnt in her youth. Even decades of democracy had been unable to erase the years she'd spent in the thralls of Hitlerian zeal.

Irène picks up where she left off.

At the trial, the guards swore they didn't know where the lorry took the chosen inmates every evening. The driver said he just went where he was told, parked where he was told. What happened to his cargo was none of his business. But how could that be true? He parked fifty metres from the gas chamber and always he kept the engine running to drown out the women's screams. Before long, everyone knew the truth, from the Auschwitz Jews who burnt the bodies to the inmates who inhaled the crematorium's vile smoke, which blackened the sky on even the clearest nights.

I don't want to lie to you, dearest. We were living through the final months of total war. Our fate was being determined just a few hundred miles away on the frontline. Our soldiers were dying by the thousands. Every day the news grew more desperate, so I focused on my task. Even though I hated the head guard. We called her Her Majesty, because she demanded we attend to her every whim. She was vicious and loved to parade past us flanked by her SS bodyguards, Stretch and Scarface. Stretch was drunk all day, every day.

The prisoners sent to Uckermark were doomed no matter what I did. We were ordered not to tend to the sick, to starve everyone, and to draw out roll calls in the cold. The weakest would collapse in the snow.

Sometimes their bodies would hit the ground without a sound – that's how light they were. Given their condition, death was a release. Every evening, fifty or so would be taken away by lorry.

One day, at the end of February, I recognised the Polish woman in a group of prisoners transferred from Ravensbrück. I didn't understand what she was doing there, alongside the old, the sick, and the mad. I thought it had to be a mistake. I thought the SS officer who culled the prisoners from their barracks had been over-zealous. At first I didn't even notice the child, but then I realised she wouldn't leave his side. She was acting like his mother. I found out he was an orphan who'd arrived in a convoy of Belgian Jews. He was a repulsive, skinny little monkey with eyes too big for his face, like all the children wandering the camp. Now and again the SS would round them up. The weakest were easy to take.

Irène puts down the letter and takes a deep breath. She is disgusted by the way this woman talks about the prisoners, especially children.

She feels an urge to call her son. When she hears his voicemail, she leaves a message suggesting he invite Toby to sleep over. 'Pizza and a movie, but please no horror films tonight.' She'd like a comedy, something light.

Irène hangs up, ready to return to Uckermark. It occurs to her that Elsie's words are a perfect match for the world she's describing. The ugly language does the horror justice.

When I returned to the SS quarters, I talked to the head guard at the main camp. She told me the Polish woman had been given the chance to work in the SS canteen. A coveted position. But she'd taken a shine to the Jewish orphan, who had been scheduled for transfer to Bergen-Belsen with the other kids. She'd hidden him in her block and stolen food to keep him alive. An informant had reported her to the camp Gestapo, so they'd put her on a Mittwerda list. It wasn't a mistake, she deserved it.

The next day I watched her. She was sharing her tiny ration with him, spooning it into his mouth. He was skin and bone and could barely stand. Then she took some snow from the windowsill and dabbed at his dirty face with her handkerchief. I was repulsed. I wanted to shake her, to scream that the little rat had no future. But I would have been wasting my time. What did a Polish woman's life matter anyway?

I had a reputation for being strict, but I never struck people for no reason. Sometimes, when inmates saw me, they would dare to ask for a little bread or water. The head guard would have killed them for far less. But the Polish woman was too proud to beg. When the boy whimpered, she spoke quiet words of comfort and gave him snow to suck on.

At the beginning of the afternoon, when the roll call siren rang, I went into a block and caught her by surprise. She was crouched in the shadows at the far end, hastily replacing a floorboard. I shoved her aside and found the pendant she'd hidden. She promised to give me something in exchange if I let her keep it, but what could she possibly give me? I laughed in her face and slipped the pendant into my pocket. She stared at me with hate in her eyes. I should have slapped her. I don't know what stopped me.

Elsie's obsession with this woman was so strange. She was Polish – the scum of the earth to a Third Reich German. Poles were barely above Jews in the pecking order. Irène wonders if Elsie is protesting too much. Was she attracted to the woman? From Elsie's point of view, the blonde hair and blue eyes would have signalled pure Aryan blood. Wherever it was found, even hidden behind enemy lines, the smallest drop of this blood had to be saved. Nazi propaganda hammered that message home. It must have riled Elsie to see the object of her desire demeaning herself further by caring for a Jewish child. Irène pictures Elsie taking the locket. Violence and infatuation hang in the air. Her failure to follow through with the slap, the closeness of their bodies, the power imbalance. In taking the necklace, Elsie is forcing the Polish woman to look at her. She's making her bow down to her authority.

Irène puts on her gloves and unfolds the Bubble Wrap to free the pendant. It's very old, both delicate and modest. She's moved by the simplicity of the bronze chain attached to a mandorla that frames a darkened enamel Virgin and Child icon. Since the prisoner worked in the SS canteen, maybe she traded food for it.

Irène returns to the letter.

During roll call, the head guard made the prisoners undress. The Polish woman was holding the child in her arms to keep him warm. He couldn't have weighed much, but after a few hours, even a feather feels heavy. She'd been smart enough to find a spot in one of the back rows. But Scarface still noticed her and shouted for her to drop the child, cracking his whip just a couple of inches from her face for emphasis. The little Jew boy was trembling. She set him down carefully, and his feet shook when they touched the snow. But it was too late, Her Majesty had seen them. She was a creature of habit. She enjoyed standing across from the prisoners as they waited naked in the falling snow and freezing wind. She would pick out the weakest among them, the ones who wobbled or had swollen legs, the loonies on the verge of a breakdown. She had plenty of time since the lorry wasn't due till six. She marched up to the child, then smiled and asked if he liked sweets. He looked at the Polish woman, hoping she would whisper the right answer. Her Majesty got impatient. 'Cat got your tongue? Don't be afraid. Come with me, I'll give you sweeties.'

She talked to him as though he were a little boy she'd bumped into at a friend's house. But he didn't play along, he looked like a baby rabbit caught in a trap. So she grazed his shoulder with her switch. The silver handle glistened. It was a present from an SS officer, as she liked to tell us. Then she drew the handle towards her. That's how she indicated which inmates were bound for the gas chamber. Then she would shout

'Links!' *and the chosen women would have to line up on her left. If they were too slow, she would whip them. If they resisted, the guards stepped in. The little Jew didn't have the strength to cry out, he opened his mouth but there was no sound. Stretch threw him over his shoulder. That's when the Polish woman stepped forward, her skinny body still muscular. She stood up straight, as if held up by an invisible thread. In a strong voice, enunciating every German syllable, she said, 'Ich bleibe bei ihm.'* I'm staying with him.

I still remember the silence. There wasn't a sound apart from the howling wind.

'You're still fit to work,' the head guard said.

'I'll go wherever he goes.'

Her Majesty stared at her, speechless.

The Polish woman realised she would have to beg. You could see how much it was costing her. She had the pride of a pure-blood German. I wanted to slap her, to tell her she didn't have the right to behave like that. Her skin was marbled from the cold. When she said 'Please,' I could taste bile in my saliva.

My boss was relishing the moment. The one able-bodied woman in this circus of cripples was asking for permission to die. She took the time to think it over, then, with a flick of her whip, signalled to the Pole to join the child and the four other women who were waiting at the side.

The rest of the selection proceeded without incident, though the women sent to the left begged to be spared. After roll call, the remaining women were allowed to put on summer dresses – hardly enough to warm them. The little Jew's eyes were glassy with fever. His teeth chattered as he stood there in a white cotton shirt, its back marked by a black cross. I asked to take them to the gymnasium, a block which served as a transit zone. Until that day I had managed to avoid leading prisoners to the lorry. I knew only what others had told me. None of us had ever gone further than the spot where the lorry parked. Gassing was the business of men.

In the gymnasium, I was close enough to hear an old woman speaking to the Polish woman in French. They seemed to know each other. The other woman may not have been so old after all. Some of them went grey in a matter of days; they aged so quickly. I didn't understand what they were saying, but I could tell it was a disagreement. The Frenchwoman kept saying the Polish woman's name, trying to make her listen: Wita. I imagined she was trying to reason with her. She was still strong, she could survive. The Polish woman put a hand on the Frenchwoman's shoulder. The Jewish boy was so tired he collapsed. She scooped him up and sang him a lullaby in her language, stroking his hair. I wanted to go see Her Majesty and ask her to save Wita if she would forget about the boy.

But I didn't. I knew she would refuse.

As we led them out, the sun was setting and the temperature dropping. They had to line up again, completely naked. 'Doktor Vera' was there. That's what we called her, though she wasn't even a nurse. She wore a white jacket because she'd completed some vague sort of medical training in Prague. In exchange for privileges, she would poison the prisoners or give them lethal injections. She'd also extract gold teeth from the dead bodies. Every evening, she wrote the numbers of those sentenced to die in indelible ink on their chests. That helped with identification, afterwards. This was the first time I'd witnessed the ritual, and it disgusted me. I remembered my father tattooing animals before he slaughtered them. The Polish woman held out her left arm, she didn't want the numbers on her chest. She had a terrible scar on her forearm. Vera wrote the numbers just below. Then the women were able to get dressed again to wait for the lorry. It always arrived at nightfall. As they climbed in, some of the prisoners screamed and fought back with the renewed energy of the truly desperate. That night I watched Scarface beat a one-legged Russian woman until she passed out, then toss her headfirst into the lorry. The Polish woman was one of the last to board. She lifted the child into the truck and climbed in behind him. I followed with another female guard and Her Majesty's SS guards. The driver started the lorry, and we drove through the dark forest. The kid craned his neck to get a look at the woods, fascinated by the reddish glow of the headlights on the snow. Stretch patted the boy's head. He was drunk, as usual. He smiled. 'You seem to enjoy travelling. Just as well, since you're about to go on quite the journey. All the way up there,' he said, his finger pointing skywards.

The Polish woman's glare went right through me.

The lorry parked fifty metres from a wooden building near the crematorium. The SS officers barked at the prisoners to hurry up. As the motor rumbled, the Polish woman said her parting words.

'Du, du bist nicht besser. Du wirst sie in der Hölle finden.' You're no better. You'll see those men again. In hell.

Her words left me winded.

Wita was the first to enter the wooden structure, with the boy. We waited in the truck for twenty minutes, though it felt like an eternity. When we set off again, there was only silence.

My darling girl, when you read this letter, I'll be in my grave, and you'll be ashamed of me. At least now that you know what really happened, you can separate truth from lies. My Uckermark days were the worst of my life.

For the first few years after the war, I managed to push it all out of my mind. I fled Ravensbrück when the Russians came. I hid on various farms, trading my help for a place to stay. My father must have been laughing in his grave. I put all my energy into surviving, and not getting raped. The nightmares didn't start until after the trial. Wita would come to me in my dreams. Sometimes I would watch her go up in flames, her bright eyes meeting mine through the smoke. Other times I was the one being led to the wooden structure. 'Let me go! Don't you recognise me?' I would shout at Stretch and Scarface, but they would just laugh in my face and force me to watch the towering flames.

I kept the locket. I never tried to sell it, not even when I had nothing. I could have made a few marks. One day I put it round my neck, but I could feel it burning my skin.

I began talking to Wita at night. 'Leave me alone. Leave me in peace. I've paid my debt,' I would say.

After a while I began telling her personal things, little things at first, then bigger things. I told her about your birth. Your father's death. Sometimes I feel like she's the only person who's ever really known me. You're going to think your old Mutti's gone crazy. I know I'm a bit of a recluse and you think I'm a bore. You want to get out in the world and live your life. I was the same at your age. But every time I see your beautiful face, I pray to the heavens you will never experience the things I lived through. I pray that life will be good to you, that it will spare you bad choices and regrets, that you'll be happy.

The pendant is yours now. Bury it somewhere alongside this letter. Remember how much I love you. Please forget the rest.

Irène realises she'd been holding her breath as she read the final pages. There's a lump in her throat as she puts them down. She knows she'll have to go back through them looking for clues. It's up to her to return the pendant to the descendants of a Polish woman she knows nothing about, except how she died and her first name, Wita. And the act of kindness for which she deserves eternal esteem: not letting that little boy face a terrifying death alone. Irène can see why the tenderness of the Virgin and Child pendant was so important to her.

Beyond that, she's left with a knot of mysteries. Her job is to untangle them.

Lazar

A BRANCH OF THE old beech tree thuds against Irène's window all night long, like a ghost demanding to come in. She decides to ask Hanno to cut it off the tree. They can burn it in the fireplace the following weekend. This morning the wind smells of snow. The days are getting shorter, the autumn colours now few and far between. Wita has preoccupied her all weekend, even as she talked to friends and watched Hanno eat an unbelievable number of sausages. Hanno hates it when her work leaves her distracted. He says she zones out while he's talking to her. 'You're nodding but you're not really listening,' he says. 'You probably didn't even notice Trump won the election.' He's wrong though. This bit of information has not escaped her attention. Yet another sign that the world is getting darker and closing in on itself, reawakening her latent anxiety.

Henning laid on her desk copies of a few lists of prisoners who were 'transferred to Mittwerda' – the only ones held by the archive. Irène is touched by the gesture. She dives in full of hope but is quickly disappointed: there's no sign of any Wita, not even a name that could be Wita, mangled by the handwriting of a distracted clerk. And nothing at all on the little boy. She reads through the names of women sent to the gas chambers because they were 'mad', 'hysterical', sick, or disabled. They came from all over Europe. Hélène, Hedwig, Charlotte, Magda, Tatiana, and so many more. The youngest were under twenty, the oldest barely sixty. Bodies and minds ravaged in just a few months, the hardiest in a few years.

'We only have a fraction of the lists,' Henning reminds her. 'Prisoners managed to save a few, but an awful lot are still missing.'

As they drink their weak office coffee, Henning's gaze seems to float aimlessly, untethered. He eventually confides that, for the past month, his three-year-old twins have been waking in turns every night. The paediatrician he took them to see concluded, 'Your children are perfectly healthy. They're just anarchists.'

'And I'm an old father with no authority,' Henning adds wearily.

'I admire you. But I'm also very glad to have a grown-up son who can help out around the house and sleep until midday.'

She doesn't mean this entirely. Much about Hanno remains a mystery to her. She doesn't know how to interpret the silences born of his aloof nature. He was so much easier to understand as a little boy. She loved the seriousness with which he formulated his first reflections on the world, and his lisp melted her heart. Her ex-husband was concerned. 'We need to take him to a speech therapist! When he grows up, he'll be a laughing stock!' Irène said a silent prayer for more time. For childhood, with its distorted and reimagined words and amusing poetry, to last a little bit longer, for it to continue reshaping reality. For the first few years after the divorce, she felt Hanno was hers alone. Her pride was so great it was sinful. She shared him with his father only reluctantly, because it meant not seeing Hanno for days. Every time he came home, he seemed changed. He'd behave like a guest. He needed time to transition between the two worlds, a neutral ground where he was no longer really her child, or Wilhelm's. By the next day he would be himself again.

As time went on, Hanno began withholding parts of his life he didn't want to share. In the silence, they disappear: a shifting, unpredictable terra incognita. When he dodges her questions, she feels as though she's up against the 'Wilhelm side' of him. And yet, in those moments she is, without a doubt, the one he resembles most. Like his mother, Hanno needs to distance himself from his parents to grow up. The important part is surely not what he hides but what he gives freely. Some days she wishes he would go back to being the child who didn't shy away from love or hurt.

Her thoughts turn to Wita's ward, his bare feet shaking as they touched the snow.

'I don't have a single lead on my Polish prisoner,' she says with a sigh.

'I know you only have her first name, but you could still try a search. If she were named Jadwiga I'd advise you to leave it, there are thousands of them in the archives. But Wita isn't a common name. It's worth a try.'

'Do you think so?'

This is the sort of task Henning adores. Looking for needles in a haystack. Dead ends awaken the Sherlock Holmes in the otherwise placid man.

'I'll take care of it,' he says, throwing his plastic cup into the bin.

Irène types the numbers written on the puppet's stomach into the Central Index and finds a registration card from Buchenwald accompanied by a photo of a brown-haired young man. His dark eyes, brimming with seriousness, seem to stare past the photographer. The face, which belongs to Czechoslovakian citizen Matias Bárta, exudes a melancholy, almost mineral beauty. He was arrested in Poland in February 1944 and transferred into the custody of the Warsaw Gestapo. A few days later he was sent to Buchenwald. He was twenty-four years old and a carpenter. He claimed he had no living relatives. As his reason for internment, the clerk wrote: *Came to Poland with Organisation Todt. Suspected of illegal activity.* His card was marked with the red triangle that denoted political prisoners.

She imagines him in his striped uniform, leaning in to give sickly young Teodor the cloth puppet.

Who are you, Matias? Why did you write your number on this puppet before giving it to the boy? So he could find you after the war? But in that case why didn't you write your name?

When Matias entered the camp all he had was a jacket, a shirt, a pair of trousers, boots, a cap, and a scarf. But the puppet would have been easy to hide. On a work certificate, she learns that Matias Bárta was put to work as a lumberjack. The SS had quite the sense of humour. 'You're a carpenter, so we'll make you cut wood.'

In spring 1944, he was admitted to the Revier for an infected wound on his right leg. Teodor was there then too, with his high fever. That's surely where they met. At the beginning of May the boy was sent to Neuengamme with the puppet. A year later, an underground network of prisoners managed to take control of Buchenwald just hours before General Patton's troops liberated the camp. Matias's trail goes cold in the upheaval that followed. Was he one of the insurgents? Had he been among the groups of exhausted inmates whom the SS sent on interminable death marches, beating anyone who collapsed?

Irène knows how to find out. After the camp was liberated, the survivors were housed in refugee camps hastily thrown up in Germany, Austria, and Italy, and run by Allied organisations. They made survivors and forced labourers arriving at the camps fill in a questionnaire to establish their identity, their backstory, and their plans for the future. Once it was all verified, they were given the protected status of 'DP', displaced person, which entitled them to material assistance, and help to return to their country of origin or emigrate elsewhere. But the wheat had to be sorted from the chaff. There were opportunists and war criminals trying to escape justice hiding among the victims. So these survivors, exhausted by years of violence and camps, were interrogated. Many no longer had any official documents to back their stories. They had only their memories to rely on, and their minds played tricks on them. The priority was repatriating those who wanted to go home. By the end of 1945, almost six million people had returned to their country of origin.

Two million displaced people remained – those who either didn't want to go home – or couldn't. Some of their countries no longer existed, others were in ruins and under Soviet control. Some of the DPs simply couldn't bear to return to the country where their families had been murdered, a place where their neighbours had pillaged their belongings and stolen their homes. For them, the past was a graveyard. The future, frail though its flame may be, could only exist somewhere far, far away.

Bárta's file contains one of these questionnaires. What disturbs Irène is that it's under a different name: Lazar Engelmann, a Czech Jew.

Frantic, she zooms in on the pencilled answers. Some of them are almost illegible. The date and place of birth are identical: 2 May 1920, Prague. Under the heading 'Other Names' he wrote Matias Bárta. One man, two identities. So was he part of the Resistance and arrested under a fake name?

In the religion section, he had decisively crossed out all the options and added Nonbeliever. Under 'Other Family Members', '*Alle tot.*' All dead.

He explained that he lived in Prague before he was deported to the Theresienstadt Ghetto. Then, in September 1942, he was sent to Treblinka. And in 1944 to Buchenwald. When the camp was liberated, he received treatment at an Austrian hospital. In January 1946 he was living in a displaced persons camp in Linz.

She can't take her eyes from the screen. A completely different story is playing out. Matias wasn't a forced labourer whose bad luck landed him in Buchenwald. He was deported to Theresienstadt then Treblinka because he was Jewish. But how did he end up in Buchenwald? Had he escaped only to be apprehended yet again by the German police?

Treblinka was a temporary extermination camp built for maximum efficiency. In under thirteen months, nearly a million Jews were murdered in its gas chambers. Then the Germans closed the camp, killed the remaining Jewish Sonderkommandos at the nearby Sobibor extermination camp, demolished the buildings, and levelled the ground. They planted pine trees and lupins atop the mass graves, built a farm with the bricks from the gas chambers, and paid a Ukrainian farmer to keep the site's secrets and ghosts at bay. When he entered the site with the Red Army in autumn 1944, Vasily Grossman noted its 'rich and juicy' soil, 'oozy as the sea bottom,' which spat out relics and clues.

The only Jews who left Treblinka alive were those who managed to escape. Some were able to sneak into lorries transporting victims' belongings. Others participated in a revolt on 2 August 1943. A few hundred weakened prisoners stood against the SS officers and their lackeys, all armed with machine guns. Many were killed in the struggle. Two-thirds of those who escaped were recaptured and shot. By the end of the war, only a few dozen were still alive.

Since Lazar Engelmann was most likely still at Treblinka in 1943, he probably took part in the revolt. He was turning out to be the hero of a desperate, epic tale. In the six months between his escape from Treblinka and his capture near Warsaw under an alias, he must have endured terrifying adventures in a foreign country, where betrayal and death were a constant threat. Only to be sent to Buchenwald.

Fascinated by his story, Irène goes back through the details. This remarkable man carried with him a tiny puppet. Then one day, he wrote his prisoner number on its stomach and gave it to a sick child.

Now Irène has to find out why.

As she goes back through his answers, she aims to glean more details about who he was and who he might have become. Before the Nazis invaded, he had lived with his parents in Prague's Old Town, at 6 Kaprova Street. His father was a paediatrician, his mother a homemaker. They must have lived the peaceful life of the highly educated, German-speaking Jewish bourgeoisie, who had long since assimilated. After secondary school, he studied law at Charles University. But the Germans refused to tolerate the insubordination displayed by students and certain professors in their new protectorate. So they closed the university. New antisemitic legislation would have prevented Lazar from continuing his studies even if it had stayed open. He went to work for his Uncle Jakub as an apprentice carpenter. Having a trade no doubt played a part in his survival.

It's likely the whole family was deported to Theresienstadt at the end of 1941, then on to Treblinka.

To the question 'Do you have any assets, in cash or property?' Matias replied, '*Keine*'. Everything had been taken from him.

He spoke fluent Czech and German, and said he also knew a bit of Polish. To the question 'Do you hope to return to your country of origin?' he replied, *NEIN* in resounding capital letters.

'Why?'

'There's no one left for me to go home to.'

The war had wiped everyone he loved from the face of the earth.

He couldn't imagine staying in Austria either. So where did he want to go? Palestine.

On the last page of the questionnaire, he had hastily scrawled an account of his final days at Treblinka, crossing out and correcting more than a few words.

At Treblinka we knew none of us would be allowed to live. The revolt broke out on 2 August 1943. A handful of prisoners managed to steal a few guns and grenades from the SS stores. We opened fire on the guards and set the camp alight. The Germans and Ukrainians shot back with their machine guns and many of my fellow prisoners died. I fled, hiding in marshes and woods. Luckily, I had some money on me. Before I was assigned to work as a carpenter, I was responsible for sorting through the belongings of our murdered brothers and sisters. We took the opportunity to gather the banknotes and precious gems they'd hidden in their pockets and in the linings of their clothes, hiding them to ready our escape. Still, I couldn't buy any food while on the run. The Germans and Poles were scouring the region for escapees, signs were plastered everywhere. I didn't leave my hiding place for weeks. I lived off what I could find. Roots and berries. Come autumn, the weather changed, leaving me cold and hungry. I was so alone. Then one day, members of the Polish Resistance found my hideout. They took all my money and gave me forged papers in return.

Afterwards, I stayed in the forest with them and took part in their operations. One of them didn't like Jews and tried to kill me, so I decided to leave. I hid during the day and moved at night. I wanted to cross the Vistula but avoid Warsaw. One evening I crossed some railway tracks near a village. Polish police were waiting on the other side. They handed me over to the Warsaw Gestapo. Thanks to my forged papers, I managed to conceal the fact that I was a Jew. They suspected me of helping the partisans, so they sent me to Buchenwald, where I was assigned to the carpentry division. That winter was brutal. I lost a lot of weight and grew weak. When the SS evacuated the camp, I was sick. My lungs were failing. The Americans sent me to recover at Bad Reichenhall Hospital.

Now I feel ready to emigrate to Palestine. I'm still young and I'm not afraid of hard work.

He wasn't yet thirty when he wrote *I'm still young*, as if trying to convince himself.

The database mentions a correspondence which hasn't been digitised. Irène will have to ask the archivists at the warehouse for a look.

The final document is his admission card from the Linz displaced persons camp. Irène hardly recognises him because he's smiling in the photograph. But the look in his eyes is devastating, full of the same sadness they betrayed in Buchenwald.

A red stamp shows the card was cancelled on 17 July 1946. The young man had set off to an 'unknown destination'.

That's where the trail ends.

All that remains are the eyes of a broken old man, set in a proud, handsome, young face open to whatever may come.

And the puppet – a few scraps of cloth at the heart of the mystery.

Lucia

Though his hair is dishevelled and he has dark circles under his eyes, Henning looks happy. After spending several days investigating all the Witas in the archives, he hands Irène a list of possible candidates. He's whittled away all the women who died too early, or too far from Ravensbrück, or who aren't the right age.

'I was right, look. Only six could be the woman you're looking for.'

Now Irène has something to go on.

'I've made copies of all the documents I've found on each of them: transport lists, medical notes, forced labour assignments and so on.'

'You're a star. What would I do without you?'

'It only took a little careful digging,' Henning replies. He likes a bit of false modesty. 'Have you found the owner of the puppet?'

'As it turns out, he's a Treblinka survivor! A Czech hero. But his trail goes cold in Linz. Simon Wiesenthal was there at the same time. I'm going to contact the Vienna Wiesenthal Institute for Holocaust Studies.'

'You're right. Wiesenthal was already helping the Americans collect personal accounts for the Nuremberg trials. But you should try Yad Vashem instead. They hold his archives from the Jewish Historical Documentation Centre in Linz. Do you think they knew each other?'

'It's possible. But to be honest I've got my sights set on the organisation which helped people emigrate illegally.'

'Brihah?' Henning cuts in. His exhausted face lights up.

'Precisely. I've checked, and they definitely had people in the Linz camp. They were gathering Eastern European Jews who wanted to move to Palestine. The British were refusing to give survivors visas, so Brihah smuggled them in. And Wiesenthal was helping them with logistics.'

'So you think they helped your man leave Europe?'

She smiles at Henning, noticing his rumpled shirt collar and the freckles on his white cheeks, which refuse to tan, as well as the healing cut on his chin – a nick from shaving half asleep.

'The way I see it, a man who managed to escape Treblinka would hardly be put off by a few British soldiers.'

*

Irène knows next to nothing about Lazar Engelmann. But his furtive figure is etched on her mind's canvas. She feels certain he wouldn't have relied on anyone's goodwill after what he went through. He owed every scrap of freedom he managed to seize to his own perseverance. No policeman or customs officer would have stopped him. She pictures him lurking in the shadows, his expert skills unrivalled. Then he climbs aboard a ship under cover of a moonless night. He leans against the railing as he waits for the sun to rise. His gaze, focused on the seemingly endless sea, is inextricably drawn to the blazing glow on the horizon. The faraway sun of a land where he may be able to live again. He'll never be able to start over, but maybe he can build something atop the ashes.

*

Irène spends the rest of the morning contacting various institutions for help, though she knows her chances are slim. When she reaches Yad Vashem, she asks if they have any leads on a Lazar Engelmann. She tells them he could have emigrated to Palestine in 1946, with the help of Brihah. The more she considers it, the more plausible this theory becomes. When the camps were liberated, Simon Wiesenthal wasn't yet the great Nazi hunter. He was an exhausted survivor languishing in a Mauthausen sick ward. Very soon after, he offered his services to the American Office of the Chief of Counsel for War Crimes, using what remained of his energy to track down Nazi murderers. He quickly realised that the displaced persons camps provided access to thousands of survivors. While they were waiting for their visas, he could collect their stories. But he had to act quickly, while the memories were still fresh. At the same time, he secured forged papers, lodgings, and transport for Brihah. He could easily have been a life-saving intermediary on Lazar's path to Palestine.

Irène's contact at Magen David Adom, Israel's first aid and disaster relief organization, advises her to draft a public appeal for information that they can post on their social media accounts. A Treblinka survivor is not likely to have gone unnoticed. Surely there are people who remember him.

*

Irène spends her lunch break going through the photocopies Henning made for her. She feels as though she could recognise the woman she is looking for at first glance. But there isn't a single photograph in the files. Wita Janowska was deported from Warsaw to Bergen-Belsen in September 1944. Wita Kryziek fell ill at a munitions factory three hundred kilometres from Buchenwald in November 1943. Wita Gorczack was sent to Majdanek in autumn 1942. Wita Sobieska left Warsaw Prison in February 1942, bound for Auschwitz. The following spring, Wita Nowicka was transferred from Auschwitz to Gross-Rosen. And last but not least, Wita Wojcik was assigned to Barth, a Ravensbrück subcamp, in January 1944. Irène's heart begins to race. Finally, the beginnings of a lead!

Just then, the new secretary knocks on Irène's door. A pretty, blushing blonde, who's constantly tripping over herself. She apologises for the disturbance and explains that there's a visitor waiting for Irène in the hall.

'I don't accept visitors. Didn't anyone tell you?'

She never meets with relatives who come to Bad Arolsen. She entrusts others with the delicate task of welcoming those who both yearn for and fear the truth, people who have grown up with shadow and darkness lingering inside them. She prefers to shield herself from their distress, and their gratitude. Irène doesn't do what she does for the recognition. She answers to a more clandestine calling. She ties together threads frayed or cut by the war and sheds light on dark fragments of the past. As soon as her task is completed, she disappears. She doesn't want to be a part of their lives or let them into hers. The only people she can't manage to keep at arm's length are the dead.

'It's just that this woman's come all the way from Argentina. She's looking for information on Eva Volmann.'

Eva.

Irène's heart skips a beat.

'I was told you knew her quite well. But I can ask someone else, if you'd rather.'

Irène can't delegate anything related to Eva. She's the only person here who really loved her. At least, the only one left. She suspects the Brain always had a soft spot for her. Was it mutual? One day she had teased Eva about it, and she'd laughed in Irène's face. *'Du bist a beheyme!* You're ridiculous!' she'd countered in Yiddish. 'What does a fool like you know about life?'

Irène had already imagined that someone might try to track Eva down, but she'd been such a solitary person. The only creature she seemed to love was a mangy old cat. Its death, months before hers, had been a terrible blow. She had few friends, and Irène was extremely proud to be one of them. Eva hated to display emotion and refused to appear vulnerable. At the ITS, everyone feared her sharp tongue, even the director. He had no hold over her.

'I've survived worse than that puffed-up operetta villain!' she would tell Irène, mischief sparkling in her eyes. 'Look at them though! They revel in the way he makes them quake. It reminds them of the sound of boots in lockstep.'

Max Odermatt had taken the reins at the ITS when many of the old guard were retiring. Most of them were former DPs, prisoners of war, and concentration camp survivors who were tirelessly devoted to their research. They healed by helping others. Over time, they began to understand the full extent of the camp system. They learned precisely how and where their own personal tragedies had panned out through tragic or providential twists of fate. They also came to see the hidden ties that bound them to so many other anonymous victims. They may even have crossed paths with the people who wrote to them. The first investigators gave the job everything they had to give, letting their work consume them. Most of them didn't want to leave, so they had been gently pushed out. 'It's time to enjoy a richly deserved retirement.' But they couldn't retire from the things that kept them up at night. They lived for their work. When it was taken from them, their ghosts returned to haunt them.

The new director hired local people to replace them. Their attitudes to the past were defined only by what they thought had been taken from *them*. They didn't want to hear about the horrific crimes committed by the Nazis. The country had been at war, and war justified everything. They were there to earn a living, nothing more. They slept soundly, untroubled by the dead.

Their apathy suited Max Odermatt, whose reign thrived on compartmentalisation and control. The ITS became a secretive place, and silent as a grave. No information was allowed to reach the outside world. Historians and descendants, who had been welcome under the former director, were not allowed past the gate. The archives were reserved for a few specialist employees. The others only had access to the Central Index. Research protocols were long and complicated, so investigations often took years. Eva had refused to leave, but she couldn't get over her anger. By hiring Irène, ten years later, she had masterfully positioned a key piece on the chessboard. Eva instilled her with her own high standards. Irène had been a tool at first, then her ally and, eventually, her friend.

'Tell the woman I'll see her,' Irène finally tells the secretary.

*

Irène finds a young brunette waiting for her in the conference room.

'Lucia Heller,' the woman introduces herself. 'It's a pleasure to meet you.'

Irène is surprised to hear her speak German and asks the woman where she's from.

'Buenos Aires. Getting here was quite a trek. Three planes, a bus, and a taxi. Luckily I found a room just round the corner, at the inn.'

'Your German is perfect.'

'My paternal grandfather was German. He was always making us practice, and there was no room for error with him.'

Irène invites Lucia to sit down. She removes her coat and hat, unleashing her brown curls and a heady fragrance with notes of amber.

'Sorry for turning up like this. I was told your job is to find out what happened to victims of the Nazi regime.'

'That's right.'

Despite the warmth in Lucia's voice, Irène can tell she's nervous.

'I know a few things about my family history. What I've been told, or rather what I've managed to discern. But it's not enough anymore. The whole thing started getting to me when my daughter was born. I realised I want to know who my relatives were. How they lived and how they died. I want to be able to tell my daughter their stories. I know all that, more or less, about my father's side. As for my mother's side, I know they were Polish Jews. My mother's father got out just before the Germans closed the Warsaw Ghetto. He fled to Japan with his wife and children. From there, they made it to Argentina. His elder brother, Medres, refused to follow with his family. He wanted to stay with their parents. Their father, who was in a wheelchair, was a veteran and very patriotic. He couldn't imagine anyone would dare harm him. No one knows what happened to them. To Medres, his wife, and their three children. Until recently, we thought they had all died in Poland.'

'Except one, right?' Irène asks softly. 'The one you're looking for.'

Lucia smiles.

'That's what brings me here. My grandfather would never talk about it. He couldn't stand hearing about

Poland. But my mum was seven when they left Europe, so she remembers bits and pieces. When I was young, she'd tell me stories about her cousin Ewa. How she fought like a boy and hated getting her plaits done for school so much that one day she took a pair of scissors and cut them right off. Her mother took away her books to punish her. They were constantly arguing. Ewa wanted the same freedom boys had, but her mother didn't have very progressive views on girls' education.'

Irène thanks Lucia for sharing these stories, in which she recognises Eva completely. It's as though, as she got older, Eva simply grew truer to the person she had always been.

'She was my mother's hero. My sisters and I had to live up to her example. But we were never clever enough, never brave enough … When I was pregnant, I started to wonder more about her. I spoke to a friend who had lost most of his family in the Holocaust. He showed me a letter his father had received from Arolsen in the late eighties. He'd requested death certificates for his parents, who were last seen at Belzec. Two years later, a woman wrote back to him from the International Tracing Service. She said the ITS had very little on the Jews murdered in killing centres. As soon as the trains turned up, they were led straight to the gas chambers. The Nazis there didn't even bother with registers. The letter was signed Eva Volmann. That stopped me in my tracks! I thought it was most likely someone else, because my mother's cousin was called Ewa, spelt the Polish way. But I wanted to be absolutely sure, and I wanted to take the opportunity to visit Frankfurt, where my father's family are from. So I decided to come all this way. The receptionist just told me an Eva Volmann did work here, but that she passed away.'

The sadness in Lucia's voice moves Irène. She asks her if she knows her mother's cousin's date of birth. Lucia checks her notebook: 30 April 1930.

'That's her,' Irène replies decisively.

One year she organised a small surprise party in the ITS gardens, inviting the few people Eva liked. At the time, her friend had seemed touched, but afterwards she made Irène promise never to do it again.

'Are we allowed to smoke in here?' Lucia asks.

'No, but I'll join you. Let's go outside.'

Walking the sodden paths with this young woman reminds Irène of the day she first came to Arolsen, though the season doesn't match. Today they're shivering in a windy drizzle. And now Irène is playing Eva's role.

'I don't know her story,' Irène says, sheltering her lighter between her hands, 'but she was a fighter. She battled illness, and always stood up to injustice. She was a force to be reckoned with.'

'When did she die?' the young woman asks, lighting a 100.

'Eleven years ago this spring. An aggressive cancer. It was bad, though I suppose cancer is never good.'

Irène studies Lucia's radiant complexion and tries to see the resemblance. Eva's face was more like a piece of dried fruit – all of the light was concentrated in her eyes.

'My father's brother disappeared during Videla's Dirty War,' Lucia says, exhaling smoke. 'He was part of a student group that published underground pamphlets. One night they came for him. They took his young wife and baby too. We never saw them again.'

These words stir a forgotten memory. Irène must have been eleven or twelve. Her parents had bought a colour television, and it was always on. She saw a crowd brandishing signs on the evening news. They bore photos of people she didn't recognise, but she remembers she was struck by the face of a beautiful young girl. The protestors were chanting slogans in a language she didn't understand. Irène asked her mother what the protestors were asking for.

'Their children have been kidnapped, and they're demanding justice. I wouldn't hold my breath if I were them! The army took them.'

Irène didn't understand how soldiers could do such a thing. She looked for Argentina on her light-up globe. To her fingers, it hadn't seemed so far away. For several months she lived in fear of being kidnapped. She'd flinch every time a car slowed near her.

'The year I was born, they set up a National Commission on the Disappearance of Persons to find out what happened to those who'd gone missing. It had been eight years, and we still had no news of my uncle or his wife. All my father wanted was to be told they were dead. In the Jewish community in Buenos Aires, lots of people had been tortured and killed fighting for freedom. The government gave the commission nine months – hardly any time at all. The investigators were meant to have access to all the archives, but the army had got rid of all the evidence and razed the clandestine detention centres where they tortured people. Despite all that, they managed to identify my uncle among the victims. But they found nothing on his wife and son,' Lucia concludes, her voice quavering from the force of her anger. She pulls a puff of smoke deep into her lungs as her beautiful black eyes take in the compact outline of the ITS buildings. 'Is that what you do here? Look for dead people?'

Irène thinks of the barefoot child in the snow, of Wita, and Lazar. She takes a drag on her cigarette and can almost taste her first conversation with Eva beneath these same trees. She remembers the tattoo on Eva's arm, the questions she swallowed out of cowardice. The memory fills her with regret but reminds her how grateful she is for that summer with Eva, which changed everything for her.

'Yes. But, sometimes, when we look for the dead, we find the living.'

Myriam

Lucia heller has gone away to visit the places her father's side of the family once lived. She told Irène she'd be back at the end of the month. Since she left, the constant pounding of cold rain has been hollowing out ruts where car tyres get stuck. Irène is bogged down too. She's growing impatient with her lack of progress.

The Wita Wojcik lead has gone nowhere. She had several frostbitten toes amputated at the Barth subcamp. The resulting limp would certainly have earned her a referral to Mittwerda, but it wouldn't have escaped Elsie's attention. The Wita she's looking for may be one of the other five, but all the trails go cold and there's nothing to link them to Ravensbrück. It's as though her ghost left nothing but a footprint in the snow on that fateful day in February 1945.

Hanno is spending the weekend in Göttingen. Irène misses him, but she's looking forward to having two days to herself. Tonight a curtain of rain and mist obstructs her view of the forest. She lights a fire, pours herself a glass of white wine, and calls Antoine, her former lover and current best friend. The sound of his voice makes her feel like Paris isn't so far after all, like if she just closes her eyes she can hop on her scooter and speed through the city streets to catch the Bresson screening at the Cinémathèque Française.

'Ah, at last! I hadn't heard from you in so long I was beginning to wonder if the Germans had kidnapped you for good. When are you coming to visit?'

'I don't know. I'm working on a new project that's pretty time-consuming.'

'If I had a euro for every time you said that, I could afford a new boiler. Mine's broken. It's so cold in my flat that I've always got a blanket round my shoulders like a sluggish old dog.'

She can hear the chuckle in Antoine's voice. She imagines him smoking on his balcony, uninterestedly watching the passers-by on Boulevard des Invalides below.

'Is the dome lit up?'

'Of course! It's always here waiting for you. In fact, it's looking a bit glum. Must miss you.'

'I'll be there. But first, I need to return a few things to their rightful owners.'

Irène tells Antoine about how she follows clues in the archives, comparing them to the little white pebbles Hansel and Gretel left behind to find their way home. Unlike the fairytale children, she's still lost and frustrated.

'So, if I understand correctly, you need to work out who owned these objects and then locate their relatives? What if they don't have any?'

'Well, I'll have put myself to a lot of trouble for nothing. But something tells me my research will lead me to someone in the end. A distant cousin, a friend . . . someone who'll find meaning in the object.'

'Do you have lots of these to get through?'

'Thousands. We're all working on different cases, on top of the rest of our responsibilities. Let's just say we're keeping busy.'

'Will you return them in person?' Antoine asks. He knows her too well.

She pauses, then replies, 'We're supposed to invite them to Arolsen. If they can't make it, we can send them the object, but it's better to have a proper meeting. It's a very different way of working for us. Usually, we only open an investigation once we've received a request from a family member. Now we're the ones reaching out. It could be a real shock for these people. I'm trying not to think that far ahead, though. You can't imagine how much I'm dreading it.'

'Your old boss would have spared you the turmoil,' Antoine says, amused.

She contemplates the golden hue her wine takes on in the firelight.

'That's for sure. He kept these objects languishing under lock and key. I can just picture his face if he came back. Digitised archives accessible to all. All the projects we've worked on with schools, historians, and memorials. The visitors who come from around the world to see what remains of their grandfather who died at Dora-Mittelbau. It would make Odermatt sick! His worst nightmare come true.'

Irène closes her eyes and Eva's smoker's laugh seeps into the crackling of the fire. How her friend would revel in this turn of events.

'An archive,' Antoine observes, 'is a little like a collection of grenades with all the pins pulled out. Digitising them and ensuring free access is a great victory for democracy.'

The change in policy coincided with the appointment of a historian as the Centre's director. Irène has high hopes for the future.

'As for your Treblinka survivor, you should watch the Lanzmann film again,' Antoine suggests. 'Remember, the one about the Sobibor uprising?'

She thinks back to a rainy autumn afternoon. Hanno must have been four or five. She'd left him with her mother and met Antoine at the Cinema l'Epée de bois on rue Mouffetard. *Sobibór, October 14 1943, 4 p.m.*. They left shaken to the core by the smile of a survivor who had managed the impossible. That day, he had bolted for the forest as bullets whizzed past and fellow escapees fell all around him. When he reached cover in the trees, he fell asleep. It was as though the idea of dying had lost all meaning after that.

'Yehuda Lerner,' she says softly.

Before the uprising he'd never taken a life. But that day it was his job to beat to death a towering SS officer – a giant straight out of the Grimm brothers' "The Brave Little Tailor". He clasped the handle of his axe. It was his only chance, his last hope. In a fraction of a second, the impossible became possible. The blood spilled wasn't his or a comrade's. The guard who'd made them suffer lay lifeless on the sawdust-covered floor, his uniform soiled.

Did Lazar learn how to kill on 2 August 1943? Did he collapse exhausted in the marshes, entrusting his life to the muddy waters which masked the smell of fear? Did he watch the black smoke from the burning camp rise up into the sky?

'Don't forget that in the Bible, Lazarus is the one Christ chooses to bring back from the dead. After that, his life is a mystery. If your Lazar is similarly elusive, you may have some trouble finding him.'

They talk late into the night. Antoine always opens up in these moments, when he's half asleep, his usual reserve waning. He tells her about his ageing mother, who makes him pay dearly for her love. Of her six children, he's the only one who betrayed her. She brought him up with good Christian values and taught him the codes of their aristocratic world. Then he turned against his family and brought shame on them. But she could never bring herself to disinherit him. When he hasn't visited for a few weeks, she invariably summons him.

'You know what she came out with the other day? "You know, even that short woman would have been better. You should have married her. What was her name again? Irène, that's it. She wasn't one of us, but we could have moulded her into something acceptable."'

'Moulded me?' Irène baulks. 'Actually, I'm not surprised she said that.'

She suspects he's toned down her language. At the time, she'd described Irène as a 'mannerless yokel with a good heart'.

Over the last few years Antoine's mother has come to terms with his sexuality, though she still prays for a 'cure' for him and doesn't want to hear about his private life.

What she refuses to forgive is his 'shit-stirring'. The fact that he revealed his family's ties to the Vichy government, including business relationships and revolting friendships. To make matters worse, Antoine even published his discoveries in an acclaimed essay on collaboration among well-to-do French families. His uncles and cousins no longer speak to him, and he's estranged from his siblings as well, except for his youngest sister, Alice. She's always been the best of the lot. She's also the only one who's met Antoine's partner, Pierre.

'What about you?' Antoine asks gently.

'Me? Nothing to tell. All I do is work,' she says, poking the last log in the fireplace.

'Come to Paris. I miss you.'

'Soon. In the meantime, since you're a good little Catholic, tell me why Jesus brought Lazarus back to life.'

'I think he did it to make himself look good.'

'I'm guessing you weren't top of your Sunday school class, huh?'

She hears him laugh.

After she hangs up, Irène lets the fire burn itself out. She wonders if Antoine helped to kindle her vocation. Is she a shit-stirrer too? Her former mother-in-law would certainly say so.

She switches on her computer and searches for the passage on the resurrection of Lazarus in the Gospel of John. One commentator stresses the fact that Jesus cries in the story. He arrived too late to save Lazarus. On purpose. His friend had to die so he could raise him from the dead and reveal his glory to the world. But Christ cried, because he knew that a person doesn't really return from a journey like that.

When Jesus opens the entrance to the cave and shouts, 'Come out!' Lazarus stumbles towards the light, his body wrapped in strips of linen. 'Take off the grave clothes and let him go,' Christ instructs the crowd. Jesus delivers him from death, but this new life is a poisoned chalice. Lazarus terrifies the living. People plot to kill him. He has to leave his homeland and live in exile. He'll never have a place to call home again.

Irène wonders how Lazarus lived his second life. Did he see it as a blessing or a curse?

Before falling asleep, she works through a few hypotheses. The branch bangs insistently against the shutters. As if to remind her she's forgetting something, or someone.

*

The Glaser household is always filled with joyful chaos. This Sunday, the smell of a long-simmered dish wafts through the kitchen as the youngest sibling massacres a Chopin prelude on the piano.

'Quiet down, please, for our guest!' Toby's mother, Myriam, shouts over the din. 'You're going to burst the poor woman's eardrums. Sigalit, stop playing wrong notes and come say hello to Irène.'

Three shaggy-haired children rush over to hug her, and Leopold, the big, honey-coloured Labrador, is so excited he almost knocks her over. Sigalit, the most impulsive of the three, takes Irène's hand and leads her to the living room. After her long solo walk through the sodden forest, the girl's affection melts Irène's heart. Ever since the day she first met Myriam at the kindergarten where they were both dropping off their sons, the Glasers have been like family. She sees them nearly every week. Hanno sometimes spends the weekend with them and even attends services at the synagogue with Myriam and the kids. When Hanno was seven, a yarmulke fell out of his backpack and provoked a diplomatic incident with Wilhelm's parents. They suspected Irène was trying to convert their grandson. Hanno didn't understand the exact nature of the psychodrama, but learnt that it was better not to mention the Glasers around his father's family. Ever since, he has led two separate lives. Irène has no idea what Hanno gets up to with Wilhelm. Could he be completely different with him?

She watches the children roughhousing and bickering, oblivious to the conflicting loyalties and avoidance strategies so familiar to children of divorce. Hanno never experienced the idyll of happy parents living under the same roof. She wonders if he's weaker or stronger for it.

Irène likes the way Benjamin looks at Myriam. The tenderness she showers him in. The humour with which they highlight one another's flaws. They are very different people, in terms of both upbringing and personality. Myriam is Mediterranean and a true believer. She's deeply committed to Judaism's rituals and symbolism. Benjamin is an ardent defender of Europe and secularism and generally sees all religion as fanaticism. He isn't circumcised but agreed that his sons could be. He lets Myriam take the children to the synagogue but getting him to observe Shabbat is a weekly battle for her.

'He's glued to his phone,' his wife complains. 'What a great example for the children! Shabbat is such a beautiful tradition if he'd just give it a try. It's about being truly present and available for the people you love. It's supposed to be a day of celebration.'

'True, but Jewish law says the Sabbath can be broken to save a life,' Benjamin replies, topping up their glasses.

'So that's what you're doing on Twitter? Saving lives? I've heard it all now!' Myriam scoffs. 'You understand, Irène. It's so important to switch off from time to time.'

Irène is glad Hanno isn't here, because he'd have said, 'My mother, switch off? She doesn't even know what that means.'

'To be honest, when I'm in the middle of an investigation, I don't always know when to stop.'

'Of course, that's *normal*,' Myriam says. 'You feel a responsibility towards the people who contact you. You know they're waiting for a reply, you know how much it means to them. You're surrounded by tragedy. If I were you, I wouldn't be able to sleep at night. I have enough nightmares as it is!'

'So let me get this straight. Irène's allowed to slave away to return a broken old watch which isn't even under warranty, and that's just fine. But it's unacceptable for me to be even a little distracted by my cancer patients,' Benjamin teases his wife.

'Apples and oranges!' Myriam retorts.

'Ben's right,' Irène says. 'His work is a lot more important than mine.'

The majority of people whose lives she investigates are long dead. Would allowing herself to live a little really take anything from them? Maybe taking her work so seriously is just her way of filling the void.

'Now look what you've done!' Myriam says to her husband with daggers in her eyes. 'You're making her question herself.'

'Sorry, Irène. I actually really admire your work. I'm just trying to best my wife. She dreams of dragging me to synagogue. Her father warned her I wasn't good news. At the time, she fell for my bad boy attitude. Now, she's trying to get me back on the straight and narrow. But you know it'll never happen, don't you, darling?'

'We'll see about that. You're not as stubborn as I am,' Myriam replies with a smile. 'Could you check on the meat, please?'

He disappears into the kitchen, and the children take the opportunity to swoop in on the nibbles: almonds, olives, and dates. Myriam chases them off, laughing.

'Shoo! You're like seagulls! Go finish setting the table.'

She tells Irène she suspects Toby and Hanno have stayed in Göttingen to hang out with girls.

'Toby's fallen back under the spell of that girl Leni,' Myriam says with a sigh. 'She's a philosophy major, but she seems more interested in organising parties than in studying. I hope he won't fail his exams.'

'Myriam is suspicious of any girl who even looks at Toby. It's a matter of principle,' Ben observes, topping up their champagne glasses.

'As for you, you're a lucky lady,' Myriam tells Irène. 'Hanno has good taste. Toby says Hermine is charming. And she works hard and gets good marks. She'll be a positive influence.'

Irène tries to hide her hurt. She's never heard of this Hermine girl. Does Hanno no longer trust her at all? The fact that Myriam is in the loop adds insult to injury.

'Do you think?' she asks, sounding as laid back as she can. 'I haven't met her yet, have you?'

'Hanno showed me a photo. She's pretty. Anyway, I'm not worried about your son, he has a good head on his shoulders. He's nothing like Toby, who lets anyone wrap him round their little finger.'

'Yes, Irène's brought Hanno up right,' Ben jokes. 'Maybe you should try letting Toby figure things out for himself for once?'

Irène listens distractedly, working out ways to convince her son to open up to her about this girl. She can't help but find it unfair that Hanno shares his secrets with Myriam, who can be an overbearing mother hen.

*

It's late when Irène gets back to her little house. She places the bag of freshly harvested walnuts Ben gave her on the sideboard. She looks for the nutcracker in the kitchen drawers and gets cross with Hanno. He never puts things back in the right place. She grabs the first knife she can find and tries to crack one open, but the shell resists and warps the blade. She realises her finger is bleeding and swears as she hunts for plasters. She wonders if Hanno might be in love. If he is, why does he feel the need to hide it? Is he trying to protect her? Is he afraid she'd feel abandoned?

She finds an old pocketknife in a drawer, drives it into the crack in the nutshell, and manages to pry it open enough to finish the job with her fingers.

She stares at the cleaved fruit, the walnut flesh tucked neatly into each half.

Something about it reminds her of Wita's locket.

Wita

First thing monday morning, while steam is still rising from her coffee cup, Irène opens the locket. It's been closed for so long that she struggles with the clasp. The excitement makes her clumsy, and the gloves aren't helping either. Inside she finds a thin, folded-up piece of paper. When she uncovers a drawing of a child's face, her pulse begins to race. She's impressed by the artist's precision. Every detail is included, even dimples and eyelashes. The hair has been lightly shaded to suggest blondness. The little boy's eyes and expression come to life on the paper. The caption reads: *Karol Sobieski, 5 Nov 1938*.

Irène immediately thinks of the little boy Wita protected. She looks at the documents Henning collated, the surnames of the other Witas: Janowska, Kryziek, Gorczak, Nowicka, Sobieska.

Wita Sobieska.

Karol Sobieski.

Her son?

5 November 1938 could be his date of birth.

In February 1942, Wita Sobieska was transferred from Warsaw Prison to Auschwitz. Could she then have been sent to Ravensbrück, to die in a gas chamber with a child who wasn't her own? Irène's fingers tremble as she types *Karol Sobieski* into the ITS search engine.

There are about twenty on file, all born before 1921. By 1938 they would have been far too old to look like the picture.

Irène opens the window and lights a cigarette.

Now she has three people to trace and only one proper lead.

*

That afternoon she goes to the warehouse. Dieter Behrens, one of the archivists, has agreed to go through the Lazar Engelmann correspondence with her. He's as aloof as a butler in a fusty BBC period drama. She follows him through the labyrinthine stacks, where the thrumming of the ventilation system is the only sound. The archives must be kept at a certain temperature, like a wine cellar. Since the end of the war, Germany has paid for their conservation. While digitising the archive's holdings, the archivists realised just how precious the documents were in their own right. Now they're only handled with utmost care.

After they put on their gloves, Irène asks to see the two photos of Lazar Engelmann. One taken in Buchenwald, the other a portrait of him as a free man. Behrens reluctantly hands them to her. She takes her time studying them. It's even clearer in the originals: the sadness in his eyes in the first photo is present in the second as well. He's smiling and his face is less emaciated, but the look in his eyes betrays his unravelling.

The correspondence, which has not been digitised, was given to the ITS by a Yad Vashem archivist in May 1978. Behrens reads it to her in a voice more suited to an undertaker. In it, the Israeli archivist explains that a certain Madame Torres in Paris sent them a letter addressed to Lazar Engelmann. She didn't know how to contact him but knew he had lived in the Land of Israel for many years. She hoped her letter might still reach him there.

Israel. So Irène had been right.

Since Lazar had left Israel in the late fifties, the Yad Vashem archivist imagined that he would one day write to the ITS for their help putting together a case for reparations. So he was forwarding the letter from Madame Torres in the hope that it would eventually reach him.

Irène is surprised to see the letter is still sealed. 'Over the past thirty-eight years no one thought to open it?'

'It's a private letter,' the archivist says, his lips pursed.

Irène remembers he was hired by Max Odermatt. And he clearly still clings to the man's methods: never take initiative without the blessing of leadership.

'And no one thought to look for Engelmann?'

'No one asked us to.'

'I need to know what's in this letter.'

'That's out of the question,' Behrens says, as if scolding an intern.

Irène raises her heels up out of her pumps to reach eye level with him. She's sickened by the smell of his aftershave.

'It's my job to find out what happened to Lazar Engelmann. The director herself entrusted me with the task. And this letter could help me find him. So now it's your responsibility to open it for me.'

They glare at each other, but Irène has said the magic word. Dieter Behrens is obedient if nothing else – the director's wish is his command. He opens the envelope with a letter cutter. It contains several pages written in what looks like a non-standard form of Spanish. *Mi querido,* which opens the letter, has become *Mi kerido.* Neither of them speaks Spanish, so Irène calls Montse Trabal, a French historian with Catalan roots who's worked at the Centre for a few months. As soon as Irène spells out the first words of the letter, Trabal has an answer.

'It's Ladino,' she explains confidently. 'A language spoken by the Sephardic Jews who were chased out of Spain in the fifteenth century. They took it with them into exile. It mixes old Castilian Spanish with Hebrew and words borrowed from the languages in the countries they moved to. Turkish, Bulgarian, Italian, French, and so on. Few people still speak it. I was lucky enough to study it at the Sorbonne. I have quite a few things on at the moment, but I'll try to translate it for you by the end of the week.'

When she hangs up, Irène wonders what could connect a Sephardic woman living in Paris to an Ashkenazi Czech who'd moved to Israel. Unfortunately, since Allegra Torres didn't know where to find Lazar in 1978, Irène is likely to encounter the same problem. Antoine was right. Like the Lazarus in the Bible, this man seems to have a real talent for disappearing.

*

When Irène joins the rest of her team in the canteen, Henning looks exhausted. He and his wife spent the rainy weekend trying to tire out their twins with games of Memory and back-to-back wildlife documentaries. But their plan was a complete failure. The kids were on such raucous form at bedtime that they were tempted to put schnapps in their bottles.

'When I'd hear people talk about the Oedipus complex, I always thought it was figurative,' Henning explains with a sigh. 'I didn't think they would actually try to kill me so soon.'

'Can you get your parents to look after them?' asks Constanze, a German colleague.

'They're too old, the kids would finish them off.'

'Why don't you separate them?' Irène asks. 'They're winding each other up.'

Henning nods pensively. 'Have you found your Polish lady?' he asks.

'I think I have.'

When Irène reveals the pendant's secret contents, her audience is enthralled. Everyone has a theory. Wita was a Resistance fighter in the Polish Home Army. She was torn from her family and sent to do forced labour. She was a prostitute with a big heart. A spy.

'What surprises me most is that she chose to die with the little Jewish boy,' says Constanze. 'Polish antisemitism is no myth.'

Irène makes sure Dorota, their Polish colleague, hasn't heard.

'It was a tradition over there,' Michaela says scornfully.

'Let's stop with the generalisations,' Henning says, irritated. 'Throughout Europe the Nazis found enthusiastic collaborators who were more than happy to help get rid of Jews. Every country had greedy neighbours eager to steal their possessions and their businesses. Antisemitism wasn't just the province of Germans and Poles. It was everywhere.'

Constanze tries to change the subject. 'You should ask the Auschwitz Museum, Irène. They may have something on her.'

'That's a good idea. And I'll ask the Polish Red Cross too.'

Irène asks her colleagues about their ongoing investigations. Most are progressing just as slowly as her own. But Renzo, who joined them from Milan two years ago, has had some luck. He's easily managed to identify the woman a ring belonged to. He even thinks he's found her daughter in Norway.

'An opportunity to visit the fjords over Christmas,' Michaela suggests.

It must be beautiful in winter, Irène thinks. *And who knows, maybe he'll find a pretty Norwegian girl to watch the snow fall with.*

Renzo's fiancée left him not long ago. She couldn't understand why he'd traded a sought-after position at the University of Milan for an obscure German archive. She couldn't imagine leaving home for the deepest, darkest corner of Hesse.

Irène watches her colleagues chat and laugh. They come from different parts of the world, but they're all under thirty. They share what Chancellor Helmut Kohl called 'the grace of late birth'—after the war. They also share a passion for their work, a commitment to both the living and the dead. She remembers what Eva always used to say. 'No one ends up at the ITS by chance.' What have they come here to seek, or heal? Irène doesn't even know what brought *her* here. But she knows exactly why she stayed.

*

Janina Dabrowska's laugh rattles the receiver.

'Irena, dearest, it seems you just can't get enough of me. We'll adopt you if you're not careful. If you fancy Warsaw, we'll find you a job here!'

Irène is taken by her energy and the way she calls her Irena as if she were Polish.

'Correct me if I get the details wrong. You're looking for a Wita Sobieska, who would have been detained in Pawiak Prison, then sent to Auschwitz in February 1942, and later on to Ravensbrück, where she died three years later. You're also after a little boy who could have been her son, Karol Sobieski. Born 5 November 1938. Is that right?'

'Exactly right. As for your invitation to Warsaw, I might just give in one of these days,' Irène replies warmly.

Next, she contacts the Auschwitz Museum. She's passed from pillar to post, then waits quite some time for a German curator to call her back.

'I have a Wita Sobieska. Same arrival date. But nothing on the child,' he says.

95

Irène's heart races. The curator apologises for not having more information to share and explains that the Nazis destroyed nearly all evidence of their crimes at Auschwitz too. Wita's name is on a Revier list dated April 1942. The museum also has her identity photographs. Polish prisoner and photographer Wilhelm Brasse was made to document every person who entered the camp, except for the Jews and Roma who were taken straight from the ramp to the gas chambers. Everyone who entered the camp proper was photographed, from the front and the side, like a mugshot. In the left side-view pictures, the men donned their caps and the women their scarves.

The curator goes on to detail Brasse's acts of resistance. At the age of twenty-two he refused to sign the Volksliste, which would have granted him 'ethnic German' status. His act of rebellion earned him a one-way ticket to Auschwitz. He was forced to spend the next four years committing to film everyone who crossed the threshold to hell. He had no choice but to immortalise the children tortured by Mengele and the martyred corpses SS officers posed with as mementos. In January 1945, the Nazis ordered him to burn all compromising material, but he risked his life to save some of the photos. Now more than forty thousand of them are held by the Auschwitz Museum. Including a picture of Wita.

Irène is overcome with emotion when she sees Wita's face on her screen. She's instantly certain it's the same face which mesmerised Elsie and haunted her until her death. The photo has been colourised. Wita's pale eyes look past the camera into the distance. Her platinum blonde curls accentuate the striped uniform's ugliness. Her beauty is so sensual that it seems as though she's stumbled into a macabre farce. The young photographer must have put her at ease because she doesn't look afraid. But in the side view, with her hair covered by a scarf, the dark circles under her eyes and her expression convey sheer sorrow and shock.

She couldn't comprehend the aim of the camp. How could screams and cracking whips coexist with this photo session? Did the simulacrum of normality rekindle hope in her? But then the photographer asked her to turn to the side, reminding her she was a prisoner. In a flash, she must have realised that her life as a free woman was over. The mere thought of everything she'd already lost must have brought a lump to her throat, but she refused to cry in front of them.

Irène prints off the photos of Wita and takes them home to join Lazar's. That night, before she goes upstairs to bed, she studies their faces in the embers' dying light. The curator told her that, after Auschwitz, Wilhelm Brasse couldn't bring himself to photograph the living. The dead took up all the space in his eyes. The people who posed for him in the camp still had faces when he saw them, still had flesh on their bones. Some would smile at him, just because he seemed human. There was nothing he could do for them. He was just a photographer, so he became their witness.

Over the next few days, Irène decides to delve into Eva's past. Lucia Heller's visit has finally overcome her reticence. Irène watched her friend fight cancer and refuse to die in hospital. Now she's ready to learn what she went through as a girl.

On a questionnaire she filled in at the Bergen-Belsen displaced persons camp, she still spells her name the Polish way: Ewa. She provides the names of her father and mother: Medres and Estera. And those of her brothers: Jacek and Jurek. She also includes their last known address in the Warsaw Ghetto. Her family moved several times between the end of 1940 and January 1943. Surprised, Irène looks up a map of the ghetto on a Polish website. She learns that the Germans kept changing the layout, adding or removing sections of road, with no regard for the people being shunted around in an already over-crowded space. In 1940, the Volmanns lived in the 'small ghetto', which was connected to the 'big ghetto' by a wooden footbridge. Elektoralna Street, where they lived next, was in the ghetto just before the large-scale deport-ations in summer 1942, but was outside its subsequently redrawn borders. The Germans made the ghetto smaller and smaller as more of its population was deported to Treblinka. Then the Uprising put a stop to the deporta-tions. Exacting their revenge, the Germans furiously and methodically reduced the ghetto to dust. They pulverised the blocks, the streets, and the squares where market sellers and beggars stood side by side.

But Eva didn't witness the last of the fighting. In spring 1943 she was hiding in a suburb of Warsaw in the home of a Catholic woman. In July she moved to a new hiding place. In February 1944 she was arrested and sent to Auschwitz. Did someone report her?

When the camp was evacuated, she was sent on a death march, which led the utterly exhausted survivors to Bergen-Belsen. After it was liberated by the British army, she mentions being treated in hospital for both typhus and dysentery.

When asked if she would like to be repatriated, she answers, *'Ich weiss nicht'*. *I don't know*. At barely fifteen, she'd survived a harrowing stay in the camps. What sort of future could she possibly imagine?

At the end of the questionnaire the Allied official wrote: *A frail young girl, suffering from the after-effects of malnutrition and typhus. The doctor has diagnosed her with stunted growth. She had her first period two weeks ago and was terrified. She says she lied about her age when she arrived in Auschwitz, making herself two years older on the advice of a man who retrieved prisoners' belongings. He also warned her not to get into any train car painted with a red cross. She learnt later that they 'took people to be gassed'. She's a smart young woman, with a tendency to provoke others. The only person here who has been able to gain her trust is Erin O'Sullivan from the British Red Cross. O'Sullivan says Eva is deeply concerned about her parents and brothers. It took everything she had to dissuade the girl from setting off to try to find them. I believe we should keep her here until we can ascertain whether they survived. If they are dead, which is unfortunately very likely, she should be entrusted to the Polish Red Cross.*

In that short description, Irène sees the Eva she knew so well: determined and completely disillusioned about human nature. But she also sees another Eva, whose distress devastates her. A poor lost girl, damaged in both body and soul. Irène wants nothing more than to take that girl in her arms.

Young Eva just wanted to find her family. She didn't yet realise quite how alone she was in this new postwar world.

Allegra

Mi kerido,

As I write these words, emotions resurface, like the heartbeat of a stunned bird. But you've been just an abstract thought, or a scar, for so long that I feel like you belong to another life. An era of light and air.

You weren't my first love. Before you I had loved and lost my parents, my aunts and uncles, my cousins, and my beloved grandmother. You weren't the first person to break my heart by leaving either. But you are the only person who ever let me believe I could find solace in another. The emptiness I felt when you left taught me something essential. I realised it was up to me to choose life or death.

I've been silent for twenty years but now I feel the need to let it all out.

Do you remember the first glance we exchanged? I do. It was in April 1958. As evening approached, a cold wind rushed down the banks of the Vardar and the sea was rough. The last of the fishermen were returning to the safety of the harbour as a few straggling patrons shivered on the terrace. I was drying glasses at the counter when you walked past me, out on the wharf. You were with Stavros, one of the fishermen who supplied my Greek mother. He was trying to explain something, speaking with his hands. You were doing your best to make it out. Then all of a sudden, you noticed me and paused for a moment. I suppose I was rather pleasant to behold back then. I was twenty-two and in my prime. Stavros came over to say hello. He'd known me forever, watched me grow up. To him, I was Anastasia Mavridis's daughter Althea. He didn't remember that I had once gone by a different name. Maybe I'd forgotten too. Before I got to know you, I found it easier to be a girl with no memory. It made things simpler for everyone involved.

When I brought the two of you a carafe of wine, Stavros explained that you were a ship's carpenter freshly arrived from Kavala. Before that, you'd lived in Israel. With a chuckle, he added that you didn't speak Greek, and he didn't speak Jew, which made for interesting conversations. But, after a drink or two, I could tell you'd found a common language from the way you were laughing together. I kept feeling your eyes on me and found it unsettling.

A little later, when the carafe was almost empty, Stavros was telling you about his boat, his gestures theatrical from all the wine. That's when I heard you say a few words in a tongue which touched my very soul. Sometimes old fishermen, with faces tanned by sea and wind, would shout to one another in that language, and tears would instantly well in my eyes, quick as waves.

My throat dry from the emotion, I went over to ask where you had learned to speak Ladino. You smiled at me for the very first time and told me you'd picked it up from the dockers at the port in Haifa – men who'd emigrated from Salonica before the town went back to its Greek name. Stavros sat staring at us in surprised silence as we spoke. Then he remembered that I once spoke Ladino too, though it wasn't something he liked to think about. When his discomfort grew too strong, he slipped quietly away. I went back to serving my customers, but it was too late, I felt the Ladino part of me begin to stir deep within. The words came back to me, like a heartrending song. It was the music of my childhood, and I had missed it so much. It was the language I felt in my skin and gut, the language of lullabies and of my mother's love. From that moment on, you and Ladino were one and the same to me. You were a stranger who came from afar to return me to myself.

Mi kerido. Let me whisper it, as if you were right here with me. I never told you, but when I met you, I stopped sleeping. Even before we began to share our feelings. Before I ever felt the texture of your skin or listened to your heart beat against my ear. From my window I would watch the stumbling steps of late-night revellers and listen to the Byzantine church bells chime every hour. Even then I was wishing for you.

In the days that followed, I stalked the harbour, hoping to cross your path. One day I found you in Demetrios's studio, where you were studying the hull of a fishing boat. You were stroking the wood, your brow furrowed. The hull was rough, worn down by the salt water. The fisherman looked worried as he awaited your verdict. When you saw me at the door, you asked me to reassure him in Greek. He'd built his boat with love. And love, you added, was never given in vain. I remember the way the fisherman's eyes gleamed with relief. He was afraid of losing his boat. He was more attached to it than to any woman.

You were surprised to bump into me so often. You didn't ask why a Greek girl spoke the language of an eradicated people. You didn't ask me anything at all. I was drawn to you, even though you were twice my age. I was sure I could win your heart. You kept your distance, but despite your reserve, I sensed you had feelings for me too.

Do you remember our first walk in the Upper Town? It was just before Holy Week. We looked for traces of old Ottoman houses and admired several mashrabiyas. Though you were a foreigner and had only just berthed in Thessaloniki for the first time, you told me all about the old Turkish and Jewish quarters from a golden age which ended long before my birth. You were Ashkenazi, but your gentle voice shared the stories you'd heard from Sephardic dockers who moved to Palestine after the Great Fire destroyed the city. As I listened, enthralled, another city took shape around me. A city where the air was saturated with different accents and smells and the skyline made up of minarets, synagogues, and masts. I imagined my parents running through the narrow streets, among spice merchants and women who covered their heads with multicoloured veils, their hair braided with pearls. It was a city that no longer existed, a place I knew nothing about. But, under the blazing sun, you gave it back to me, like a crown returned to an exiled queen.

Our walk had been so lovely that I worked up the courage to kiss you. You pushed me away gently and said you were too old. Embarrassed, I ran off.

During Holy Week, we avoided each other. For my Greek mother, Anastasia, it was the most important week of the year. She kept hovering around me, saying something about me was different. Stavros had told her about the man called Lazar, who'd come from the land of the Jews. She was on her guard, surprised I seemed so unaffected by my week's fast. I used what remained of my energy to pray to the Christ in the icons, who would be resurrected in a few days' time. I prayed he would give me you. During the silent vigils, I readied my soul to love you. Everything had changed! Until I met you, I'd never felt such desire. Before, when men complimented me or smiled at me, I'd seen nothing but a cage reflected in their eyes. Somehow, I knew you wouldn't lock me away. You were free. You were even trying to keep me at bay.

Easter was my favourite holiday, maybe because it reminded me of Passover and the joy of preparing for it, my parents, aunts, and sisters busy in the kitchen. I was helping Anastasia to make orange-flavoured koulouria *when a memory suddenly surfaced. I was sitting on my mother's knee while she helped my clumsy little hands cut out circles of dough for the* borekitas. *I was trying very hard, and she peppered my cheeks with kisses of encouragement.*

I was so overcome by emotion that my hands began to tremble in the flour. Anastasia saw the look on my face but said nothing.

At midnight on Saturday, when the Holy Fire was lit at Hagios Demetrios to symbolise the resurrection of Christ, I felt the flame burn my body and my soul, consuming the lies I'd accepted. Warmed by the crowds of people embracing one another around me, I let my tears run down my cheeks.

When we got home after the ceremony, I told Anastasia that, from then on, I would go by the name my mother gave me.

She was so angry she cut me off. 'This is about him, isn't it? I know it's about him. He's got you all muddled up.'

'You don't understand,' I replied. 'It's my name.'

She was furious. 'I forbid you from seeing that man again. He's not right for you.'

I suppose the two of you agreed on that point.

I shouted that I was an adult, that she couldn't tell me what to do any more.

The streets were lit up and full of people dancing as I ran through town. Laughter rang out in Aristotelous Square, and music blared from the bright tavernas. I looked for you everywhere. At two in the morning, I finally found you at the back of a smoke-filled room.

You were listening to rebetiko, *your eyes closed. I took your hands in mine and whispered: 'Look at me. Don't be afraid. I'm not scared of you.'*

This time you didn't push me away. I told you my real name. Surprised, you repeated it. Allegra. Joy.

That night, you finally gave in to joy.

It was true, nothing about you scared me. Not even the scars that ran the length and breadth of your body. I shivered when I first saw them in that candlelit room. But later, I dared to trace their contours with my fingers and lips. I didn't know that the story etched into your skin would eventually separate us forever. But from that first night, the shadow of it was there.

Your sleep was interrupted by nightmares and sudden jolts. Tears slid down your face and you moaned in a language I didn't understand.

One summer day, we went to the beach in Halkidiki. I watched you walk towards the great expanse of water, then become one with it. The shimmering blue surface enveloped your wounds, and I dozed off in the sun. Later you woke me by dripping cold, salty water on my warm stomach.

We ate the koulouria, *cheese, and olives we'd bought at Modiano Market, and drank the wine you'd left to chill in the sea.*

I asked who had hurt you, and you whispered a reply: Treblinka. SS officers and Ukrainians. Every day for a year.

I repeated the sinister name. I'd never heard it before. 'Where's Treblinka?' I finally asked.

'In Poland', you told me, stony-faced.

After that, you were silent for a long time.

Mi kerido, I don't think you were ever truly mine. But in your arms, I felt reborn. After my relatives died, I pushed Allegra to the deepest, most hidden part of myself. You brought her back, and with her, my joy. My world was finally opening up, it felt limitless. At last it seemed possible to go on living without them.

But it was different for you. It was as though you carried the war with you wherever you went. You were still its prisoner.

Despite all that, you had a gift for having fun and making friends. Demetrios and the fishermen had adopted you after just a few days. In the evening, when you sat with the gang, I'd watch as you told them stories in a mix of Ladino and Greek, laughing as you drank. I always wondered if I was the only person who could see the sadness in your eyes.

I thought I could heal you.

By then, Anastasia wasn't talking to me unless she was giving me orders, at home or at the taverna. Even little things I did would make her furious, and she'd send me to bed like a child. The second I heard her footsteps recede I'd hurry out the window to find you. One night her son saw me climbing back into my room just before dawn. He called me a whore and said, 'I'm ashamed of you,' his voice full of disdain.

The next day, Anastasia was waiting for me after the lunch service. She told me I'd dishonoured myself, that no Greek man would want to marry me after that.

'So what?' I replied. 'I don't want to marry a Greek man anyway.'

Her rage exploded. 'That foreigner! I knew that Jew was leading you astray!'

'I'm Jewish too!' I shouted. 'Have you forgotten?'

She slapped me as hard as she could, then stared at me, petrified. My cheek stung, and I was torn between anger and pity. 'You're my daughter,' she said softly. 'I don't want him to take you away from me.'

I mumbled that I wasn't going anywhere.

But when I said it, I realised, for the very first time, that I was planning to leave.

'It's so moving, isn't it? How much she loved the man,' Montse Trabal remarks, interrupting Irène and bringing her back to the present, still troubled by her foray into another stranger's private life. 'Are you looking for her or him?'

The young historian is dressed in a colourful patchwork jacket and roomy trousers. She gets up to turn on a light. The sky is so heavy with clouds that it feels like night is falling in the middle of the afternoon.

'Him. His trail went cold in Austria and now he's in Thessaloniki, in love.'

'He's just so broken. I felt so bad for them while I was translating the letter. Their story's like a Greek tragedy. And the fact that it's happening there, in Thessaloniki. Have you ever been?'

'No, I haven't.'

'It's built like an amphitheatre facing the sea. It's as though the stone and water are engaged in an eternal dialogue.'

'I'd like to visit. Did it have a significant Jewish community?'

'Yes, an extremely influential one!' Montse exclaims. 'During the Ottoman Empire, Salonica was known as the Balkan Jerusalem. For centuries, Jews, Muslims, and Orthodox Christians lived alongside one another in harmony. That's the city's golden age Lazar is telling her about while they stroll through Ano Poli, the old Upper Town. It's surprising to see an Ashkenazi telling a Sephardi all about her ancestors! Unfortunately, once Greece seized Thessaloniki, it erased many traces of its Jewish past. For example, they built Aristotle University on top of the Jewish cemetery! The biggest Sephardic cemetery in the world ... The current mayor seems to be trying to revitalise the town's multicultural heritage. I hope he's true to his word.'

'It must have been so hard for this girl to live in a city which erased all trace of her people,' remarks Irène.

'Allegra's Ladino expresses her ambivalence very clearly,' Montse replies. 'I don't know if it's come across in the translation. Allegra survived because a Greek woman risked her life to hide her. She adopted Allegra and, from the looks of it, loved her like her own child. But the price of survival was erasing her Jewish heritage. Taking a Greek name, pretending to be an Orthodox Christian. Allegra may have felt she was betraying her parents.'

'And meeting Lazar stirred up everything she'd suppressed.'

'To use a Greek word, it sounds like she had an epiphany,' says Montse. 'But I suppose love often reveals us to ourselves. Don't you think?'

'Maybe,' Irène says, her thoughts turning to Wilhelm.

'Do you think this letter will help you find him?' Montse asks.

'It should help me find out what happened to him, at least,' Irène says. 'I doubt he's still alive.'

*

Until now, Lazar has been nothing but a shadow, lurking behind the trees. Thanks to Allegra, he has a body. A wounded body, riddled with scars. A body which hurts, breathes, swims, and makes love. Now Irène knows that, despite it all, he knew how to have a good time and never lost his zest for life. Perhaps his exuberance helped him to overcome the memories from the camp that caught up with him every night. Irène is impressed that such a young woman picked up on this duality, though it's difficult, of course, to disentangle the girl from the more mature woman writing seventeen years later to the man she loves still.

As a ship's carpenter, he had stopped building structures that helped men put down roots, choosing instead to repair boats, which carried them to distant lands. He chose to live in ports, among those who preferred the high seas to dry land.

'Is his daughter the one who asked you to find him?'

'His daughter?' Irène asks, looking confused.

'Ahh, you haven't got to that bit yet,' Montse explains with a smile. 'I'll let you read on. That letter is quite the odyssey. Let me know if you track down Lazar. I'd like to find out what became of them, all three of them,' she says as she walks Irène to the door.

Elvire

WHEN IRÈNE GETS BACK to her office, she takes the phone off the hook so she can read the rest of the letter in peace.

. . . I realised, for the very first time, that I was planning to leave.

But the ground beneath my feet connected me to those I had lost. I was clinging to memories that were beginning to fade. Late-night parties where the air was saturated with enticing aromas, games of hide-and-seek with my friends from the Alliance Israélite Universelle school, the long tables set out on Shabbat, the nape of my mother's neck as she sat at the piano. Had I really been that cherished, carefree child?

For years, I awaited their return. Sometimes I feel like I spent my entire childhood waiting for the Simplon-Orient-Express to pull into the station. That was the line my father would take to sell his fabrics in all the European capitals. When I was little, my mother and I would go to meet him and I would jump into his arms, inhaling the smell of leather and tobacco at his neck. For me, that's still the smell of travel. After the war, the Orient-Express came through town less frequently. The world had been sliced in two, with some countries stopping all traffic at their borders. Its arrival was always a bit of an event in Thessaloniki.

Whenever it pulled into the station, my heart would pound. The travellers hailed from Paris, Venice, Vienna, and Belgrade. I would study the businessmen, tourists, and young couples on their honeymoons. But it was never them. *The people always walked right past me.*

One winter evening, Anastasia found me on the platform, my skin hot with fever. She wrapped me in her coat and took me home. She ran me a bath, put me in her bed, and watched over me until my temperature came down. I was twelve.

'You're a big girl now,' she said to me the next day. 'It's time I told you the truth. Do you remember the day your mother left you with me?'

It was the spring after I turned seven. My mother had just given Anastasia a piano lesson. She was no longer allowed to teach, but some pupils came to her in secret. After the lesson, they spoke for a long time in hushed voices. Afterwards, my mother announced that I'd be staying with Anastasia for a while, in the Upper Town. I was to be a brave girl and obey her every word.

I quickly gathered a few prized possessions: my old teddy, a notebook, and the pen my father had given me for my birthday. I reluctantly let my mother kiss me goodbye. I didn't understand why she was hugging me so tightly.

That very evening my parents were forced out of our home. The Germans penned them in a ghetto by the station with hundreds of other Jews. Anastasia had a fish stall at Kapani market. A few days later, a teenage boy slipped her a folded piece of paper, which she'd kept. She showed it to me now. My mother had written, in Greek, 'We're leaving tomorrow. Rabbi Koretz says they're sending us to Kraków, Poland. Before I go, I need you to return the package I left in your care. I don't know how long we'll be staying in Kraków, so I'd rather take it with me.'

I remember reading and rereading those Greek letters, unable to put together what they meant. Anastasia explained that my mother had changed her mind. When she realised how soon they would be deported, she couldn't imagine leaving me behind. She wanted Anastasia to return her daughter, me.

But Anastasia had a premonition and couldn't bring herself to do it. She chose instead to risk her life, and her son's, to keep me safe. She would send me to join my parents when she was sure they were all right.

After the war, a handful of survivors returned, so haggard and emaciated no one dared meet their eyes. Most of them later sought out more welcoming countries. But before they left, they described how their brothers and sisters had been murdered in a Polish camp called Auschwitz. The elderly, mothers, and children were murdered as soon as they arrived.

'They're not coming back,' Anastasia repeated again and again until I listened.

They're not coming back.

From then on, she was the only family I had. She hadn't chosen me. She had accepted a perilous burden and ended up with an orphan. She saved me.

Every day since, I've imagined my mother waiting for me at the station. The thought breaks my heart. She must have believed I'd abandoned her. So, every day, part of me is relieved to be alive, but another part wants to go back in time to join them. To die with them.

When I met you, something I couldn't express had been keeping me trapped in rough waters just below the surface.

One night as you moved inside me, their buffeting finally stopped, as if a switch had flipped. A sense of peace washed over me and moved me to tears.

The dawns that summer were enchanting. We spent the mornings fishing in a quiet so pure only the seagulls' cries could breach it. On the way back to shore, the fish blood and rolling waves would leave me feeling sick, so you'd take me for a walk on dry land. Sometimes we'd climb up the old ramparts to look down over the rooftops and watch black cats slink along them like shadows.

Since the infamous slap, Anastasia and I hadn't talked in any meaningful way. The heat was suffocating from ten in the morning. It felt like everything was on hold, as though we were all waiting for a release that never came.

One evening, I joined you in a taverna near the White Tower. I wanted to savour an ouzo which I hadn't poured myself. You were exhausted and happy since you'd just finished repairing Stavros's boat. You guided me to the dance floor. I let you lead. I remember thinking, 'There is one Lazar during the day and another at night.' Then, all of a sudden, my head was spinning, blood throbbing at my temples, and my legs gave way. You carried me outside to breathe in the cool night air. You laid me down gently on a low wall, your hand warm against the back of my neck. Ninia, I heard you whisper again and again, your voice full of worry, but I was too far away to respond. The lapping of the waves lulled me to sleep. When I finally opened my eyes again, your drawn features immediately brightened.

'Are you all right, Ninyeta?' you asked me tenderly.

I'd felt tired for a while. After my long workdays, I shared your fragmented sleep, waking every time you did.

I smiled to reassure you.

Anastasia had hoped your stay would be brief and that our lives would soon return to normal. But after a while, since you didn't seem to be going anywhere and you had made Greek friends, she reasoned that a Jewish son-in-law was better than bringing shame on the family. She resolved to talk to you, with a determination that came off as arrogance. You never told me exactly what she said to you, but I can imagine. That I was even more stubborn than the goats she had tended up in the mountains as a child. That she would give in if you married me and promised to stay in

Thessaloniki. I don't know what you said either. Did you give her a glimmer of hope?

Later, when we were having dinner, just the two of us, you laughed about her overbearing tone. Your worried eyes never left my face, and I could read in them a question.

I drank too much, to take the edge off the awkward moment.

'If you're leaving, take me with you,' I finally said.

'Really?' you asked softly.

I said it again and downed the rest of my drink.

At your side, I felt ready for adventure and faraway lands. I was tired of Thessaloniki. I wasn't sure the city even liked me.

'I want you to show me the world,' I added.

You smiled, amused. 'Very well then,' you replied, refilling our glasses. 'Where would you like to go?'

'I want to see Istanbul, Venice, and . . . Paris.'

I was embarrassed to realise my horizons were limited to stops on the Orient-Express. The places my father had described, where he'd bought me exotic trinkets which set my imagination on fire.

'I'd also like to visit Israel,' I said, a little too quickly. 'And . . . I want to have your baby.'

I blushed at my audacity and turned away. On the quay in the distance, a couple held hands as they walked towards the White Tower.

When I dared to confront your silence, tears filled your eyes. Your sadness terrified me.

'Ninia,' you implored almost inaudibly, 'don't ask that of me. I can't do it, do you understand? It's more than I can bear.'

My last period had come back in July, but I wasn't brave enough to tell you.

After that evening, sadness was always by our side, casting a shadow over the late summer days and long evenings awash in the scent of jasmine and fig trees. You still sat with your friends and laughed from time to time, but it was hollow.

And then there was our last night. Do you remember the words you drove into my heart like a dagger?

'I'm leaving, Ninyeta. You have your whole life ahead of you. You'll love another man. He'll give you the life you deserve.'

And the next day you were gone.

I turned your words over and over in my head until they almost killed me, trying to put myself off you. But then I'd remember your defeated face. I'd remember your confession: 'It's more than I can bear'.

You weren't my first love. But you were the first person I ever loved as a woman, not a girl. I never let anyone heal the wounds you left behind.

I finally resolved to write to you because I kept the child. Initially, I did it out of despair. I didn't know who to turn to or what to do. When the baby began to move, the presence of a new life inside me upended my world. It was as though she were stamping her feet to say 'From now on, I come first'.

Your departure confirmed Anastasia's prejudices. She was relieved when I returned home. But it wouldn't take long for her to realise I had a secret passenger. And once she did, I knew our uneasy peace would shatter.

One September day the Vardar wind blew so furiously that walking became a struggle. I had climbed up to the fortress, though the baby protested. I had to stop often to catch my breath. I hadn't been up there since you'd left. On the ramparts, I had to brace myself against the wind. People here say that the wind washes your heart and clears the dust from your soul. The wind brought you to this part of the world, then took you away again. As I looked out over the white roofs which stretched all the way down to the sea, I realised that this moment was my kairos. *The ancient Greeks depict Kairos as a young winged god with a single lock of hair. Could I catch him by that lock and climb onto his back? If not, this town would become my cage.*

When I got home, I dug out the notebook I'd taken from my parents' house, which held my postcard collection. A few years earlier, a postcard of the Eiffel Tower had come unglued. I'd read the lines written mostly in French on the back.

Preziada mia,

For your birthday, I'm sending you a beautiful doll from Paris. When you come to visit, I'll take you to the top of the Eiffel Tower. Your mother told me you're making good progress on the piano. It sounds as though you play like an angel.

The whole family works in the schmatte business, as we say here, and business is booming! I've bought a big apartment. And Cousin Saltiel lives opposite!

Give everyone a kiss from me and tell your parents to bring you to Paris during the summer holidays.

The card was signed Your Uncle Rafo *and dated 7 April 1920. The sender's name was familiar. My mother sometimes talked about her beloved uncle, who had gone to live in France when he was seventeen, after the Great Fire. It devastated me to imagine my mother as the little girl he was addressing. I had slipped the postcard back into my notebook and put it away.*

Now it was time to open it again.

It sounds as though you play like an angel.

Those words broke my heart all over again. I would give anything to hear her play now. I can still see her hands flying across the keys, but all I hear is silence.

On the back of the postcard, my great-uncle had written his address:

Rafael Ferelli, 31 rue Saint-Lazare, Paris, VIII

Rue Saint-Lazare. Kairos was pointing the way.

In a single breath, I told Anastasia about my pregnancy and my decision. I had expected shouting and tears, but she just stared at my belly in silence, as if she'd always known this moment would come. Regaining her composure, she gently laid her hand on my stomach. After a little while she felt the baby move, and she smiled.

She met my haste with admirable poise and pragmatism, helping me to choose clothes for every season. I thought she would try to convince me not to go, but she accepted my choice. Uncle Rafo's postcard tipped the scales. Perhaps she thought it was only fair to return me to my family, if any of them were still alive. She asked me to send word when I'd arrived safely. If things didn't turn out as we hoped, I was to take the first train home.

I gave her my promise. On the platform, I clasped her in my arms. I told her I'd come back to visit, with the baby.

She abruptly cut off our goodbyes.

So, mi kerido, that's how I finally ended up on the Simplon-Orient-Express. Through the window, I watched the city I'd grown up in fade into the distance. A city which had ripped my life in two. I felt excited and afraid in equal measure. But I still savoured every moment of the journey. It felt as though it were bringing me closer to you.

Miraculously, Uncle Rafo had survived the war. Roaming from one safe house to the next had cost him what little money he had left, but he was alive. Cousin Saltiel wasn't so lucky. He was reunited with his parents, his cousins, and his niece from Thessaloniki at Auschwitz. Rafo didn't want to talk about those terrible years. He worked as hard as he could to forget them. When he returned to Paris, he built his fabric business back up, and by the time I arrived, he ran three tailor shops in the Sentier neighbourhood. He'd only recently managed to reclaim his apartment on rue Saint-Lazare, after a long struggle. The people who'd lived there since Occupation had torn out the wood panelling and skirting boards before they left.

My uncle was so moved to welcome the granddaughter of his preziada ermana, *and the child in her belly. In his eyes, the baby was a source of hope, not shame.*

In his world, I found a family, what remained of the pre-war Sephardic community. They adopted me without question, and I took comfort in their warmth.

Here too, I find myself up against a wall of silence. They don't talk about the dead. The main thing here is to work hard and live discreetly. Sometimes we get together for a Shabbat meal or share a recipe for borekitas *or* pastellicos. *Occasionally a few words of Ladino work their way into conversation, sometimes a tear or two is shed. But mostly, we keep secret what the war took from us. If we were to talk about it, who would listen?*

One Sunday, I was taking a stroll when a choir of male voices stopped me in my tracks. The door to an apartment building was open, and I entered. In the middle of the courtyard, stood a small wooden church built around the trunk of an oak tree whose branches reached skywards, higher than the building's roof. Inside, candlelight revealed the icons that covered the walls and a group of believers praying on either side of the trunk, as if in a forest. I thought I was dreaming. I closed my eyes and let their deep, bass voices take me back to Thessaloniki.

When I left, I felt a pang so intense it knocked the breath out of me. I suddenly realised how much I missed Anastasia. I wished she were with me. I wanted to put my head in her lap and hear her tell me that I'd manage, that I was strong enough.

The next day, I gave the central switchboard the taverna's number. Anastasia's voice sounded so distant and frail. 'Mamma,' I said, 'the baby will be here soon. I'm scared.'

She arrived the day before I gave birth.

Our daughter was born in Paris on 12 March 1959, under a fitful sky, mi kerido. I named her Elvire. On some days, in a certain light, I think she looks like my mother.

Yesterday she turned nineteen. Her hair is as dark as yours. Like you, she loves a good party and is always laughing. She teases Uncle Rafo, who's getting on in years now, for losing his glasses when they're right there on his nose. She's a brilliant student, and she fills us with pride.

Today I'm finally writing to you, despite the risk of stirring up these old memories, because lately, when I look into Elvire's eyes, I sometimes think I see a sadness which concerns me.

All these years, I've respected your wishes. She doesn't know anything about you, only that we loved each other, and that she is the product of that love.

She peppers me with endless questions, but I've never given in.

But now I think she needs you in her life. It's as if she's looking for you. And it's not just her, mi kerido. I'd like to know where you live now, too, and whether you still think of me. How you're doing. If you're feeling any more at peace.

I know you didn't have the strength to raise a child. But maybe one day you'll want to meet this young woman who looks like you. Elvire will soon be able to look after herself. She's strong and has never wanted for love. I think you'd like her if you met her.

And I'd like to see you again too. I'd like to sit across a table from you and listen as you tell me about other journeys and other boats. I don't want you to feel obliged, but life can pass us by so quickly, so I wanted to write to you before I get too old. To tell you that I can't stop thinking about you. And to thank you for sparing me false promises and empty words. You didn't destroy me, and I want you to know that. You gave me Elvire. She's my anchor.

I have no idea where you are, so I'm sending this letter to Yad Vashem, in the hope that they'll pass it on.

Mi kerido, whatever you decide, please know that I won't resent you. What we had together is a gift that endures.

Allegra

Irène stares at a blot of dried ink next to the word *gift*. Knowing that this letter never reached its intended recipient leaves her distraught. She's touched by the way they pieced their ravaged lives back together with love.

In a notebook she writes *Allegra Torres* next to *Lazar Engelmann*. On the line below: *Elvire Torres. Born in Paris, 12 March 1959.*

Irène wonders if Allegra is still alive and what she should do with the letter and the revelations it contains. She works out that Elvire will be fifty-eight this spring. Is there some sort of a link, even a symbolic one, between the cloth puppet and Lazar's refusal to have children?

To answer these questions, Irène will have to pick up his trail.

Karol

'SO SORRY TO HAVE KEPT YOU WAITING, Irène,' says Charlotte Rousseau. 'They're setting up the Christmas market in town and traffic's all backed up. My, it's cold this morning! Between this rotten weather and sunset at four in the afternoon, I'm flirting with a case of seasonal affective disorder. No wonder they call this place Little Siberia.'

This year the snow has come late. In the streets, Christmas decorations are going up everywhere, some kitschy, others rather tasteful.

'How are you getting on with returning those objects? Are you enjoying the work?' the director asks as she hands Irène a cup of tea.

'Our enquiries are raising certain ethical dilemmas.'

'Tell me. And take a biscuit, they're homemade. My elder daughter is in a baking phase.'

Irène tells her about Lazar. Ever since she read Allegra's letter, she hasn't been able to stop thinking about the couple. She starts with the puppet and the number written on its belly, explaining how it led her to the Czech survivor with a dual identity: Matias Bárta and Lazar Engelmann. She wonders aloud if the middle-class, would-be law student was outraged when the diplomats gathered to sign the Munich Agreement, sacrificing his country for provisional peace. Irène explains that after the invasion of Czechoslovakia, Lazar was banned from university by the Nazis and became a carpenter. His fall in social status accelerated as more antisemitic laws were passed. Soon he was deported to the Theresienstadt Ghetto, then on to Treblinka.

'Did he die at Treblinka?' the director asks, an eyebrow raised in resignation.

Just the mention of that place extinguished any light.

'No, he took part in the revolt and managed to escape. He hid in the forest for a few weeks, until the Polish Resistance found him.'

'Ah,' Charlotte says. 'Survivors have said that some of those soldiers didn't hesitate to denounce Jews, or kill them themselves.'

'Some helped Jews, others betrayed them. The ones who found Lazar Engelmann got him false papers, and almost certainly saved his life. Luckily, the Polish police officers who found him a few days later never uncovered his true identity. Treblinka escapees were murdered upon capture. Lazar was sent to Buchenwald instead.'

'Every story of survival contains happy accidents. But he could have died in Buchenwald, or on a death march.'

'He almost did. By the time the Allies came, his lungs were in dreadful condition. He was treated in Austria. From there, he illegally emigrated to Palestine. I think he stayed in Israel until 1958.'

'Why do you think that?'

'Because in 1958 he fell in love with a young Jewish woman in Thessaloniki,' says Irène, smiling at Charlotte's surprise.

Irène tells her about the letter in the archives, and the sparring incident with Dieter Behrens.

'Behrens acts as though Odermatt's still here,' Rousseau says with a frown. 'I'll make sure he knows not to get in your way again. Now tell me how this Treblinka survivor ended up in Greece.'

Irène wasn't sure. All she knew was that he became a ship's carpenter in Israel and had lived in Haifa, where the dockers from Salonica had taught him Ladino.

'So, once he got to Thessaloniki he met and married this woman?'

'Not quite.' Irène tells Rousseau about the end of their relationship, Lazar's retreat, and Allegra's pregnancy and exile.

'So he never knew he had a daughter?'

'I'm pretty sure he died without knowing.'

'Then you'll have to find this daughter and give her the object.'

Irène sets out the counter-argument. It's possible Elvire knows nothing about her father. So is it right to reveal the secrets the letter contains? Irène feels she doesn't know enough about Lazar to conclude her investigation.

'Irène,' Charlotte says, taking her hand, 'I think you're asking a lot of questions in one. Should we reveal to descendants what we discover? The people who contact us want an answer, even if it raises questions about what they thought they knew. It isn't unusual for a detainee's child to discover they had another wife, or other children – people they knew nothing about and who died in the camps. How old is Lazar's daughter?'

'Fifty-eight.'

'She's old enough to know the truth. Trust your instincts. The younger generations want to know.'

'Yes, but the thing is, she hasn't asked for any information.'

'Doesn't the letter say she constantly asked her mother questions?'

'It does,' Irène concedes.

'You're perseverant, and your hunches are eerily accurate. But your perfectionism too often leads you beyond the scope of your mission. You know who owned the object and you've found a descendant. You've got everything you need. Now all that's left is to find her and give her the puppet.'

'But I don't know what the puppet meant to Lazar.'

'You have to accept the fact that some questions can never be answered. You're giving a woman her father. Isn't that enough?'

Feeling powerless, Irène keeps quiet. Wrapping up her enquiry at this point feels like abandoning Lazar.

'You have three thousand objects to return, and a single lifetime to do it,' Rousseau says with a smile. 'You have to learn to let things go. Anything else?'

Hiding her frustration, Irène talks Charlotte through the confession which Elsie's grandson sent, Wita's decision, the Virgin and Child pendant, and the pencil sketch of the boy's face.

'Did you locate her just from her first name?' Rousseau asks, impressed.

'All thanks to Henning.'

'If the child in the drawing is the prisoner's child, how old would he be now?'

'Seventy-eight. If he's alive, that is.'

'It's such a brave thing to do,' Rousseau says quietly. 'To go to your death with an orphan. It reminds me of the Warsaw Ghetto paediatrician, Janusz Korczak. He had well-connected relatives who were desperate to save him. But he refused to abandon the children in his orphanage and was murdered with them. But your Polish woman had a son . . . That should have stopped her. Maybe he was already dead, so she had nothing left to lose?'

Irène shakes her head. She's convinced Wita wanted to live. The drawing alone is proof of that. But the orphan boy somehow derailed her. She just couldn't bring herself to abandon him.

'How many objects is your team working on at the moment?'

'About twenty.'

Charlotte's pleased, it's a good start. She'd like to brief the press about the project, a little publicity could help things along. Why not put out a call for volunteers? They'll need to think of a catchy hashtag.

'Thank you,' she concludes, 'your presentation was fascinating.'

Irène stands to leave. On her way out, she asks, 'Could you grant me access to Eva Volmann's file in the staff archives? The other day a young woman from Buenos Aires came looking for her. I'd like to gather all the information I can before she comes back.'

'Remind me when Eva Volmann started here?'

'1948.'

'Of course! She was one of the first DPs to join the ITS,' Rousseau remembers, her eyes lighting up. 'As it happens, I'm reading up on the Centre's early years at the moment. Are you free at the end of the afternoon? We can look through her file together.'

Every meeting Irène has with Charlotte Rousseau makes her feel as though she's been plugged into a generator and fully recharged. But the idea of abandoning Lazar saddens her. Of course she can imagine why he didn't want a child. But she doesn't know what brought him to Thessaloniki, or what became of him after he left. She hopes his daughter will ask her to investigate further.

*

Janina Dabrowska rings Irène after lunch. She has good news: She's found Wita Sobieska in their records. When her husband asked the Polish Red Cross to look for her in 1945, they told him she'd died in Ravensbrück according to a survivor from Lublin.

Janina has also gathered more information about her husband, Marek Sobieski. Before the war he owned a farm near Lublin. During the Occupation, the Nazis expelled Poles from their farms, replacing them with Volksdeutsche farmers. To escape deportation, thousands of the displaced farmers joined Resistance groups hiding out in the forests. Marek joined the Polish Home Army. In summer 1944, Lublin was the first major Polish city to be liberated.

Immediately afterwards, the communists seized power. In the eyes of Stalin, members of the Home Army were criminals, destined for Siberia. Marek was jailed and accused of collaborating with the Nazis. The Soviets were in the habit of using this sort of argument to tarnish the reputation of the Resistance. Marek had just been released when the Red Cross informed him of his wife's death.

'The strange thing,' Janina continues, 'is that he remarried three weeks after he found out.'

Irène feels a pang of sympathy for Wita. He hadn't grieved her for long. Was he just a pragmatic man, or was he desperate for a new start after five years of horror?

'What about the boy?' Irène asks.

Janina confirms their son disappeared during the war. 'Wita's sister tried to track him down in 1949. She said he was kidnapped by the SS.'

'As part of the Germanisation programme?'

'Apparently. But the search led nowhere. Your Child Search Branch ended up closing the file. That happened often with children stolen from their parents in the occupied territories.'

'Do you think he was put up for adoption in Germany?'

'Probably. He couldn't have been more than two or three.'

'So why don't I have any record of this in our archives?'

'Maybe the file got lost?' suggests Janina. 'I'm going to see if we have anything about other members of the family. With all this, it looks like you'll be coming for a visit sooner than you thought, Irena!'

After Irène hangs up she studies the portrait. The boy's features are in perfect harmony, and he's so blond. He clearly inherited his mother's 'Aryan' beauty. For both mother and son, what must have at first seemed like a blessing turned out to be a curse. Irène looks again at the inscription: *Karol Sobieski, 5 Nov 1938.* The first time she saw the drawing, it made her think of a missing-person poster.

As Irène continues her search, Wita comes to life more and more. Irène feels close to her somehow. She sees herself in the woman whose little boy was taken, who was thrown into prison, then deported to Auschwitz and later Ravensbrück. Irène imagines her during those years. Trying to save her strength, doing her best to go unnoticed. In the half-light of her barracks, she sketches her son's face, writes down his name and date of birth. After the camp, she'll find him.

Then she meets the little Jewish boy, who's nearly the same age as her son. He's all alone. Against her better instincts, she's drawn to him. She tries to save him but fails. Together they're sent to Uckermark. The terrifying head guard chooses the boy during the evening roll call. Wita can't bring herself to leave him. They can't take *this* child away from her.

Not once but twice her short existence was derailed by maternal instinct. She had the classic qualities of a fairy-tale princess: beauty and a big heart. Except in this story, the gifts bestowed by the fairies led to her downfall.

Irène studies the portrait, feeling the weight of her duty to find the boy. To retie the loose threads, to do Wita justice.

Eva

WHEN IRÈNE STEPS into the conference room, it's already dark outside. Charlotte Rousseau's hair is dishevelled, and her glasses have slipped down her forehead. As she emerges from a heap of boxes and files, she looks like a caver coming back up to the surface after a very long day.

'I thought all this might help shed some light on Eva's documents,' she says. 'I've recently begun an inventory of all archives relating to the history of the Centre itself. I'd like to set up a permanent exhibition. You know as well as I do, there's always been an invisible wall between us and the town. It's time to knock it down. The people here need to realise that we're an integral part of their history, that having us here is a real asset, that we bring something important to the community. I'm working on the project with a historian who grew up here. Her uncle worked at the ITS for ten years, but before she decided to write her dissertation on us, she had no idea what we did! Can you imagine?'

Irène isn't surprised. For the twenty-seven years she worked under Max Odermatt, their mission was clouded in secrecy, which was ideal for people who refused to confront the past.

'Here's Eva's personnel file.'

Irène looks for her friend's familiar features, but in this picture, she looks like a wary mouse. The green of her eyes is clearer, and her short dark hair makes her look like a schoolgirl, but the shrewdness in her eyes clashes with that image. The employment contract is dated February 1947. She wasn't yet seventeen. Perhaps her frequent use of irony was the only defence mechanism she had left to keep the ghosts of her shattered life at bay.

In another photo, Eva is posing with friends in front of the entrance to the Centre. She's staring directly at the camera as the others, in modest skirts, smile broadly. One of them is even sticking out her tongue. They look like any other postwar girls, rediscovering what it means to be carefree, but something about the photo bothers Irène. Undoubtedly because the semi-circular sign above the gate, which reads ALLIED HIGH COMMISSION FOR GERMANY, INTERNATIONAL TRACING SERVICE, strangely echoes the curved ARBEIT MACHT FREI sign at the entrance to Auschwitz.

'Where was the ITS back then?' Irène asks.

Charlotte explains that the American army requisitioned lots of buildings in the town. Their headquarters were in the former residence of the Nazi prince. In its early years, the International Tracing Service, which was still called the Central Tracing Bureau, was located on the estate as well. Hundreds of displaced people, washed up by the tumult of war, lived in nearby barracks which had previously housed SS garrisons. Most of the DPs wanted to emigrate, so they were learning languages and skills which could earn them visas to countries of their choice. They were an international enclave right in the centre of the town, and the locals were hostile. They viewed the DPs as parasites sponging off the Allied occupiers' generosity. The Central Tracing Bureau hired some of the survivors, especially the multilingual ones, like the Brain. After his plane crashed near Arolsen in the last bouts of combat, he spent two years in hospital, floating from one operation to the next on a cloud of sedation. He left missing a leg but with a job suited to his linguistic talents.

Eva had arrived one morning with Erin O'Sullivan, a young woman from the British Red Cross who'd managed to earn her trust. In Arolsen she discovered a welcoming community of survivors who resembled her in many ways, so she decided to stay. They banded together to start their lives afresh. They organised balls, sporting events, holiday parties, and picnics by the lake. Though it felt like a fragile interlude, people coupled up, and children were born.

'It looks like Eva's room was in block F,' Irène says as Charlotte unfolds a map of the barracks.

Every morning, Eva would walk across the old SS training field. Irène can't help but wonder if it felt like a cruel joke. Maybe she saw it instead as a symbolic victory over the people who tried to kill her?

'She was already working at the Tracing Bureau,' Charlotte says. 'Her first appraisals were glowing. Her boss writes that she actively participated in field investigations and showed "remarkable intelligence in her analysis of documents." Despite being so young, she kept being given new responsibilities. She was good at her job, that much is clear.'

She looks up from the file.

'Look, Irène.'

In a letter addressed to the American director, Eva explains that she wants to carry out investigations in Poland, but she's concerned her statelessness might leave her vulnerable. In his response, the director agrees that the communist government would likely detain her and advises her to reconsider until she has a solid lead.

From the end of the war, the Western Allies opposed the forced repatriation of displaced people to the new Soviet bloc. The diplomatic tension in the air was a harbinger of the Cold War. Eva must have been torn between her desire to find her family and her fear of being stuck in a country where she couldn't see a future for herself.

'She must have changed her mind,' says Charlotte, 'because I can't find any record of a trip to Poland in the following years. But I do have her correspondence with the head of human resources. Did you know Johanna, Irène?'

'I didn't, but Eva held her in high esteem. If I'm not mistaken, she was pushed out after Max Odermatt arrived?'

'There were irreconcilable differences in their approaches. She was one of the first Germans to be hired here. She started as a typist. She was in her early twenties and knew nothing about Nazi atrocities. She and other young German women were utterly shocked by what they typed up. Johanna fell in love with a Polish DP who wanted to emigrate to Canada. At the time, she had to give up her German nationality to marry him.

Can you imagine? And she paid a high price: the whole town ostracised her. In the end they stayed here. She was an incredible HR manager for over thirty years, devoted to the employees. I would have loved to meet her.'

Me too, thinks Irène. For so many years, her aversion to asking Eva about her past deprived her of precious conversations with the people who lived through it all.

'Sorry, I've got to go,' says Charlotte, looking at her watch. 'I'll leave you with Eva's file. Just get it back to me when you're done.'

*

With Eva's precious file in hand, Irène exits the building. She slips on the icy ruts that tyres have left in the staff car park. When she gets home, the dark entryway smells of cold ash. She hangs up her wet parka, turns on the dim tabletop lamps, and starts a fire. She drinks in the cosiness of her home and admires the pictures Hanno drew as a child, which are framed on the wall, adding a joyful note to the decor. Her plush green velvet armchair is waiting for her. Irène pours a glass of wine, puts on some jazz, and takes a few bites of pizza before diving into Eva's correspondence.

For weeks after arriving, Eva battled intense fatigue, terrible joint pain, migraines, and insomnia. Even on a high-protein diet, she struggled to achieve a normal weight. She retained her gaunt figure for the rest of her life, like a tree with no sap. In summer she forced herself to swim several times a week at the pool or in nearby lakes. She rediscovered the happiness she'd felt as a child, splashing in the Vistula. Johanna's replies to Eva are full of warmth and kindness. She encouraged her to adapt her hours and to take proper breaks during her long workdays. In another pair of letters, they discuss an altercation Eva had at the bakery, when a German woman insulted her. Things became heated and Eva ended up punching her. Johanna assures her that management will support her if legal action is taken.

It's no stretch of the imagination to picture the scene. Eva always knew how to stick up for herself.

Irène's phone interrupts her. 'How are you, Mummy dearest?' Hanno asks sweetly.

She's ashamed to realise she hasn't called him since Myriam told her about Hermine.

'I'm just drowning in work. You know how I am.'

'You're impossible to be around,' he teases.

'Is it that bad?'

'Even worse.'

'I've really put you through a lot, haven't I?'

Hanno laughs and agrees, then tells her he'll be home for the weekend.

'I'd like us to spend some time together, just the two of us. Is that cool?'

Irène feels a rush of secret joy. For the past few months, Hanno's been all about the Glasers.

She's cosy by the fire when she rereads the beginning of a letter Eva wrote to Martin Talbot in May 1951. He ran the ITS as the representative of the Allied High Commission.

Irène can't believe what she's reading.

Eva writes that she suspects one of her German colleagues, Holger S., was in the SS.

One morning she chanced upon him as he was leaving the archives, though she knew he didn't have authorisation to go inside. Ever since, she'd been watching him from afar. He never spent time with the DPs, preferring the company of a small group of German staff. Ten days later she passed him in a lane at the swimming pool and noticed a letter tattooed on the inside of his upper arm, right below the armpit. She knew that SS men had tattoos of their blood group in that exact spot. Ever since, she'd been unable to sleep, tormented by the idea that a former SS officer was hiding at the ITS.

She was asking Talbot for authorisation to investigate him.

'At night, I'm back in the camp. If I don't find out for sure what he's up to, I'll never be able to sleep again,' she wrote.

Talbot's response is not in the file. But a letter from Eva, written three weeks later, implies they discussed the matter in person, and he allowed her to access relevant documents.

'I don't understand how the employees of an Allied organisation could have been so negligent. You say they're not like the people who welcomed us when we were liberated from the camps, that they don't realise what the Nazis were capable of. But how could they have hired Germans without due diligence? The fact that this murderer has hidden out here for months, no, years, that he's had the opportunity to destroy all records of his crimes, makes me sick. I know you understand how I feel. I fear there are more like him, sir. Give me more time and I'll unmask them all.'

The replies are missing. Did he sign off on a discreet investigation? Was he worried a public scandal would sully the ITS's reputation? Irène stares at the words, incredulous, until they blur before her eyes. How could they have hired former SS men to guard archives on Nazi persecution? Were there sympathisers at the heart of the Centre?

Irène logs on to the Central Index remotely and does some research on Martin Talbot. The American ran the ITS at a time when the Allied High Commission was ready to hand off such a heavy responsibility. Talbot was tasked with ensuring a smooth transition.

'We are here to serve the millions of victims of this war, regardless of their background, nationality, politics, or creed. We serve the living as well as the dead. This is our duty and our honour,' he said at the inauguration of the new buildings. He didn't seem like the sort to take his mission lightly.

Eva had written, 'I know you understand how I feel'. Eva trusted no one, but she had put her faith in this German-speaking Jew from Czechoslovakia, who had fled Central Europe in 1938, then returned to fight the Nazis in an American uniform.

Irène takes a closer look at a message he sent to his superiors in the winter of 1952. The heading reads THE FUTURE OF THE ITS. She is stunned to learn the Americans were thinking about transferring its management to the

German government. Focused entirely on the new political realities of the Cold War, the Western Allies were prepared to hand over evidence of the Third Reich's crimes, and clues to the fate of its victims, to Adenauer's Federal Republic, which hardly saw denazification as a priority.

Using methodical arguments, Talbot aims to persuade his superiors that this idea is heresy. If the Germans ran the ITS, they could destroy evidence and invalidate the Nuremberg verdicts. They would push out the DPs and replace them with German employees who were far less trustworthy. *Oh, the irony,* Irène can't help but think. The last argument laid out exactly what Max Odermatt did nearly thirty years later, with the blessing of the International Committee of the Red Cross.

'I have recently discovered that forty-five of our German employees held senior positions in the SS or Gestapo,' Talbot writes. 'Our investigation has revealed that one of them tried to set fire to the entire archive. All these men were hired to work at the ITS by agents of Allied organisations, with no regard for due diligence or denazification laws. I dismissed them all immediately, but I cannot stress enough the danger of giving war criminals access to our archives. If this mess ever became public knowledge, the reputations of the Allied High Commission and International Tracing Service would be irreparably damaged. It is my recommendation that management of the archives be relinquished to an international body, which would oversee the mission and its staff.'

Irène takes a sip of wine. The secret has been well kept. Did Talbot make some sort of deal with Eva? He'd allow her to investigate in return for her silence?

A conversation comes back to Irène. It took place a few months after she joined the ITS. She and Eva had just had lunch with the Brain, who'd regaled them with a series of amusing anecdotes. Irène found him irresistibly charming.

'He's such a lovely man,' Eva had conceded. 'He's so modest and brave. Very few of us from the original team are left. Most wanted to leave Germany when the Allied troops pulled out.'

'So why did you two stay?' Irène asked.

'I can't speak for him. As for me, I had nothing left. At least I feel useful here. And someone had to keep an eye on the archives. You've heard of Cerberus, the dog who guards the Underworld?'

'I have. Why?'

'Don't you see the resemblance?' Eva replied, her smoker's laugh filling the corridor.

Irène can hear it still.

Karol

Irène sits in the corridor massaging her temples. Last night, she dreamt Eva was warning her. *They're coming back.* It was impossible to get back to sleep after that. Her usual anxiety – an irrational fear that someone would harm Hanno – clamped onto her and wouldn't let go. It was three in the morning, so she tried to resist the urge to call him. 'Calm down, he's fine,' she said aloud to loosen the grip of the vice on her chest. She visualised the tranquil paths that ran through his campus, students engaged in deep discussions beneath the trees. A real and reassuring world which could not be shattered.

In the end she gave up trying to sleep, put a log in the fireplace, and binge-watched *Fleabag* until dawn. She loved the tormented heroine and her trenchant humour. When Irène woke, having finally dozed off, her car was snowed in. As she shovelled the hardened snow, she felt the fresh air in her lungs chase away her dark thoughts. Clad in a mantel of powdery white, the forest shimmered in the morning sunlight. When Hanno still lived at home, this chore was his. They'd always end up having a snowball fight punctuated with fits of uncontrollable laughter. She suddenly wonders if she should adopt a dog. The Glasers' Labrador is so affectionate.

Silke Bauer is on time. She's been with the Child Search Bureau for two years. Before that, she taught contemporary history in Berlin, where she specialised in the Nazi process of 'Germanisation'. She discovered the ITS while doing research for a book she was writing. For eighteen months, she spent all her days off going through the archives. After she published, Charlotte Rousseau convinced her to stay.

Silke welcomes Irène into her impeccably tidy office. There are no precariously balanced files here, no mugs of cold coffee dregs on the shelves. An Advent wreath – a keepsake from her childhood in Berlin – enjoys pride of place. She misses the bustle of the capital. It's too small here, she says. So small it feels like living in one of those little painted wooden villages you put out on Christmas Eve. She's about fifty, with short faded blonde hair and the dark circles of an insomniac. A reformed smoker, she's invariably holding an electronic cigarette in her hand. Silke focuses on 'unaccompanied children': displaced minors who ended up in the German-occupied zones. When the war was over, the Allies were suddenly responsible for millions of 'lost' children. Orphans, kids who'd survived the camps, teenage forced labourers, and so on. Aid agencies had to look after them, identify them, and organise their repatriation. The majority were malnourished, traumatised, and unable to speak. The volunteers, many of whom were just arriving from Britain and America, had no first-hand experience of war. But they quickly realised that this task would require absolute devotion. It took them considerably longer to understand that they were merely pawns on a huge chessboard and to fully comprehend just how little they could do.

'I'm looking for a Polish boy,' Irène explains. 'He was taken in late 1941 or early 1942. The Polish Red Cross looked into his case but couldn't find anything.'

'Do you want to reopen the file? Do you have any new leads?' asks Silke.

'It's too early to say. His mother died in Ravensbrück.'

'Was she part of the Resistance?'

'I don't think so. I'm not sure why the Germans deported her.'

'Maybe they just wanted to get rid of her,' Silke suggests.

'So how did investigators first get wind of this Germanisation programme?' Irène asks.

'In the beginning there were just rumours. But the rumours were persistent. It seemed the Nazis had abducted children with "good racial standing" from the occupied territories and sent them to be raised by German families. It sounded like a bogeyman story designed to scare children into good behaviour. But later, thousands of photos of missing children flooded in from Eastern Europe and the Baltic states, and there was no longer any question. Today we think two hundred thousand children were kidnapped.'

'Two hundred thousand!'

'Dizzying, isn't it? Himmler told the SS to "take purebloods" wherever they may be. They identified children between two and twelve who had "Aryan features". Then, with the help of Nazi nurses, who were called the "Brown Sisters", they stole them from schools, orphanages, or right off the street.'

An image of Wita on a snowy pavement pops into Irène's mind unbidden. Blond little Karol is giggling and running beside her. She scolds him, tells him he mustn't get so close to the road. A black sedan slows a few metres away and a nurse gets out. She smiles at the child, asks how old he is and strokes his hair. Wita takes him in her arms. The nurse looks back towards the car and nods. Immediately, two SS men emerge to wrest the child from his mother's arms. Wita fights hard to keep hold of him, screaming all the while. They hit her, hurry back to the car, hand the child to the nurse, and take off.

But Irène will never know if that's really how it happened.

'Who were these Brown Sisters?' she asks quietly.

'Women who were uncommonly devoted to the Nazi cause and volunteered to serve in the east. They would locate desirable children, then tell the parents they had to go for medical tests. And if they refused, the SS got involved.'

'Were the children sent to Germany immediately?'

'First they were sent to "race experts", who subjected them to all sorts of tests: measuring the distance between their eyes, the shape of their noses, and their body proportions. They also searched for birthmarks and any diseases or genetic abnormalities they might be carrying. Those who weren't deemed Aryan enough were either sent home or dumped at forced labour camps. Those who passed were transported to special "re-education" centres. There were lots of these in Poland. The goal was to produce perfect little Germans. If the children spoke their native language they were severely punished. The youngest were sent to *Lebensborn* centres, before being adopted by Nazi families. The others were made to work for the Reich.'

Irène is fascinated by how meticulous the process was. By this chain of command where everyone – the SS brutes, nurses, and doctors – was so corrupted by ideology that they all happily played their parts without ever questioning what they were doing. They were all convinced they were acting in the children's best interests. They weren't stealing these children; they were ensuring they fulfilled their destiny.

Since Himmler wanted to be certain there was no evidence of these crimes, the abducted children's birthdates and names were systematically falsified. This made the investigators' task a difficult one. Teenagers still had some childhood memories, but the youngest children had completely forgotten both their parents and their native tongue. They no longer looked like their baby photos either, or at least not enough for the investigators to make definitive matches.

Immediately after the war, Allied military authorities gave people searching for missing children permission to enter German homes when they suspected an illegal adoption. Posters in the streets reminded German parents they were legally bound to answer questions. The Germans hated the foreigners for invading their privacy. To them, there was something sinister about the young British and American women who would turn up with chocolate bars and fake chumminess. Their presence felt like a harbinger of further misfortune, after all the bombs, rapes, and deprivations they'd already suffered. Sometimes the interloper spoke German. Families would share their meagre rations and a bit of schnapps and beer, to relax. They'd talk about how difficult times were, about how their children played in the rubble. After a while the parents would let their guard down and agree to discuss the child. The boy had brought a smile back to the father's face. Kids were life, more resilient than weeds.

Then the visitor would ask more probing questions. The parents refused to believe the insinuations. They were always convinced they had adopted a German child. Nothing could change their minds. Surely the party hadn't lied to them.

If the investigators had any doubts about the child's true identity, they could remove the boy or girl to an Allied centre to await repatriation. But very quickly the American military government began demanding proof of nationality before authorising transfers. In the majority of cases that was impossible, and the authorities were increasingly reluctant to repatriate children to the Soviet bloc.

Irène wonders why the Americans hindered the investigations. 'The Cold War?' she eventually guesses aloud.

'Precisely,' Silke says with a nod.

After the unprecedented bloodshed of the war, children were a cherished prize. The two sides even fought over children born of liaisons between German women and prisoners of war. French soldiers scooped them up as they were returning home. The only children who were not in demand were the frail youngsters who had survived the camps. Switzerland reluctantly accepted Jewish children who had made it out of Buchenwald alive, but only for a few months – just long enough for the Alps' healing air to work its magic.

'These stolen children became a fiercely contested point between the Germans, the American military government, and representatives of the countries they were taken from,' continues Silke. 'Basically, German families had no desire to return these children. Many of the adoptive parents were deeply fond of them. Others saw them as free labour. And the Americans didn't want to indispose their new West German ally. They baulked at the idea of sending these children back, adding to enemy ranks.'

The investigators were torn between their instructions from the military authority and their own ethical concerns. What *was* in the children's best interests? Removing them from their adopted families would create more upheaval, it would mean uprooting them to take them back to a homeland they'd forgotten. But leaving them where they were meant condoning war crimes and legitimising adoption by theft. Was it better to leave the children with their former enemies or condemn them to a life of misery in the Soviet bloc?

'After the war, the journalist Gitta Sereny tried to track down the stolen children,' Silke explains. 'In an interview she mentions an official directive from the American military government, which ordered children whose parents now lived in the Soviet bloc to be sent to the US, Canada, and Australia.'

'So their parents were waiting for them but they were sent elsewhere . . . just to keep them out of the Soviets' hands?'

'Exactly. In an interview she gave many years later, she couldn't help but wonder, "How could anyone think of ordering that children who had twice suffered the trauma of losing parents, home, and language should, like so many packages, be transported overseas and dropped into yet other new and entirely strange environments?"'

The two women step out onto the balcony so Irène can smoke. The melting snow reveals a smattering of slate roof tiles.

'It's inhumane what they did to those kids,' Irène exclaims once she's inhaled. 'Do you think that's what happened to Karol?'

'It's possible. Unless the investigation really did hit a dead end. What we know for sure is that, out of two hundred thousand missing children, only twenty-five thousand were returned to their home countries. By 1949, it was really quite convenient for most people to leave them in Germany. Maybe your Karol stayed with his adoptive family. In which case the Polish Red Cross would have been told he was untraceable, and the file would have been destroyed.'

'What I need is to talk to some of the people who investigated these cases.'

'I met a few when I was writing my book. I can give you their contact details,' Silke says as she walks Irène to the door.

*

Afterwards, Irène drives to Kassel and finds a book by Gitta Sereny in a high street bookshop. Its Conradian title – *Into That Darkness* – promises to show her the dark heart of Treblinka, where she hopes to find clues about Lazar.

She eats dinner alone in a little Greek restaurant, far from the bustle of the pubs. She orders a glass of ouzo and thinks of Allegra. She struggles to imagine her as an old woman.

A notification lights up her screen.

Janina Dabrowska has emailed to say she's found Wita's husband's children. She attaches an address near Lublin.

Irena, I hope you'll enjoy my little surprise. It was misfiled in another case, so finding it was no easy task! Hopefully it will brighten your days until you can find time to come to Poland!

Irène impatiently enlarges a photo Janina attached. A young Wita is holding a small blond boy. Her lips brush his ear as she whispers a secret, and he laughs, tickled by her breath, forgetting the big black eye of the camera. He can't have been more than eighteen months old. A blonde curl slides over Wita's right eye. The expression on her face, as she meets the photographer's gaze, is mischievous but tender. She is glowing. Irène thinks of all the ways her light was dimmed between this instant and the moment she had her photograph taken at Auschwitz.

The child's chubby hand is resting on his mother's neck, and this tiny detail breaks Irène's heart. He's so calm and sure in the knowledge he is protected and loved.

Irène decides to make them both a promise she hopes she'll be able to keep.

Eva

Lucia and Irène stare at each other in silence, intimidated by the tape player. On the tape's label, the words *Eva Volmann, 7 November 1978*.

'When I set out, this is not where I imagined I'd end up,' Lucia Heller admits.

Since their first meeting, her face has acquired a new gravity. The lives of long-lost relatives have left their mark. She sought out their traces on a school playground, in a courtyard, in the window of a jewellery shop which had once been a kosher deli, and on the tombstones of an unkempt cemetery overgrown with brambles.

'Are we really going to hear her voice?' Lucia asks once more.

Irène nods. She didn't have the courage to listen to the recording beforehand.

When she arrived at work this morning, Irène was almost certain Lucia would be disappointed. Everything she had on Eva pertained to her postwar life: a thin envelope of photos, performance reviews, and a few letters. But, a few hours later, the director placed the tape on her desk and said, 'Mark Epstein.'

'I'm sorry, what?' Irène asked, puzzled.

'He's an American author of German descent. He came to the ITS in 1978. He was writing a novel and needed information on the death marches.'

'And they actually let him in?' Irène asked, surprised.

'This was before Odermatt's time. The director back then believed in the importance of partnerships and the free circulation of ideas. Anyway, Epstein met a few of the former DPs who worked here and decided to record them. For decades, no one paid the recordings any notice. They've been at the bottom of an HR filing cabinet. You see, inventory isn't all bad—'

'So, this is Eva?' Irène gasps.

'I don't know how he did it, but he got her to talk.'

And now here she is with Lucia, opposite this old cassette player and its crackling recording. Amid the static, Eva's voice emerges from beyond the grave. It's less hoarse than Irène remembers, somewhat distorted, and slightly defensive. But it's definitely her. Irène remembers that sardonic tone, her inimitable way of disarming whoever she was talking to. The interview is all in German.

'Do I really have to say that? I feel like I'm on trial! Do I have to swear on the Bible too? My name is Eva Volmann. I was born in Warsaw on 30 April 1930. I've been working here since 1947.'

'What brought you to the ITS?'

His voice is gentle. Like an outstretched hand to be taken or refused.

'I wanted to find my family. I was obsessed. I knew that I would have the means to look for them here. At

first, they wouldn't even consider hiring me. They thought I was too young.'

'How old were you?'

'Nearly seventeen, but what's in a number? That age was the one I'd been given, like the rags on my back. All I cared about was finding my family.'

'How did you get them to let you stay?'

'How do you think? I refused to take no for an answer.'

Eva's laugh fills the room as if she's standing right next to them. The illusion is so true to life that it brings tears to Irène's eyes.

'No one was as stubborn as me. You've no idea.'

Epstein joins in with a muffled laugh.

'So they kept you on. And you quickly became one of their best investigators, didn't you?'

Irène can hear the pride in Eva's voice.

'I was pretty good at my job, yes. I worked really hard. But I had competition too. I remember a guy from Kraków. In Buchenwald he had sabotaged medical experiments and saved quite a few people. He was an excellent investigator. We were a team. I learnt a lot just by watching him.'

'What became of him?'

'He emigrated to America in the early fifties. Lots of people left back then. The Allied armies were leaving Germany, and they'd recently closed the last DP camps. I remember a town hall meeting on the church square. Everyone was there. We were completely segregated, you see: us on one side, them on the other!'

Eva laughs again.

'The American officers declared that, from that moment on, DP status no longer existed. We could either stay or emigrate. The Federal Republic of Germany, in its great generosity, was offering us the status of "stateless foreigners". This would give us the right to live and work in Germany, without ever becoming citizens. I know what you're thinking, but it was a step up from Untermenschen! In fact, all the locals were furious. And they didn't keep quiet about it either. We parasites had no right to stay in their precious fatherland, no right to a slice of all the Marshall Plan cash flowing in.'

'Even though you'd all been working here for years?'

'In their eyes we were just muckrakers, stirring up the filth they'd willingly wallowed in for twelve years. They were hoping we'd bugger off with the Americans.'

'What about you? What did you want to do?'

'Most of us couldn't imagine living in Germany without Allied protection. It was obvious the old Nazis were still here. Some of them didn't even hide it. In the next village, former Waffen SS men would hold rallies. They wanted to do away with the Republic and create the Fourth Reich! Can you imagine? So most DPs preferred to start afresh somewhere else.'

'But you stayed.'

'I never believed that my life would be better elsewhere. I knew moving wouldn't change anything. And I loved my work. Others chose to stay too, like the

Brain. We understood each other. We didn't have to pretend.'

'*What about your family? Did you ever find them?'*

Epstein asks this question casually, even though he must know it will sting. The silence that follows vibrates in the staticky air for a long time.

'*I never found a single lead. It's as if they never existed. Did you know they didn't even record the names of people sent to Treblinka from the Warsaw Ghetto? They were erased before they even arrived.'*

'*So they're not listed anywhere?'*

'*No. When they began deporting everyone, my father and his friends built a hiding place for my grandparents in the attic above their apartment. He was in charge of getting provisions to them, though all of us were starving. One morning he went up to see them and the partition had been torn down. The wheelchair was overturned on the floor. A neighbour told them that a Jewish policeman from the Judenrat had come with some Trawniki men. You know, eastern POWs who joined the SS. They were just as cruel as the Germans. They'd thrown my grandparents in a cart with other people deemed "untransportable" and shot them in the Jewish cemetery. My father didn't want us to find out, but we all lived in one room. I overheard him telling my mother.'*

Lucia Heller's expression doesn't change. She simply listens, and every word falls, as if down a well, into the deepest part of her.

'*Did your parents escape the deportations?'*

'They were killed during the Uprising. My brothers too. I don't know where or how . . . I'm sorry, I just can't . . .'

Irène can't bear the pain in Eva's voice.

Mark Epstein apologises gently. The tape stops with a click, then restarts after a pause.

'How did you manage to escape the ghetto?'

'My parents had a friend on the other side of the wall. She knew a network which passed children to the Aryan side. Once they got out, the network hid them in someone's house, or in a convent. But this only worked if the child spoke Polish, knew Catholic prayers, and didn't look too Jewish. My brothers only spoke Yiddish. They were both dark with very curly hair. But I could pass. A Jewish woman from Dresden lived with us in the ghetto and gave me German lessons, and I spoke fluent Polish. For weeks, my mother made me learn prayers and practice Mass rituals. I hated it, I didn't want to go live with the goyim.'

'Did you understand it was a matter of life and death?'

'What do you think?'

The words ring out like a slap in the face. Irène can just imagine the look Eva is giving him.

'We lived with death, we saw it every day. There were bodies in the stairwell, in the courtyard, on the pavement outside. We weren't allowed to leave the building, the street was too dangerous. When the deportations started, we'd stay still for hours on end, our bodies folded into the most unlikely shapes. Don't

cry, don't breathe too loud. We were always listening for footsteps or barking. We were afraid every second of every day. I was twelve and I eavesdropped on the adults' conversations. I knew going to the Umschlagplatz meant death. I knew all that, but I still didn't want to leave my family. My mother didn't give me a choice. One night in early winter 1943, a man came to get me. He led me through the sewers. We walked for hours in the darkness. Sometimes we had to crawl through the black water, and I clung to his coat. When we finally made it to the other side of town, I was soaked and couldn't stop shivering. Someone wrapped me in a big blanket and hid me in the boot of a car. All I really remember is how hungry and afraid I was. I was handed over to a strange woman, along with other children. She gave me a bath and did what she could to comfort us. But all the children were crying, it was so upsetting.'

'How long did you stay with her?'

'I don't know, maybe two weeks. One morning a young woman came to get me. I called her Kasia. She was part of the Resistance. She gave me a birth certificate in the name of Renata Sliwa, and a Kennkarte. I couldn't have gone anywhere without an identity card. She made me recite the life story of the real Renata, who must have been dead, then took me to where I would be living from then on.

'And where was that?'

'In Wola, in the western part of Warsaw. The woman who took me in was a real bitch who spent all her time

shouting at me. She was afraid I'd attract the neighbours' attention, so she made me stay in my room all day with the shutters closed. She didn't like me, but she needed the money. It was worse than being in the ghetto. One Sunday she went to Easter Mass. I took my chance and escaped, making my way back towards the city centre.

'Did you want to go back to the ghetto?'

'Yes. I was certain I could find the entrance to the sewer. But when I was still very far away, I saw smoke in the sky. As I got closer, I realised that the Uprising had begun. There were tanks everywhere, and soldiers armed to the teeth. The worst thing was the Poles who'd come in crowds to enjoy the show. Some were cheering that Hitler was getting rid of the Yids. Others were mocking the Wehrmacht for sending tanks and an army to defeat a handful of starved Jews. As for me, I wanted to cross the wall and fight with them.'

'Was your father among the rebels?'

'No, he wasn't a fighter. He was an intellectual, a humanist. He organised cultural events in the ghetto, concerts, secret classes, and such. My mother was more rigid in her thinking. To me, she was the epitome of rules! I hated following the rules. My father would always defend me. When they began deporting people, it broke his spirit. All the young people on the block committee had been sent to Treblinka. All our neighbours and friends, one after the other. My father lost all hope, he was a shadow of his former self. But my mother was the opposite, her anger galvanised her. She

became the head of the family. She sold our last, most meaningful possessions for scraps of food. She even sold her wedding dress to some unscrupulous Poles. In the end she joined the Jewish Combat Organisation. The whole time she was planning my escape, she was attending secret meetings to prepare for the Uprising.'

'*She was very brave.*'

'*Yes. It was strange, as if she'd become a whole new person. A person I'd never met before. Taking action made her stronger. She was no longer afraid. She even made me think that they could win, and that afterwards she would come to find me. But she was only saying that so I'd agree to go. She knew they didn't stand a chance.*'

Eva's voice breaks.

The tape stops.

*

Irène and Lucia go out for a cigarette in the park. They shiver without their coats as the fresh snow soaks their shoes. Both are thinking, *I couldn't have done this alone.* Then they return to the room, which now feels like a crypt. The voice of a whole world destroyed continues to echo through Eva's account.

Lucia

THE TAPE STARTS UP AGAIN. Eva's voice is firmer, and she's the one asking the questions now. She's gaining the upper hand.

'*Why are you doing this? What's the point? Poland's one huge cemetery, and no one cares.*'

Now the writer's the one who finds himself struggling for words.

'*I guess I'm doing it . . . so these people don't disappear. Through your story, they live on.*'

'*Do you really think so?*'

'*I hope so.*'

Then the novelist takes her back to spring 1943, that day of smoke and fear.

'*So what did you do once you got to the ghetto?*'

'*I couldn't get close, it was rammed with policemen and soldiers. Kasia had warned me that blackmailers hung around just outside the ghetto walls, trying to spot Jews. She had told me that if I was ever in trouble, I was to go to a haberdasher on Mostowa Street and ask for the blue ribbon my mother had ordered. The shopgirl made me wait for hours in the storage closet until Kasia came to get me. She hid me in her attic room for a few days, but it was too risky. So she took me to Praga, on the other bank of the*

Vistula. A widow there had agreed to take me in. Filomena. Since no one could see into it, I was allowed to use the garden. She was very pious and tried to convert me. She kept telling me, "The good lord has sent you this test to save your soul."'

Eva laughs.

'And did she succeed?'

'Oh, I was a lost cause! But the good thing about Filomena was she let me read the newspaper. That's how I found out the ghetto had been destroyed. The German papers said all the insurgents had been killed. But Filomena said some had managed to escape through the sewers. I desperately hoped my family was in hiding somewhere on the Aryan side. Sometimes Kasia would come by to keep my spirits up. In autumn 1943 she stopped coming. Filomena stopped receiving payments from the network as well, but she kept me anyway.'

'Do you know why Kasia stopped coming?'

'I only found out ten years ago, when I tried to find her. One morning the Gestapo turned up at her door. Someone had turned her in. They executed her in the ruins of the ghetto. That's where they took people to kill them. She was nineteen. Before the war she was a girl scout. Poor thing.'

'Did you stay with Filomena for a long time?'

'Almost a year. In February 1944 I took off again.'

'Did she not want you any more?'

'Oh, it wasn't that. I'd been holed up for over a year and I just couldn't wait any longer. I'd convinced myself my parents were still alive. So I climbed out the window. It was so cold my teeth chattered. I remember the black clouds

over the frozen Vistula. I crossed the river to get to the Old Town, taking the back streets. I went back to Królewska Street, near the university, where we'd lived before the war.'

'That was very risky!'

'It was downright stupid. I thought maybe my parents would go back there to hide. I didn't dare knock, though. The neighbour's curtain twitched, and I realised my little expedition was crazy, that I had to go back to Filomena. I remember forcing myself not to run. At the street corner I bumped into a boy I'd gone to school with. "Arrest her, she's a Jew!" he shouted, and I slapped him. He rounded up the other local thugs and they chased me down, then handed me over to the German police. From there I went to Pawiak Prison and on to Auschwitz.'

'Would you like to tell me about that?'

'No, I'm tired.'

'Let's stop for today. But one last question: have you found any survivors from your family?'

'My father's brother managed to get out in 1940, with his wife and children. They live in Buenos Aires.'

Lucia Heller opens her dark eyes wide. Irène knew this moment would come. An investigator of Eva's calibre would surely have managed to find what remained of her family. She is sure Lucia is going to be hurt by what follows.

'Have you tried to contact them?'

Eva is silent, seems to hesitate.

'I wanted to, but I've never been able to bring myself to do it. They left before the ghetto closed . . . when we all believed we could just grit our teeth and stick together. That

this violence would go away as suddenly as it started. When I think back to the girl I was ... At my house there were always endless discussions and arguments. Sometimes I felt suffocated, I wanted my own life. It's ironic, isn't it? Now I have that life. Only it's empty because my family aren't here. The girl I was is long dead. So I can't see them again. If they didn't want to know what happened, I would be devastated. But if they did, my answers would destroy them. So, you see, it's better this way.'

'Do you feel at home here now?'

'At home? I don't know what that means. My childhood was my home. I'll never feel at home again.'

'Thank you, Eva, for trusting me with your story.'

Irène's eyes meet Lucia Heller's, red and rimmed with tears. She stops the tape and tries to think of something to say to ease her pain. 'The younger generations want to know,' as Charlotte said. But truth can be brutal. Eva had cut the ties to her past. She chose to stay in Arolsen with a handful of displaced people, people who would remain so wherever they went. Ripped from everyone and everything they loved, they knew the poisonous scorched earth that lived on within them could not be shared. But their mission gave them a reason to keep on living.

Lucia suddenly feels cold. She puts on her coat and says, 'Thank you, Irène. Thanks to you, I feel as though I've met her. It makes me terribly sad to learn she didn't want to meet us. I hope you know we'd have welcomed her with joy and open arms. She wouldn't have been a burden, quite the opposite. She could have rebuilt a life for herself, surrounded by the warmth of her family.'

'You heard what she said. She just couldn't.'

'I understand, but it still makes me sad. There are so few of us. We would have loved her with all our hearts. Can you make me a copy of this recording? I want my children to listen to it when they're old enough.'

'Of course I can. Now come, I have some other things for you too.'

*

'You knew her. What was she like?' Lucia asks at the foot of the main staircase.

When the word *ferocious* comes to mind, Irène shares it with Lucia. Her fondness for her friend is plain as day. 'I like how you talk about her,' Lucia says. 'You were very close, weren't you?'

'As close as she allowed people to get. She didn't give much away. She kept her distance. Except with her cat!'

As she says those words, she remembers the photo her son took in secret one Sunday, when Eva invited them over for lunch. The old tabby cat had fled when they arrived. In the end he returned and jumped down from the windowsill onto Eva's lap. Hanno captured the moment. Irène finds the photo in her desk drawer. She likes this portrait because the creature has coaxed a softness from Eva, a softness she was always reluctant to show.

'Here we go,' she says as she hands the picture to Lucia.

After the camp, but before her illness. This is how Irène remembers Eva, this is the image etched in her memory.

'She's beautiful,' Lucia murmurs.

The cat is purring on her lap, triumphant. Eva's smile is one of willing capitulation.

Irène spreads other photos out on her desk, mysterious sepia pictures from another age. Young girls in floral print sit on the steps, a look of poignant vulnerability in their eyes. Couples dance at a holiday party in 1947. Under the International Tracing Service sign, next to a man leaning on crutches, Eva raises her chin defiantly, as if to say 'What are you looking at?' In another photo she's just won a swimming competition. She's so very skinny in her bathing costume, with her nimble grasshopper legs. Behind the smiles Eva puts on for the camera, there's an underlying melancholy she's trying to hide, like a limp she didn't want anyone to notice. Later, in 1965, Eva is posing with her colleagues on Christmas Eve. She must have been thirty-five at the time but looks a lot younger. A lot older too.

Visibly moved, Lucia leans in to inspect her face.

'The people with her in this one, were they camp survivors too?'

'Not all of them,' Irène replies. 'But they had all lost everything, that's what they had in common. The one on the right was a fighter pilot. I always thought he was in love with her.'

Lucia finds him rather dashing. 'Were they a bit like family to her?' she asks pensively.

Irène wonders if that word would have hurt Eva.

'I can't tell you that.'

'I'm glad she wasn't alone at the end.'

'She wasn't alone,' Irène says, even though she knows it's a lie.

*

As they cross the park, Lucia tells Irène she acted on an impulse that originated in the very core of her being. She's here in defiance of her grandfather's silence. A silence built like a wall, from terror and unfathomable anguish. She didn't come to knock that wall down, she explains, but to form connections with the people who didn't survive. To listen to *them*. She knows the experience will change her, even though she fears that much about these ravaged lives will remain hidden. She's worried that now her love for her children will be most keenly felt through her fear of losing them.

'When my son was born,' Irène says, 'I'd dream of his tiny dead body and wake up in tears. Even now I worry someone might hurt him, physically or emotionally. It keeps me up at night. Love makes you strong, but it makes you vulnerable too. Eva fought against all forms of attachment but was disarmed by the love her cat showed her. What would life be like without love?'

'Colourless.'

'That's why you came here to find out about your family. They're a part of you now. Don't let their deaths overshadow their lives.'

Irène finds herself saying these words as if she's talking to herself. She feels privileged to have known Eva. In her mind she will store the image with the cat next to the image of teenage Eva in the Warsaw Ghetto, and the skinny young woman who hunted down former Nazis. A woman who would not back down from a fight, but who couldn't talk about her brothers without reopening a terrible wound.

Irène watches as Lucia makes her way towards the gate, the evening wind ruffling the feather in her hat. Before she disappears, she turns and smiles.

Piotr

'Have you tried separating them?' Irène asks sympathetically.

Henning nods wearily.

'It takes an hour and a half to put them down, and then they sleep for a single cycle before waking up inconsolable. And once I'm up, I can't get back to sleep. I lie there thinking about global warming, mass extinctions, and Trump in office. To tell you the truth, I'd rather they kept me busy the whole time from nine to two,' he explains.

'Make yourself another coffee, go on.'

Together they sip their watery coffee with a strange, freeze-dried-soup aftertaste, studying the psychedelic patterns the sunlight casts on the wallpaper.

'How's your investigation going?' Irène asks, changing the subject.

Henning has spent a few weeks trying to find the owner of a wedding ring with a Cyrillic inscription.

'The ring belonged to a deported Bulgarian,' he replies. 'He died in the Dachau Revier. I think I've found his daughter in Gabrovo. I just need to check a few things with the Red Cross before I get in touch.'

Technically, Henning should invite the relative to Bad Arolsen or ask if they'd prefer the object to be sent, but he's hoping for a few days of leave to take it to her.

'It looks pretty. The town's nestled in the foothills of the Balkan Mountains. But if I leave my wife alone with the twins, she'll leave me.'

'Take her along. Dump the twins outside your parents' house, and speed off before they can say no.'

Henning looks tempted as he stares into space.

'What about Wita, any news?' he asks, as if it's perfectly normal to get updates on a woman who died seventy-one years ago.

Irène shows him the photos taken in Auschwitz, and the one with her son.

'Poor woman. Do you have any leads on the kid?'

Irène explains that she's called several of the people Silke Bauer interviewed for her book. One died just a year ago. Another worked in a centre for unaccompanied children after the war. She recalled how the children who had been torn from their adoptive families cried all night and began wetting the bed. It made the woman doubt the purpose of her mission. She remembered that there had been Polish children, but she couldn't recall any names. It was so long ago, and they all had German names anyway. One boy had been returned to his biological mother, who lived near Gdańsk, but a few weeks later he ran straight back to his adoptive mother. 'Cases like that were heartbreaking,' the woman concluded. 'We ended up thinking the best thing to do was leave them where they were, if they were doing well. But Piotr didn't agree. He would move heaven and earth to find the kids' real parents.' Piotr Waliński, she went on to explain. A Polish man who had helped Allied organisations in the field. His tenacity was exhausting.

A woman Irène reached in London the night before had said the same thing. She'd laughed and said, 'A relentless shit-stirrer, that one. Piotr was the bête noire of American soldiers and German child protection agencies alike. He was never taken in by their promises and never let anything go. They nicknamed him "Bull". He cross-referenced every piece of information and opened every envelope in the massive pile of mail himself. Before long, everyone knew to hand off the most complicated cases to him.'

'Well, looks like you need to find this "Bull" then,' concludes Henning.

'He moved to the US. And is most likely dead,' Irène replies with a sigh.

Henning accepts the challenge. Persistent people can do incredible things.

*

Two days later, Irène gives him what looks like a conch shell.

'Plug it into the wall in the twins' room and they'll fall asleep to the sound of waves, whale song, or the wind rustling through a stand of bamboo. It can make womb sounds too. I tried it. It's hypnotic.'

'And where did you find this gem?' he asks.

'Göttingen.'

'You're a star. Actually, I have a little something for you too,' says Henning. He hands Irène a postcard of the Golden Gate Bridge at sunset. On the back, a few words are scrawled in expansive handwriting.

Sending warmest wishes from San Francisco to all my friends at the Child Search Branch. The sloping streets here keep leading me back to you, in heart and mind. I live in a little red house overlooking the rooftops. I can't wait for you to visit.
   Fondly,
   Bull

The card is dated 11 April 1965 and has a return address.

After a quick search, Irène turns up a Piotr Waliński in San Francisco. If it's the same man, he's reinvented himself as an anarchist bookseller. She finds a few pictures of him from the seventies: red bandana, unbuttoned shirt, moustache, and long hair. He looks more like a hippie than a bull. In one he's posing with Tom Wolfe for the release of *The Bonfire of the Vanities*. In another, he stands beside Leonard Cohen under an arch made entirely of second-hand books. In the most recent photo, he's tanned, with a grey buzzcut, a bomber jacket, and vintage jeans. He looks like an old adventurer who never unpacked his bags. His bookshop, A Tale of Two Hippies, still stands in Haight-Ashbury – the heart of the old beatnik district. Its plum façade is covered in brightly coloured posters and graffiti. A true temple of counter-culture. A place of pilgrimage for ageing punk rockers and anyone else looking to feed their nostalgia for failed revolutions.

Later that night, Irène rings the shop. It's ten o'clock in the morning in California, and the bookshop has just opened. A young woman answers the phone, apologising for the noise. They're doing a soundcheck for the gig that evening. She makes Irène repeat the Polish name.

'Oh, you mean Peter!' she exclaims. 'He used to own this place. He sold it two years ago, but he's still around.'

Irène remembers what Henning said. 'Does he still live in the small red house?' she asks.

'Of course!' the woman replies. 'He's never wanted to leave, even though it's a nightmare with his arthritis. It's so tall and narrow, way too many stairs.'

Irène gets his number. Apparently, Peter has routines. Every morning he has a coffee at Pablo, on Castro Street. Then he takes a stroll round the neighbourhood with his dog, Digger. Right now, the bookseller thinks, Irène should be able to reach him at home.

Irène presses her forehead to the bay window. It's a restless night; she hears gusts of wind and creaking branches. She imagines a café in the sun, a cable car climbing a hill, its bell tinkling, Piotr's Victorian house stretching skyward, its red siding a little faded, and the cries of seagulls skimming the roofs on their way to the sea.

'Oh gosh! The International Tracing Service . . . You're the Ghost of Christmas Past!' Piotr Waliński exclaims when she introduces herself.

His voice is warm, and his English still has traces of a Polish accent. He chuckles to learn he's the one who's been tracked down this time, says he's getting a taste of his own medicine. But behind the bonhomie, Irène senses the shock he's feeling now that this part of his life has suddenly resurfaced, the good memories with the bad. After all, he did put an ocean between himself and his past. Plus fifty years of exile, new stories, and plenty of marijuana. And now a call from Germany has taken him straight back to the war and his youth.

'I've heard an awful lot about you, Bull. Is it true they called you that?' Irène teases to break the ice. He laughs. He'd forgotten that old nickname. He tells her about German towns in ruins, headquarters set up in bombed-out cinemas, the endless queues for everything, and often for nothing. He remembers Shirley, Dee, Janet, and Alice, who came from Boston or Kent to save the world. How quickly they were overwhelmed by the complexity of the situation, how tangled they were in red tape. As for the children, they were sad, unmoored, feral, and ever so disarming. They were herded into makeshift camps, like parcels without labels, their origin and destination unknown. He couldn't sleep at night, tormented by what lurked in their silences. Tracking down stolen children became his obsession. The American soldiers he relentlessly pestered eventually got fed up with him.

'Give it a rest, Bull! Those kids are hardly the worst off!'

Piotr would lose his temper. 'They were kidnapped, for God's sake! What more do you want?'

Their names and lives had been stolen, and now he was supposed to just leave them with their kidnappers? Be content they were treated well? Some were unscrupulously exploited. Others were surrendered one morning to the Allied organisation on the pretext that they'd become 'difficult'. Or just because they were an extra mouth to feed when no one had enough to eat.

'The adoptive parents were deceived too,' Irène objects.

'Of course,' says Piotr. 'And the majority genuinely loved their children. Loved them as much as they'd loved their own, who were sent by the Nazis to fight in a ravaged land and died in uniforms too big for them, next to guns they couldn't even hold. But the plight of these children shouldn't fade in importance against the backdrop of all-encompassing tragedy. And nor should the question of reparations.'

Piotr spent hours studying Red Cross photos and knocking on doors. He would estimate the age of the children and compare their features to those in photos taken several years before. A birth certificate from Poznań or Gdańsk and adoption papers which mentioned a Lebensborn centre often indicated a stolen child. Usually the SS gave them a German first name which was close to their original name. Fransciszek became Franz; Tomek, Thomas; Brygida, Brigitte; Jadwiga, Hedwig . . .

'What about Karol?' Irène interrupts.

'Karol . . . Then you're looking for a Karl. I'll have a look at my notebooks. But it's such a tip in here. If I find anything I'll let you know!'

*

Piotr calls her back two days later, just as she's leaving for work. It's late at night in San Francisco. He turned his house upside down to the sound of the dog's snoring, with a good aged whisky to keep him company. She recognises in his voice the fervour of a successful investigator.

'Gertrud Fischer. She wrote to us in 1947. Back then, I was the one who opened the mail. Most of the time there was nothing to go on. But with Gertrud's letter there was. She had been expelled from East Prussia at the end of the war and put in a refugee camp, where she'd seen big posters with pictures of stolen children. She must have thought that sending us a tip might earn her a favour or two, so she wrote that during the war, she had lived next door to a family named Winter in Königsberg. Fervent Nazis, in her view. Otto, the husband, was a Wehrmacht officer. His wife, Irma, was involved in the party's charitable arm. In 1943 a little boy appeared out of the blue. He couldn't have been more than three or four. To be neighbourly, Gertrud would sometimes look after him. He was a good kid and could play alone for hours without a peep. One evening, when Irma came to collect him, Gertrud told her how surprised she was that the boy would sometimes sing Polish songs. Irma went ashen and mumbled that he had stayed with Polish farmers at the beginning of the war, for his safety. She never left him with Gertrud again. Then, in the spring of 1944, they moved without leaving a forwarding address.

'I knew immediately that I was on to something! I asked a friend at the ITS to find Otto Winter. I got lucky, the Allied military government had questioned him in Munich, as part of the denazification programme. He wasn't classed as a dangerous Nazi. Obviously, that meant nothing, since it was a huge whitewashing operation! They all had each other's backs. So I went to Munich. At the time, Bavaria was withholding information, but I was more stubborn than they were. I ended up on the Winters' doorstep. They'd gone down in the world, but they hadn't come out of the whole thing too badly. The kid was about ten. He was tall for his age and seemed to be doing well. They were fond of him, that much was obvious. They wouldn't leave me alone with him. I said a few Polish words just to see . . . The father tensed up and mumbled the usual cover story: Karl was a German orphan who'd been found in the eastern territories. His adoption papers were in order. I sent his photo to the Polish Red Cross, but they weren't able to identify him. I wanted to admit him to one of our centres, but the Americans refused. They said I was only working off assumptions.'

'A request for an investigation into Karol's whereabouts was submitted to the Warsaw Red Cross in 1949,' Irène says, her heart pounding.

'Indeed it was, my dear. I wrote that in my notebook. At the time, I seriously thought this could be the Winter kid, but the photo was too old to help. It's not easy to match the photos of eighteen-month-olds with those of the same kids as teenagers. But I refused to give up. I gave the Americans hell for weeks. I kept telling them we had enough to remove the boy from the home. Eventually the major took me to one side and told me the evidence just wasn't conclusive. Back then, the military was in charge, and they were always one step ahead. He advised me to drop the case if I didn't want my ass kicked all the way back to Poland. I couldn't go back there. I distrusted the Soviets as much as the Germans. So I kept my mouth shut and closed the case.'

'I understand,' Irène says.

'Not my proudest moment. But it happened all the time. They buried certain files, especially on kids from Eastern Europe. That's why I started taking notes. Names and dates. I thought one of them might knock on my door one day. I often wonder about what they've made of themselves. It was clear little Karl was a good kid. And you're going to say, *At least he was loved.* And that's true. But do you think a tree grows up tall and strong in poisoned soil? That love overcomes war crimes and lies? See, I think that sooner or later everything falls apart. I hope I'm wrong, though. Do you think you'll be able to find him?'

'Thanks to you, I finally have a proper lead. Can you give me the last address you have for them, please?'

She writes in her notebook:

Karl Winter. Adopted son of Otto and Irma Winter. Last known address (1949) 11 Rosenstrasse, Munich.

Hanno

It hits Irène that Hanno seems different. It's almost imperceptible, but he's more confident. When he was little, he styled himself as her protector. He would offer up his pocket money when they needed a new boiler, and he worried about what she'd do to pass the time when he was with his father. He seemed uncertain she'd survive without him. Even today, she senses that his affection is laced with concern. She wishes he'd worry less and is delighted to watch his independence grow. She never wanted to give him the impression that he was the only thing in her life, but if she's honest, that was the case for a long time.

For the first years after the divorce, she hated seeing him constantly shuffled around. She felt as though he wasn't at home anywhere, always in transit. Yet another thing to feel guilty about, in addition to destroying her marriage. So she invested a lot of energy in being a good mother. She came up with little holiday rituals, always went on school trips, and organised punishingly elaborate birthday parties.

Very quickly they adopted the Glasers, or perhaps the opposite was true, and Irène felt less alone, less over-whelmed. On the weekends Hanno spent at his father's, she reacquainted herself with the pleasures of going to sleep at dawn, chatting for hours on the phone, and reading in her pyjamas in front of the fire. She accepted invitations to dinners and drinks and had a few flings. But she always put her son and their fragile equilibrium first. Hanno only ever met one of her lovers, and he'd hated the man so much that he rebuffed all efforts to win him over, his demeanour as icy as the Prussian winter outside. None of the others had meant enough to her to risk an introduction. Compartmentalising her life suited her, though. She wouldn't risk loving anyone outside their little tribe.

Her work became another backbone of sorts, restoring her confidence and authority. But now that Hanno lives in Göttingen, she finds it increasingly difficult to let go of her work. Tracking down and following leads is what makes her tick, and nothing else in her life can match the rush she gets from doing her job well. Sometimes Hanno takes offence. But this weekend he has her all to himself. After spending weeks with her nose in her files, she's savouring the joy in every second with her son.

After a long walk in the forest, they warm up over mugs of mulled wine at the Christmas market. The smell of cinnamon, beer, and grilled sausages wafts through the air.

'So when are you leaving again?' Hanno asks.

Her reply is drowned out by hearty laughs at a neighbouring table. 'The first week of the holidays!' she repeats.

'Doesn't sound like a fun trip to take solo. Why don't I go with you?'

He says it with such little conviction that she bursts out laughing. For him, Poland means Auschwitz, which he visited once on a school trip and once with her, two years ago in November. After seeing the camp, they spent a few days in Kraków, but all Hanno remembers is the smog which cloaked the monuments, hiding their architectural splendour. The fetid, yellow fog clung so tightly to the city that people wore masks in the streets.

'Don't you worry,' Irène reassures him. 'This time I'm going to Lublin and Warsaw.'

This information seems to ease his concerns. He wishes she were less invested. The ITS is still just a job, after all. It would be nice if she could leave it at the office.

*

After loading a Christmas tree into the car, they make their way home through the forest.

'I've met someone,' Hanno suddenly says, with a clumsy sort of haste that Irène finds terribly endearing. He's trying – and failing – to make the news seem trivial. And then, in the interlude their nighttime drive provides, he asks point-blank if she ever loved his father.

Irène hesitates, realising he expects her to answer him as an adult. She barely knew herself when she met Wilhelm. At almost twice her age, he was mature and knew exactly what he wanted. She was flattered and let herself be wooed. The park where they'd met resembled him: elegant, romantic, and a little old-fashioned. Her attraction to Wilhelm was quiet. It was the sort of love she associated with a serious life – one that would finally wrest her from the insular world she'd been trapped in. She looked down on passion as being puerile, so she opted for a more solid foundation. She loved the intimate rhythms of married life. It wasn't a risky love and didn't take up much space; she still had free rein. She could have blown up her marriage by becoming a Madame Bovary in exile or a Lady Chatterley of Hesse. Instead, she did it by following her calling. And it all happened so quickly, she wondered if their love had ever been real.

When she thinks of her ex-husband, the tale of Bluebeard comes to mind. Wilhelm could accept anything she did, as long as she followed his rules and didn't pry into his secrets. Only in Irène's story, Eva was the one to hand her the metaphorical keys, which led to the archives and the books she hid in the attic. Eventually, her curiosity grew too strong to resist. Did she betray her husband? In some ways, she supposes she did. By violating their silent agreement, she revealed that she had never truly been his and that she didn't see herself as a member of his family. Their quiet love held until the silence was broken, though it would undoubtedly have waned over time regardless. Their son would have been the glue that bound them. Maybe she should have stayed silent to protect him.

Once she's completed this mental inventory, she tells Hanno she did love Wilhelm. She feels that's what he needs to hear. She can't help but wonder if his father confides in him. If he's rewritten the story of their relationship to match the tone of its demise.

*

Hanno's grandfather died when he was eleven. Irène remembers she was helping him into a black turtleneck when he looked into her eyes and asked, 'Why doesn't Dad want you to come?'

Sometimes funerals reconcile old enemies. But she knew that Wilhelm would never bury the hatchet.

'Well, I'm not part of the family any more. And your grandfather and I didn't get on so well. But he loved you deeply, and it's important you say goodbye.'

'Oma says you tell lies about Opa being a Nazi.'

'I never said that he was,' Irène replied, swallowing her anger.

She was so angry at that ornery old woman for bringing her son into this mess. Trying to make him take sides in a situation he didn't understand. Hanno's grandparents talked about her behind her back, oblivious to how much their insinuations were hurting their grandson. That was when she realised that as he got older, Hanno would eventually need to be told the truth about the incident that had destroyed their family. *He'll want to know someday*, she thought, *but I hope not for a very long time.*

*

'How do you know if you're in love?' Hanno suddenly asks, just as Irène shuts off the engine.

By opening up, she's encouraged him to follow suit. He laughs and admits things are never straightforward with Hermine. One minute she's strong, the next she's vulnerable. She teases him for being chivalrous, then calls him

185

in the middle of the night, plagued by anxiety about the end of the world. He doesn't know how to be present without suffocating her.

'You'll learn, don't you worry. The important thing is to stay true to your feelings and be fully yourself with her,' Irène replies. 'Are you happy?'

He nods and smiles. He and Hermine often talk for hours. She encourages him to dive deep into topics, to look beyond the surface of things.

'For example, everyone wants to plant trees. So when you fill up a tank of petrol, they tell you you're funding reforestation if you pay thirty cents more. And you think you're making a difference, helping the environment. Your very own car will have done its part to help save the planet! But in reality, the fossil fuel industry is just using you to keep on polluting unchecked. They plant trees to distract you from the wells they're drilling in Africa! And they don't give a shit about biodiversity, so they plant the wrong sort of trees in the wrong places. Which messes up ecosystems and leads to further environmental collapse. There's no benefit for the planet. Instead, they're using your money to buy themselves a clean conscience!'

'That's awful,' Irène says, thinking of all the times she's secretly patted herself on the back for contributing to some revolutionary environmental initiative and her fantasies about reforesting the Amazon from the comfort of her home.

'Today the biggest polluters boast about producing renewables. But it's a smokescreen, pure marketing. We've got to outwit them, develop tools to catch them out. Establish new norms. That's what Hermine and I want to do. We have loads of plans!'

Irène listens to him as she pokes the fire, then while they grill chestnuts and decorate the tree. When he's passionate about something, he becomes so talkative and gesticulates a lot. He has lovely, strong hands – a man's hands, she notices for the first time. The environment, he says, is his generation's battleground, where everything could be won or lost. He knows they're up against the old guard, who are clinging to their power and poisonous ideas, but it doesn't scare him. He's itching to bring the whole system down. Hanno's enthusiasm reminds Irène of the young woman she once was, a woman with absolute faith in her own strength.

Hermine's influence seems to be everywhere in Hanno's speech. She seems to have channelled his energy into tangible goals. Myriam is right, she's a good influence. But Irène would prefer he grow up at his own pace. She keeps the thought to herself, though. It's so rare for Hanno to confide in her.

'So when are you going to introduce us?' she finally asks.

He laughs, showing his dimples, and she's suddenly intimidated by how handsome he is. He may have inherited her big black eyes and long lashes, but he's also got his father's curls – the locks of a fetching Italian shepherd in a Renaissance painting.

'We talk about you a lot,' Hanno says. 'Hermine admires the way you raised me alone while working full-time. Her mother is more . . . traditional, you know what I mean.

She's a stay-at-home mum, like Oma. I explained your job to her, and she was very impressed.'

Flattered, Irène says there's no rush, but she'd be delighted to meet her when they think the time is right.

In the meantime, they need to decide what they're doing for Christmas. She wants to go to Paris. She's been dreaming of long walks, afternoons at the arthouse cinema, and animated discussions with Antoine before their traditional window-shopping excursion at the fancy department stores on Boulevard Haussmann. Hanno's quite fond of Antoine and gets on board immediately.

'Where will we stay? With Mamie?'

The word intrudes on Irène's lovely holiday tableau, reminding her of her old bedroom with its faded wall-paper. The idea alone makes Irène feel as though she's putting on clothes which are so tight they cut into her skin.

'Not this year,' she decides. 'That way, we won't have to do Christmas Eve with your uncles either.'

With a complicit glance, it's settled.

*

On Monday morning, she leaves the house before daybreak. She puts on the big soft wool scarf Hanno gave her to keep her warm on this trip east.

Just last night, she received an email from the archivist at Yad Vashem, informing her that Lazar Engelmann was a witness at the first Treblinka trial in 1964. Irène will take advantage of her trip to consult the transcripts before she meets with Elvire, the daughter he never knew.

When the small plane takes off from Düsseldorf, Irène feels as if she's taking Wita, Lazar, and Eva with her. She's counting on them to guide her once she reaches her destination.

Agata

Irène's first impression of Warsaw is hostile – a cold city under a leaden sky. Gusts of freezing wind blow right through her as soon as she steps outside. Thankfully her scarf is long enough to wrap round her neck three times. She takes the wrong bus, wanders through the streets, gets on the subway, and eventually makes her way to Central Station where she manages to find a train for Wschodnia, on the other bank of the Vistula River. She gets there a few minutes before the train to Lublin departs and runs to the platform, exhausted and dripping with sweat. Janina Dabrowska has offered to accompany her and is waiting outside the carriage.

'Welcome to Poland, Irena!' Janina exclaims as a smile spreads across her frozen face. Blonde strands peeking out from her hat frame her face. 'We meet at last! I pictured you as an austere blonde, like a Hitchcock heroine. But you're pretty and brunette. Quite the opposite!'

Irène shakes Janina's hand and notices her red lipstick matches her hat.

They climb aboard the yellow train. The heating is broken, so they keep their coats on and buy sandwiches and tea from a man making his rounds with a trolley. As they leave the Warsaw suburbs, Irène watches pine forests unfurl on the other side of the window. The reddish trunks look poised to attack the sky. A few silver birches stand guard on the edge of the woods. Every now and again, she glimpses the polished red roofs of farms that look like Lego buildings, but they're quickly replaced by more trees, like something out of a dream. The carriage is so empty it makes her feel as though she's travelling back in time. Janina is in good spirits as she shares the story of Marek, Wita's husband, whose family they are due to meet tomorrow.

At the Yalta Conference, after the war, Stalin demanded Poland, and he got it. The Allies sacrificed the exiled Polish government and the country's Resistance fighters on the altar of a fragile peace. It was a gross betrayal of all the people who had led such a desperate fight against the Nazis. They still hadn't forgotten the way Hitler and Stalin divvied up Poland at the start of the war either. Or that the Red Army watched Warsaw burn from the far bank of the Vistula, waiting for the city to be reduced to dust, its population massacred or deported, before they crossed the river. The Home Army was ordered to fall in line in exchange for Stalin's pardon. Those who believed him were tortured, imprisoned, or deported to Siberia. Others returned to the forests where they had conducted their clandestine operations during the war. Marek rejoined the National Armed Forces, or NSZ, which were fiercely anti-communist. During those years, the 'cursed soldiers' waged guerrilla warfare against the Soviets. In the summer of 1945, Marek was locked in the dungeon of Lublin Castle. Fortunately for him, his future father-in-law had influential contacts among the local communist intelligentsia, and he was spared the gulag.

'So his future father-in-law supported the communists?' Irène asks, surprised.

'Let's put it this way, he used his connections to keep his sawmill. After the war, the country had to rebuild. His business was thriving, and he had just one child, a daughter. Marek had lost everything. For him, this marriage was an unbelievable opportunity. And for his father-in-law, it appeased his conservative friends so he could continue making opportunist deals with the communists. He'd got a Resistance fighter out of prison and made him his son-in-law and heir. He didn't boast about it, but people knew. At the time, the Polish Resistance was being written out of history. Of course, it's quite the opposite now! Now the "cursed soldiers" are national heroes. Particularly among government supporters.'

'Are there a lot of government supporters here?'

'The region is divided,' Janina explains with a frown. 'The head of the local government is in the ruling party's pocket, but the mayor's from the opposition.'

Ever since the Law and Justice Party rose to power in 2015, two very different Polands have been facing off. Their opposing views on the country's past and future are irreconcilable. Janina says she's very worried about the future of democracy in her country. 'Open debate and compromise are impossible with such obscurantists,' she adds. 'But don't get me started on this, Irena! It gets me so worked up!'

Irène leads the conversation back to Marek. Do his children know why she wants to meet them?

'I told his eldest son that you were looking into his father and his first wife. He's looking forward to meeting you.'

*

The next morning, Irène looks out of the hotel window, savouring this interlude, which almost feels like a holiday. The castle, the Renaissance façades in the Old Town, and the snow-capped baroque bell towers shimmer in the morning light. She calls Hanno, who's still in bed, to tell him all about the lovely hotel and beautiful city.

Janina knocks at the door. 'The car's here,' she says when Irène opens it.

Taxis don't cost much in Lublin, but the drivers like to talk. Theirs goes on and on in Polish. There's a glint in his eyes as he studies Irène in the rearview mirror. When they leave the city behind, Irène notices the countryside has already shed its colourful autumn veil. Beneath low skies, bare fields extend as far as the eye can see. The woods on the horizon look to be full of ghosts and shadows. The Sobieski brothers' sawmill is half an hour's drive south. Irène imagines Wita and little Karol in this landscape.

As they pull in, she notices a group of buildings at the end of the dirt road – some brick, others prefabricated. Mountains of tree trunks are piled up behind lorries loaded with logs. Some distance away stands a white house surrounded by flowerbeds which must be spectacular in season. Its pillared porch, crowned with an ox-eye window, exudes ostentatious elegance. The taxi drops them in front of the house, where Marek's son Janusz welcomes them warmly. He must be in his seventies, but age has been kind to him. His thick white hair and moustache remind Irène of Lech Walesa. His voice is deep and resounding, his handshake firm.

'I don't often get to talk about my father,' he says over raised voices that reach them from inside.

In the entryway, Janusz shows them a sepia photo of a wooden building. His maternal great-grandfather founded the sawmill in 1910, he explains proudly. Today, his two sons manage three sites and a hundred and forty employees, supplying Poland's largest construction companies, whole-salers, and wood workshops. His younger son has been called to a different site, but Wladeck, the elder, has invited some friends whose grandfathers fought alongside Marek. Unsettled, Janina interprets for Irène. They would have preferred a small, private meeting, not an Armed Forces Day celebration. But they'll have to make do.

A dozen men are sitting in the spacious living room, which has exposed beams and a view of the forest through bay windows. Most of them are wearing jeans and checked shirts, but there's also a teenage boy in a hoodie bearing Poland's coat of arms – a white eagle – and the letters NSZ on a black background. On the walls, hunting trophies and prints of knights in armour compete for space with a huge kitsch painting of a Polish flag adorned with a wrathful eagle perched atop the *kotwica*, the anchor symbol of the Polish Underground State.

The atmosphere is jovial as they introduce themselves. It's all Irène can do to remember a stream of names made up of musical consonants: Milosz, Taddeusz, Michal, Bronislaw, and Wladek. Janusz's wife walks round the room full of men, dishing out smiles and biscuits. Without asking, Janusz serves his new arrivals a shot of vodka.

'Let's drink to the memory of our "indomitable soldiers",' he says.

Janusz is visibly moved as he delivers a speech, which Janina interprets for Irène in a whisper.

'This morning, I was thinking of my father, whose courage sets an example for us all. Marek and his comrades fought, and some even laid down their lives, to defend Poland's independence against German and Soviet occupiers. Today, our traditional values are under threat yet again. Now more than ever before, it is our duty to protect their legacy.'

He concludes with a moment of silence. Then everyone raises their glasses and downs their shots in a single gulp. Irène follows suit, though the sting of the vodka brings tears to her eyes. The man next to her, a dark-haired fellow with handsome Slavic features, looks at her fondly, his eyes full of laughter. It's Wladek, the host's elder son.

'Irena,' Janusz declares, 'has come all the way from Germany to learn more about my father.'

An enthusiastic roar rings out, dotted with a few laughs. Irène clarifies that she's French, and that she's also looking for information on Marek's first wife, Wita. There's not a flicker of interest when Irène mentions her name. But everyone has a story to tell about Marek's bravery and loyalty. Janina's cheeks are red from the vodka, and so many people are talking that she doesn't know where to begin interpreting. Wladek proudly shows Irène a frayed red-and-white armband which belonged to his grandfather. It bears the initials of the Home Army: AK. He points out a speck of dried blood on the yellowed white fabric. The fighting went on into the late 1950s in the surrounding forests, he explains. At the mill, they still find bullets in the trunks today.

Irène looks through a photo album, hoping to find pictures of Wita and the little boy. But all she finds are photos of Resistance fighters smoking or smiling as they pose with their guns. As she focuses on Marek's face, she can imagine Wita falling in love with his decisive gaze and sensual mouth – a kind of love that could survive the exhaustion inherent to such a dangerous life.

Irène asks Janusz what he was like as a father, and Janina translates his reply.

'He was strict. The war hardened him. Boy, was I afraid of him when he got angry! He taught me how to be brave. And all about nature and animals. He wanted me to be able to survive in the forest. He was an old-school man. A hero. I never saw him cry, even when my mother died. He had scars from when the communists tortured him. He would always say to me, "Be a man, regardless of the circumstances". And I tell my sons the same.'

Irène reaches for a biscuit, hoping to sop up the alcohol, which has gone to her head. The other guests are filling and draining their glasses at a steady pace, their conversations dotted with hearty laughter. They seem to have forgotten Irène and Janina are even here. She takes the opportunity to ask if there are any photos of Wita, any keepsakes from Marek's first marriage.

Janusz says he's never seen any. Perhaps his father took them with him when he joined the Resistance in the forest. After the war there was nothing left. Marek never talked about his first wife. He avoided all mention of the war, of those he'd lost. He thought it was better to focus on the present.

'And my mother was jealous, of course. So he had to watch what he said,' Janusz adds with a wink.

'He never talked about the boy either?' Irène persists.

Janina, who's made the mistake of accepting another vodka, interprets clumsily.

Their host frowns. *'Ta dziewczynka?'* he asks.

'Nie,' Janina responds.

They keep talking and seem unable to agree. Irène wants to scold Janina for getting tipsy and failing her at a crucial moment.

'He says the child was a girl,' Janina says, looking at the ceiling.

'He must be confused,' Irène replies, clearly tense.

Janina interprets for her, and the man looks annoyed. He goes on a long tirade, during which his paternalistic cordiality wears thin, revealing a temper he must have inherited from his father.

'He says he's not senile yet. The child was a girl. A teenage girl with blonde hair. He only met her once, when he was four or five. After that, his father would go and visit her in Warsaw. He remembers those visits well, because Marek would come back late and lock himself in his study. His mother would leave his dinner outside the door. He remembers her shouting,

"If it works you up so much, just stop going! What's the point?"'

Suddenly, it clicks.

'And this teenage girl was Marek and Wita's daughter?' Janina translates, looking perplexed.

'*Tak!*' Janusz exclaims. 'Her name was Agata.'

'Where did she live? Who looked after her?'

When he replies, there's less anger in his voice.

'He doesn't know who looked after her,' Janina translates. 'All he remembers is that she lived in Warsaw. He only met her once. He thinks his mother didn't want her around. He was too young to understand, but he remembers his parents arguing over her. After that, his father started going to visit her in Warsaw.'

'Have you ever heard anything about another child? A boy?'

He shakes his head and replies, '*Nie*'.

Irène shows him a photo on her phone, of Wita and little Karol. '*Nie,*' he says in a softer voice, staring at the child in his mother's arms. He seems destabilised and turns to Janina once more.

'He's asking if the boy died with her.'

Irène realises the surrounding conversations have died down. The tension of their exchange has shifted the atmosphere. The men have come nearer to listen. She watches them while Janina translates her answer: 'No, she was murdered at Ravensbrück with a little Jewish boy.'

She sees a combination of stupefaction and anger in their eyes. One word, *Żyd*, surges through the gathering.

Janusz's voice seethes with anger again.

'He says she wasn't a Jew. That's a lie,' Janina interprets.

Irène rushes to clarify. 'She wasn't, no. But the little boy was. She took care of him in the camp. She tried to save him. They were killed together.'

Janusz's scathing reply makes Janina go white.

'What does he think I said?' Irène asks, shocked.

Janina reluctantly translates. 'He says these claims are slanderous. He refuses to let us sully his father's name under his roof. He's asking us to leave. He says no one in his family has ever been at the beck and call of Jews.'

Irène is silent, completely stunned.

Janusz's change of mood seems to have infected the others. Their voices merge, steeped in aggression. One word keeps being repeated, but Irène doesn't quite catch it.

Janina is increasingly uncomfortable. She gestures to Irène that they need to go.

The handsome Wladek is embarrassed as he walks them to the door and calls a taxi. He asks them to forgive his father, whose temper has only worsened with age. 'The war is a sensitive subject around here. It brings up too many bad memories.'

'I don't understand what upset him,' Irène whispers, as the taxi sets off down the gravel path.

'I'm sorry, Irena. Sometimes I'm ashamed of my country.'

'Well, let's focus on this teenage girl. Agata. I never imagined that Wita could have had another child. How old would she be now?'

'About eighty,' Janina calculates.

'If she's alive, we need to find her.'

Stefan

To ease their shock after the incident, Irène and Janina go for a long stroll through the Old Town during a fleeting moment of clear skies. But at the end of the afternoon, snow forces them back to the hotel. Now Irène is enjoying some time at the spa while Janina rests in her room. Once she's settled into the Jacuzzi, Janusz's anger begins to feel less frightening, more like a symptom of generational trauma. She wonders if Marek mourned Wita for the rest of his life. Or if he forbade himself to think of her and little Karol, fighting hard to keep the door to the past firmly closed. Maybe his gruff exterior was simply an expression of his vulnerability, which he kept hidden away at all costs. She can't help but think of Wilhelm, who banished her from his life overnight, dropping their baby on her doorstep as if at a crèche and communicating exclusively through terse, infrequent voicemails about things like vaccination appointments and chicken pox outbreaks. Irène has never been able to erase anyone or anything from her life. She carries her past on her shoulders, and the weight of her mistakes equals the joy of her proudest moments. When she looks back, she sees in her wake all the little choices she's made – nearly imperceptible oscillations in the current.

*

Janina has booked a table for three. On the walls of the restaurant, silhouettes of rabbis dance between portraits of Hassidic men in dark clothing. One of the waitresses, who all have waist-length hair, brings them menus. Guidebooks speak highly of this place, and the people at neighbouring tables are speaking Lithuanian, Russian, and English.

Janina's guest apologises for being late. He's tall, with an open, almost boyish face and wavy, golden-brown hair that falls in his eyes. Irène thinks he can't be more than forty. He introduces himself in English. He's called Stefan and works at the Grodzka Gate – NN Theatre Centre.

'Stefan does quite remarkable work,' Janina says. There's been a sparkle in her eyes ever since he arrived.

He goes on to explain that his job is to preserve the memory of the city's Jewish Quarter. The Lublin Ghetto was one of the first to be liquidated, in spring 1942. After the war, there were fewer than three hundred survivors.

For the past fifteen years, Stefan and his colleagues have been collecting accounts from these survivors, and from their 'Aryan' neighbours outside the ghetto. The Centre is home to the recordings, as well as another invaluable treasure: thousands of photos of the ghetto and its residents.

'Where did they come from?' Irène asks.

'I knew you'd be keen to learn more!' Stefan replies with a gleam in his eye. 'Well, first there are the colour photos taken by a German soldier. They're surprising, because the photographer's gaze is so full of empathy.'

'I would love to see them.'

'Of course, I'll show you! But that's not all. When we began renovating an old residential building, we found almost three thousand glass plate negatives wrapped in old rags. Images from the Jewish Quarter before the war. Portraits and intimate scenes of everyday life. It's a miracle they survived! We had no idea who had taken them. He had to have been a part of the community because he documented private gatherings and religious ceremonies. We spent years trying in vain to identify the mystery photographer.'

He senses Irène is impatient to know how the story ends, but he pauses to heighten the suspense, a smile playing on his lips.

'In the end we found him by cross-referencing census data. He claimed on the form to be a carpenter. His name was Abram Zylberberg.'

'What an extraordinary story!' Irène exclaims.

The waitress suggests the Shabbat set menu, which is only available on Friday evening, and they all follow her recommendation.

'Their goose cholent is just marvellous. It's an authentic Ashkenazi recipe, cooked and served by goys,' Stefan says sardonically.

'I thought this was a Jewish restaurant,' objects Irène.

'There are barely any Jews left in Poland, Irène. In Lublin there are no more than thirty. And they keep to themselves.'

'So few?'

Stefan's smile disappears. 'Unfortunately, antisemitism didn't die with Auschwitz. A quick look through the archives of the Central Committee of Polish Jews, which helped the survivors after the war, makes it patently clear.

When they returned, survivors were threatened or even killed. They received a very hostile welcome, and the communists were no help. The police and high-ranking civil servants even took part in pogroms in Kraków and Kielce. That's when most of the Jews who had survived the Holocaust left the country. They were afraid. Then, in 1968, the government expelled those who'd remained, following concerted efforts by the media to ostracise them.'

Irène tells Stefan about their encounter with Janusz, how heated it became.

'What was that word they all kept saying towards the end?' Irène asks Janina.

'*Żydokomuna*. It's a slur, an allusion to a "Judeo-communist plot". Those men are nationalists. To them, Jews and communists are all one and the same.'

Irène can't believe this old myth still holds water for some.

'It sounds crazy, but some people still believe Jews bleed Christian children to make matzoh,' adds Stefan.

'It doesn't help that a segment of the clergy's been feeding antisemitism,' Janina continues. 'Even after the postwar pogroms, their position was ambiguous.'

Their meals arrive, interrupting their discussion. Irène thinks the cholent is almost as good as Myriam's.

'I always ask myself whether people really believe this nonsense or if it's simply a smokescreen for something else,' Janina says.

'What do you mean?' Irène asks.

'The murder of the Polish elite, and the Holocaust, made space for middle-class Poles. They moved into

Jews' homes, helped themselves to Jews' possessions and businesses.'

'That happened in all the occupied countries,' Irène adds. 'In France, Germany, Austria, and the list goes on.' She feels self-conscious when she realises the Americans at the next table are listening in.

'That's true,' Janina replies, lowering her voice. 'But in France people often didn't know what was happening to people after they were deported. Here it was happening *in* our villages, on our doorsteps. When Germans rounded up Jews here, their neighbours watched as they were murdered in the middle of the street. Babies were being tossed out of windows. Some Poles even helped track Jews down. Others swooped in to loot freshly emptied homes. Everyone knew what was happening, many saw it with their own eyes.' Janina's voice trembles slightly and she pauses to take a sip of wine. 'Beyond the collective trauma lies buried guilt. And hatred of anything that might awaken it.'

Janina explains that the Righteous Among Nations found themselves in a particularly difficult position. They risked their lives, and their families' lives, to hide Jews from both the Nazis and their own neighbours, who wouldn't think twice about turning them in. Even today, most of these Good Samaritans keep quiet about what they did, out of fear of reprisal. Many had to emigrate after the war.

'The height of the irony,' Stefan says, 'is that now the government has instrumentalised the Righteous, making them a symbol of Poland. They keep telling us we need to stop teaching World War II through a "lens of shame". That we were a country of heroes and martyrs.'

'But Poland *was* martyred,' Irène counters. 'The violence the occupiers inflicted here was unheard of. And hundreds of thousands of Poles still fought back! In France, right after the war, we just wanted to forget the Vichy regime and pretend everyone had joined the Resistance . . .'

Stefan nods in agreement. 'Every country has its own national myths, and casting heroes and villains is always a political move. But this official narrative doesn't help people come to terms with the past; it feeds denial, and silences dissent.'

Irène has experienced this firsthand. Since the end of the war, the work of the ITS has been wedded to various iterations of Germany's version of events. After the war, only certain categories of Jewish victims received compensation. It took years for political prisoners and Resistance fighters to be eligible for reparations, and several more decades for forced labourers. Each additional victim was seen as an additional cost for the state.

The American couple has left, and the other diners are absorbed in their own conversations. The atmosphere is cosier now, more intimate.

Janina clears her throat. 'One day, when I was round at my grandmother's, I found a small cup at the bottom of a cupboard.'

She tells them she must have been eleven or twelve at the time. The pewter was engraved with cryptic symbols. She'd been reading Tolkien, so to her it looked like something from Middle-earth. She ran to show her grandmother, who snatched it from her hands and banned her from touching it ever again. After her *babcia*'s death, Janina found the cup in a hat box. By then she was working for the Red Cross and knew that the inscriptions were in Hebrew. Feeling something was amiss, she gave the object to the Jewish Historical Institute. How had her grandmother got hold of it? The unanswered question still haunts her today.

'I loved my grandmother, but she didn't have nice things to say about Jews. It's strange because she loved klezmer music. And she was the one who introduced me to Ashkenazi cooking. But this incident complicates my love for her.'

Irène is touched by Janina's candour and wonders what Hanno thinks of Wilhelm's father. Does he go back over happy memories, looking for traces of inner struggle or attempts at redemption?

Stefan chimes in. 'People always ask why I've devoted my life to Jewish studies. "You're not even Jewish!" they always say. I tell them Jews didn't just die on our soil. They lived in this country for almost a thousand years, they shed their blood in our battles, fought in our failed revolutions. They are an integral piece of our history. Their music, ways of thinking, cooking, folklore, and more. Their absence has left a hollow in each of us. We can try to fill it with silence, ghosts, and hate. But none of that will ever fill the hole.'

After dinner, they take a stroll through Old Town. Janina takes a call from Warsaw. Her husband has thrown his back out and can't get out of bed. Though she's sorry to leave Irène, she has to take the first train home in the morning. Tomorrow they're meant to meet with Sabina Marczak, the Ravensbrück survivor who testified that Wita was dead.

'Can I go on my own or will I need an interpreter?'

The castle's silhouette stands out against the dark sky. Irène tries to light a cigarette, but the wind is too strong. Stefan wraps his hands round hers to shelter the flame. Their fingers brush.

'She speaks French and German,' Janina says.

'No need to worry then,' Irène says cheerily, trying to hide her apprehension.

They're due to meet at Sabina's home, near Ludowy Park, at ten o'clock.

'Tomorrow I'm having lunch at my parents',' Stefan says. 'But we could have dinner together if you like.'

The offer reassures Janina but flusters Irène.

She tells herself it will be comforting to have company after her meeting.

Erwin

SLEEP ESCAPES IRÈNE. Disturbing phrases swirl through her head. *Żydokomuna. In their eyes, Jews and communists are one and the same.*

She pictures Hanno on that November morning five years ago. The questions in his eyes. She immediately knew there was no getting out of it. The time had come. He had just come home from school, where they'd been learning about the Third Reich. He bit into an apple, then placed it on the worktop.

'What did Opa do during the war?' Hanno began.

Stalling, Irène asked what his father had told him.

'He says Opa fought in the war but wasn't a Nazi. It was his duty to fight, he didn't have a choice.'

She nodded, tempted to leave it there even though she sensed this explanation hadn't satisfied him.

'Why did you fall out with Opa?' Hanno persisted.

Instinctively, he'd realised the two things were related. He was fifteen by this time. How had he grown up so quickly? Irène had to tell him the truth. She wasn't sure if he was ready to hear it, but lying wasn't an option. If school thought he was old enough, she couldn't deflect the question. She took a deep breath and told him what she knew.

*

When she first met Wilhelm's parents, her main impression was that they were very old. Wilhelm was sixteen years older than her, after all. Her father-in-law was born in 1920. To her younger self, the sixty-nine-year-old man was intimidating, with his moustache and glasses which made him look like an owl. She didn't dare call him Erwin. The first few times she met him, she called him Herr Meyer.

His wife was pleasant and plump, and seemed much more approachable. But Irène was quickly disabused of the notion that Magda was a friend or ally. In her view, a woman should devote herself entirely to homemaking. She claimed Irène worked so hard she'd made herself sterile. Five years of marriage and no child to show for it. Irène stoically endured her insinuations and superficial kindness.

Erwin was more direct. He had married late in life and spent his career working in the car-making industry. Now he was enjoying a well-deserved retirement in his pretty half-timbered house. He spent his time going for walks and bike rides, though he had struggled with rheumatism and tinnitus since the war. Erwin railed against the individualism of the modern world. He had cried as he watched the fall of the Berlin Wall, and raised funds to help East Germans move to their region. He had welcomed his French daughter-in-law with open arms too. Irène was sometimes bothered by the fact that he had lived through the Nazi regime. He was twenty at the beginning of the war and had fought in it, though she didn't know exactly what that meant. She'd only dared to ask Wilhelm after their wedding. He told her that his father had nothing to be ashamed of. He'd fought in an infantry division, the war had stolen his youth, there was nothing more to say.

They never discussed it again until one Easter lunch. It had begun under the best auspices, with slow-roasted lamb and a pregnancy announcement. Finally! The grandparents-to-be were overjoyed, though Magda didn't understand why Irène was still working. Exhaustion caused premature births, why take the risk? All of a sudden Irène was desperate for a glass of wine, but she talked herself out of it. She and Magda would never be friends, but she would be a good grandmother, and that was what mattered. Pregnancy was making Irène more emotional. She was feeling unusually conscious of the distance separating her from her parents and resolved to be grateful for her in-laws' kindness. Opposite her, Wilhelm was smiling, touched by his parents' response. He was looking handsome in a royal blue shirt. She noticed that his lovely dark hair was beginning to grey at the temples, and it only bolstered her affection for him. He clasped her fingers in his. She hoped the child would inherit his hands.

'You'll be an older father, just like your dad,' Magda joked, toasting the baby's health.

'I had no choice. I had to wait for the Russians to let me go. What's your excuse?' Erwin asked with a laugh.

As their crystalware clinked, something occurred to Irène. *That means he must have fought on the Eastern Front.* Her smile went stiff, and she took a swig from Wilhelm's glass. She imagined the child frolicking round this garden, decorating the trees with painted eggs, making nests of leaves and moss for the Easter Bunny. And a year or two from now, they'd probably start thinking about a little brother or sister. The idea of two children was a little frightening, but she had plenty of time. She was only twenty-eight, after all.

The tone of the conversation had changed. Was it because Erwin had brought up a POW camp? Listening more closely, Irène realised her father-in-law was now talking about an exhibition which had been touring the country for months: "War of Annihilation, the Crimes of the Wehrmacht, 1941–1944." It had caused a huge outcry and triggered heated debates throughout the country, even at the Bundestag. Legions of veterans had organised protests. Erwin had attended one and was still furious. He swore they'd get the libelous nonsense banned. Explained they had political support.

Irène should have kept quiet and let the storm pass. But that day a little bit of Eva seemed to have got into her. She was itching to confront Erwin, to force him to break the silence that surrounded his part in the war.

'I don't understand what you find so objectionable,' she said calmly.

Her father-in-law was taken aback. He shouted that the exhibition was a pack of lies, that it defamed the Wehrmacht, that it tarred everyone with the same brush.

Wilhelm sent silent signals she chose to ignore.

'That argument doesn't hold water. There are fifteen hundred photos in the exhibition, as well as letters, written orders, and execution reports—And that's only a fraction of the material available.'

Erwin went red in the face with indignation. 'It's all made up to sully the Wehrmacht! To insult the dead!

Do you think the French spit on their soldiers' graves? That they have *exhibitions* on what they did in Algiers?'

Irène countered that the crimes had largely been documented by soldiers themselves. There were photos of infantrymen posing merrily in front of hanged men and mass graves – memories they immortalised for posterity, kept in their wallets, or sent to fiancées. Obviously, it was much harder to stand by what they'd done once these souvenirs were shared with the public.

'What do you know about any of this?' he shouted.

'It's my job, Erwin. I spend my days in archives from the war.'

She hadn't meant to let this slip. They all stared at her in shock, as though she'd just revealed she was a spy and had been recording their every word for years.

'You know nothing. You're just a child. You've no idea what it was like.'

'That's true, I don't know. So tell me. You fought on the Eastern Front, right? When exactly?'

Wilhelm's gaze burned her skin. She was no longer the dutiful young wife or shy daughter-in-law. She was righting wrongs, exposing lies. The time had come to dispense with the myth that the Wehrmacht kept its hands clean. That the poor little soldiers only realised what horrors had taken place in 1945, when it was all over. That they'd known nothing about it before. She didn't understand how the myth had endured despite decades of research and piles of proof. In the six years she'd spent at the ITS, she'd discovered the extent of the Wehrmacht's crimes and complicity. They played their part in plundering, deportation, and forced labour. How many sleepless nights had she endured after reading certain documents? The dry language of their bureaucracy turned bodies into *units* and murder into *liquidation*, or even a *solution*.

'If you must know, from spring 1941 to the end of 1942,' Erwin replied. 'I spent nineteen months on the front. I *earned* my Iron Cross. Do you know what we were fighting? When we arrived in the east people would cry with joy because we were saving them from Stalin. What do you know about the Bolsheviks? Do you know what they did over there? Are you as interested in *their* atrocities? Yes, it was an appalling war. All wars are appalling. It stole my youth. *Gott sei Dank* my son didn't have to go through that. It's true the SS were brutal. Those men have blood on their hands. But the Wehrmacht always conducted themselves honourably.'

'No, Erwin. An army that helped to exterminate Jews and murder civilians has not behaved *honourably*. You need to find another word. You've seen the photos.'

'It's all a lie,' he muttered, his gaze unfocused. 'We were fighting communism. We had no choice. It was us or them!'

'*They* were children, mothers, and the elderly. Unarmed civilians who couldn't defend themselves. You saw them with your own eyes,' she pushed, as if forcing him to look down into a mass grave.

Magda got up brusquely, knocking over the bottle of wine. A scarlet stain spread over the white tablecloth. She shouted at Irène to get the hell out, and followed her, still screeching, to the door. When Wilhelm tried to calm his mother, she burst into tears. 'I never want to see her again!' she'd hammered. 'Never! Do you understand? As if your poor father hadn't suffered enough!'

On the path outside, Irène felt her baby move for the very first time. She placed a hand on her stomach to protect it, even though it was too late. Now that her anger had faded, she felt conflicted. She wanted Wilhelm to understand and forgive her, she wanted to cry in the comfort of his arms for a very long time. But he just opened the passenger door, his gallantry a perfunctory reflex.

'What got into you?' he asked as they left town. He looked devastated.

She didn't know how to explain. Pregnancy had put her on edge, heightening even the slightest annoyance. All she wanted were words of comfort from him, but they never came. She was willing to admit she'd gone too far, but his mother had reacted so violently.

'She won't stand for anyone attacking my father,' he replied, as though that justified throwing their pregnant daughter-in-law out into the street.

He kept his eyes on the road.

Later, she wrapped her body round his with anxious urgency. She wanted to make love, to get him to reassure her. He rebuffed her gently and turned to face the other way. He was tired.

For the next few days, he claimed he was stressed, that he was overworked. Weeks passed without a single touch between them. His desire seemed to have evaporated, he'd pulled away. For six years he had needed to take her in his arms as soon as he came home. To hold her and breathe in her scent. Now he kept his distance from the body carrying his child, though he tended dutifully to her every need. He was thoughtful and would fuss if she felt even the slightest twinge. He even knew the midwife's number by heart. But with every passing day, silence devoured what was left of their love, as greedy as the Nothing in *The NeverEnding Story*. Something inside Irène shut down, but the life inside her continued to grow, her body expanding despite the scorched earth. She wished Wilhelm would yell at her or hurl plates across the room. His polite indifference was torture.

Irène held out hope that the baby's arrival would reconcile them. Hanno came into the world on 4 September, and from the moment Wilhelm set eyes on the boy, he adored him. Though he thanked her for such a marvellous gift, his affection for her was gone and his expression was drained of all warmth. Irène struggled to accept the situation, breaking down whenever Wilhelm left the room. The midwife told her she was suffering from postnatal depression. Her belly and heart were both empty. That fateful Easter lunch was the crack that eventually toppled the life she had built.

The moment they got home from the hospital, she realised she couldn't live with a stranger. In the middle of the night, she told him she was leaving him. Wilhelm objected that the baby was too little, that she hadn't even recovered from the birth. But she couldn't wait, and he didn't fight her for long. If she wanted a divorce, so be it. She would have to live with the consequences.

*

Sharing every disastrous detail of her failed marriage with her son was out of the question. Fifteen years later all she could do was recount, in broad brushstrokes, the argument with his grandfather, and admit that Wilhelm never forgave her.

'So Opa was a monster who killed innocent people!' exclaimed Hanno.

There was so much pain in his voice, on his face.

'Darling, I don't know. Maybe your grandfather did nothing wrong. Some men refused to commit atrocities, others were never put in that position. There were soldiers who deserted and were shot or sent to disciplinary battalions.'

'The people who refused to shoot were shot?'

'Not if they refused to kill civilians. That wasn't a punish-able offence.'

'So why did they do it?'

He looked so vulnerable just then. His fingers were smudged with ink, his red glasses askew, and his curly hair in disarray. *Don't you worry, it's all make-believe,* she desperately wished she could say. *The giant dies at the end, and little Tom Thumb gets away.*

'Because it's hard to disobey an order,' she finally replied. 'It's especially hard for a soldier. And it's even harder to reject groupthink. They were constantly being told these people were subhuman, that their lives were worthless. That Jews were all partisans, all communists. And that if they didn't kill their children, those children would grow up and take revenge.'

Hanno thought for a moment.

'Why didn't Dad stick up for you?'

'I'd hurt him by arguing with your grandfather.'

'But you were telling the truth!'

'You can be wrong even when you're telling the truth,' Irène conceded with a sad smile.

She still remembers how lost she felt after deciding to leave. The next day she packed her suitcases and boxes of books, but she was exhausted and didn't know where to go. That morning, Eva came to visit and found her in tears in the kitchen as she nursed the baby. An hour later she was putting their things in her car, dismissing Irène's objections. She had a guest room that was never used and a misanthropic cat – but that was his problem.

For three months, Irène and her son upended Eva's peaceful existence, and Eva looked after them, in her own way. Though she hated to admit it, she became attached to Hanno. When she was in a good mood, she would speak to him in Yiddish, calling him *tatele*. She would have let them stay longer, but Irène didn't want to take advantage of her friend's hospitality. She found a studio to rent in the town centre.

As soon as she was on her own, her sadness returned. She drifted for a few weeks, going through the motions of motherhood. Gradually, Hanno forced her to come back to herself. She still remembers the intensity of his shortsighted stares and the strength in his tiny fingers. He won her over bit by bit, with his shrill cries and angelic smiles, the smell of skin and milk. It wasn't just her anymore. It was time for her to face the facts and fully embrace her new life.

She went back to work at the beginning of the following year. Every investigation was an intellectual challenge which allowed her to escape her worries and guilt. She felt better. Sometimes she was shocked to be doing okay. The pain of losing Wilhelm dulled, like falling onto fine sand. Her days were intense and taxing, leaving no time to think about herself, but that proved to be a comfort.

Then, late one night, she turned on the television. A perfectly coiffed host was interviewing a Wehrmacht veteran live. The touring exhibition was still a source of controversy. In every town it visited, crowds of right-wing extremists filled the streets with banners. GLORY AND HONOUR TO THE GERMAN ARMY. ANYTHING FOR GERMANY, YESTERDAY AND TODAY. Veterans were giving interviews to newspapers, vying for a moment in the limelight. That night, an old man sat trembling beneath the harsh studio lights.

'How did the exhibition make you feel?' the journalist asked, her smile unreadable. She'd either caked on the foundation or just returned from a ski holiday.

'It brought it all back as if it were yesterday. It's all true, you know,' he admitted with a sigh. 'It's all true. One day I went into a church in a village near Tarnopol. The people stared at me, their eyes full of hatred. And they were right. I'll never forget what we did over there. They told us we should be proud, that we'd done our duty as soldiers. If that's what duty means ... I'm ashamed of Germany's soldiers. I'm ashamed of myself.'

He broke down in sobs, giving the host the striking image she'd been looking for.

Irène cried in front of the television.

She felt compassion for the man. After the war, soldiers who had committed war crimes were absolved of all responsibility. All this time, as the Wehrmacht was glorified for its bravery and values, all this time, people like that man were left alone to confront what Nazism had done to them. What they had done to themselves.

She thought of Erwin. Of the wall he'd built to separate himself from his memories. She'd knocked down that wall, without knowing quite what lay behind. Now she'd never know. In the same way she didn't know what haunted Wilhelm, what he was pushing away with all his strength. In her crusade against Holocaust denial, she had forgotten all about his feelings.

She did her best to explain all that to Hanno, but she's not sure he understood.

Tonight, as she watches the snow fall noiselessly on the Old Town, she can't help but dread the thick silence.

Sabina

SABINA MARCZAK'S FLAT SITS on the third floor of a new build that overlooks the park. Dressed in an elegant mauve silk shirt and black trousers, she welcomes Irène with detached politeness. Her birdlike eyes, accentuated with liner and mascara, scrutinise Irène. She's very old and so frail her bones look as though they might snap. Holding tight to the crutches that keep her upright, she invites Irène to follow her into the sun-filled lounge.

One side of the room is home to a large book collection. The walls are decorated with old theatre posters. In hesitant German, Sabina asks if she would like tea or coffee. Irène helps her to prepare the tray and two plates of *szarlotka*. Sabina carefully lowers herself onto a purple velvet armchair. Irène sits across from her on a sofa festooned with embroidered cushions. So far, they've barely said a word to one another.

'The woman from the Red Cross let me know she couldn't come. Are you German?'

'French.'

Sabina seems relieved by this response. 'Ah, what luck. My German has never been great,' she replies, quickly switching to French.

'Where did you learn French?' Irène asks, intrigued.

'At Ravensbrück. From the political prisoners. A young Frenchwoman, Anise, taught me how to conjugate verbs. I was already finding French difficult. She always said, "Well, it's easier than Polish!"' Sabina's voice quavers but her diction is firm and precise.

'You speak it very well,' Irène says as she sips the tea, which is too strong for her taste. She takes a bite of apple cake to combat the bitterness.

'I've made progress,' Sabina replies with a smile. 'After the war, I went to the Catholic University of Lublin. I wanted to study. It's very important to me. Under the Occupation, teaching was . . .' She pauses, searching for the French word. 'Forbidden, punishable by death. Our teachers hold classes in secret. That's how I graduated at seventeen. But then I was arrested.'

'You were so young,' Irène can't help but interject.

'Other girls were arrested with me. The youngest, maybe fifteen. Some were my friends, we had a secret Girl Guide troop. With our parents, we do things to help the Home Army. It wasn't called that yet. The Germans arrested us, but they couldn't find our parents. It was winter, I remember the snow.' Sabina thinks for a moment and her features darken. 'Maybe was February 1941. It was so cold. I didn't know all the girls. But afterwards, in prison. The Gestapo interrogations . . .'

'Where were you detained?'

'At the castle,' the old woman replies, setting down her teacup. 'We thought they are going to shoot us. We were afraid, of course. But we were willing to die. For us, death was . . . abstract. We knew our parents will be proud. We didn't think about our shattered lives.' Sabina pauses again, choosing her words with care. 'But they didn't shoot us,' she continues, her lips upturned. 'They sent us to Ravensbrück.'

Ever since Sabina started talking, Irène has been struck by the way she says 'we'. As if all of the women are speaking through her.

'Sorry, I'm talking too much,' Sabina says. 'Tell me about yourself.'

Irène tells her about her work as an investigator.

'You come across terrible stories. It's hard, isn't it?'

'Let's just say it's not the kind of job you can forget the minute you get home.'

'Why choose to work there? Do you have a personal connection to the war?' the old woman asks Irène, paying close attention to her reaction.

'It was pure chance. I saw an advert. I'd just got married and was looking for work.'

'Chance . . . you believe in that? I think we're pushed towards certain things. Moulded, like iron in the fire. Is your husband German?'

'Ex-husband.'

'Do you ever wonder what his family did during the war?'

'Sometimes,' Irène replies, embarrassed. 'They never talked about it.'

'Yes, but it's your job! You never talk to him about it? Very strange.'

Irène wants to say the omertà didn't bother her. That it was her haven, her secret garden. Sometimes she can't help but think of those silent years as a paradise lost.

'My husband died,' says Sabina. 'He didn't want me to talk about the camp. He cuts me off as soon as I start. "You're alive! You came back! Just focus on that." So I stopped talking about it. I could see he didn't understand.'

'What didn't he understand?'

'That I never came back. I'm still there.'

Irène wonders if Eva felt the same way, if all survivors remain trapped in the camps as if caught in the gravitational field of a black hole.

They sip their tea in silence.

'You came because you're looking for someone, right?' Sabina finally asks.

Irène nods and shows her the picture of Wita with her son. 'Wita Sobieska. You testified that she died at Ravensbrück.'

Emotion floods Sabina's face.

'Oh, Wita . . . I don't recognise her in this picture. She's so pretty. She lost a lot of weight at the camp, but she still had her face. Lots of people lost their faces. We were all afraid of that. Is the boy her son?'

'Yes. I'm looking for him too. He was kidnapped by the SS.'

'Yes, that's right, I know that. She hoped to track him down after the camp.'

'How did you meet her?'

'It's a long story,' Sabina says softly as she stares into the distance.

Warm rays of sunshine stream through the bay window. Irène doesn't want to rush the slow pace of their conversation. She waits patiently, deeply moved to be talking to someone who knew Wita. Through Sabina, she feels closer to Wita, almost close enough to touch her. She looks at Sabina's hands, at the maze of veins under her diaphanous skin. Sabina is the link between Irène and Wita. Her voice, her memory.

'If you want to understand, I have to tell you what happened to us,' she says apologetically.

Sabina puts on her glasses and struggles to her feet to retrieve a notebook from the bookcase. 'My cheat sheet,' she explains. As soon as she came back from Ravensbrück, she forced herself to write everything down. She was torn between wanting to forget and dreading what would happen if she did.

That summer, they were no longer new to the camp. They'd been at Ravensbrück for a little more than a year. The extraordinary beauty of the surrounding countryside felt cruel. The lake gleamed, indifferent to their suffering. The forest was shelter beyond their grasp. And the townspeople went on with their lives, pretending not to see or hear. Though alive, the prisoners had been erased from the world, forsaken by all. First they lost weight, then they began to grey, their faces coated with a strange layer of fuzz. Some fell ill. Others were covered in weeping abscesses. The young political prisoners from Lublin were among the *Verfügbaren* – prisoners who could be called upon for any task. They unloaded heavy stones arriving by boat and carted sand. Their hands would bleed, and the sand worked its way into the folds beneath their striped cotton uniforms as well as into their mouths and nostrils. They were so exhausted they could barely stand at roll call every morning and evening. The sturdiest inmates would hold up the sick, because those who collapsed disappeared aboard 'death trains', whose name alone chilled them to the bone. Despite it all, they learned to survive. They knew which watchwomen were the most sadistic, which prisoners were Gestapo informants, and what a morning summons really meant. Some of their friends had been murdered at dusk. They had no doubt their turn would come. But in the meantime, they held on. Sometimes, in a fit of terror, one of them would ask the others, 'Do I still have a face?' They weren't certain they truly existed anymore. They felt more like scarecrows in uniforms. But they held on to their dreams and desires, their hunger for life and for the world outside. Sometimes they would trade a day's meagre bread ration for a book. It was an insane thing to do, but those stolen moments reading gave them strength. They'd fall onto their pallets in the dying light and tell each other stories which made them forget the walls around them. It was summer, but that year – 1942 – it was cold until late June. Then a heatwave descended on the barracks and quarries.

One day at the end of July, six of them were summoned to the Revier. The infirmary was often a staging post before death by firing squad, lethal injection, or whatever followed the death trains. Sabina still remembers how warm it was, how the sky glowed purple. *This is my final morning*, she'd thought, almost relieved.

In the infirmary barracks, they were made to take a bath – with hot water and soap. An unheard of, terrifying luxury. Sabina's thoughts went to the tradition of the last meal, but the SS had no regard for its inmates. A prisoner working as a nurse brought them each a clean nightdress. Sabina asked her what was going on.

'You're all ill. They're going to operate on you,' she replied, though her eyes were full of terror and could not meet Sabina's.

'No, we're not sick,' Sabina replied. The prisoner nurse turned and left without another word.

Then an SS nurse led Sabina into a room and ordered her to lie down. When she saw the row of white beds she froze. They seemed so out of place. But the idea of lying down on those crisp, white sheets gave her such a sense of wellbeing, she felt as though she were entering a dream. She were so very tired. The *Schwester* gave them each an injection. Panic rushed through her when she realised she could no longer move. Terrifying questions swirled round and round in her head. Then everything went blank.

When they woke up, they were burning up and dying of thirst. They each had a cast on one leg. For the first few hours, all Sabina could feel was a bad headache and weakness. The pain came in the night.

'What have they done to us?' Basia gasped. She wasn't yet sixteen. They were delirious with fever. Occasionally, the *Schwester* would open the door and watch them.

She's waiting for us to die, Sabina thought. Through the window, she could see barbed wire. If she could only touch it, *this* pain would stop. She reached out in vain.

The next day, their legs were so red and swollen that the casts cut into their skin. An SS doctor came to examine them.

'He taunted us,' Sabina recalls. 'I can still hear him! *"Seid brav, kleine Kaninchen . . .* Be good, my little rabbits, be good," he would chuckle. They often blindfolded us. The SS doctors would come in and take off the casts. Then they'd reopen the wounds, put something nasty on them, and give us new casts. I will never forget the agony.'

'Why did they blindfold you?' Irène asks, horrified.

Irène is familiar with SS medical experiments, but she can't get her head around what this woman went through.

'They didn't want us to see their faces.'

They stayed in the Revier for an eternity, too weak to get up or even choke down the revolting soup the *Schwester* gave them. Foul-smelling pus oozed through their casts.

'On the second day, our friends turned up outside the window to see how we were doing. After that, everyone knew what they'd done to us.'

Their fellow prisoners were overcome by compassion. Even in such an inhumane place, people were still shocked that these young women had been treated like guinea pigs, so they brought them treats through the window: a few slices of apple, a handful of currants, a few crumbs of sweet bread.

'Wita stole them from the SS canteen,' Sabina says with a smile. 'She doesn't know us but she takes such risk! She could be killed for it. Do you understand how valuable those apples were? I have never forgotten how they tasted.'

'So you didn't know each other?' Irène asks.

'No, we only knew she is from Lublin. At the beginning of autumn, I was allowed to leave the Revier on crutches. Some of us died but the operations continue. One evening,

Wita managed to visit us because our block leader was Polish too.'

The Rabbits wanted to give her a gift, but they had nothing. At the time, the women who survived experiments were assigned to the camp's sewing workshop. They spent weeks collecting scraps of fabric under the German foreman's nose. As for those who'd been operated on more recently, they were allowed to stay in their blocks and sew. So they made a handkerchief for Wita out of the scraps, and every *Kaninchen* embroidered her name on it.

'That's what they called you? The Rabbits?' Irène is shocked.

'We hated the name at first. But that's how everyone knew us, so—Just a second, I'll be right back.'

Sabina doesn't take the arm Irène offers, relying instead on her crutches to get up. Irène doesn't dare to imagine the state of her legs.

She comes back with the handkerchief.

It's a patchwork of pastel triangles that have faded over time. The embroidered names form a constellation: *Sabina, Basia, Wanda, Grażyna, Weronika, Halina*, and so many more. And at the centre, some Polish she can't decipher.

'It says: *For Wita, so generous and brave.*'

'It's beautiful,' Irène replies softly.

These words, generous and brave, sum up the death she chose.

'Do you know how she died?' Sabina asks. 'The SS sent her to Uckermark. It had a gas chamber, right next to the Ravensbrück crematorium. The Germans take her there at nightfall. One of our group works in the laundry. The next morning she find Wita's uniform in a pile of washing. The handkerchief was in the pocket. That's how we know.'

Irène thinks back to Elsie's letter, which she must have read a dozen times. In particular, the passage where she described the way Wita looked after the little boy. She'd taken a bit of snow from a windowsill and was wiping his face with her handkerchief.

'You're not in a rush, are you?' Sabina asks. 'Oh, good. I'll make some more tea.'

Léon

Sabina leans her crutches against the bookshelf and sits back down slowly.

'You know, I don't think of myself as a victim,' she says.

Irène nods, admiration and compassion competing for dominance in her head. 'Do you like the theatre?' she asks, pointing to the posters.

'I do. Before the war I used to dance. I wanted to join a ballet troupe. My parents thought that's not an acceptable life for a girl. When I left the Revier I knew I would never dance again. When you're young, you think you're immortal. But by eighteen I knew that life is short. They operated on me eleven times. The pain comes and goes. When I talk about the camp my leg hurts. It stirs up bad memories. I met my husband after I'd returned from Ravensbrück. He led a theatre troupe. At first I just watch, but then I wanted to join in. I loved it. When I act, I use my body, with its shortcomings. When I'm a character, I forget everything else. I can be anything on stage. A woman with disabilities, a femme fatale, a witch . . .'

Irène does everything she can to avoid looking at Sabina's legs, hidden beneath the fabric of her black trousers. How did she manage to survive in a place where the first sign of weakness was a death sentence? She works up the courage to ask.

'Do you know what saved us?' Sabina replies. 'Solidarity and revolt.'

Their misfortune had made them famous. By then, Polish women occupied key positions throughout the camp. Some were in charge of blocks, others worked at the Revier or in administration. Those who had a little power used it to protect the others, and especially the *Kaninchen*, who inspired so much compassion. They made sure Sabina and the other Rabbits could rest and save their strength.

One day, the SS came to choose girls for the soldiers' brothel. Those who volunteered were promised they'd be set free sooner. But they knew how much an SS promise was worth. Was maiming them not enough? Now the Germans wanted to turn them into whores? 'Over our dead bodies,' one of them said. Another translated it into German. She may as well have spit in the guards' faces. That moment was their Rubicon. They no longer wanted to survive at any cost. They were better than that. Realising it helped them to feel like their old selves again.

'At the beginning of winter, it must have been 1943, February, maybe . . . they start killing us.'

The Nazi doctors were destroying the evidence, and the Rabbits realised they were next.

'We are caught in a trap,' Sabina says. 'What to do? We didn't know. It was terrifying. One evening another prisoner told us we are cowards for letting them do these things to us. And we were ashamed, because she is right.'

'But what could you have done?'

'Resist,' Sabina says, with fire in her eyes. 'Even if death is the price.'

At the beginning of March, a young woman from their group was summoned to the Revier, but she refused to go. That 'no' was just the first of many. They began to realise there was power in numbers.

'The commandant ordered his men to drag us to the Revier. So we wrote a petition.'

Sabina flips the notebook's pages to find the passage she is looking for. As political prisoners, they condemned the operations carried out on healthy women, resulting in mutilation, disabilities, and deaths. International law prohibited performing such experiments on humans. They demanded the commander put a stop to it, though they were under no illusion that he would comply. What mattered was standing firm, no matter the cost.

'One Sunday we held a protest in the centre of the camp,' Sabina says with a glint in her eye. 'Everyone watch as we march past on our crutches. No one ever seen anything like it at Ravensbrück!'

The commandant responded that these so-called operations were a figment of their imagination, a lie dreamt up by hysterical women.

As punishment, the *Kaninchen* were sent to forced labour. They could wear themselves out carrying bricks and stones. But they took advantage of the opportunity to tell the other prisoners what they'd endured. The next day, the SS confined them to their block. This victory encouraged them to talk more. If the outside world learnt what had happened, maybe the SS would think twice before killing them. One of them came up with the idea of hiding secret messages in the letters censored by the Nazis that she sent to her parents. She used urine as invisible ink. Her mother passed the information on to the Home Army, who relayed it to the exiled Polish government in London. Before long, a BBC news bulletin reported on the suffering endured by the young women from Lublin.

They were locked in their barracks for days without food or water. The camp commander was furious. He threatened to reduce their block to dust. How dare a bunch of cripples stand up to him! At Ravensbrück, the Rabbits' revolt was all anyone could talk about. Their resistance galvanised the other prisoners as well.

As Sabina relives this epic tale, her voice grows stronger, tinged with a fierce sense of humour. Completely caught up in the story, Irène wonders how she ever could have thought this woman was frail. 'How did you find the strength?' she asks.

Sabina tells her the first 'no' was the hardest. It got easier after that. The camp taught her that freedom comes from within. They had to reject their own powerlessness and ignore their fear. Freedom can reach through even the thickest walls, but only if you rise up to meet it. And once you start down that path, there's no turning back.

'The SS had no idea what to do with us,' Sabina explains, delighted. 'They were absolutely furious.'

For months, they went after them, inventing novel punishments. Since the SS couldn't break them, they eventually decided they were insane, and moved them to block 32, at the very edge of the camp.

'There were all sorts of people in our block,' Sabina says. 'Members of the French Resistance, Red Army prisoners, Polish women . . . and Wita.'

'Will you tell me more about her?'

'She didn't talk much about her life,' Sabina says, taking off her glasses. 'She was in Auschwitz first, it's even worse than Ravensbrück. She was on her guard, afraid of informants. But she was someone you could trust.'

In early winter 1944, Sabina was laid low with a sudden fever. She didn't know what the SS doctors had injected her with and was afraid she'd die. It was too risky to go back to the Revier. So Wita watched over her for nights on end, making her drink medicinal tea she'd managed to steal.

Eventually the fever abated, but those tense hours had brought them closer. One day, Wita finally opened up about her son. The Germans had taken him away, on the pretence of compulsory medical tests. With no news of his whereabouts, she gone all the way to Warsaw to find him. She wandered from one office to the next, questioning stony-faced clerks. In the end, the German police threw her in prison. She endured weeks of solitary confinement and humiliations, and was eventually sent to an unknown destination at dawn. Another Pawiak prisoner had seen a group of children board a train destined for Germany. She clung to the hope that her son was still alive. As soon as she was released, she would go and find him.

'Did she ever mention her daughter?'

'Yes, but she was mostly worried about the little boy. Her daughter was safe, with her sister.'

'And that was in Warsaw?'

'It was a long time ago, you know. I didn't write the place down, but yes, I think it was Warsaw. With her sister.'

'Sorry, excuse me, I need to make a call.'

Irène goes out onto the balcony, lights a cigarette, and calls Janina. 'What was Wita's sister called again?' she asks.

Janina looks through her papers. It should be easy to find since she's the one who was looking for Karol in the first place. 'Ah, here we go. Maria Koslowa. She gave an address in Wola. It's not far from here. I'll drop by. How's it going with Mrs Marczak? She has a reputation for being rather . . . difficult.'

'She's absolutely extraordinary,' Irène whispers.

*

'You asked about Warsaw,' Sabina says when Irène returns. 'That reminds me of something. In our last autumn at the camp, a huge number of women and children arrived from Warsaw. The Germans were burning the city to the ground and deporting everyone. They left them outside, in a tent, with no food or water. Wita was worried about her sister and her little girl. She asks everyone but no one had seen them.'

It strikes Irène that Wita died without knowing what had happened to either of her children. The only tangible

235

thing she had was the Jewish boy that fate had placed in her path. Dying with him meant giving up on the ghosts and hopes that had kept her going until then.

'Wita was killed with a little boy. Do you know his name?' Irène asks.

'I can't remember. Maybe it's in my notebook,' Sabina says, leafing through the pages. 'At the end of 1944 lots of prisoners from other camps are sent to Ravensbrück. The camp was full of kids. God, the state they were in . . .'

By then, the *Kaninchen* were in charge of guarding the new anti-aircraft ditches. This strategic posting allowed them to walk freely through the camp and expand their network of supporters. The SS knew they were losing the war. They were more nervous and unpredictable than ever. The chaos and violence were reaching a peak. The Rabbits felt they had to protect the new children, so they got their supporters involved.

Some of the prisoners adopted orphans. The children called them their camp mothers. At first Wita said her own two children were enough, but she eventually agreed to help out. When they were granted permission to organise a Christmas party for the children, they spent weeks making presents and even put together a little play complete with costumes. Wita managed to steal enough bread and margarine to give each of them a piece. But the party was a disaster. The children were terrified of the costumes and so skinny they couldn't swallow a mouthful. It was devastating. They'd thought that celebrating Christmas would do everyone good, but it broke their hearts instead. Sabina remembers Wita leaning against a wall, watching a little boy who hadn't even touched his food. His big dark marble-like eyes seemed to swallow his entire face. He didn't make a sound, he didn't even move. Wita had knelt down to talk to him. A few minutes later, he held out his arms to be picked up and she left with him. When she was at work, she gave him to the other women in the block to look after. When she returned, he stayed glued to her side. He was so tiny they could hide him under the covers.

She didn't need another child, thought Irène, *but she got one anyway*. 'Where was he from?' she asks aloud.

While Sabina flicks through the pages of her notebook, deep in concentration, Irène studies a picture of a group of women in front of the statue of a camp prisoner.

'That photo is from 1959,' Sabina volunteers. 'There was a ceremony. It was the first time we went back to Ravensbrück . . . Aha, I've found his name, Léon Gartner. He arrived with his mother in a convoy of Belgian Jews. She didn't last long, the poor thing.'

'Do you know why he was sent to Uckermark?'

Sabina takes off her glasses and rubs her eyes. 'He fell ill. An SS officer would go hunting for weak prisoners, with his whip. He rounded the boy up with the oldest women from our block. I wasn't there. When he hunts, we have to hide too.'

In winter 1945, the Eastern Front was getting closer. Auschwitz had been evacuated. Long lines of emaciated survivors had walked hundreds of miles through wind and snow, almost naked, to reach Ravensbrück. The SS high command drove ahead of them. They took in the big muddy tent – where women and children who hadn't even been registered were wasting away – with a combination of interest and disgust. Then they toured the barracks and walked through the new camp slums filled with Roma, the wounded and disabled, beggars losing their minds, and wild children. The newly arrived Germans had been afraid they'd be bored in Brandenburg, but they clearly had work to do. They emptied Uckermark to turn it into a sort of pre-extermination holding pen and built a gas chamber. The firing squads continued as well, but at a quicker pace. If they had to empty the place, they may as well travel light. With that in mind, they had to work out a priority system. As the biggest thorn in the commander's side, the *Kaninchen* were at the top of the kill list.

Halina was the first to be shot, leaving her friends full of rage. They couldn't make peace with the idea of dying when they were so close to freedom. Luckily, they were no longer anonymous victims. Their bravery had won them the sympathies of every woman in the camp: German prostitutes, soldiers from the Red Army, French Resistance fighters, Czech nurses, fortune tellers, and British spies. They decided they would all work together to hide the Rabbits. An ambitious plan took shape – to protect them for not hours or days, but for weeks or even months. However long it took to liberate the camp.

'And they succeeded?' Irène asked, impressed.

'Yes.' Sabina smiles. 'They hid us all over the place. Even in beds with contagious patients! We were constantly changing hiding places.'

Some got tattoos with the numbers of women who had died in Auschwitz. Others dressed up like Roma or beggars.

'They saved us. With their bravery and their imagination.'

'It's incredible,' Irène exclaims softly.

In twenty-six years at the ITS, she has encountered many tales of survival, solidarity, and sacrifice. But she is still amazed by the way these tortured women found the strength and wherewithal to save the *Kaninchen*. And touched by the way Wita, who was so disciplined and focused on her goal, was so disarmed by a lonely child.

'But we didn't save the children,' Sabina whispers. 'We didn't save Léon or Wita. So many others died. We left them there.'

The lump in Irène's throat keeps her from speaking. She knows there's no cure for survivor's guilt.

*

Before Irène leaves, Sabina insists on giving her Wita's handkerchief embroidered with all their names.

'In the end, it brought me luck. But I don't need it for my final voyage. It should go to Wita's children. Will you give it to her daughter, if you can?'

Irène promises she will. Impulsively, she clasps the older woman's hands in her own, squeezing them tight. She doesn't know how to thank her.

'I'll be thinking of you. I hope you find her children,' Sabina says as she closes the door.

Irène walks for a long time, letting the falling snow wash away her tears. Her heart beats painfully in her chest. She feels useless, unfit for the task. What right does she have to meddle in these broken lives? She can't fix any of it. She can't even repair the damage she's done to her own life.

Stefan is waiting for her in front of the castle under a black sky dotted with snowflakes. When she reaches him, she's in tears again. It's as though a valve has opened in the very core of her being, and she has no idea how to shut it off.

He looks at her without a word, then pulls her close and holds her tight.

Jacek and Jurek

BACK IN WARSAW, the sky is so pale that Irène can barely discern where it begins and ends. The cold takes her breath away. For a moment she thinks of Stefan. Of how spontaneously he pulled her close, as if holding her back from a ledge. In her mind, his gesture will forever be associated with the dancing rabbis on the restaurant wall, Sabina's smile, and the Christmas carol that echoed through the night of a faraway city. They held one another for quite some time, jostled though they were by groups of tourists in parkas. Then their lips found their way to one another's and their embrace took on a new layer of complexity. Mounting desire cut through Irène's weariness, offering her a night free of consequences – a tried-and-true option for keeping the spectre of death at bay.

Before turning to ice, they took refuge in Stefan's small apartment, just a few streets from the Grodzka Gate. They drank a local white. She told him that though she found him attractive, she couldn't sleep with him. That night she was after something else. So they talked and smoked until daybreak. He confided in her that he'd felt the same emptiness she was feeling now. That reading and listening to so many terrible stories often left him feeling porous. Wondering whether there was any point to what he did.

To be putting so much effort into conserving traces of a murdered people, in a world where war and destruction raged on. A world that hadn't learnt any lessons, one where barbarity and indifference had reached new heights. For a few days, he'd think seriously about leaving Lublin, about travelling as far away as he could. But then the feeling would pass as quickly as it had come. Lots of people visited the museum. Families would come all the way from Israel, worried they'd find nothing about their loved ones. When they left, they were invariably overcome by emotion. If just one person experienced that, his work was worthwhile.

Early the next morning, Stefan gave Irène a private tour of the museum. He told her the story of Henio, whose portrait hung on a wall. A cute little boy with a side parting looked down at them with the gracious smile of a well-behaved child. He was born in this building and died at the age of nine in the Majdanek gas chambers. Every year, local children sent him letters and pictures, which the museum preserved as precious artefacts, he explained. They also sent the children replies: 'The recipient no longer lives at this address.'

When they said goodbye, Stefan told her that the time they'd shared had probably forged a deeper connection between them than if they'd made love.

*

As she looks up at the Hebrew letters engraved on the Jewish Historical Institute, Irène calls Stefan to thank him for pulling her back from the brink.

'Where are you?' he asks.

'In the old Warsaw Ghetto. It's so cold, I feel like I'm in Siberia.'

'You're already so far away,' he says softly.

*

Before her appointment with the curator, Irène visits the Institute's museum wing. During the war, Warsaw's extensive Jewish library was concealed here. And this is where the story of Oneg Shabbat, literally 'the Joys of the Sabbath', began. It was a terribly risky clandestine operation led by the historian Emanuel Ringelblum, who set out to create a secret archive of life in the ghetto, complete with diaries, theatre tickets, German decrees, Star of David armbands, children's drawings, popular jokes, and underground pamphlets. Ringelblum and his friends included the most insignificant, everyday things, knowing that together the objects would tell the story of their experience. The archive would speak of their hopes, their acts of resistance, and their pragmatism. It had to be kept absolutely secret. Only three people knew where it was hidden. That way, if the other members of the group were arrested and tortured, they couldn't compromise its location.

They hoped to survive the war one way or another, to tell the story of the ghetto in their own words. If they failed, all that would remain would be propaganda films shot by their murderers, which cast Jews as dirty creatures who were indifferent to their own suffering. The organisers of Oneg Shabbat risked their lives to safeguard an invaluable treasure: the final glimmers of their world and its extinction.

Irène stares at the last words of nineteen-year-old Dawid Graber, inscribed on the museum wall: WHAT WE'VE BEEN UNABLE TO SHOUT OUT TO THE WORLD.

In summer 1942 they decided to bury the collection. *Grossaktion Warsaw* had begun, and the ghetto was being emptied of its residents. By then, nearly all the Oneg Shabbat organisers had been sent to Treblinka. Those who remained harboured no illusions about their fate. They understood that the archive would be their last will and testament.

Of the three people who knew the archive's location, at least one would have to survive. That particular prayer was answered. After the war, the survivor returned to a Warsaw in ruins. The Germans had burnt the ghetto to its foundations, but it was easy to make out its perimeter. And luckily, Saint Augustine's still stood at the heart of the stony desert. Thanks to the church, the sole survivor of Oneg Shabbat was able to locate the hiding place. Using pre-war aerial photos, he calculated the distance between the church and the cellar of number 68 Nowolipki Street. Then he started digging.

Later, the second cache was located, but the part of the archive hidden at a third location has never been found.

Irène takes her time in the exhibition, studying the drawings and fragments of text. A quote from Emanuel Ringelblum catches her eye: 'We wanted the experiences of every Jew – and every Jew during this war is a world unto himself – to be conveyed in the simplest, most faithful manner.'

The curator's office window looks out onto the street and the biggest synagogue in Warsaw, which stands across the road. The Germans destroyed the original during the Uprising.

'It's not every day we get a visit from an ITS archivist,' the curator says with a smile.

She speaks English with just a hint of an accent, and looks like a university student, with her turtleneck and ponytail. A small gold cross sits on her chest.

'You submitted a request for information about a Polish Jew who survived the war.'

Irène nods, then sums up Eva's story, from the Warsaw Ghetto to the ITS.

'Your friend wrote to us in the fifties. She was looking for information on her parents, Medres and Estera Volmann. Her letter also mentioned two younger brothers. We wrote back at the time saying none of their names appeared on lists of survivors from the ghetto.'

Were those few lines enough to discourage Eva? It seems unlikely since the curator is certain Eva visited the centre in person after the fall of the Berlin Wall, just a few weeks before Irène met her for the first time. She spent a whole month combing through the Oneg Shabbat archives day in, day out. The archivist assisting her mentioned in a report that Eva was overcome by emotion when she found some of the documents.

'I've made copies and translated them into English. The originals are in Hebrew.'

The curator shows Irène to an austere office. There's a wooden table and a chair. The snowy sky isn't letting much light through, so she turns on a lamp. Here, the hustle and bustle of the city is muffled and distant.

'The first document is an extract from the testimony of a man who took part in the Uprising. He survived and emigrated to Israel after the war. He was a member of the Jewish Combat Organisation.'

'Eva said her mother was too.'

'Precisely. This man mentions a fighter called Estera. We think he was talking about her mother. And it seems your friend agreed.'

Irène remembers that the ghetto rose up on 19 April 1943. On Passover. The commander of the insurgents, Mordechai Anielewicz, was only twenty-four years old. They had a handful of guns and some explosives given to them by the Home Army. The soldiers they were facing were armed to the teeth, with tanks, artillery, and flamethrowers. On the third day, the SS began burning the ghetto to the ground. They went from block to block, setting buildings alight.

Irène has read accounts and seen photos from the Uprising. The insurgents held every position as long as they possibly could. Parents clasped their children to their chests as they jumped from the fourth floor of burning buildings. Lovers held hands as they threw themselves into the void. So many people burned to death or suffocated. Smoke blackened the Warsaw sky for weeks on end. Anyone captured was shot where they stood or sent to a killing centre. Survivors hid in caves or bunkers they had dug out in advance. The SS general in charge had vowed to end the Uprising in three days. But the Jewish fighters held out for four weeks against an army. The chaos was apocalyptic. They forced the enemy to retreat several times. *What's happening has surpassed our wildest dreams*, Mordechai Anielewicz wrote. A few days later, the Germans encircled the Jewish Combat Organisation's base, and the young commander killed himself.

'Even after the Germans had taken the JCO base, there were still pockets of active resistance,' the historian explains. 'Thanks to this survivor's account, we know the Volmanns tried to reach the Aryan side. We also know how they died.'

She leaves Irène alone with the text. In the first paragraph, the survivor recounts his escape through the sewers with a group of others. He knows that the Germans are blowing up or backfilling manholes. Sometimes they use them to fill the tunnels below with toxic gas. Columns of exhausted people are wandering endlessly through the darkness of the city's entrails, lost in a maze.

That night there are ten of them, led by a smuggler. The narrator is walking behind a couple with two children. The water comes up to the adults' calves and the boys' knees. The mother keeps her gaze focused on the dancing light of their guide's lamp; the father brings up the rear. They've been trudging through the sewers for hours, when one of the boys begins to moan. The mother tells him to be quiet, that the SS are listening.

'Medres, calm him down,' she whispers. The survivor recognises a woman he fought alongside and calls her by her first name, Estera. He also mentions the revolver in her belt.

Irène stops to wonder if the weight of the gun reassures her and if she's thinking of her daughter, who took the same route months earlier.

They're all dying of thirst. To keep the children from crying, the father gives them some fetid water to sip. Hours pass and they lose track of time.

Eventually they find a passable manhole, but the smuggler hesitates. He's not sure they've gone far enough. He's worried he's taken a wrong turn. But he decides to climb the rusty rungs. The Volmanns are just behind him. Estera helps one son up, Medres follows with the second. The narrator waits with the rest of the group, listens as the cover scrapes against pavement. The Volmanns pull themselves up to the fresh air, one after another. The rest of them wait in the darkness.

The group listens intently, hoping for a sign the coast is clear. The silence lasts an eternity, growing more sinister with each passing second. Then there's a gunshot, immediately drowned out by a volley of machine-gun fire. The group below the surface remains silent, stops breathing. Instinctively, they start moving again. They carefully move away from the opening, then retrace their steps and take a new tunnel at the intersection. They walk aimlessly for a long time. In the middle of the night, they have better luck than the Volmanns. They find another manhole. This time it's the right one. Friends are waiting for them with a car.

The story ended well for the narrator, but reading it must have ripped Eva's heart to shreds. Perhaps she felt pride in the fact that her mother had fired the first shot when she saw they were surrounded. Eva had always felt so unlike her mother, but now she had caught up with her daughter, surpassed her even. Her mother had always told her that fighting wasn't ladylike, but when push came to shove, she took up arms nonetheless.

Irène knows nothing about the second document, other than the fact that it's from the Oneg Shabbat archives. She doesn't really grasp what she's reading at first. She looks to the Hebrew original for clues and notices the diligent, childlike penmanship as well as the lined paper.

My Father

My father is the person I admire most in this world. He is very knowledgeable and rarely gets cross. Instead of shouting at us, he takes the time to explain important things. Before the war, he was a professor at the university. When we had to come and live here in the ghetto, he lost his job. He was always sad and tired. Then the neighbours came and asked him to be chairman of the block committee. Now he organises shows and cultural evenings and collects donations for those in need. He's hardly sad anymore. He tells us incredible stories about the Jewish people and very funny jokes. Even Jacek can't keep a straight face. It's impossible not to laugh.

My father always says he wants us to grow up righteous, even though the world has been led astray. We're luckier than some, so we should set an example. Jacek doesn't understand why he isn't allowed to beg with the other children. He admires the scoundrels who steal bread from the rich women on their way home from market. My father tells him that the people we see begging on the street were chased from their homes. They used to live in other parts of Poland, until the Nazis took absolutely everything from them. So they have to beg. As a result, some of them have lost all moral compass. We should pity them instead of judging them, because we are lucky enough to have a roof over our heads, and parents, and more than one meal a day. 'I know you are hungry. I am too. So let me give you a tip: when you occupy your mind with something interesting, you'll find your next meal comes sooner,' he always says. Jacek finds that hard to believe because he's always so hungry that he can't think of anything else. Even when we tell him funny stories.

Now that our school on Nowolipki Street is open again, my little brothers and I all attend. Jurek loves his teacher, who is kind and gives him buttered bread every morning. They grow beans from seeds in pots to decorate the classroom. In May they're going to put on a play about the seasons. Jurek will be a snowflake and Jacek a daffodil. He doesn't like that at all! Grandmother is making them costumes from old pieces of fabric, and I have to help them run their lines, even though they don't listen to me. The other day they were playing Germans with the neighbour kids in the courtyard. Jacek shouted, 'Jude, raus sofort!' and the others were meant to put their hands in the air. Jurek burst into tears. He said he didn't want to play a Jew. I comforted him and punished Jacek, because he was older and should be setting a better example.

Yankele, who lives in the attic, slips through a hole in the wall around the ghetto several times a week to bring back food. He promised he'd take me with him next time. I really wanted to go, but at the same time I was scared, so I discussed it with my father. He said Yankele is as brave as Roytkepele, the robin in the poem. Because every time he flies to the other side of the wall he risks being shot by a hunter. My father looked sad. 'Bubele,' he said, 'if you got yourself killed for a piece of bread, I couldn't bear it.'

He explained that everyone has a talent which makes them unique, a talent they can choose to share with others. He says sharing it makes us happier. He mentioned Chana, who sings at the block committee concerts. Her voice is so beautiful that it comforts those who are feeling down. I thought about Chana and told my father I wasn't sure I had a talent which made me unique. I do know how to fight, though, and I'm stronger than some of the boys. Last week, I protected Jacek when the bullies from the next street over started to gang up on him. But Mame doesn't think that's really a talent for a girl.

My father thought for a moment. He told me my talent was hidden in my name. In Hebrew, Ewa means 'life'. And you, bubele, are a little beacon of life. You see, thanks to you, it shines on us all.'

When he talks to me, it's like he knows what I'm thinking. I stop being angry and my sadness melts away.

The text stops there. Beneath the last line, the historian has written by hand, 'Text by Ewa Volmann, April 1942. The prompt said, *Write a portrait of someone you love.*

Agata

AFTER SHE LEAVES THE INSTITUTE, Irène spends hours walking through the old ghetto, despite the squalls of snow. She doesn't want to leave twelve-year-old Eva behind quite yet. She needs to walk in her footsteps.

After the war, the Old Town was reconstructed exactly as it had been, but not these streets. There's no extravagant trompe l'oeil here. In Muranów, the cityscape bears brutalism's stamp. Before Irène took her leave, the curator warned her that many of the streets from that time no longer exist or have new names. Others have been relocated. So Irène's on the hunt for the rare vestiges that remain. She goes quite far out of her way to spot small sections of the ghetto wall, plaques, and monuments. The old courthouse and the block which served as Judenrat headquarters are still standing. Saint Augustine's Church no longer towers over fields of rubble; instead, it's surrounded by quiet streets and snowy squares. The Volmanns lived nearby, on Nowolipki Street. Eva and her brothers went to the school at number 68. The first section of the secret archives was buried there, in a tin box.

This is the place where Eva's childhood came to an end. Irène passes two bundled-up figures braving the gusts to walk their dog. She can't help but wonder who still remembers the four seasons play and the children dressed as daffodils and snowflakes. Who would recognise the faces of those who somehow managed to get by in these streets? This sleepy residential neighbourhood is their cemetery. It was built from the ruins: concrete mixed with earth and the remains of the dead. 'Nothing is lost, nothing is created, everything is transformed,' as famed Enlightenment scientist Antoine Lavoisier said. As she treads the graveyard, ghosts of the forgotten streets and the people who once filled them with life coalesce into feelings of melancholy that assail her like damp eating away at a wall. Do they haunt the neighbourhood's current residents? The curator told her some say they hear violin music in their flats at night. Others wake in the dark to the sounds of children crying. Irène is only passing through, but her emotions are so intense she feels the need to talk to Eva. The little girl she was intimidates Irène less than the survivor she became. 'I was a coward,' she confesses. 'I was afraid of your secrets. But I'm here now.'

She is freezing when she crosses Avenue Jana Pawła II to reach what used to be Pawiak Prison. She steps from Eva to Wita, forming a bridge between their lives and their suffering. When Wita was imprisoned here, Eva and her family were still managing to make ends meet a few hundred yards away. The museum is closed, so she walks on to the Umschlagplatz. The gusty site sits at the end of an ugly, congested street. This is where the Nazis packed Jews tightly and left them to wait for hours on end before pushing them into trains in a crush of tears and screams. The monument's sober design conveys the feeling of being trapped, of power-lessness and dread. Just an empty space and the rushing wind. The black line on the white walls evokes the dark stripes on an Ashkenazi tallit, while the frontispiece depicts a forest of felled trees, symbolising annihilation. Irène stops to contemplate the names engraved in the stone.

Her phone vibrates in her pocket.

'Irena,' Janina says, 'I've found her.'

And just like that, life triumphs over death.

*

Irène heads to the nearby Wola district to meet Janina at a milk bar and get the full story over lunch. While tending to her husband over the past few days, she's managed to find time to track down Wita's sister, Maria Koslowa.

Maria's husband was killed during the Warsaw Uprising. In 1944 he was working as a surgeon at Wolski Hospital, treating injured Resistance fighters. The Germans executed him, along with the rest of the staff and all their patients. In the first days of the Uprising, they massacred tens of thousands of civilians in the city's western districts. Plaques erected in their memory still dot the neighbourhood's streets. But Maria and her children were comparatively lucky. They were arrested a few days later and sent to a forced labour camp. That was still a step up from Auschwitz or the Ravensbrück tent.

When the city was liberated, Maria returned home with her three children and little Agata. Well, home wasn't the right word. The blocks on her street were empty shells, gutted by fire. The buildings which were still standing had been vandalised. Like many Varsovians, Maria Koslowa and her four children found themselves living in a cellar with no water, electricity, or heat. She worked for Warsaw social services, which were overwhelmed by the scale of their task. When she asked the Polish Red Cross to investigate what happened to little Karol, she still lived at the same address. She died there in 1976 having never remarried. At her burial, a member of the party gave an impassioned eulogy. She was held in high esteem by everyone in the neighbourhood. In a photo Janina found in a contemporary communist newspaper, a crowd of mourners stands round her grave, which was completely covered in candles and flowers. Irène is intrigued when she spots a blonde woman in the background. Her sad eyes remind her of Wita in the Auschwitz picture. A bearded, dark-haired man has his hand on her shoulder. The caption mentions the children of the deceased – including Agata Nowik.

'I couldn't believe it when I read her name,' exclaims Janina. 'She was my paediatrician, believe it or not!'

'That's unbelievable! But wait, how old are you?' Irène asks, surprised this could be possible.

Janina blushes. 'Forty-six.'

With her smooth skin, platinum-blonde hair, and multi-coloured mohair jumpers, Janina looks much younger.

'Dr Nowik was lovely. She had the most magnificent eyes. I was in love with her son, who was as handsome as they come. They lived in the block across the road. I could see their balcony from my bedroom window. Her husband was arrested in 1981, under martial law. One day, just after he was freed, I passed him in the street. He looked like Rasputin with his long black beard.

'Was he a Solidarity activist?'

'Yes. He wrote in underground papers. He died about ten years ago. But she's still alive. She lives just round the corner. Shall we?'

Irène is full of doubt. Wita's daughter has survived the war, a labour camp, and two dictatorships. How will she talk to her without reopening old wounds?

'Let's,' Irène says, to force her own hand.

*

In the tranquil, tree-lined street, nothing distinguishes Agata's block from the neighbouring cream-coloured rect-angles between freshly salted footpaths. A passing resident lets them in, and they climb four flights of stairs. Janina rings the bell.

At first Irène can hear nothing but silence and the thumping of her racing heart. She forces herself to breathe calmly, then notices a rustling noise. Someone is watching them through the spyhole. The lock turns and the door opens, revealing an old woman with Slavic features and soft blue eyes.

'Janina Tarnowska!' Agata exclaims.

Then there's a rush of Polish words which make Janina laugh, and Agata invites them in.

The decor is simple and warm: a brown sofa dotted with a collection of cheerful crocheted cushions, a worn armchair, overflowing bookshelves, and an old sideboard topped with pictures and plants. Agata offers them a very strong cup of tea. Irène supposes this must be the Polish way and adds a sugar cube. Janina and Agata chat away. It's been so long since they've seen one another that there's much catching-up to do. As she listens, Irène's nerves get the better of her. She wonders how best to talk to Agata about Wita. How will she even bring her up? Lost in her own thoughts, she inadvertently meets the old woman's gaze. Her eyes are full of questions. Janina's tone grows more formal, and Irène imagines they're talking about her.

Agata turns to them and says, in stiff English, 'Dear madam, Janina tells me you have come from Germany, and that you have information about my mother.' Her features betray what she's feeling: equal parts hope and apprehension.

'I'm very pleased to meet you,' Irène says. 'Is it okay to continue in English?'

'I spent years translating the articles my husband wrote for the Western press. I'm a bit rusty now, but if I don't understand, Janina will help me.'

Irène pauses, taking the time to choose her words carefully. She paints a picture of Wita's time in the camp. All Irène has from her months in Auschwitz are the photos. Beneath the outward signs of her circumstances, you can still see the woman she was before. At Ravensbrück she was stronger, hardened from her time in the camps. Irène thinks of the metaphor Sabina used, of iron forged in flame. The camp forged Wita, its effects profound and irreversible. They'll never truly know the person she became, which parts of herself she killed off to survive and which ones she clung to. All Irène can share with Agata are the impressions Wita left on others. The impact she made on the lives of a Nazi guard and a woman from the Polish Resistance. That's all she has to offer after weeks of obsessive research: a few fragments, unanswered questions, and a handkerchief.

Irène tells the story of the martyred Rabbits of Ravensbrück and the slices of apple Wita stole from the SS canteen. She stresses her empathy and generosity. She talks about that bleak children's Christmas party, the Rabbits' revolt, and how their fellow prisoners protected them. Finally, she mentions the vulnerable little Léon. She doesn't want to tell Agata that her mother chose to die with a child who wasn't her own, so she simply says that Wita took the boy under her wing. That they were sent to Uckermark and then to their deaths.

'They were gassed,' the old woman says under her breath. 'I thought only Jews were gassed.'

Irène explains that initially only Jews and Roma were targeted for extermination, but in Germany they began to gas people with disabilities and mental illnesses as well. At Ravensbrück, that was how they got rid of anyone who was weak or ill. The gas chamber was only in operation for a few months, but it kept running until the final days before liberation. The SS made it their top priority.

Agata asks the question Irène has been dreading.

'If Wita hadn't tried to save Léon, would she have had a better chance of surviving?'

Irène says it's impossible to know. Sometimes strong, healthy inmates only lasted a few weeks, while frailer people survived. There was no way to pierce the sinister logic of the camp. In any case, Sabina confirmed that Wita clung to the hope of reuniting with her children. And that hope sustained her.

Overwhelmed with emotion, Agata replies in Polish. 'The day I left them, the train to Lublin was delayed. There were German soldiers everywhere. I was so scared. My little brother was screaming in my mother's arms. She kissed me and said, "Have fun, Adzia." We were supposed to be reunited just a few days later. I never saw her again.'

Irène thinks of her own son. She was in good spirits when she left him, safe in the knowledge she would see him soon in Paris. The idea that she could lose him shakes her to her very core, but she stifles the urge to call him and make sure he's okay.

'My mother was so affectionate. Even after the Germans took over, when our lives were so frightening and full of hardship, we had moments of joy. One day I realised I'd forgotten the sound of her voice. That hurt so much. I listened to my Aunt Maria. Their voices were similar, but my mother had more of a lilt. She would sing us lullabies. How on earth had I forgotten her voice? I would turn round whenever I saw someone who looked like her on the street. I was terrified of forgetting her face as well. Luckily, my aunt had photos. I kept them under my pillow.'

Irène can hear the pain of the little orphan girl in Agata's voice, as if it's still fresh. Her childhood had been trampled by the clamour of war, but she couldn't complain, everyone had suffered. In 1945 the city and its residents were both in ruins, but they had to hide their sorrow and choke down their anger. The new masters demanded obedience. The country had to be rebuilt. Feelings of rage, grief, and betrayal couldn't be spoken out loud. Her Aunt Maria believed in socialism at first, but the communists cured her of her taste for utopia. Eventually, the only thing she trusted was her own goodwill. So she devoted her life to helping orphans and the slews of girls who sold their bodies on the streets to survive.

Maria raised Agata as one of her own – with the same gruff manner and high expectations. In the evening, while the older children cooked dinner, she taught them the history of Poland. She raised them to cherish the country's fleeting interwar period of independence, to decode propaganda, and to think for themselves. Living under Stalin's boot meant having a different personality in the outside world, a façade that hid their guiding truth as well as their hopes and dreams. Only when Poland was finally free again could they be their authentic selves.

'She trained us to be successful dissidents,' Janina translates. 'She taught us to hide our feelings. Usually, I'm very good at it.'

'Did she ever talk about your little brother?' Irène asks. She looks into the woman's pale blue eyes, searching for Wita's gaze.

'Never. No one even mentioned his name. It was as though he was dead. As though he'd never existed.'

'Did you know she asked the Red Cross to look for him?'

Agata's face betrays her surprise. She's shaken to learn of her aunt's efforts to reunite the family. 'But since they didn't find him, does that mean he's dead?' she asks.

'Not necessarily. Did your aunt tell you he was kidnapped?'

'She explained that my mother couldn't come and find me immediately. I don't remember very well. She must have told me there was an issue with my brother. I assumed he was ill. That must have been in November or December, because I was hoping to be home for Christmas. She didn't tell me my mother had been arrested until later.'

After the war, they got on with their lives as best they could. One evening Maria came back late, looking particularly tired. She told Agata her mother had died in a German killing centre.

'My aunt was an austere woman. She'd lost her parents, her husband, and her sister. She said, "I'm going to have to adopt you, because your father's likely to spend the rest of his life in prison." I felt absolutely terrible. It was like being ripped from my family.'

Irène is struck by her choice of words. It's as though she's invoking her brother as well, without saying his name.

'But Maria was still a godsend. She looked after me and pushed me to pursue my education. I became a doctor, met my husband, and had my son. And now I have two wonderful granddaughters.'

Their tea gets cold as the light from outside dwindles. They exchange the odd smile as they chat. Occasionally, Agata has a question or asks for clarification, but her voice is so hushed it's hard to hear. When she's finished, Irène hands Agata the handkerchief embroidered with the names of all the Rabbits of Ravensbrück.

The old woman unfolds it carefully and stares at the Polish inscription. Then she retrieves a bottle of vodka and downs her glass in a single gulp, her eyes rimmed with tears.

'It's so silly to be crying about my mother, at my age,' she says, wiping away her tears with the handkerchief. When she realises what she's done, she apologises, as if she's just desecrated a sacred relic.

'That's what a handkerchief's for,' Irène says. 'It's yours now. You can even blow your nose with it if you like.'

The joke brings a shy smile to Agata's face.

She fills three glasses, and Irène and Janina are too polite to refuse. This time, the vodka chases away death. Sadness too.

Once outside, Irène calls her son. They talk for a long time as she walks. The sound of his voice quells her worries, but it also makes her miss him more. The sparkling skyline on this icy night leaves Irène with a strange feeling. The city pulses around her in a din of traffic, police sirens, and thumping bass from open windows. Before she hangs up, she tells Hanno she loves him and can't wait to see him in Paris.

'What's going on with you? Are you dying?' he asks teasingly. 'I'm looking forward to seeing you soon too, Mummy dearest. Christmas in Paris is going to be ace. Next weekend I'm popping over to Berlin with Hermine and Toby. I'll pick up something for Antoine at the Christmas market.'

Reassured, she catches up with Janina, who's waiting on the corner.

The outline of the Palace of Culture and Science looms before them in the dusk, bathed in ghostly light. A gift from Stalin to the people of Poland in the fifties. He was determined to outdo American skyscrapers, so he tore down sixty blocks of flats in a city in ruins where thousands of people had no roof over their heads. Thirteen construction workers died building it too, Janina explains. 'A poisoned chalice,' she concludes. 'We call it Stalin's Finger. After the fall of communism, lots of people wanted it knocked down.'

'If we tore down every monument to a despot, there wouldn't be much left!' Irène exclaims.

'You're right. We got used to it in the end. I dare say we even like it now.'

Janina says she's surprised Irène didn't mention the locket.

'Well, I left it in Germany. I think it should go to Karol.'

'So you think he's still alive?'

'I hope so. Wouldn't that be a nice gift for Agata?'

Julka

Agata's son has invited them over for lunch with his family, so Janina has swapped her mohair jumpers for a smart black dress with suede ankle boots. When Irène teases her for getting dressed up for her old crush, Janina shares the details of her unrequited love story. If only Irène had seen Roman back then! There was something so free and sensual about him, half poet, half renegade. He had all the appeal of the hero in that Wajda film, *Man of Marble*. He'd even gone to prison for attending underground meetings. To the tubby, sentimental girl living in communist Poland, Roman embodied the dangerously charming rebel archetype. In bed at night, she'd dream of him wrenching her from her boring existence. But he never even noticed her. She was just a child desperate for his attention.

Then, fifteen years ago, she spotted him at a charity gala. She looked gorgeous that night, on the arm of her husband-to-be, but she still hadn't dared to talk to him. As if she were suddenly that awkward girl again.

Today, Roman is an esteemed corporate lawyer, and the owner of a spacious duplex in a part of Wola where skyscrapers and luxury flats abut gyms and Ayurvedic centres. He welcomes them warmly, touched to see his old neighbour. Irène struggles to see the dissident poet in the immaculate fifty-something wearing cufflinks and brogues. His thinning hair is greying and the beauty of his once-handsome face has faded, but his bright eyes fill it with life. He's relaxed as he speaks to them in fluent English. He remembers that the last time he saw Janina, her hair was red and Poland was still communist.

Janina bursts out laughing. She'd completely forgotten about dyeing her hair red. She introduces Irène and tells him all about their work together and what a good friend she's become through it all.

As they wait for Agata, the three of them smoke and take in the view. The balcony overlooks towering glass buildings and the snow-dusted canopies of leafless trees. Roman tells Irène he hasn't seen his mother so emotional for a very long time. It isn't just learning more about Wita, it's the fact that her brother might still be alive. He asks if they can reopen the search for him.

'That's just what I've done, in a way,' Irène says. 'If I have a solid lead I'll get in touch. But I don't want to give you false hope.'

'Well, the hope's there now,' Roman says with a sigh. 'I'm glad someone could testify that my grandmother died in the camp. With her brother there's no explanation, no grave. She's never managed to silence the voice in her head telling her one day he'd come back. And then, as if that weren't enough, she had to deal with an absent father who started a new family in order to forget his first. At first Marek would come and visit her in Warsaw after he was released. They would spend the day together and have lunch at the same place every time. But she started to get in the way of his fresh start, so he stopped coming. They lost touch long before he died, and she's never got over it.

'My mother found it very difficult to accept my divorce,' he adds. 'She was worried about my daughter. One day I finally told her to stop worrying, that Julka would always be at the centre of my life, even if I remarried. I married Edyta fifteen years ago, we had a little girl a year later, and everyone gets on well. But my mother's still afraid that Julka might feel left out or unloved,' he says with a smile. 'It's visceral for her.'

Agata and her granddaughter arrive arm in arm, their cheeks flushed from the cold. Agata's place is only a few streets away, but she says coming here makes her feel as though she's travelled through time. She laughs and they all raise their glasses. Julka is slender and blonde. She has a wide forehead, pale blue eyes, and high cheekbones. Her hair is tied up in a tight bun. At twenty-seven, she teaches English at a secondary school. She bombards Irène with questions about her job. Since the people she's looking for are long dead, does that make her an investigator or an archivist? Irène is troubled to realise she's meeting a freer, more buoyant version of Wita, in trainers and black jeans.

'A bit of both,' Irène replies. 'In the early fifties, an American article on the ITS ran with the headline A DETECTIVE STORY IN REVERSE. It's not totally off the mark.'

'Do you hunt Nazis too?' Julka asks.

'No, the Central Office in Ludwigsburg handles that. But our archives are often used as evidence to convict them.'

All of a sudden, Irène remembers the day when Eva told her that the new director, Max Odermatt, had decreed the ITS would no longer share documents with the Ludwigsburg prosecutors.

'But why?' Irène had asked, taken aback.

'That's a very good question,' Eva had replied. 'Why indeed? Why refuse to help bring the Third Reich to justice?'

The uneasiness she felt that day returns, undimmed.

'What about *Babcia*'s brother?' Julka asks. 'Are you going to find him?'

'Even immediately after the war, tracking down stolen children was very tricky,' Irène explains. 'Now we're looking for a seventy-eight-year-old man who goes by a different name and has spent the vast majority of his life living as a German.'

Julka likes the idea of having cousins abroad. Her family feels just as European as they do Polish. Roman has lots of German clients. Agata keeps quiet; her feelings are no doubt conflicted. For her, Germany is the enemy that destroyed her childhood.

Agata carefully removes the handkerchief from a velvet pouch and passes it to her granddaughter. In awe, Julka studies the signatures, then reads the inscription aloud.

Julka has only ever known her great-grandmother as a sepia face in old photos. Now this piece of fabric has brought her to life. A life she risked to bring the Rabbits something nice to eat.

'That makes me so proud,' Julka says, her eyes welling with tears. 'I'd never heard of this group of young women from the Lublin Resistance. I imagine most of them died in the camp?'

Irène assures her the majority actually survived. Together, they found the strength to resist. Every act of revolt reminded them that they didn't belong to their persecutors. She tells Julka how they got under the camp commander's skin, how he began calling their barracks 'the bandit block'. Though they were designed to break them, their punishments only strengthened their bond. They even protested in front of the *Kommandantur*, crutches and all.

'That's incredible!' the young woman says. 'The women participating in the Black Protests have to hear this story!'

'Julka, you can't compare that sort of resistance to your abortion march,' Roman objects, shocked.

'Do you really think I'm stupid enough to compare what the Law and Justice Party is doing to what happened at Ravensbrück?' she immediately counters in Polish. 'The context is different, of course. But these Resistance women found the courage to protest in a place where the only right they had was the right to die. I can't help but find them inspiring. Today we have no excuse to be cowards. We have to defend our rights when they're under attack.'

As Irène listens to Janina's translation, she remembers seeing images of the march. Crowds of women in black carrying umbrellas.

The black, Janina explains, is a historical reference to when Poland was partitioned and women took to the streets dressed in mourning for their country. Now it's become the symbol of the Black Protests, along with the red lightning bolt, which symbolises their anger.

'Are you telling me *you* protested?' Roman asks Julka, surprised.

'Of course I did!' she replies with a smile. 'I bought this black parka for the occasion.'

Julka explains that it all started when an international NGO – Catholic extremists with close ties to the government – proposed passing a law to ban abortion in Poland. They claimed they wanted to 'protect the country from moral decadence'. Really it's just a power-grab by the most radical elements of the Church, she concludes.

'They're xenophobic, misogynistic, and homophobic,' Julka says in English, to sum things up. 'Have you noticed these things often go together?'

She recalls the emotion she felt when she saw the ocean of black umbrellas on the streets of Warsaw. She'd never seen so many women, of all ages, come together like that. That October Monday was the first time she'd ever protested. She's never been very interested in politics, but since the conservatives have been in power, the two sides of the political spectrum have been fighting over all of the country's symbols: the national flag, the story of the Warsaw Uprising, and Solidarity. In the school where she works, new curriculums have been foisted upon them. They're supposed to discourage the spread of 'gender ideology'. The government pays families five hundred zlotys for the birth of the second child and has instrumentalised the popular measure to stifle objections to its conservative platform. As soon as the party was elected, it took control of the state broadcasters, began weakening the Constitutional Court, and started chipping away at reproductive rights. So Julka and her friends dressed in black and went out to protest.

On social media, tens of thousands of women posted photos of themselves dressed in mourning, with the hashtag #czarnyprotest. Across Poland, nearly two hundred thousand took to the streets. It was the biggest public mobilisation since Solidarity. Julka's *babcia* even came out to march with them. There were so many of them, their anger swelling like a wave. Julka felt as though nothing could stop them. A girl standing next to her let off balloon effigies of President Duda and Jarosław Kaczyński. She watched them rise into the sky, wobbly and absurd, then retreat from sight. That day, she felt she was taking part in a revolution. She felt the crowd was waking up after a long sleep, remembering how powerful they were. She drank her fill of chants, laughter, and war paint.

Later that day, a journalist handed her a microphone and Julka said, 'I'm protesting today so I can keep living in the country I was born in. Because my body belongs to me and me alone. Not to the Church, and certainly not to Mr Kaczyński.'

Her interview was broadcast by an independent network.

'I see I've upset my father,' Julka says, turning towards Roman. 'He says the movement lacks diplomacy.'

'I don't see the point in provoking people,' Roman replies. 'You've omitted the fact that your slogans are plays on ones used by Solidarity. And you even disfigured the emblem of the Home Army.'

The conversation continues in English, which they both speak fluently, although Agata occasionally seems to have difficulty following. Sometimes Janina leans over and translates.

'It's our history too, isn't it? In this country we're always referencing the past. But when women allude to the past, everyone's outraged.'

'Do you really think you need to invoke the Home Army to defend the right to abortion?' Her father is cross. 'I don't see the connection!'

'It's about refusing to let other people control our lives. Whether that's Nazis, communists, or priests. You wouldn't let anyone dictate how *you* live. Women just want that same freedom.'

'You can't reduce this to a question of freedom,' Roman objects. 'The Church objects to abortion because of the sanctity of life. That's its role, and it's unfair to condemn it. I grew up under communism. I know what I owe the Church. Your generation has forgotten.'

'Dad, the Church you're talking about defended people against the State's abuse of power. But now it's supporting that very same power.'

'Irena hasn't come to listen to us argue,' Roman says, his tone calmer. 'In any case, you've won. The government has backed down. What more do you want? Let's eat.'

They sit down in a minimalist dining room where the sun shines bright on the white walls and big, vibrant abstract paintings. The warm light showcases the pensive expression on Agata's face as well.

At the end of the meal, she addresses her son in English. 'You're being unfair to your daughter. Please forgive me, Irena, it's easier for me to say this in Polish.'

Janina leans in to translate.

'When I see the pictures of Solidarność, I see only men. But lots of women supported the union. Without us, who would have found the hideouts and supplies? Who would have checked and printed articles for the foreign press? *Our* history has been erased! Do you not see that? When I was Julka's age, I was proud to live in a country where women fought alongside men. I didn't mind not being in the spotlight. But maybe we grew so accustomed to the shadows that we got used to being ignored. And men have got into the habit of ignoring our needs and desires. If you came on a march with us, Roman, you'd see women from the Home Army protesting with their medals on. You would hear them shout, "We didn't fight so our granddaughters could be deprived of their rights!"'

Irène can still hear the rebellion in Sabina's voice too. Her affection for the younger generations, her wariness.

Dodging his mother's attack, Roman goes to fetch dessert from the kitchen. Julka kisses her grandmother.

'I can't have children,' Janina says. 'And I hate that so much. But I don't believe motherhood should be forced on anyone.'

Irène is moved by Janina's honesty and directness, by the modesty with which she shares her pain.

She can't imagine her own life without Hanno.

As she marvels at the three Polish women from three different generations, who all love their country fiercely, with a mixture of rage and hope, Irène can't help but imagine Wita and Sabina sitting next to them.

Lazar

AN OLDER WOMAN CATCHES Irène's eye across the carriage. She's dressed in a belted grey coat and a black felt hat. When their eyes meet, Irène is reminded of Audrey Hepburn in her final years. Are they heading to the same place? The countryside unfurls on the other side of the window: snow-covered fields in a hazy glow. She's left behind the tumult of Warsaw for this solitary journey to her last meeting on Polish soil.

What a strange feeling it is, to be travelling the very same rails Lazar's convoy took in 1942, through a landscape which can't have changed much.

The passenger in the hat alights behind Irène at Małkinia Górna station. On the opposite track, a rusty freight train catches their eyes. Irène's grandfather was a railway worker. As a child, she loved playing by the tracks with her brothers. Now trains have more sinister connotations in her mind.

Deportation transports passed through this station regularly from the summer of 1942 to the autumn of 1943. Sometimes they would sit unmoving on the tracks all night. Other times, they came and went incessantly. They would arrive with loads they could hardly contain, then leave, empty, a few hours later. The Nazi bureaucrats needed the railways to transport their 'cargo'. They needed a station away from prying eyes. In this region, the narrow tracks are bordered by forests and marshes. Nothing nearby but tiny villages and a few farms.

A taxi is waiting for the woman in the hat in the car park.

'Are you going to the camp?' she asks Irène in English. 'Come with me!'

Irène detects an accent in her travelling companion's warm voice. She thanks her but says she'd rather walk.

'But it's so cold!'

Irène smiles as she points to the black parka Janina has lent her for the occasion. The taxi sets off without her.

Her GPS says the memorial is less than eight kilometres away.

From Małkinia, the transports would go south, taking a spur which no longer exists, then disappear into the woods. The trees were so close to the tracks that mothers would lift their children so they could see the branches. Carefully reaching their fingers through the barbed wire stretched across the tiny opening, the children could almost touch the trees. It was the first forest many of those who'd grown up in the ghetto had ever seen.

Irène walks for a long time, snow crunching beneath her feet. When she breathes, her lungs burn. All she can see is snow, mud, and rows of bare trees. She crosses a bridge over the Bug River and leaves the road behind. When she sees the Treblinka sign, it sends shockwaves through her body. The fact that a village still bears the name, and that people live here, going about their lives as they always have, is too much. The wooden houses are quite dated. Irène passes an old woman bundled up in a shapeless coat. She must have been a child when the camp commander ordered two excavators to dig up the mass graves, then made his Jewish slaves pile the bodies onto metal grates to burn them. On windy days, the smell carried for miles. The woman gives Irène a hostile look, as though she's just read her mind.

The memorial is only four kilometres away now.

Irène doesn't know when Treblinka station was destroyed. It was still standing in the late seventies, when Claude Lanzmann came to film scenes for *Shoah*. Irène's bag contains Gitta Sereny's book on Franz Stangl, the commandant of Treblinka. In it, the old stationmaster tells Sereny that he counted the transports and informed the Home Army, scrupulously jotting down the number of passengers the Nazis had scrawled in chalk on the side of each wagon. His final tally came to over one million victims. A few thousand were Roma, the rest Jews. Every train had thirty to sixty wagons, but the tracks to the camp could only accommodate fifteen or twenty. The rest would sit at the station, their passengers dying of thirst, burning up or freezing to death, depending on the season. At first the wives and children of some of the rail workers would bring water for the captives stuck inside. But before long, there were Lithuanian conscripts – bloodhounds, as they were called – posted atop the wagons, firing warning shots to scare them away. Irène wonders what it must have been like for those children, their childhoods upended by such an unthinkable reality. The dead bodies of those who tried to flee lying there on the platform. The fear. The foul smell of the fog that rose up from the camp. The stationmaster explains in the book that it made people physically ill. Irène thinks of her grandfather, who was a railway worker in France at the same time. Would he have sent his children to carry water to the trains? He never said a word about the Occupation.

As she draws closer to the camp, a black wall of trees obscures the horizon and darkness surrounds her. She keeps walking along the tracks until she reaches the old fork. The section of tracks the Nazis added is now just a path through the woods. She starts down it, breathing in the smell of damp earth and tree sap. Her boots snap pine needles and slip on slushy snow, breaking the silence. The tall trees sway gently in the wind. Their red trunks seem to be ablaze, as if the light were emanating from the depths of the forest itself. The place has a spirit so strong that Irène can't help but feel intimidated. The trees that were cut down to build the barracks and watchtowers have made space for saplings to grow strong. The forest is encroaching on the camp – a shroud for its victims.

As the camp entrance nears, granite slabs mark the path of the phantom tracks. The Nazis destroyed everything they could. Stone foundations mark the position of the platform. She thinks that here, right here, couples and families were still together, for the next few yards at least. Once they passed through the gate, they would be separated for eternity.

The men undressed in the courtyard, the women and children in a building to the left. Once they were naked, the Germans would pick a few of the most robust young men. That's when Lazar must have been chosen. Did he tremble when the SS ordered him to get dressed and follow them? He wouldn't have known he'd just been given a reprieve. He wouldn't have known what a high price he'd pay to stay amongst the living. He'd only just arrived, and he'd already been ripped from his loved ones. Irène thinks back to a survivor who told her about the moment he saw his wife and little boy being led away. Months later, in the darkness of the barracks, he remembered being afraid his son would catch a cold. 'A *cold*,' he repeated, stunned.

Lazar and his family had come from the west. They were most likely welcomed with reassuring words. 'After your bath, we'll get you to work. Hurry up, the water's getting cold. Don't you worry, you'll get your things back soon.' They would have been given a small piece of soap, and a towel, so they'd walk confidently into the trap. Later, Lazar must have learned how differently they treated the terrified, half-starved survivors of the Polish ghettos. The SS terrorised them as soon as they got off the train, so they didn't have time to think. They ran to escape the blows and the dogs – right into the gas chambers.

But, regardless of where they'd come from, the people who reached this platform were dead two hours later.

Irène steps into the camp and walks towards a stone memorial which marks the location of the gas chambers. When the site was operational, the gently sloping path which led prisoners to their death was completely hidden from view by towering walls topped with barbed wire and interlocking pine branches. The SS called it 'the road to heaven'. There was a bend in the path, so prisoners only saw the building at the very last moment. There was a Star of David painted over the entrance to make it look like a ritual bath house. Irène remembers reading that the men were killed first. The women and children waited outside, naked. In winter, the children's feet would stick to the frozen ground. Their mothers had to pry them from the icy earth.

Countless stones stand upright in a snowy field near the memorial. Each of them represents a shtetl or town whose Jewish residents were murdered here. In the distance, Irène spots the woman in the hat, immobile, her head slightly bowed. They are alone in the disconcerting quiet without so much as the beating of a bird's wings.

The camp spanned sixty acres of sandy earth bounded by hedges, *chevaux-de-frise*, and watchtowers. From the outside, all you could see were green walls, the tops of wooden barracks, and the towers. Irène studies the map and tries in vain to imagine just how big the camp was. A pine parapet has grown up all around the site, as if standing guard.

Irène thinks of the moving forest in *Macbeth*, come to avenge the murder of innocents, then suddenly realises she's freezing.

Through the silence she feels the vibrations of the dead. Their solitude and terror. She whispers a prayer for them.

*

Later, she walks to the car park. In the little museum she notices an article in the local paper that features the picture of a handsome old man. 'Who's this?' she asks the attendant.

'Samuel Willenberg. The last survivor of the Treblinka revolt,' he replies in English, rolling his *r*s.

'The last?'

He nods. 'He came here often. He was a great man, an artist.'

Irène's heart sinks to learn that the last witnesses are now dead. The heroes of the revolt. It seems unlikely she'll unlock the secrets Lazar took to the grave.

The museum's centrepiece is a model of the camp made by Polish survivor Jankiel Wiernik. She pauses in front of his portrait to take in his grey hair, pointed ears, piercing black gaze, and Cossack moustache. He was fifty-three when he was rounded up in the Warsaw Ghetto. It was a miracle that he survived. But he was in luck: the SS needed a qualified carpenter. He became a tireless builder: watchtowers, barracks, even a zoo. Lazar was initially chosen to sort belongings but must have become part of his team at some point. As master carpenter, Wiernik was the only worker permitted to move freely through the camp. He became the central cog in the revolt.

The model is a copy of the one he made for the Eichmann trial. Irène stares at the mountains of belongings in the courtyard. She reads the descriptions, imagining Lazar hunched over them, running from pile to pile as the SS berate and beat him. He quickly sorts the items, ripping hems open, rifling through pockets, closing suitcases, and tying up bundles. And all without thinking, because thinking about these piles was certain death. She pictures the piles of clothes, all sizes, all sorts. Pairs of shoes tied together, canes, crutches, hats and pocket watches, but also cooking utensils, menorahs, prayer shawls, and toys . . .

Toys.

She sees him leaning over the cloth puppet.

Not a single child survived Treblinka. Their remaining possessions were given to German children. But Lazar saved this puppet, concealing it from the murderers.

Irène opens Sereny's book to a page she's marked. An interview with a Czech survivor. He tells her that by the end of winter 1943, the transports grew rare. 'Then one day, there was nothing left for us to do. You can't begin to imagine how we felt, the *things* were the only reason we still breathed. Without these *things* to sort, why on earth would they keep us alive?'

So maybe, Irène thinks, *the puppet was a talisman of sorts for Lazar.*

She walks over to join the woman in the hat by a display case that contains objects retrieved from deep beneath Treblinka's surface. The sign explains that just two years ago, a team of British archaeologists uncovered the foundations of the gas chambers and a few ceramic wall tiles. As well as bones and hair. A ring in the shape of a flower, a rusty pendant, and a comb with broken teeth.

'They wanted to erase them from the face of the earth. But they didn't quite succeed,' the woman from the train says.

When she and Irène step outside, large snowflakes are fluttering to the ground. This time, Irène accepts her offer to share a taxi. The ride gives them a chance to properly introduce themselves. The woman's name is Ruth Greenberg, and she lives in Tel Aviv. Her mother, who grew up nearby, lost her entire family to Treblinka, so she visited the site every year, and sometimes Ruth would accompany her. She died two years ago, so Ruth decided to make the journey on her own. It was cathartic for her to say the Kaddish for the departed.

'What about you, dear, who did you lose?' she asks, placing her hand on Irène's.

*

Later Irène will remember that Ruth Greenberg jotted down *Lazar Engelmann* in a small black leather diary. That they exchanged addresses, and that the lady in the hat invited her to come visit her in Israel one day.

She'll remember that she was running late to meet Janina in a restaurant behind Piłsudski Square. On the way, she got a text from Hanno asking her opinion on a wooden pyramid he was thinking of getting Antoine at the Berlin Christmas market. She glanced at the picture distractedly, typed *Wunderschön*, then put her phone back in the bottom of her bag, where it had been on vibrate all day.

She'll remember that Janina was sad to see her go, but glad to have shared so many important moments with her, however heavy some might have been. 'It's gone by so quickly,' Janina said, and, even though Irène agreed, she felt relieved to be leaving a country whose wounds still seemed so fresh. She needed time to process the past few days while relaxing with Hanno and Antoine. Her thoughts were already in Paris, really. Her spirits rose as she shed the sadness that had inhabited her since Treblinka. They drank cocktails and enjoyed trivial small talk. Once the alcohol had loosened her up enough, she might even have mentioned what happened with Stefan. She couldn't be sure.

'Will you come back?' Janina asked as they left the restaurant.

Irène promised she would. She suspected her journey was only just beginning.

To give them more time before they said goodbye, they walked to the Tomb of the Unknown Soldier. A handful of tourists were studying the guards' impassive faces, looking for signs of fatigue. Janina asked Irène what time her plane left, and when she took out her phone to check, she was shocked to see how many missed calls she had. Her older brother, who never called, Myriam, and Antoine. They'd all rung several times. At eight thirty, Antoine had texted.

I've just heard the news. How are you all doing?

Irène's blood turned to ice. She called him back.

A lorry had just barrelled into Berlin's Christmas market, lights off, destroying everything in its path. At least twelve people were dead and fifty injured. The black lorry was registered in Poland – a gruesome coincidence.

Irène tried to call Hanno but couldn't get through. She dialled his number dozens of times, sick with worry. Janina spoke softly, trying to calm her down, but Irène couldn't hear her. A red mist seemed to envelop everything before her. She wanted to be taken to the station or airport, but there were no more flights or trains to Berlin. She chain-smoked as she called Myriam, Wilhelm, and Hanno. They all went straight to voicemail. Janina suggested they go inside the nearby Sofitel – at least it would be warm there. But the fear that had been more or less latent inside Irène since Hanno was born was finally devouring her. Nothing could stop it. There was nothing to ground her.

Antoine tried to reassure her over the phone. 'If Hanno were hurt, you'd have been notified by now. The network's overwhelmed, you've got to be patient.'

She couldn't stop refreshing her newsfeed. There was no information on the dead and wounded. An English university student explained to a news crew that she'd been drinking mulled wine with her friends by a market stall when they heard muffled bangs followed by screams. Her voice was still shaking from the shock.

The Polish lorry driver had tried to overpower the man who had taken him hostage. His body was found in the cab. The killer had disappeared into the Tiergarten night. A search was underway.

Irène will remember spending a sleepless night in the Sofitel lobby, glued to her phone as if it were her distress beacon, her only hope of survival. It felt like an eternity. Myriam's text arrived at 10:35.

They're okay, they're at Hermine's cousin's house in Schöneberg. Benjamin's on his way to get them. The mobile network's still down, but you can reach them on Facebook Messenger.

Irène had a Facebook account, but she never used it and didn't have the app on her phone. She couldn't even remember her password. When she finally managed to open Messenger, a slew of messages from Hanno popped up.

We're okay, Mum, don't worry. I'm trying to call you but it's not working. Toby, Leni, and Hermine are with me, we're at Hermine's cousin's.

Still can't get through, the network's overwhelmed. I hope you're not too worried. Love you.

I hope you're okay, I've sent you a few texts but I don't think they've gone through. We're still at Lotte's, we're going to stay here tonight.

Irène burst into tears of relief as her fingers stumbled across the touchscreen keyboard. Janina looked at her, eager for an update.

'He's absolutely fine,' Irène said, smiling through her tears.

'I think you need a drink.'

Janina ordered two vodkas, which they downed in a single gulp: Agata's recipe for banishing misfortune.

'Are you going to change your flight?'

Irène nodded and explained she'd take the first flight to Berlin in the morning.

'The terrible thing about children,' she mumbled, 'is that you can't always protect them.'

He could have died tonight, and your evening would have been exactly the same, Irène thought. *You wouldn't have known or felt a thing. And even if a sixth sense* had *somehow alerted you, it wouldn't have changed anything.*

Allegra

THEY ONLY SPENT forty-eight hours in Berlin. The city she and Hanno both loved – a place synonymous with freedom and acceptance – had been shaken to its core. Shock and heartbreak subsumed everything else. When Irène rang the doorbell of Hermine's cousin's flat, on a quiet street in Schöneberg, she found five young faces looking very relieved to no longer be enduring it all on their own. Irène and Benjamin shopped, cooked, and consoled. All while reassuring Myriam, who called every half hour. Knowing the killer was still out there had kept Hermine and Leni up all night. Hermine sat nervously twirling a lock of her long chestnut hair. There were dark circles under her eyes, and the jumper Hanno had lent her seemed to swallow her whole. Irène felt her feelings towards Hermine soften. She'd never seen her son in love, except back in kindergarten, when he'd harboured a possessive affection for his teacher. *For him, love is about taking care of the other person, being the strong one,* Irène thought.

*

'So, what do you think of her?' Antoine asks once they're settled in at his place in Paris.

'I like her,' Irène replies.

Hanno's slipped into Antoine's office to call her.

'He seems like he's doing well,' Antoine observes.

'It's difficult to know for sure. He keeps so much to himself. Even when he was little, he was always the one comforting me. "Don't worry, Mummy, it will be all better thoon" he would say with his lovely little lisp. Once he even tried to fix some water damage with a toy wrench.'

'He knows you're the least chill mother in all of Europe.'

'I know, but I go to an awful lot of effort to hide it. I hate how it impacts him.'

'You're a terrible actress,' Antoine teases. 'It's a good thing you opted for your job in the archives.'

He puts on a jazz record and pours golden rum into two tiny crystal glasses – a gift from the man he loves. The two of them don't live together though. Antoine wouldn't know how to share his space. He's set in his ways and has no desire to share bad moods or washing up. Some of Pierre's friends annoy him, and most problematic of all, he's a doting uncle. He takes his nephews to football practice and music lessons every Wednesday afternoon and even some weekends. The youngest is learning the viola, and the screeching of his bow on the strings is enough to make anyone's ears bleed. So Antoine prefers the quiet of his lair. Sometimes he feels bad for making Pierre put up with his solitary nature, particularly since he suspects Pierre would like them to live together. He might even be secretly dreaming of getting married.

'We met at a conference,' Antoine says.

'How romantic!' Irène giggles.

'It was, actually.'

In a sea of spotty students and grey beards, he only had eyes for Pierre. He exuded charm and spontaneity.

'But what about you? I thought I'd be hearing all about your plans to move to Silesia to be with a certain Pole.'

'Do you really think I'm destined to make the same mistakes again and again?'

'Not at all! I think you're quite capable of making new mistakes.'

Irène laughs, then stares at the pyramid-shaped candle-holder that could have cost them so dearly. Hanno had just left the market with the gift to join the others in a Kurfürstendamm bar when the black lorry crashed into the stalls.

Since arriving in Paris, Irène's anxiety has loosened its grip. She likes Antoine's apartment – clearly the home of a scholar. An ageing, eternal student. Piles of records and books are gathering dust in every corner, and an expansive collection of highbrow mystery novels is yellowing on the mantel. Tartan throws are draped over Directoire armchairs alongside a Chinese lantern, a Louis XVI chest of drawers, and faded Oriental rugs. That night Irène leaves the shutters ajar to fall asleep enveloped in the golden glow of the Dôme des Invalides. The sounds of Parisian traffic are like a lullaby. Having grown up with the constant din of the city, it makes her feel at home.

The next morning, they walk along the Seine, then stroll through the Latin Quarter and Montparnasse. The crammed avenues make them nervous. The mindless, febrile crowd, drawn to the Christmas displays in shop windows like flies to a lamp, puts them on edge. Just over a year ago, the 13 November attacks turned Paris into a bloodbath. In the weeks that followed, Antoine recalls, Parisians made a point of sitting on café terraces. Having a drink with friends became an act of protest. The slightest unfamiliar sound sent everyone rushing under their tables. But you can't live in fear forever.

Irène nods in agreement with Antoine's assessment. But right now, she still feels a surge of panic at the idea of taking the Métro or going into a department store. So they put the soles of their shoes to the test and avoid crowded places. In the café where they stop, she watches a young bearded man from the corner of her eye. He's sitting alone at a table in the back. It looks like he's mumbling prayers, with his bag on his knees. When their eyes meet, she's ashamed of her assumptions.

Thanks to a fake passport the police found under the seat of the lorry used to attack the Berlin Christmas market, the authorities have identified the suspect as a Tunisian asylum seeker, whose name was on a list of potentially dangerous individuals. 'His victims are Merkel's victims,' the far right is saying as it demands the resignation of the chancellor who welcomed over a million migrants into Germany.

Irène had volunteered to help welcome thousands of people to Hesse. In spring 2015, Merkel's gesture had kindled a wave of solidarity throughout the country. But widespread optimism went up in smoke at the end of the year, when dozens of women were sexually assaulted in Cologne on New Year's Eve. Ever since, the far right has been gaining momentum, racist discourse has become commonplace, and several migrant shelters have been set on fire. Afterwards Merkel curtailed access to asylum status but refused to completely change her liberal stance on migrants. Irène hopes the chancellor will be able to weather this new storm.

'At least Germany has been brave enough to confront its history,' Antoine says emphatically. 'Here, the entire political class dances to the far right's tune. When you guys were taking in two million refugees, we reluctantly accepted a hundred thousand, then went around patting ourselves on the back for our magnanimity! The reality is that we left Germany to navigate the refugee crisis alone.'

'I grew up behind barbed wire fences. I refuse to build new ones,' Irène says, paraphrasing Merkel.

'The terrorist's asylum request had been denied,' Hanno cuts in. 'The problem is that he was still in Germany. If you don't deport dangerous people, you lose all credibility.'

'That's true,' she says. 'But no matter how careful you are, people slip through the net. After the war, criminals hid in displaced persons camps and duped even the most vigilant investigators. We even hired former Nazis at the ITS!'

Hanno's eyes widen.

'Forty-five high-ranking members of the SS and the Gestapo. Can you imagine? One of them tried to set fire to the archives. When you take in refugees, there's no such thing as zero risk. That's why some people want to close our borders. But do you really think the people you've been helping should just be abandoned to their fate?' Irène asks.

At university, Hanno and Toby help asylum seekers learn German and fill in their paperwork.

'No,' he says quietly.

The people he's met have walked through hell to flee countries ravaged by dictatorships, poverty, and war. And when they finally reach Germany, their qualifications and training are meaningless. They have to start all over. They take menial jobs and spend years waiting, terrified that their applications might be rejected.

'If my work's taught me anything,' adds Irène, 'it's that it can happen to anyone.'

*

On Christmas Eve, Irène and Antoine visit their mothers, who are both masters of emotional blackmail. Irène has it a little easier though: hers is madly in love with her grandson, who is absolutely perfect in her eyes. When he's there, she hardly even complains about how rarely she sees them.

'I missed you, Mamie!' Hanno cries.

She hugs him tight.

'My, you're so handsome! You've got even taller, or maybe I'm getting shorter. It's such a shame you're not staying. Your cousins will be so disappointed.'

To deflect, he shows her a photo of Hermine. His grandmother engages instantly, eager to know where he met her and who made the first move. She can't resist a good love story and is obsessed with the private lives of pop stars and royals. She and Hanno have a lovely chat while savouring the éclairs Irène brought.

'Why aren't you staying here?' Irène's mother finally asks her. 'You're so stubborn. There's plenty of room! You know, your brothers were so worried when they heard about the attack. So where *are* you staying? Really? You still see him? You certainly are forgiving!'

Irène's mother has never understood why she's still friends with Antoine. She's convinced that she lost her daughter the moment she met him. She's still completely oblivious to the fact that her daughter had been suffocating, wasting away, for years before that. Antoine helped her to escape from a life without prospects or horizons. The books he lent her gave her wings. But she mistook the joy of diving into someone else's words and thoughts for love. He was her soulmate, the person who gave her the confidence to take her fate into her own hands.

In the end he admitted he couldn't love her the way she wanted. He was sorry, but he wasn't attracted to her. Irène was angry at first, then dejected for a long time, but when her heartbreak subsided, their connection and affection for one another were still intact. Antoine decided to embrace his sexuality, and she found the strength to leave, even though her move to Germany left her feeling a little guilty for abandoning him.

No one in Irène's family understands what they see as her whims: moving to Germany, getting divorced as soon as her son was born, then insisting on raising him alone in a foreign country. Dedicating her life to the horrors of Auschwitz and the like. So many morbid commemorations and old people in tears. Wasn't everyday life bad enough, without having to relive all that? If someone told her brothers Irène had been swapped at the hospital, they'd be relieved. They're forced and awkward with her, as if she's just any other guest. They forget they shredded their knees on the same brambles as Irène, and make crude, out-of-character jokes. This year, she's spared herself the drama.

*

When Hanno and Irène get back to Antoine's, he's opening a bottle of champagne. The Clash are blaring from the record player.

'Christmas has a disastrous effect on my mother,' he explains.

He'd spent a bit of quiet time with her that afternoon since she'd made it very clear he was persona non grata at Christmas dinner. But still, she just had to unbury the hatchet. Every now and again, she just can't resist the urge. Listening to her, you'd think Antoine hadn't just written a book, he'd committed a mortal sin. It may not be a bestseller but still, it exists. It even got good reviews in *Le Figaro*, the conservative paper his mother reads religiously every morning. Seeing her father and uncles called Nazi collaborators in its culture pages over 'a few compromising friendships' sticks in her throat. During the Occupation, they prioritised their family and employees. How dare he judge them for that? Thanks to them, he'd never wanted for anything.

In his defence, Antoine said he was just telling his side of the story. She threatened to disinherit him, as usual.

'I'm never going to see her again,' Antoine says. 'I'm done.'

Irène nods, even though she knows he'll go back. He loves her too much not to forgive her.

He smiles and shifts gears.

'I'm so happy to see you! Now for some champagne.'

They film themselves toasting, then send the video to Hermine and to Pierre, who is spending Christmas with his family in Touraine. Antoine and Hanno sing out of tune as loudly as they can, making Irène laugh so hard she cries.

Later they take a stroll up the avenue lit by the dome, then cross the esplanade and Pont Alexandre III, to reach Place de la Concorde. Right when they arrive, the Eiffel Tower begins to sparkle, as if it were waiting just for them.

'Merry Christmas,' says Antoine.

On such a perfect night in Paris, which was her first true love, Irène feels torn between two countries. Germany is no longer a barren place of exile. It's her son's home and a country that welcomed her, the place where she's put down roots. And, like Eva before her, it's where she feels most useful.

*

A few days later, after leaving Antoine and Hanno at the Gustave Moreau Museum, Irène suddenly remembered that rue Saint-Lazare was just around the corner. The street immediately turned her thoughts to Allegra, her Uncle Rafo, and the winged god Kairos you had to grab by the hair. Now, standing outside an unknown building, she's unsure how to proceed.

She looks up at the freshly renovated façade of the Haussmann block. At the friezes of plants and animal heads crowning the gentle arches of the tall windows. The heavy wooden door is ajar. She steps inside.

'Can I help you?' asks a surly voice.

The concierge comes down the steps she's cleaning. With her grey skirt and black apron, she looks as though she's stepped straight out of an Eugène Atget photo where she'd have figured alongside turn-of-the-century gangsters and lamplighters. Her expression is unwelcoming, her hair tied up in a tight bun.

'I'm looking for a man who lived in this block. Rafael Ferelli,' explains Irène.

A flicker of interest appears in the concierge's narrowed eyes.

'That was a long time ago. Mr Rafo's been dead for years.'

'I'm looking for his niece, Allegra Torres. Do you know her?'

The concierge looks Irène up and down with curiosity now. 'And what might you want with her?'

Irène attempts a conspiratorial smile. 'I have something that belongs to her.'

'She's dead,' the woman says bluntly. 'Twenty years ago or so. It was just after Lady Di's accident, in the tunnel.'

Princess Diana died in the late nineties. So Allegra would only have been in her sixties, Irène calculates.

'She was young . . .' Irène whispers sadly.

'Her heart gave out. It was so sad. I really liked Madame Allegra. She wasn't arrogant, like some people here. Sometimes she'd invite me in and we'd have a chat.'

'Which floor did she live on?'

'Fourth floor, on the left, by the courtyard. Back when Mr Rafo was still with us, it was a duplex. Madame Allegra sold the top floor when her daughter got married. She said it was too big for her. When she died, her daughter rented the flat to some Italians. They only came once a year, the shutters were always closed. It was heartbreaking to see a lovely flat like that go to waste. Fortunately, Madame Elvire came back after her divorce.'

'So Madame Torres's daughter still lives here?' Irène asks breathlessly, her heart pounding in her chest.

'Of course she does. I watched her grow up. When I was fifteen, I lived on the first floor, with the Pelletiers. I looked after their children, did the housework and shopping, plus a bit of sewing. Sometimes I looked after Madame Allegra's daughter too.'

Irène wonders how old this woman must be, put to work at fifteen. She follows her into the courtyard, where the bare trees yearn for spring. The concierge points out two windows on the sunny side of the building.

'You can go up if you'd like. It's the holidays, she'll have the children.'

Irène stares at the red curtains in the windows. For a few seconds she imagines climbing the steps and ringing the bell. Stepping into a stranger's home, meeting her family. But what would she say? She'd hoped to find Allegra first.

Her death has upended her plans. If Elvire knows nothing about her father, Irène will have to reveal the truth. She can't turn up unprepared and empty-handed.

Irène changes her mind.

'I'll come back,' she tells the concierge.

She joins Antoine and Hanno as they're leaving the museum.

'Where did you disappear to?' her son asks, surprised to see her dripping with sweat.

'I found her!' she says, with fire in her eyes.

'Who?'

'Lazar's daughter.'

Karl

'HERE HE IS!' Henning exclaims, pointing at his computer screen.

A young blond man is running between cars on a Berlin street, brandishing a red flag. He's wearing a leather jacket and bell-bottoms. The wind has tousled his wavy hair, and a big smile has narrowed the corners of his blue eyes. He isn't yet thirty and still looks so young.

Irène stares at him, fascinated, until he passes the flag to another extra as if it's a relay race, and disappears from the shot. She can't believe it. Is this really him, Wita's son, the stolen child she's been obsessing over for months?

Henning went to a lot of trouble to find these images of Karl Winter, since he's usually the one holding the camera. After several fruitless days of research, he finally stumbled upon an obscure film buff forum and learned that Winter had appeared briefly in a short film called *Die rote Fahne* in the late sixties.

'You, Henning, are a genius!' Irène exclaims.

In mid-January, Irène received a letter from the German Red Cross informing her that Otto and Irma Winter had died in the early eighties. Their house in Munich had been sold, and there was no trace of a Karl Winter anywhere in Bavaria. The next step would be to track down the solicitor who had officiated the sale, but they were experiencing very high demand, and the investigation could take months. Irène's time was also in demand: she'd taken on an urgent project to locate the descendants of forced labourers to whom a company in Hesse wanted to pay reparations.

So Charlotte Rousseau suggested Irène ask for help from volunteers. The ITS had just opened its #stolenmemory site, designed to help the archives return the objects in their possession. Some of the team had already used it with good results. Volunteers reached out from all over the world, eager to put their amateur sleuth skills to the test. So Irène posted Karl Winter's last known address, his adoptive parents' names, and his date of birth on the site.

Two months later, amid a pile of useless responses which were too vague or off the mark, she stumbled across a message from a retired doctor in Hamburg. *In the sixties, I knew a filmmaker by that name in Berlin. He was about thirty, so it could be him.*

Irène sent him an email and learnt that, in 1966, when the doctor was at university, he had taken part in a demonstration against the Vietnam War. A stranger had filmed them. Afterwards, they'd all gone for a beer together. The man told them he made films to challenge people's world views. After that, he never saw him again. But a few years later, a film club in Hamburg-Mitte screened a film by Karl Winter. When he saw the name on the sign, he made the connection. He went to see the film with his then girlfriend. They found it confusing and boring. *But I have good memories of that night because we spent the whole time kissing. We were young, you know*, he concluded.

Irène decided that tracking down an obscure avant-garde director from the sixties would be right up Henning's street.

'It really wasn't that hard,' Henning boasts. 'My parents were 68ers. I'm very familiar with counterculture. I grew up surrounded by the smell of incense and marijuana.'

'So that's where you got your yogi-level patience,' Irène teases.

'Maybe, but if so it's a form of rebellion. My parents wanted to blow everything up. They met at a Molotov cocktail-making class! I wonder if it's simply skipped a generation . . . Last night, the twins staged a sit-in in the living room. They were fighting for their right to an extra bottle and a cartoon.'

'Don't your parents spoil the budding activists?'

'My mother can't stand more than two hours with them, and even then it has to be outdoors. My parents have really changed. Now they're model citizens who sort their rubbish and criticise my lack of authority. But back to your chap. No one remembers him today, but at the time he was quite a well-known figure on the radical left. He was one of the people behind the Oberhausen Manifesto.'

'Doesn't ring any bells for me,' Irène says.

'It ushered in the age of New German Cinema! What about Alexander Kluge, Volker Schlöndorff, Fassbinder, Margarethe von Trotta? Do any of them sound familiar?'

Irène recognises a few names and nods.

'Initially it was activist, experimental filmmaking, inspired by New Wave cinema in France. They combined documentary and fiction within a single film. Lots of voiceovers, static shots, and agitprop,' Henning explains with a smile.

'So you're saying Karl wanted to change the world?'

'That dream was pretty widespread in 1968. But in Germany, there was also the terrible legacy of Nazism. Parents had lost all credibility in the eyes of their children, for supporting Hitler.'

The generation born during the war learned about the crimes of their parents and grandparents at the Auschwitz trial. The horror and shock they felt kindled a particularly visceral form of anger. They wanted to hold people to account. But their parents always dodged the subject. The country refused to confront its past. Former Nazis were present at all levels of society, even in the Bundestag. They'd converted to capitalism: the economic miracle the younger generation saw as alienating mercantilism – the final form of undying fascism.

'In the sixties, the majority of policemen were former Nazis,' Henning recalls. 'As were half the judges. They were hardly impartial arbiters when sentencing war criminals.'

Media outlets belonging to the Springer group called for the ruthless suppression of demonstrations. Some of the students became so radicalised that they took up arms.

'If Karl is our kidnapped boy, he had good reason to be angry,' Irène says quietly. 'Even if he'd forgotten Poland and repressed the rest.'

'Yes. But he was an artist, he didn't plant bombs. Back then, people like him were called sympathisers.

He carried on making films. They were screened at art house cinemas and foreign festivals . . . Not exactly blockbusters. Then he went on to teach filmmaking in Berlin.'

Irène is impressed by Henning's research. 'Do you think he's still alive?'

'It's impossible to say. Here's the last trace I found,' he says, handing Irène a copy of an article from 2012.

It's a clipping from the French regional daily *Sud Ouest* about the Bordeaux Independent Film Festival. In the picture, a man in his seventies poses next to a tall middle-aged man with long brown hair and a relaxed demeanour. His grey eyes sparkle behind thinly rimmed glasses. The photo is captioned: 'Karl Winter, invited to present a retrospective of his work, alongside his son, documentary filmmaker Rudi Winter.'

Irène looks from father to son.

She wants to rewatch the footage of Karl running with his flag, making a show of his rebellious joy against the dreary grey backdrop of the city.

'Henning, I don't know what I'd do without you,' she says.

*

That evening she drives along the slippery forest roads in a fog so thick that the yellow glow of her headlights can't pierce it. It's hard to imagine that the first buds will appear in just two weeks' time. *That's winter's ruse, making us believe it will last for ever,* she thinks.

When she arrives home, she's happy to be back in her warm haven, with her son's childhood drawings on the walls. Little men with outsized arms and smiles. She lights the fire and puts on the Dafné Kritharas album Antoine and Hanno gave her for Christmas. Some of her songs are in Ladino. Cradled by Dafné's melodic voice, Irène imagines a young woman standing on the ramparts of a blinding-white city. She wonders if Allegra thought of Thessaloniki as she took her last breath.

Slowly but surely, her daydream wends its way back to Wita's son. When she rang the German Film and Television Academy in Berlin, the woman on the telephone asked which Winter she meant. Karl Winter had retired in the early noughties and hadn't attended the German Film Award ceremony for years. Rumour was that his health was failing. But his son Rudi taught at the Academy. She gave Irène his work email.

She finds articles online about Rudi's latest documentaries, as well as a few trailers. The state broadcasters regularly air his work. She's seen at least one of his films: a documentary on Greta Thunberg. In the past few years he's been exploring the deep-seated fears at work in German society, making films about the environment, immigration, and discontent among those living in former East Germany. She writes:

Dear Mr Winter,

I work at the International Tracing Service, where I aim to locate the descendants of people deported to Nazi concentration camps. One of my current investigations may concern your father. I would be very grateful if you could spare a moment of your time. I'm more than happy to come to you.

She adds a polite sign-off, then presses send.

*

Irène is waiting for Rudi Winter in a café on Friesenstrasse, in the southern part of Berlin's Kreuzberg neighbourhood. It's a cold, rainy evening, just a few days before Easter. He's shooting a few streets away, in what used to be Tempelhof Airport. The site has been a welcome centre for refugees for several years now.

Setting up this meeting wasn't straightforward. His first response was curt: her request was intriguing, but he was in the middle of a shoot and couldn't spare the time. But Irène couldn't stop thinking about Agata, who was getting on in years, and about Rudi's father, who could be battling cancer. So she lobbied hard and prevailed. But now she's been hanging around in the draughty café for an hour and fifteen minutes. Spring clearly hasn't come in Berlin. A few months have passed since the Christmas market attack, and the city seems quiet, at least on the surface. She orders another mint tea. The deep blue of dusk is overtaking dull grey in the sky. Puddles on the pavement reflect the glow of the streetlights.

Just when she thinks Rudi Winter has stood her up, a shapeless figure in a poncho shakes off the rain in front of the door to the café. Once he's removed the poncho and cumbersome rucksack, she recognises the face from the photo, although his hair is greyer, and he has a three-day beard and a few more wrinkles. She notes he no longer wears glasses. In his all-weather outfit and gear, he could easily be mistaken for a hiker freshly returned from the wilderness.

'Irène Martin?' he asks as he holds out his hand. 'I'm so sorry, we finished late because of this bloody rain.'

'Are you filming at the refugee centre?'

'Yes, it's a TV documentary,' he explains. 'Just after the Christmas market attack, the police searched the centre looking for a Pakistani man, though they released him after a few hours. The refugees are scared. Gangs of far-right extremists are always prowling around. They were here again this morning. They reeked of booze, you could smell it twenty metres away. They were looking for a fight, trying to start a fire. Their idea of hospitality.'

Irène can't stand the way the far right has instrumentalised the attack to place asylum seekers at the centre of every political debate since. It makes her sick.

'But you're not here to listen to me talk about asylum seekers,' Rudi says, cutting her off. He's clearly in a hurry. 'I've never heard of the International Tracing Service. And I don't really understand what my dad could have to do with a camp prisoner.'

She feels he's trying to get rid of her. He isn't receptive, but she continues. She hasn't come all this way to leave empty-handed.

Irène unfolds her napkin on the table, removes the pendant from its envelope, and carefully places it on the table in front of him.

He looks at the representation of the Virgin and Child in its enamel mandorla, the blue of her dress, the faded gold halos, and the tarnished bronze chain.

'This locket belonged to a woman named Wita Sobieska, a Polish prisoner at Ravensbrück,' she explains. 'Before she was deported, the Nazis kidnapped her son. He wasn't yet three. I have reason to believe he was given to a Lebensborn centre, then adopted by a German family.'

Now she has his full attention.

She opens the locket carefully, and shows him the portrait. 'See, she drew the boy's face and wrote down his name and date of birth. Tragically, she was murdered before they could be reunited.'

'It's a moving story, but I don't see what this has to do with me.'

'It's very likely this boy is your father,' Irène replies, ignoring the furious beating of her heart.

'No,' he says abruptly. 'You've got the wrong person. My father's German.'

'But he was adopted, wasn't he? By Otto and Irma Winter. They lived in East Prussia, then moved to Munich in 1944.'

'How do you know that?' he asks. His eyes betray his astonishment.

'After the war, an investigator took an interest in them. He worked for the Allies, tracing stolen children. Their former neighbour testified the boy would sing in Polish.'

'No,' he repeats. 'My father was a German orphan. I've seen his adoption papers. That's what they say.'

'The SS lied to adoptive parents. They falsified children's identities. The good news is that Wita Sobieska also had a daughter, who survived in Poland. If your father agrees, we could do a DNA test. That would give us irrefutable proof that they're siblings. Proof that wasn't available to the investigator at the time.'

'That's out of the question. Don't even dream of bothering my father with this absurd story, do you understand me?'

He shoves the necklace back across the table.

His hostility comes as a surprise. Blood pounds in Irène's temples and she loses her cool.

'Isn't it up to your father to decide? Maybe he needs to know where he's from. Maybe he's been haunted by doubt his whole life. He should at least be consulted.'

'If you really want to know, my father is very unwell,' he says in a hushed voice. 'He has Alzheimer's. He lives in a home, and the very last thing he needs is someone upsetting him with this sort of thing! So forget your little detective story. Go back to your archives and leave us alone.'

Irène stands up as though she's just been slapped. The meeting has been a complete disaster. She puts on her coat with a lump in her throat. As she goes to put the locket away, she changes her mind.

'I'm sorry about your father,' she says, looking him in the eyes. 'These things aren't easy to say, and I'm sure I've been clumsy. But this is also your story, and your heritage.

Your father may have been kidnapped, but he's not the only one impacted. The crime has upended several lives. A woman in Warsaw has spent seventy years waiting to see her brother again. She'd give anything to be reunited. All I'm asking you to do is think this through.'

She walks out, leaving the locket on the table.

Hanka

THE DAYS PASS and she doesn't hear a word from Rudi Winter. His silence leaves Irène crestfallen. Eventually, she confides in Myriam.

'You know what? I get it,' says Myriam. 'It must be so shocking to realise the foundations your life was built on might all be . . . a lie. He wants to protect his father. Just give him time to digest what you said.'

'But what if he refuses to find out the truth?'

'He has every right to. You need to be prepared for that.'

'Yes, but if he refuses, he's depriving Agata of the chance to reconnect with her brother. That isn't fair.'

'What's unfair is what these children went through. Your guy's doing what he can with the information he has. Everyone develops their own strategies to overcome trauma,' Myriam counters. 'Benjamin's great-aunt survived Auschwitz. When the camp was liberated, she took two years off her age. She erased the two years she'd spent in the camp, just like that. Acted like they'd never happened. So no one else talked about them either, they respected her decision. We realised it was a question of survival.'

Irène knows her friend is right. Even though she dreams of reuniting Agata with her brother, it's not her job to tend to their wounds. Her job is to give descendants bits and pieces of a story which they are free to refuse.

That night she has a terrible nightmare. Rudi Winter never wants to see her again and refuses to let her speak to his father. His icy grey eyes judge her in silence as she desperately tries to do up the buttons of her coat. She can't manage it, her pregnant belly is already too big. She wakes with a start.

*

When she arrives at the Centre, Irène makes a copy of Allegra's letter, with the translation by Montse Trabal, and slips them into an envelope addressed to Elvire Torres. She writes that she found it in the archives and invites Elvire to take it all in at her own pace. She adds that she hopes it doesn't leave her too shaken and tells her she's free to get in touch if she has any questions. Before signing off, she also mentions that the International Tracing Service holds an object belonging to Lazar Engelmann.

She hesitated for a long time about whether to simply send the puppet as well. Perhaps it's simply cowardice, but this time she's decided she doesn't want to force things. She would rather Elvire come to her.

The same day she receives a letter from Lucia Heller.

Dear Irène,

I don't know how to fully express our gratitude. The documents you sent me have had such a resounding impact on our lives.

You apologised for finding so little in Warsaw, but you can't imagine how precious what you did find is to us. Don't forget that we have nothing else to remember them by. We don't even have a grave where we can pay our respects.

Reading Eva's words reunited my mother with her Uncle Medres, whom she remembered as being just as gentle and wise as Eva said. She's so sorry that her father died without being able to read it, because he missed his beloved brother every day of his life. My grandfather was the businessman and Medres was the intellectual. They admired each other but they were always bickering.

My mother remembers Eva rebelling against her mother. She still remembers Estera as a reserved woman, overly attached to the idea of propriety. It was quite a shock to find out she'd taken up arms in the ghetto! Estera and Eva both showed great courage through those tragic times. I hope my daughter and nieces will keep their memory alive and find strength in their example.

The passages where Eva talks about her brothers were so touching as well. The last time my mother saw them, the youngest wasn't yet walking. My mother insisted on gathering all her children and grandchildren to hear her read Eva's piece out loud. By the end, we were all in tears. It was like a memorial service.

I often think back to what you said. 'Don't let their deaths overshadow their lives.'

Thanks to you, a little of that life has been restored to us.

I've had the pictures of Eva framed, so she can live on among us. I've told my family an awful lot about you and your work. Everyone here wants to meet you! We'd be honoured if you'd accept our invitation to visit us here in Buenos Aires.

Irène writes back immediately.

Dear Lucia,

The day we listened to the recording of Eva, I tried to find the right words to console you and ease the journey to reunite with your lost loved ones. And today you've returned the favour, just when I needed it most. Thank you for so generously reminding me of my purpose here. A purpose your aunt passed on to me.

Estera's bravery, Eva's strength, and Medres's gentle wisdom all find their expression in you. It's a beautiful legacy. I'm sure that your children will be inspired by them in their adult lives. And I'd be delighted to visit you, just as soon as my work allows.

It's still dark when Irène leaves for Ludwigsburg the next morning.

Four hours later she's ringing the bell of a building that blends discreetly into the cityscape. From the outside, you'd never guess that it's protected by reinforced doors and a steel frame, nor that it houses nearly two million files on Nazi war criminals.

The Central Office for the Investigation of National Socialist Crimes was established in 1958. Back then most former Nazis went about their business quite openly, with no fear of prosecution, or had been pardoned after a few years behind bars. They returned to their previous positions in society, and even demanded back payment of their pensions. The German people were fed up with Nazi trials. So the Central Office received a welcome about as warm as the ITS's in Bad Arolsen. The young prosecutors assigned there found themselves in a hostile town, where they weathered daily insults and threats. The circumstances were united against them to ensure their work remained purely symbolic. But the prosecutors' youth was a double-edged sword. They were a fresh set of eyes on crimes unprecedented in their nature and scale. Some were so traumatised they only lasted a few weeks before asking to be sent back to their previous posts. But the ones who remained proved surprisingly pugnacious.

Until the early eighties, the ITS helped them to find witnesses and collect evidence. Then suddenly, without warning, Max Odermatt decided to bar them from accessing the world's most extensive archives on Nazi persecution. The thought alone makes Irène furious. It's been more than ten years since Odermatt was dismissed, but she still hasn't forgotten.

The Central Office continues to hunt Nazis around the world, combing through thousands of pages of dossiers to find one name, one neglected clue. Nearly all the perpetrators are dead now, most of them having passed peacefully in their own beds. Most witnesses are gone too. The survivors are getting on in age, and their memories are failing. No other place embodies the limits and powerlessness of justice as well as the Central Office. But no other place embodies the nobility of the mission so well either. The Ludwigsburg lawyers have never given up.

Today, the Central Office employs barristers, historians, and archivists. It was conceived as a temporary entity, but its closing date was pushed back so many times that it eventually became a hallowed institution of the new democratic Germany. It's a place where memory is tangible, enduring, and troubling. A place that invites you to venture into the darkness, to probe the shadows.

Irène has come for Lazar.

The staffer lead Irène to a room where other researchers are already hard at work in monastic silence. She puts on the handling gloves. Several boxes have been laid out for her. They contain witness statements from the trial of Kurt Franz, which began in October 1964 in Düsseldorf. Ten SS officers from the Treblinka killing centre stood trial for almost a year. The eleventh defendant died before the trial began. As the camp's last commandant, Kurt Franz was the biggest fish. He was always so immaculately dressed that the prisoners called him Lalka, 'the Doll'. A doll who was constantly coming up with new games, new ways of making people suffer before their inevitable death. After the war, Lalka went back to his old job as a cook in Düsseldorf, where he lived in peace until he was arrested. In his home, the police discovered an album of photos from the camp entitled *Schöne Zeiten*. Good Times. He'd clung to Treblinka for as long as he could, then went to hunt partisans near Trieste.

One or two of the men in the defendants' box showed glimpses of humanity. They would beat the prisoners, but unenthusiastically, or even reluctantly. This nuance made them look like lambs among wolves. They'd been obedient soldiers, hoping to hide out in the camp for long enough to avoid the front. The killing centre operated until October 1943. For fifteen months, cruelty had been the rule, humanity the exception. Dozens of survivors came to testify, including Lazar.

Reading his testimony makes Irène feel as though she is leaning over the opaque surface of a lake. All she can make out is a dark, moving surface. Underneath there's an abyss she can't fathom. Lazar dredges his words up from the depths. Eerily steady, they slice through the silence like so many sharp blades.

He describes the crowds pouring out of the train cars. He remembers himself back in that crowd, dazed and confused when he saw the mountains of belongings in the yard without understanding what they meant. He recalls the speed with which everything happened. The separation of men and women, being forced to strip. Having been assigned to the Sonderkommando at the lower camp, he never set foot beyond the leafy hedges. But he heard the screams. Later, he saw huge diggers, untold bodies in their jaws, raising their cargo towards the sky. He breathed in the foul smell of burning bodies.

Sometimes that smell comes back to him, like a ghost. 'We were walking dead men,' Lazar remembers. This certainty inspired their revolt.

In his first months, he was sent to sort belongings – the domain of Lalka and his henchmen. They'd suddenly appear out of the blue, beating whomever they liked until a bloody corpse was all that was left.

Later, Lazar was recruited by the carpentry team. He helped build a zoo to amuse the SS men, and a smart-looking fake station called Obermajdan designed to trick arriving victims. There was even a clock with stationary hands. He was occasionally seconded to the Tarnungskommando, which tended to the hedges. In the winter of 1942–43, the number of arriving transports dropped off drastically. Lazar and his colleagues became useless mouths to feed. So the SS starved them, leading to a typhoid epidemic. Prisoners who couldn't keep pace were executed. Hundreds of them died. If the transports hadn't started up again in March, they would all have been dead before the revolt.

He describes the torture and executions to the judges in great detail, holding each of the defendants accountable for his actions. He calls them by their nicknames: Lalka, Kiwe, Frankenstein, the American, and the Angel of Death.

After a while, Lazar and the others could no longer feel anything.

One autumn morning, Lalka sent them to secure the ramp. A large transport had just arrived. They were sent to reinforce the Sonderkommando prisoners assigned to welcome new arrivals – the Blues, named for the colour of the armbands they wore. They unloaded dead bodies and belongings from the trains, then had half an hour to clean the cattle trucks before they went off again, clearing the way for the next convoy.

The SS and Trawniki men were waiting on the ramp, armed with whips, revolvers, and growling dogs. The terrified crowd cast fearful glances in their direction. Lazar helped stragglers to jump onto the platform.

He saw an SS officer approach a woman carrying a little girl in her arms. The officer was lean and strong, his cheeks as rosy as a babe's, his eyebrows bleached by the sun. The Polish prisoners called him *Kelev*. 'The Dog' in Yiddish.

The little girl was holding a cloth toy, a puppet. Lazar had seen puppets like it before, in Prague. This one was dirty, but the girl clutched it tight. She was so afraid of the dogs and the men.

*

Irène stops short at the mention of the doll. She wanted to know where it came from, but now she's not so sure. Something tells her this story destroyed Lazar. For a fleeting moment, she regrets having come.

But there's no turning back now.

*

Kelev reached out to snatch the puppet from her, but the girl held on tight. Lazar remembers her saying *'Neyn! Neyn!'* her big black eyes, full of fury.

So Kelev took out his gun and shot the girl's mother in the head. She crumpled to the ground. As the little girl fell, she dropped the puppet. The officer beamed as he picked it up.

The prosecutor asks whether Kelev is one of the men on trial.

Lazar says he doesn't recognise Kelev among the accused. He doesn't know the man's real name, but he has never forgotten his face.

Kelev saw Lazar watching the little girl weep next to her mother's lifeless body that day.

'Take that one to the Lazarett,' he ordered.

The prosecutor asks Lazar to explain what the Lazarett was.

He tells the court that it was a roofless building surrounded by hedges. At the entrance there was a big white flag with a red cross, to make it look like an infirmary. The elderly, disabled, and sick were taken there, along with unaccompanied children. Anyone who would slow down the death machine. The Lazarett was also the only end in sight for Sonderkommando labourers. That's where the SS got rid of them, as punishment or simply because they'd outlived their usefulness.

'If I understand correctly, you were being asked to lead this child to the place she'd be executed?' the prosecutor presses.

'That's right,' Lazar replies.

He knew that behind the walls there was a mass grave, where a fire raged all day and night. Sometimes the SS sent one of them to burn piles of the victims' photos and papers in it. He'd seen what happened to the people taken there. The Angel of Death would order his victims to sit on the edge of the trench, and Frankenstein would walk past them in a lab coat and shoot each of them in the back of the neck. Their bodies would fall straight into the flames.

At this point, he has to pause regularly, unable to finish his sentences as his memories tear down his calm façade.

He scooped the girl into his arms and carried her to the Lazarett. He says she reeked of fear. The girl had curly black hair, and her face was smeared with snot and tears. He consoled her and felt her relax a bit in his arms.

'What could I have done?' he asks.

His arms held her tight, but they were useless. They couldn't save her.

He would never forget her name. Hanka.

He remembers thinking, 'When I am in the ground, who will remember her?'

He couldn't imagine surviving Treblinka.

When they reached the Lazarett, the Angel of Death was guarding the entrance. Frankenstein suddenly appeared with his hideous face and white lab coat.

He wanted to take the child from Lazar, but she clung to him. The murderous look in Frankenstein's eyes terrified her. She started crying again, so Frankenstein simply snapped her neck with his rifle butt. Her black curls were sticky with blood. 'No point wasting bullets on that,' he snarled as he carted Hanka's body behind the wall.

Lazar was unable to move.

In his oddly high-pitched voice, the Angel of Death said, 'Get lost unless you want to join her in the Bosom of Abraham!'

*

Irène closes her eyes, her heart heavy. She pictures Lazar, the devastation on his face. His arms are empty but still warm from her heat.

*

'Every night I hear her,' Lazar continues. 'I hear her screaming inside me.' He explains that she was the reason he'd come to the trial, the reason he was putting himself through it. To confront her killers.

At the end of the trial, the Angel of Death and Frankenstein were sentenced to life in prison. The former died in jail; the latter was set free fourteen years later.

*

The next day, in the morning light, the puppet looks so sad, with its faded tears and droopy mouth. Maybe because now Irène knows about the ghost it protects.

I hear her screaming inside me.

Rudi

'It's funny,' Antoine says over the phone, '*Lazarett* means field hospital in German, but it must be related to the word *lazaretto*. You know, the place where they used to quarantine lepers? And Lazarus is the patron saint of lepers.'

'The one Jesus brought back to life so he could show off?'

'The very same. Lepers were seen as the living dead. Giving them a patron saint who'd come back from the dead makes sense. It's kind of funny, really.'

'Someone had a dark sense of humour,' Irène says, looking out at her little garden, where the moonlight is putting on a shadow puppet show.

She's come across so many horrors since she started at the ITS, but she still can't get over Lazar's testimony. Perhaps this is just one too many. How many crimes and massacres can a person's mind absorb before it's poisoned? Sometimes she thinks she might lose all faith in humanity. She sees people through the lens of genocide sociology: quite a few as potential killers, a minority as Resistance fighters, and the rest as bystanders, oscillating between fear and active participation in murder and theft. She wonders which category her neighbours would fall under.

Never again is a mantra the deaf chant for the blind. What's the point of exhausting yourself to give a name to a victim, when all over the world people continue to brutalise, exploit, and destroy everything they touch. She thinks of Stefan, who said something eerily similar that cold night in Lublin.

'What's the point, Antoine?' she asks, lighting a cigarette.

'Oh dear, you really are struggling, aren't you? You know very well what the point is. You help people to tie up the loose ends the war left behind. You give them back what was taken from them, meaningful things they don't even know they want.'

'Things that could wreck their lives. Do you think my old filmmaker with Alzheimer's will feel better if I tell him the SS kidnapped him and sent his mother to die in Ravensbrück?'

'Well … he might, actually,' Antoine says after a moment. 'Maybe he'll finally realise that his mother didn't abandon him. And that he needn't have taken that out on all the women he met!'

Irène laughs, exhaling smoke. 'God, you do know how to cheer me up. Unfortunately, it's a little late for his exes. If he did take it out on them, that is.'

'It's never too late to learn an important lesson,' Antoine replies. 'That's why I continue to hope my mother will find her way to the light. Maybe a near-death experience would do the trick. They say you come out of it a new person.'

'Preferably before she disinherits you.'

'Obviously. But how's it going with your churlish filmmaker?'

'Not a peep.'

'He sounds perfect for you,' Antoine teases.

'Very funny. I thought I was so clever leaving the locket with him. Now I have to go and collect it.'

'No, you were right. He can tell *you* to get lost. But it's more complicated with an object. Especially yours— they're haunted!'

After hanging up, Irène streams one of Rudi Winter's films. The title grabbed her attention: *Vergissmeinnicht*, forget-me-not in German. The documentary was shot at a memory care facility in Dresden, where they'd recreated East German interiors, with wallpaper and furniture from the time. The facility director explains that the familiar surroundings soothe the patients. When they pick up utensils like the ones they used to have, they remember how to complete certain tasks. The camera zooms in on the faces of men and women whose memories are ebbing away. It lingers on the expression of an old man captivated by a story his granddaughter is telling. The mulish look on a woman's face as she refuses to leave her room. The tears an old man sheds while listening to Chopin.

Irène feels Rudi Winter is trying to understand what this illness does to people, what it erodes and what it reveals. His own voice narrates certain shots. 'They resemble islands gradually drifting further away from the continent. Until the moment they're so far from shore that all their moorings snap. Maybe it's best to put aside what we know about them so we can get to know them anew and learn to love them differently. As they are, laid bare, fragile, cruel, or scared. With every gesture, in every layered moment.'

Irène imagines this heartbreakingly beautiful film is also a love letter to his father, in absentia. It reawakens a sense of urgency in her. Eva's words surface once more, demanding her attention. 'Every minute, every hour, is a lifetime to the people waiting for answers. Life is fragile. We're all just hanging by a thread.'

Irène knows she can't abandon Karl and Agata. She begins drafting an email to Rudi Winter, lets verbose justifications hijack her message, and starts over several times. Every word feels like a trap. She imagines them turning against her. In the end she scraps them all and makes do with a few, very simple lines. She writes that she was deeply moved by his film. That she understands why he's afraid for his father. Afraid of reawakening a pain he has suppressed for a very long time.

> In return, I'd like to recommend a documentary you might like. One of the protagonists contacted the ITS a few years ago. Unfortunately, we were unable to give him the answers he was hoping for.

The film follows the fate of several children kidnapped by the Nazis. One of them, who was snatched in Lithuania in 1941, says the thing that hurts him most is not knowing where he came from. Even time hasn't healed the wound. He hopes to learn the truth before he dies.

*

Two days later Rudi calls.

'You don't let up,' he says gruffly.

Irène senses a softening nonetheless. She listens to what he has to say.

'Three years ago, my father was unmanageable. No one could come close to him. He'd send the nurses out of the room. He's calmer now, as if somewhere inside he's admitted defeat. They take good care of him at the memory care facility where he lives. His decline has slowed. I don't want to disturb such a fragile peace.'

'I understand.'

'Maybe you're right, even though your theory sounds crazy,' Rudi says. 'But, in any case, it's too late for him. Some days he doesn't even know he has a son.'

He goes on to admit that he wanted to return the locket straight away. He wrapped it up carefully, went to the post office, paid the postage, and left. But, after less than five hundred yards, regret set in. He went back. The man at the counter didn't understand what was going on. Neither did Rudi.

'I took a closer look at the drawing,' he says. 'It *could* be my father, but it could also be any blond child at that age. My life is complicated enough as it is.'

He pauses for a moment, then asks, 'Are you free on Friday night?'

'That depends.'

'I was rude to you the other evening. I'd like to make it up to you.'

'Really?' she asks. 'I'm not driving four hours round-trip for dinner without some sort of guarantee.'

'I promise I'll be there. I want to hear more about this Polish woman.'

The next day she goes to pick up Hanno and Hermine from the bus stop. After their exams, they worked in a brasserie for a month to save for a trip to Austria and Italy. They've just returned and are spending the final days of their holiday in Bad Arolsen, before the start of the spring semester. To celebrate, Irène has organised dinner with the Glasers and some of her son's other friends.

Ever since the attack, Hanno has texted her every evening. A gesture to assuage her anxiety. He hasn't missed a single day, not even during their trip. She received messages from Vienna, Salzburg, Bad Ischl, Bolzano, Padua, Verona, and Venice. Through them, she felt as though she were sleeping in a different city every night. Her dreams were full of clear skies, mountain peaks, and sunsets over the Venetian lagoon.

When she picks them up, they're tanned, excited, and talkative. Their rucksacks are full of pecorino and truffle salami. As she watches Hermine help out in the kitchen and welcome guests, Irène is surprised by how naturally she's managed to find her place in their lives. It's as though she's always been there, with her gentle determination and disarming spontaneity. At the station, she ran towards Irène to hug her. She can't help but admit she's growing quite fond of Hermine. When she's there, Hanno seems almost embarrassed by how happy he is. As though he's worried that it may bother his devoted mother who's married to her job, anxious, and celibate. He only sees her outward façade, but she's also quite the opposite:

carefree and impulsive. She realises she's sacrificed parts of herself to give Hanno stability. She let herself fall into an ancestral role, let dust gather on certain aspects of her personality.

Later, she steps back to take in her friends and their children, the Glaser Labrador dashing between their legs, a tornado of yellow fur. Benjamin tops up her champagne. She feels a bit tipsy.

Hanno's doing well. Perhaps it's time to let herself live a little.

*

As Irène climbs the steps to the restaurant on Friday evening, she realises that all the time she spent on her hair has been wiped out by the torrential downpour she's just braved. She does her best to wipe the mascara from the corners of her eyes. She'd love a cigarette, but her pack is soaked. The restaurant overlooks Weisser See. It was a nice idea, but maybe not the right time of year.

Rudi Winter is sitting at a table, contemplating the lake. The room is empty, apart from a few elderly couples who are already enjoying dessert. The decor exudes a dated sort of melancholy – a cross between a retirement home and the Côte d'Azur out of season.

When he gets up to shake her hand, he's taller than she remembered. A collared shirt and jacket can really change a man.

'Sorry about the weather,' he says when he sees her pathetic demeanour. 'It was a lovely day until an hour ago.'

'At least we won't be disturbed,' she says optimistically.

'True. In a quarter of an hour they'll all be asleep,' he jokes.

'Do you live nearby?'

'No, but sometimes I come here for a swim. When my children were little, we had an apartment near here, in Prenzlauer Berg. My ex-wife loved the area. It was still nice back then. Now it's just tourists, yuppies, and French expats.'

'*Quelle horreur*,' she says ironically.

'I have a knack for putting my foot in my mouth,' he says with an awkward grin. 'How long have you lived in Germany?'

She's enjoying watching him walk on eggshells.

'Twenty-six years. Your country and I go way back.'

'So, was it always your dream to hide away in the middle of nowhere in Hesse and spend your days tracking down the victims of Nazi persecution?' he asks with a chuckle.

'No, I applied for the job by chance. Then I found out I liked it.'

'Liked the war?' he asks, perplexed.

'No. Looking for people. I like *that*.'

He studies her face. At their last meeting she annoyed him, but now he's intrigued.

They order two Wiener schnitzels. He says it's the only dish the restaurant consistently gets right.

Outside, dusk is blurring the line between lake and sky.

'Would you say you're a good investigator?'

Irène remembers the way Eva laughed at this same question.

'Pretty good, yes. I was taught by the best.'

'So what's your secret?' he asks, pouring her a glass of wine.

'Instinct and patience. I spend a huge amount of time thinking about the people I'm looking for. Day and night. When I'm walking, when I'm driving. My son's always scolding me for it. My investigations are always there, in some corner of my mind. I follow my intuition, then put it to the test to see if it holds up. I try to put the pieces together, which is often slow going. But then, all of a sudden, I can tell I'm close. It's an utterly unique feeling.'

'I understand,' he says. 'I can shoot all day long and still be unable to capture what I'm looking for. I get annoyed, but that doesn't help either. Then I go for a stroll round the neighbourhood, and suddenly I see the thing I was missing. I start the scene over and it all clicks into place. Sometimes all you need to do is move the camera to change your point of view. Other times, the person I'm filming shows me something I wasn't expecting, and it all becomes clear.'

Now he wants Irène to tell him about the woman who owned the locket.

An image of Wita comes to her. She's naked, standing tall in the snow. That's how Wita made her first appearance in Irène's life, through Elsie's description. So that's where she starts. All the things she hid from Agata and her family and would hide from Karl Winter come pouring out for Rudi.

'She really did that? She died with the boy?'

Now he wants to know who Wita was before she made the ultimate sacrifice. Where she mustered the courage to survive two camps. And the courage to die.

Irène doesn't know much about Wita's early years in Lublin. She imagines her parents belonged to the educated middle class because they sent their daughters to the Catholic University. The elder one was more ambitious, more intellectual. Wita was beautiful and would have turned heads. People probably imagined she'd succumb to the fate of many pretty girls: beauty dulled by early motherhood and a boring, provincial life. She quit university for a love match, but she was content with her simple life and traditional role. She seemed to have been well and truly happy. Wita certainly didn't seem trapped in any of the prewar photos or in Agata's account. If war hadn't reduced her life to dust, she would surely have continued to savour every moment of her uncomplicated existence.

Then came the firestorms, bombs, and constant terror. Their horizons retracted with each passing day, becoming increasingly fragile and unsteady. A constant onslaught of violence drew their eyes in the street. Wita couldn't protect her children from it. She sent her daughter to stay with her sister. At the time, Warsaw seemed the safer option, though it was all relative, of course. Poland had been dissected by a butcher's saw and no part of it offered true sanctuary. The country seemed to belong to hunters and vultures.

Her son was still so young, so she kept him with her. If she'd let him go to Warsaw, maybe he wouldn't have been kidnapped. But there was no way to know. She thought they'd give him back if she asked nicely. Instead, the SS punished her insolence with a one-way ticket to Auschwitz. A few months later she was transferred to Ravensbrück. While there, Wita helped other women. She was still capable of tenderness, though her joy had dried up. In its place, a tough outer layer of courage and resilience formed. Cold rage and strength.

'This story is incredible,' Rudi says enthusiastically. 'I've always been obsessed with lives like this. Lives which look unremarkable, lives we brush against without noticing. But when we get closer, we realise we've got everything wrong. Our point of view just makes them *seem* simple.'

Irène notices there is no one left in the room apart from the waiters, who are giving them annoyed looks.

'Come on, let's get out of this dreary place,' he says, taking out his bank card. 'I'm starting to feel like we're trapped in *The Kingdom*. Did you ever watch that Lars von Trier TV series?'

She snorts, remembering the evenings spent watching it while waiting for Wilhelm to come home. She would jump at the slightest noise.

Outside, a chilly wind has blown away the rain clouds, but the car park is a swamp. Rudi explains that he came by tram and lives in the Kreuzberg neighbourhood. She offers him a lift. It's early and they don't want to say goodbye quite yet, so she accepts his invitation to have a drink in a bar near the Landwehr Canal.

He hasn't mentioned his father once the whole night.

She can tell he's wavering and full of questions.

When they say goodbye on the pavement, he admits, 'You know, I like this country, with all its faults and its scars.'

But he's afraid to find out it's betrayed him. He's afraid he might not be able to forgive it.

Matias

A FEW DAYS LATER, a mail clerk hands Irène a large envelope with an Israeli postmark. Inside she's intrigued to find old postcards written in Hebrew. She rifles through the papers and finds a letter in English.

Dear Ms Martin,

My name is Sarah Schwarz and I'm from Lohamei HaGeta'ot, a kibbutz in Galilee founded by fighters from the Warsaw Ghetto Uprising. A few weeks ago, a woman named Ruth Greenberg came to visit. She was just back from Poland, where she met you at the Treblinka memorial. She told me you were investigating a survivor named Lazar Engelmann, and it just so happens he was an old friend of my father, Hershl Morgenstern. They met at Treblinka and both participated in the revolt. As they were escaping, they decided it was safer to go their separate ways. They were reunited in Israel ten years later.

My father grew up in Poland, near Łódź. After his escape, he returned to Warsaw, where he was hidden by a group of partisans. He met my mother, and they married in secret. I was born in winter 1944. He was seriously wounded during the Warsaw Uprising.

Fortunately, a brave doctor treated him and hid him until the Russians arrived. We emigrated to Palestine after the war. Antek Zuckerman and other survivors had just founded the kibbutz. My father wanted to join him, so we did. He lived here until his death. I remember his friend Lazar staying with us for a few months. It must have been 1956 because he came to my twelfth birthday. He and my father saw a lot of each other, and other Treblinka survivors too. They had such a strong bond which we, their wives and children, couldn't share. Once we'd gone to bed, they'd stay up late into the night talking quietly. I was jealous of the men my father confided in. He was mostly silent around me.

Lazar left Israel in the late fifties and never returned. But he sent my father postcards. Then one night, the phone rang very late. My father told us that his friend Lazar had just called from New York, where he'd been reading about the Eichmann trial here in Israel. He felt guilty he wasn't here to testify. A few months later, my father wrote to Lazar, telling him a German prosecutor was looking for witnesses who'd testify against SS officers stationed at Treblinka. My father put him in touch with a prosecutor in Düsseldorf.

When Mrs Greenberg told me you were looking for Lazar Engelmann, I remembered I still had these post-cards. I didn't know if you read Hebrew, so I've translated them and numbered them in chronological order. The first was posted from Thessaloniki in 1958, the last from Mar del Plata in 1975. Unfortunately, you may not glean much from them. Lazar and my father weren't big talkers. The bond between them went much deeper than words.

There is one strange detail I noticed about these postcards though. From the end of the sixties onwards, Lazar signs off with a different name. I don't know why.

The postcards stopped in May 1975. Sometimes my father would talk about his friend, but in the past tense, as if he were dead.

I hope this information will be useful to you. If you ever come to Israel, I would be delighted to give you a tour of our museum, the Ghetto Fighters' House, and to tell you our story.

All best wishes,
Sarah Schwarz

Irène thinks back to Ruth Greenberg, her hair teased into a voluminous bun and the elegant way she turned up the collar of her coat. She kept her promise.

Irène examines the postmarks and finds the first postcard. *Thessaloniki, 17 June 1958.* The image is of a sailing boat, its boom visible in the foreground. Beyond it, there's ocean as far as the eye can see. The reflection of stately buildings with awninged balconies takes shape on the water's surface.

At the end of the sun-drenched quay, you can just make out the White Tower. Irène imagines Allegra and Lazar taking a sunset stroll. She locates the translation of the scant Hebrew lines. 'The wind here burns like the sun, brother. I've met a dark-haired girl who speaks to me in a forgotten language. At night, the waves of her hair rock me to sleep like the sea. Her heart is full of tears and secrets. If only I could repair people as well as I can boats.'

The next card was posted from Florida in winter 1959. Wooden sailing boats moored to the jetty of a placid marina. 'Your old friend Gustav says hello, Herschl. We drank a glass of bourbon to your health. During the day, Gustav gives tourists walking tours. At night, he berates the alligators in German. The world keeps turning, spinning so fast, my friend, but I'm not sure things are going the right direction. For us, the hands of time stopped long ago.'

Irène thinks back to the fake station in Treblinka, the clock meant to fool new arrivals.

In April 1960, Lazar sends Herschl a picture of the Brooklyn Bridge, with the message 'Samuel still remembers us, brother. Although he drinks a lot in the hope of forgetting. Esther has to help him into bed every night. I count the stars over the East River from my window. Given how bright they shine, who would ever guess they're already dead?'

There's a sombre sort of poetry to these little messages, scrawled on the backs of idyllic views. Lazar's wanderings trace an archipelago of insomniac survivors, united by the inescapable pull of a black hole called Treblinka.

From San Francisco he writes, 'A beggar woman asks me where I'm from. "Where I'm from no longer exists." She bursts out laughing, tells me the same is true of her. I take her for lobster in a restaurant on the port. Sometimes, my friend, life gives me a pat on the back, and I can't help but respond in kind.'

Between this postcard and the next there's a gap of several years, an ocean, and a trial. He's travelling across Europe now: from Hamburg to Vienna and Trieste. Did his wanderings have a goal, some guiding logic? On 7 April 1967, on the back of a photograph of the port in Genoa at dusk, he writes, 'When I wake in the morning, I think of the girl with the long dark hair. Her soft olive skin. The skin of a Greek girl, a Jewish girl. The morning light makes you believe in impossible things. It's at daybreak that men invent gods. And declare war. *Shalom*, Herschl, the boat is waiting for me.'

So he hadn't forgotten Allegra.

From the Genoa postcard onwards, Lazar signs off as Matias Bárta. The name on his false papers. His fugitive's alias. Is he trying to hide or disappear?

The gaps between his postcards keep getting longer. In 1970 he sends an image of Valparaíso Bay lit up at night, with the message 'Behind each speck of light lies an enduring hope. I count them at night to get to sleep. There's always a drunk bawling outside my window. I know his tune by heart: you are no longer alive, and you cannot die.'

In 1975 he posts a final message from Mar del Plata. 'Here the setting sun is the colour of blood. I've found Kelev. Drink to my health. L'chaim, brother. Do you think we'll ever find peace?'

Kelev.

Irène feverishly rereads the notes she took in Ludwigsburg.

Transport arrives. Lean and strong SS man, rosy complexion, eyebrows bleached by sun. Kelev. The Dog. Wanted to take girl's puppet. Shoots mother in head, orders Lazar to take child to Lazarett.

Not among accused at Düsseldorf trial. <u>Doesn't know his real name but has never forgotten his face</u>.

After the war, thousands of Nazi war criminals found refuge in the Americas and the Middle East. They fled via ratlines, escape corridors which ran through South Tyrol to other parts of Italy with help from representatives of the Vatican. The International Red Cross was too distracted to do much about them. The Cold War had upended the political chessboard, and many people were now willing to lend a helping hand to yesterday's enemies. They were the first to take up arms against communism, after all. The Swiss took this view and issued travel documents for Germans quite liberally. Certain prelates were also happy to forgive the excesses of Hitler's devotees, particularly if they returned to the Church's fold. And American intelligence wanted access to the information former Nazis who had spent time in Eastern Europe could provide. There were also plenty of dictators – in Libya, Paraguay, Brazil, and Argentina – eager to welcome Nazis with open arms. Realpolitik might have been hiding behind patriotic narratives, but it was clear to anyone who got close enough that judgment day was a long way off. Industrialists who had made a fortune from forced labour during the war were prospering in democratic nations. And the scientific community quietly congratulated itself on the discoveries made thanks to camp experiments. The Nazis' genocidal expertise was even rolled out for use in other conflicts. The Holocaust victims' ashes were swept under the carpet of new alliances and promising markets.

By 1975, Lazar couldn't have been under any illusions as to the efficiency of Allied justice. Is the red sky he evokes in his last postcard a vengeful one? Irène has a hard time picturing him as a vigilante. Who else could he have turned to?

She goes for a walk in the park and lights a cigarette, barely noticing the birdsong or the first smells of spring. With pinpoint focus, she goes back through Lazar's travels after Treblinka. The forest, the arrest, Buchenwald, the hospital, the displaced persons camp in Linz. Suddenly, her eyes light up.

She calls the Simon Wiesenthal Center in Los Angeles and asks if they have a file on Lazar Engelmann or Matias Bárta. If he met Wiesenthal in Linz, he may have remembered him thirty years later, when he tracked down the Dog of Treblinka.

*

A hesitant voice has left Irène a voicemail.

'Hello . . . Elvire Torres calling. I received your letter and I . . . I'd like to talk to you. Call me back when you can, preferably in the evening. Thank you.'

Irène returns her call just after dark. At first she can barely hear Elvire because of the thunder and heavy rain pounding her terrace outside. Spring storms have turned her garden into a paddy field. 'Six months of winter, and now this unrelenting rain,' Charlotte Rousseau groans every morning as she folds up her umbrella.

'I don't understand how that letter came to be in your possession,' Elvire says on the line.

'Your mother sent it to Yad Vashem, an Israeli archive. They passed it to us in the late seventies. If I hadn't been looking for Lazar Engelmann, it might never have been opened.'

'Would it be too nosy of me to ask why you're investigating him?'

'I'm responsible for returning objects we have here to their rightful owners. One of those objects belonged to your father.'

'Sorry,' Elvire says sharply. 'I'm struggling with that word. It's all been a bit of a shock, you know . . . the truth just turning up like that. My mother always refused to tell me who my father was. I suspected he may have been a camp survivor. On some level I always knew.'

Both women go silent for a moment.

'That letter you sent, it wasn't just about him,' Elvire continues. 'It was about her, about all the things she hid from me, you know?'

'Of course.'

Elvire pauses, then asks, 'Do you think we could meet? If I understand correctly, you live in Germany, right? I'm drowning in work at the moment, it wouldn't be easy for me to get away—'

'I can come to Paris,' Irène replies instantly.

*

That night, she's too excited to sleep. She gathers her notes on Lazar, copies of ITS documents, and the postcards, spreading them out on her desk like puzzle pieces. When what's in front of her isn't enough, she grows impatient. She heads downstairs, puts a log on the fire, and looks for the *Shoah* DVDs on her shelf.

To better understand Lazar, she has an urge to hear from people who suffered a similar fate. The Birkenau Sonderkommandos, who were forced to sleep above crematoriums. The Treblinka hairdresser. Szymon Srebrnik, the boy forced to sing for the Nazis at Chełmno. She needs to see their faces, their vulnerable expressions, and broken smiles. She needs to hear the words they manage to say though they know full well how much it will hurt. It feels like they're speaking from a place which isn't quite death but is no longer life. They are ghosts. The last remaining witnesses able to recount how a people were reduced to dust, living archives of their final breaths and acts of resistance at the brink of eternal night. Their words pull the victims back from beyond and invite them to face the world. Men who ran, sick with fear. Women who waited, clutching the warm bodies of their children to their chests. Women who laughed in the guards' faces. Prisoners who sang the Czech national anthem as they walked into the gas chambers. The naked woman who fought armed men to the death. Another who said, 'You can't kill yourself. If you do, no one will know how I died.'

Two Jews from Chełmno tell Claude Lanzmann that the SS officers made them call the bodies they burned *Figuren* or Schmattes: dolls and rags. Irène shudders at the terms.

She remembers Lazar's Auschwitz number on the stomach of the puppet in Buchenwald. It was more than a keepsake saved from oblivion; it was his own reflection. A schmatte caught between life and death.

Just as Irène is about to stop the film, her hand freezes on the remote. A Czech survivor is talking about the 'dead season' at Treblinka – that winter of 1943 when almost no new transports arrived. When there was nothing left to eat and typhus was spiriting them away, one by one. They were losing hope they'd be able to hold out for the revolt. One evening at the beginning of March, Lalka, the doll-faced monster, came to announce that the convoys were starting up again. The prisoners felt a terrible sense of relief that they wouldn't have to go hungry any more.

The next day, he explains, a train arrived from Salonica.

Irène sits up straighter.

Wealthy Jews from the Balkans and Macedonia who had travelled in compartments stocked with provisions, luxurious sheets, and Oriental rugs.

He recalls being handed cases of biscuits and jam. He and his companions dropped them on purpose, tripping over one another to fill their hands and stuff their mouths. Afterwards they were overcome by feelings of shame and powerlessness.

When he saw the people from that transport, he finally fully grasped his role. They were workers in a death factory, invested in its yield.

These new arrivals were nothing like the Jews from Eastern Europe. They were still strong, they radiated beauty and health. Out of two thousand four hundred people, he doesn't remember seeing a single one who was sick or disabled. They had no idea of the fate which awaited them. They were blissfully ignorant.

As for the workers, they knew that their bodies would be cold in less than two hours. *Figuren, Schmattes.*

Never had the cogs of the slaughter machine turned so efficiently, so quickly and perfectly.

He says that was the day they decided they would find the strength to revolt. They had to destroy the death machine, whatever the price.

Irène feels a mix of adrenaline and fatigue. Before she goes upstairs to pass out in bed, she writes *Salonica* in her notebook, then circles the word in red ink.

Elvire

An early-may heatwave has enveloped the city in a white haze. Irène has come directly from the airport and is sweating through her lucky blue dress. She can hear piano music through the stairwell windows as she climbs the steps. In the courtyard, a beam of sunshine is reviving an olive tree numbed by winter. She imagines how pleasant it must be to live in this little oasis in the heart of Paris.

Elvire Torres has taken the day off work. She must be nearly sixty, but her full face is relatively unmarked by age. Her glossy red hair is cut in a wavy layered bob, her thin lips accentuated by red lipstick. She exudes self-assurance, but she's nervous too. Her dark eyes are veiled with worry. Irène takes in the spacious room – the antique furniture and exposed beams, one crimson wall, another anise green. Her gaze is drawn to a grand piano and a grey cat sleeping on a cushion nearby.

'So that was you I just heard playing,' Irène says with a smile.

Elvire explains that she couldn't take lessons until her mother died. She'd dreamt of learning to play ever since she was a child, but any mention of the instrument made her family sad. In the end she realised the grandmother she'd never known, the grandmother she'd been named for, would be forever associated with the piano.

'This is her here, my maternal grandmother,' she says, handing Irène a sepia portrait of a little girl in a smart dress and tiny polished shoes. She's looking straight at the photographer with mischief in her eyes, a pale satin bow in her hair. 'She's only two here. She began playing piano a year later.'

'Did your mother talk about her?'

'Not much.'

Among the few keepsakes Uncle Rafo managed to save, there are photos of family celebrations in Thessaloniki, and Allegra's parents' wedding portrait. Elvire has always admired the handsome couple for their elegance. She remains fascinated by her grandmother, the way she's dressed in the latest Parisian fashions, with her pretty pearl tiara and her dreamer's smile. But she's never been able to fill in the blanks between the little girl with the bow, the child pianist, and the young bride. After this photo, there was nothing else. Just a void. She doesn't know much about the bridegroom with his slicked-back hair and a camellia in his lapel either. Just that he was called Albert. In addition to Ladino, he spoke Greek, Turkish, French, and Italian, which he used when travelling Europe for his fabric business. She would have loved to know more, but her mother couldn't talk about her parents without shutting down.

'So I stopped asking questions. It was strange when I was little. I didn't even know I was Jewish. My *yiayia*, my only living grandmother, was Greek Orthodox. We saw her once or twice a year, when she came to Paris.'

'Anastasia!' Irène exclaims, moved to learn that the bond between this woman and the child she saved has been passed down to the next generation.

'That's right. I adored her, and she spoiled me silly. I called all Uncle Rafo's friends *tio* and *tia*, and I thought Yiayia was my real grandmother. But I knew that Uncle Rafo was Jewish, as were most of his friends. They weren't all observant, but they celebrated Passover and Yom Kippur. We lit candles for Chanukah, but we also had a Christmas tree. My school friends were Catholic, and sometimes my mother took me to services at the Orthodox Church. It was all pretty confusing for me at times.'

'I can imagine,' Irène says empathetically.

'My mother refused to let me receive my first Holy Communion with all my friends. I thought it was very unfair, because I wanted the pretty dress and the cake with the little figurine on top. When Yiayia died and my mother took me to Thessaloniki, I finally started to understand.'

Elvire doesn't have fond memories of the city. She felt harassed by the bustle, whipped by the wind and sun, and suffocated by the relentless heat. She kept complaining she was thirsty, tired, and seasick.

Elvire interrupts her story for a moment to think about the dual connotations in French. *Mal de mer, mal de mère.* Seasickness, mother sickness. Because her mother was different in Thessaloniki. Nervous and on edge, as though she weren't quite there with her daughter. Now that Elvire's read the letter, she understands. The people she had left behind treated her like a stranger. She can see how painful that must have been. The day before they left, Allegra dragged a sleepy, grumpy Elvire up steep streets to the ramparts which overlooked the bay. She pointed out the roofs of villas she'd visited as a child and gardens where she'd played hide-and-seek with her cousins. 'We felt at home here,' she said. 'We were happy here.'

That day she told Elvire about the German soldiers who had forced Jews from their homes and sent them to die in camps in Poland. With a strange blend of sadness and frankness, she revealed that Yiayia wasn't her real grandmother. At twelve, Elvire realised her life would never be the same again. The reassuring world she'd grown up in was collapsing around her.

When they returned to Paris, Allegra didn't want to talk about the war any more. She turned back into the vibrant woman she had been, a woman who hid her deep scars from everyone. A woman who had suffered so much from the silence but had never managed to escape it.

'This letter,' Elvire says softly. 'Seeing her vulnerable and in love . . .' She admits that reading it reconciled her with her mother and gave her a sense of peace.

'I didn't understand why she continued to protect him from his own daughter! A man who'd abandoned her when she was pregnant with his child . . . Now it's clear he never knew. It's silly, but knowing that helps.'

As the conversation turns to Lazar, Irène remembers her bag, and the puppet inside.

'Do you think he loved her?' Elvire asks.

'I know he did. But he had lost his entire family. Getting close to someone would have meant reliving that and risking even more loss. I still believe he really loved your mother though.'

Irène tells her about the postcards, the mentions of his love for her up until the end.

'There *was* something irresistible about my mother,' Elvire says.

She retrieves some photos and hands them to Irène. In the first, a young brunette is standing on the banks of the Seine, roaring with laughter. Her long wavy hair seems to dance in the wind. There is wild joy and a kind of contentment in her eyes. In the second picture, Allegra is in her fifties. Her hair is short and tousled and she's wearing a sailor's jumper and a red clown nose. She's sticking out her tongue and crouching, arms wide open, next to a small giggling boy.

'We were celebrating my son's third birthday,' Elvire explains.

'They look like proper little partners in crime.'

'They were. My mother spoilt Raphaël so badly.'

'Did you name him after your great-uncle?'

Elvire nods. 'I may have been trying to make up for marrying a goy,' she jokes. 'My mother didn't hold it against me, but I got the sense she wasn't thrilled either.'

Allegra never told her daughter what being Jewish meant to her. Did she feel a sacred loyalty towards her people, a spiritual and emotional bond? As a girl, Elvire would have liked to have had help pinning down the meaning of a word which seemed vague and troubling to her. No one in her circle pushed her to identify as Jewish, but whenever she took a step away from Judaism, she could tell it hurt them.

'Tell me about him,' Elvire says, carefully avoiding the words *my father*. She still can't manage it.

Irène tells the story of the student who became a carpenter, but feels that though she's walked in Lazar's footsteps, she's never managed to get a full sense of who he really is. She's been afraid for him and empathised with him. She's been on quite a long journey to find out what happened to him, but she's still waiting for a few replies. She never imagined she'd find herself here, handing a stranger a puppet without a proper explanation.

'Did he and his family live in Prague?' Elvire asks.

'They did,' Irène replies, showing her a copy of the questionnaire he filled out after the war.

'He mentions his parents and an uncle. They were sent to live in the Theresienstadt Ghetto together. A month later, he was deported to Treblinka. Here, you see, he states that they were all dead. They may all have been on the same train. When he arrived at Treblinka, he was assigned to a Sonderkommando.'

A wave of concern unfurls on Elvire's face. She's heard about these prisoners who were forced to burn the bodies.

Irène reassures her that unlike many Sonderkommando prisoners, Lazar's job was to sort the possessions of the deceased.

The explanation doesn't seem to put Elvire's mind at ease.

'The only choice they had was this reprieve or death. The SS would have executed them in any case when the camp closed. No one would have survived Treblinka if it wasn't for men like Lazar, who found the strength to mount an insurrection. Some managed to escape, then evade all the dangers awaiting them in Poland. These men did everything they possibly could to resist their own annihilation. In a sense, they became custodians of the memory of these people they'd watched walk to their deaths. They carried this impossible burden for the rest of their lives.'

'Well, at least he didn't work in the gas chambers … that's something,' Elvire says quietly, after a pause.

'It's impossible to imagine what they went through,' Irène says softly. 'Burying their people, their wives and children. They were made to sift through the ashes and mix them with the soil. Nothing could remain of the victims. They worked under the surveillance of SS officers who would kill them if they made the slightest mistake. Despite all that, they managed to bury some bodies intact, along with messages to tell the world the truth.'

Elvire says she's never heard this before. She's always been too afraid to read survivors' accounts, afraid she might never get over their reality.

'I understand,' Irène says. 'But you'd be surprised by how much humanity and beauty their stories hold.'

She tells Elvire about the dead season in the camp, and the arrival of the transport from Thessaloniki.

'Do you think it was guilt that drove him to Thessaloniki?' Elvire asks.

'Maybe,' Irène muses.

Elvire is lost in her thoughts. She stares at the photos of Lazar: one from Buchenwald, the other taken after the war.

'My son looks like him,' she says, with tears in her eyes.

*

Later they drink lemonade and talk about inconsequential, everyday things. They realise they have a lot in common. They're both divorced with grown-up children, and love lives they prefer to joke about. Elvire has an important job and earns a good living. Since her divorce, she can't help but feel her independence scares men off.

It's left her shaken to finally see the face of the man she's imagined since she was a child. When she was at school, she would dream of him coming to pick her up in a convertible. She imagined him as an adventurer, wearing an Italian shirt and sunglasses – a cross between Al Pacino and Robert De Niro. She'd come up with extravagant alibis so his absence wouldn't amount to abandonment. He was in prison, stranded in a faraway land, an accident had left him with amnesia. She went through her mother's drawers and scrutinised her male relatives' faces. But Allegra kept her secrets close to her chest. One day, when Elvire was particularly persistent, Allegra let slip, 'The war destroyed him too.'

'He's dead, isn't he?' Elvire asks, hoping she's wrong.

'I think he died in the seventies, although I've no proof,' Irène replies.

Elvire's face crumples. 'If he had received my mother's letter when she sent it, maybe ... But there's no point trying to rewrite history. You mentioned an object in your letter,' she says, returning to the present.

Irène opens her bag and delicately removes the puppet with the faded ruff. It's so old and worn it's hard to imagine it was ever new. She places it in Elvire's hands.

Elvire remains silent as she takes in the toy.

'Look under the clothes,' Irène suggests.

Elvire's heart skips a beat when she sees the digits. She runs her fingertips over them.

She wants to know what they mean.

It's finally time to release the ghost imprisoned in the faded cotton fabric.

As Irène guides Elvire back to Treblinka and up the ramp, the air around them seems to thicken. Elvire's hands tense round the puppet's body as she listens. The story of the child who died in Lazar's arms is unbearable. Irène can't soften its blow or give it a happy ending. The father he might have been died with Hanka that day. She doesn't need to say it for Elvire to understand.

This little girl is what always stood between Lazar and Elvire.

Now there are only tears.

Max

When Irène opens the door, Antoine hands her a glass of Bourgogne. He's looking trim and in high spirits, and the flat is unusually spotless.

'I decided it was high time you met Pierre!' he exclaims.

A handsome, dark-haired man in a linen shirt, black apron, and pleated trousers leans in to kiss her cheeks with a broad smile on his face. She is tickled to learn that Antoine, who usually lives off tinned vegetables and fried eggs, has fallen for a man who cooks and dresses up for guests. She expects she'll get on quite well with the pleasantly plump professor. He spends most of his time poring over Vichy archives, but he looks more like the sort of person you'd find behind the wheel of a minivan full of kids.

He tells Irène how chilling the Vichy documents are. A note scribbled on the bottom of a form can speak volumes about a bureaucrat's opportunism and complete lack of empathy for the people his signature condemned to deportation, begging in the streets, or exile. The dry indifference of these forms cuts like a knife. It contradicts all the postwar justifications. There is no evidence of any inclination to save people. Just murderous disregard.

'The archives don't lie,' Pierre says with a smile. 'That's why so many people want to keep them under lock and key.'

'Irène knows quite a bit about that,' Antoine says. 'Tell Pierre what a struggle it was to take the ITS archives public. He'll love it.'

She recounts the years she spent working for Max Odermatt, the toxic environment where all initiative was discouraged and even seen as suspect. While Eva was still alive, Irène could handle the situation. Her friend knew how to bend the rules. But when Eva died, it all became too much. She was exhausted from constantly having to swim against the current, battling bureaucratic delays and the director's whims. She tells Pierre how he boasted about not hiring anyone who was actually qualified and banned employees from discussing ongoing investigations – even amongst themselves.

'That amounts to sabotaging your work,' Pierre replies, shocked.

'Divide and conquer,' Irène says. 'He thought of the ITS as his kingdom.'

'But someone should have been holding him accountable,' Antoine interjects. 'He worked for the International Committee of the Red Cross! And above them, there was an international commission.'

'He also refused to give documents to prosecutors building cases against Nazi war criminals,' she continues for Pierre. 'In the name of "Red Cross neutrality"!'

'Ha! Their "neutrality" was notoriously one-sided during the war!' Antoine adds.

The Swiss were so obliging towards Nazi dignitaries that they refused to protest when the Germans started rounding up Jews. Then, when they sent observers to the camps, they found the conditions perfectly acceptable. In Antoine's view, this diplomatic blindness was motivated by antisemitism. The foundations of neutrality were built on compromises. After liberation, the International Red Cross went to a lot of effort to make people forget that. Administering the ITS was part of their rehabilitation plan. They had worked hard to secure a lasting peace and ratify new Geneva conventions. But humanitarianism and political agendas weren't mutually exclusive. By the time the Cold War came around, the ICRC had very clearly chosen a side.

Irène gets up to have a cigarette at the window. 'In the eighties,' she says, 'we started to talk about extending reparations to forced labourers.'

'The financial stakes must have been very high for Germany,' Pierre chips in, enjoying the discussion. 'What if Odermatt was slowing down investigations to delay payouts? Running out the clock so there would be fewer survivors to pay?'

'That was Eva's theory,' Irène replies. 'When he took over, our response time went from a few months to several years. Then, when the wall fell, we were inundated with correspondence from the former Soviet bloc. There was a backlog of nearly four hundred thousand letters.'

'That's when Paul Shapiro came into the picture. He was director of the Holocaust Memorial Museum in Washington, DC, and had spent ten years trying to convince the International Commission to open the ITS archives to survivors and researchers. He came from a family which had been all but wiped out by the Holocaust, but his "unseemly" request still raised eyebrows. Back then, eleven countries were responsible for the fate of the archives, but the majority were entirely uninterested. Others, like France and Germany, were determined to keep their secrets locked away in filing cabinets. They opposed opening up the archives and used personal data protection as an excuse to keep them classified.'

'But at the Centre, none of us knew any of this until Shapiro was granted authorisation to visit the ITS with members of the International Commission. We were told not to answer his questions! It was all very awkward. It felt like a state visit to the USSR! Shapiro wanted a list of our different collections, and Odermatt pretended we didn't have one. Tired of the endless quarrelling, Shapiro mobilised Holocaust survivor associations and the media and declared that banning access to these documents was tantamount to Holocaust denial. I was so shocked I fell ill.'

'I remember that,' says Antoine. 'You had a thirty-nine-degree fever and couldn't get out of bed.'

'I'd been at the ITS for more than ten years, and Eva had just died. That article ripped the blinkers from my eyes and got me to realise that the Centre was withholding crucial information from survivors. Many of them died waiting for answers. I'll never forget that.'

'In the end, Paul Shapiro won. Merkel's election was a turning point. Her new justice minister cleared the final legal hurdles, and the International Committee of the Red Cross accepted defeat.'

'What a story!' Pierre exclaims. 'At least it ends well, which is certainly not always the case.'

'Too true,' Irène agrees. 'Today our doors are open to researchers and descendants alike. Teachers bring their classes. When I bump into them, I think of the survivors who worked at the Centre after the war and how happy it would make them to see the place now.'

Despite the way it was instrumentalised during the Cold War, the Centre had always been a haven for diligent researchers dedicated to finding the truth for the Nazis' victims. *They are the true face of the ITS*, Irène thinks as she contemplates the brightly lit dome. *We are.*

Pierre expresses his amazement that, in a world governed by profit, an international archive centre is taking so much trouble to return objects with no market value. 'It's such a wonderful project,' he says admiringly.

'When the director asked me to lead it, I was apprehensive because it involved meeting with relatives. As it turns out, the meetings are a far cry from what I imagined. They're more complex and unpredictable. More intense.'

Irène's thoughts return to Lucia's lovely face. To the emotion Agata and Elvire felt when she told them their families' stories. To Rudi Winter's distress when they parted on that Berlin street.

'Now, even though I'm still not sure how these objects will impact them, I'm glad I accepted. Antoine says they're haunted, and he's right.'

Rudi

'SO HOW WAS GABROVO?' Irène asks Henning as she opens her office blinds.

'Wet. But pretty.'

He tells her about Orthodox monasteries nestled into mountainsides, Bulgarian sopranos with long plaited hair and floral crowns, and narrow, winding streets lined with wooden houses.

'Now imagine all that soaked by cold, unrelenting rain. My subject's daughter was so moved she wept. Luckily, I'd brought tissues.'

Irène's surprised to see Henning looking younger under his thatch of red hair. He even looks a little tanned, though he claims he only burns.

'In any case, the trip did you good. You look great,' she says. When she studies his face more intently, she notices his wrinkles have disappeared. 'Have the twins finally started sleeping through the night?' she asks incredulously.

He nods, his lips upturned in a smile that betrays both triumph and caution. After a long battle, his parents agreed to look after them. On the first night, they almost handed them over to social services. But the next day, his mother rigged up Irène's MP3 conch and played them Grimm's fairy tales. An hour later they were fast asleep. The miracle was repeated on the next nights. The womb sounds made them anxious, but apparently decapitated ogres and plump children in cages really did the trick.

'Did you find your Czech survivor?' he asks Irène.

'The guy from the Wiesenthal Center called me back yesterday.'

In spring 1975, Lazar had, as Irène suspected, contacted Wiesenthal to confide he had recognised one of the Treblinka killers in a bar in Mar del Plata. He managed a canning factory near the port and went by the name Guillermo Cabral. He spoke with a strong German accent, and his appearance was so distinctive he was impossible to mistake: his skin and eyebrows looked as though they'd been bleached by the sun. Wiesenthal thought it could be Lothar Kunz, a Bavarian SS officer who went on the run after the war. Before he was sent to Treblinka, he'd cut his teeth in Hadamar, developing the process for exterminating people with disabilities and mental illnesses. When the killing centre closed, he followed his bosses to Trieste. Later he was captured by the Americans, but he managed to escape from the prison camp.

Wiesenthal advised Lazar to proceed with caution. Perón's death had plunged Argentina into a storm of escalating violence. The instability favoured the military, who were known to have close links to the Nazis. Argentina used asylum rights as a pretext to protect war criminals and refuse their extradition. Lazar would have to be patient and build an iron-clad case.

A few weeks later, Lazar sent him photos he'd taken of Cabral with a long lens camera. Wiesenthal compared them to the picture on Lothar Kunz's SS identity card. The resemblance was striking. Lazar missed their next scheduled call.

In early May, the Nazi hunter had stumbled upon an article in the Argentinian daily *La Capital*. Guillermo Cabral had been found dead in the basement of his villa along with a Czech carpenter called Matias Bárta. A bullet from a Luger had gone through Bárta's shoulder, and another had grazed his cheek. The gun was found several yards away. Both bodies showed signs of a struggle involving a knife. Cabral's throat had been slit, and Bárta had bled out after being stabbed several times in the abdomen. The villa was set back from the road in a quiet part of town, and the neighbours swore they hadn't heard a thing.

So Lazar bowed out on a mysterious note. Irène will never know if he took justice into his own hands, or if the SS man realised he was being followed and caught Lazar by surprise. Or maybe he even recognised the former Treblinka prisoner despite the trappings of a free man.

Irène sent the postcards to Elvire, with copies of Sarah Schwarz's letter, and the article. 'Your father's courage and strength were exceptional,' she wrote.

'And what about your stolen child?' Henning asks.

'His son is still saying no to a DNA test. I'm going back to Berlin and taking him to Ravensbrück tomorrow.'

*

As Irène and Rudi make their way towards Brandenburg, she wonders how likely it is she'll convince him to change his mind. She feels she has a reasonable chance. After all, he was the one who called to suggest they visit the camp. She hopes the sheer power of the place will sweep away his reluctance.

They savour their coffee and watch the lush countryside flash past. The train is filled with Berliners in shorts, with rucksacks and bikes, taking a long weekend for Ascension. Rudi is wearing a black polo and cotton trousers. He's finished shooting his documentary and is in a chatty mood. A few days ago, the producer organised a press screening at an independent cinema in Kreuzberg, he explains. Afterwards, a war correspondent whose work he admires interviewed him. She's covered Kosovo, Lebanon, and Iraq for *Der Spiegel*. She told him she'd like to work together on a major project focussing on migrants, he tells Irène excitedly. They'd be building an 'archive of exile' by interviewing asylum seekers, taking inspiration from what the Spielberg foundation did for Holocaust survivors. 'It would send a powerful message,' he says. 'It's a way of writing them into our history.'

As Irène listens to Rudi talk about this woman, she feels a pang of jealousy that catches her off guard.

A couple gets off at Oranienburg station, dragging their sullen teenager in headphones behind them.

'I bet they're off to visit Sachsenhausen,' Rudi says as he watches them disappear down the platform. 'When I was a kid, my father took me. It made a big impact.'

Irène took Hanno there when he was in secondary school.

'How old is he now?' Rudi asks. 'With you as a mum, I imagine he's ticked off *all* the camps, poor thing.'

She admits she hasn't skimped on pilgrimages to memorial sites, then feels obliged to explain the sort of family he grew up in and the existential questions about obedience and free will it kindled in him. Her son is convinced that everyone has the potential to become a murderer, given the right circumstances. So she seeks out examples of people who refused. She wants to show him it isn't inevitable.

'I'm not judging you,' he says with a smile. 'My dad was obsessed with the war.'

Rudi leans in and confides that his father cut all contact with his adoptive parents when he accidentally found their Nazi Party membership cards, before Rudi was born. For ten years, Karl didn't want to hear any mention of them. Then one day, young Rudi noticed an old woman in a grey coat and fur hat waving at him from behind the school gates. She was smiling but her eyes were rimmed with tears. His grandmother had come from Munich to meet him.

In the end, Karl relented. But their sporadic interactions were stormy and unpredictable. Rudi doesn't remember the family reunions fondly. Nothing seemed to quench his father's rage.

'It must have been even harder for him than anyone else,' Rudi says softly. 'The only thing that soothed his temper was filming, focusing on a shoot.'

Irène listens, convinced this unquenchable anger is a sign of repressed childhood trauma, but she keeps the thought to herself.

*

The small town of Fürstenberg is huddled on the banks of the Schwedtsee, which a branch of the Havel River links to two other lakes. Before the war, this part of Brandenburg was a favourite holiday spot. Berliners would come to recharge their batteries in its crisp blue waters and dense woods. Irène explains to Rudi that Himmler chose the site for its beauty, ease of access by train or boat, and because his mistress lived nearby.

As they get closer to the camp, she recognises the chalets where the female SS guards lived, with their wooden balconies and dark shutters. She freezes when she notices two young blonde women leaning on a balcony balustrade as they chat, enjoying the warmth of the sun on their pale skin. For a few seconds, the past blends with the present and Irène imagines she sees Elsie and her colleagues.

Now it's a youth hostel.

On their way to the memorial, she and Rudi walk past the prim wooden houses where the SS officers lived on a wooded hill. When they reach the esplanade by the lake, an imposing bronze statue is perched on a promontory.

'She's called the *Tragende*, "the Burdened Woman",' Irène says. In 1945 the Soviets liberated the camp and raped the women, including those too weak to be moved, whom they had come to save. They destroyed the barracks and set up their own garrison. 'In the late fifties, they unveiled this statue. Ironic, don't you think? To brutalise so many women, then choose this image as the symbol of Ravensbrück?'

Moved by the moment, Rudi studies the statue: a prisoner holding an unconscious companion in her arms. Her sad face looks towards the town nestled on the other bank, where the tip of the church steeple seems to pierce the azure sky. Her left foot is suspended in midair, poised to cross the lake. She holds out her weary charge in the direction of Fürstenberg, as if to make its residents face their own indifference. *Look, look what they're doing to us here.*

They say that the *Tragende* was inspired by Olga Benário, a German communist activist. Before she was transferred to Ravensbrück, she gave birth to a little girl in a Gestapo prison. She was murdered in a gas chamber when she was thirty-four. Her crime was being Jewish. But the cause of her death was of no interest to the Soviets, who chose her as their anti-fascist muse. The only women who mattered to them were the valiant comrades sacrificed for the cause.

Only after German reunification did a new narrative emerge. One that recognised other female victims: prostitutes snatched from the streets, Jehovah's Witnesses who refused to take part in the war effort, Roma girls sterilised against their will, Jewish women who survived death marches, women who were caught shoplifting, female English spies, women who no longer believed the Reich could win, women who loved other women, women who hid outcasts – any woman who'd crossed the Nazis or dared to disobey. All of them were sent here to endure every conceivable suffering that can be inflicted on a woman's body and a mother's heart.

'And now we're taking down plaques to true German Resistance fighters under the pretext that they were communists,' Rudi says, looking disillusioned. 'People try so hard to make history black-and-white.'

From where they're standing, the lake looks murky, almost frightening. Beneath the blue-green surface, the dark, slippery depths are carpeted with ash. All of the light seems to be focused on the other bank. There's a clear demarcation between the far side, where pleasure boats glide peacefully across the surface, and the side which housed the camp. Standing on this bank, the beauty of the landscape is biting. It takes your breath away and shreds all hope. It whispers in your ear that no one is coming to save you.

Rudi and Irène turn away from the statue and enter the belly of the camp. The place where Elsie, Wita, and Léon's fates became entwined. There's not a single building, just black gravel which clings to their soles like volcanic rock. Whoever designed the site clearly didn't think about the elderly survivors who come to pay their respects. Signs erected here and there mark the location of the old barracks. Irène finds block 32, where Wita tended to Sabina when she was delirious with fever. Two rows of linden trees mark the main camp thoroughfare where the *Kaninchen* marched on their crutches to protest the operations that had crippled them. On the horizon, Irène and Rudi can just make out the buildings which housed the sewing workshop, where the Rabbits stole scraps of fabric for Wita's embroidered handkerchief.

Irène evokes for Rudi the exhausting roll calls the prisoners endured, their survival strategies, solidarity, and acts of resistance. At times, she senses that he wishes he had his camera. That he wants to film what he's seeing and make the place speak the only way he knows how. He wants to find the tent where Elsie and Wita crossed paths for the first time. They walk towards a remote part of the camp where a sign pays tribute to the thousands of women and children who no longer have names or faces. No one is even certain whether they died here or elsewhere. On the side of a road while being transferred to another camp, or in a gas chamber at Ravensbrück. So many things remain unknown, so much evidence was lost or destroyed.

Inside the former Kommandantur they find a room dedicated to the stories of Revier patients. In one photo, a *Kaninchen* displays her ravaged leg. The photo must have been taken in secret. As proof of the crime, in case the Rabbits didn't make it. One display contains a card written to a girl who had just undergone the operation. It's a drawing of a rabbit with a bandaged paw surrounded by a wreath of flowers. She's lapping peacefully from her bowl, though there's barbed wire in the background. On the back of the card, the girl's friends have signed their names. Irène is moved when she makes out Wita's signature next to Sabina's. She senses it suddenly dawning on Rudi that this woman really existed. This woman who could be his grandmother has written her name with a steady hand.

'Did she die here?' he asks as they leave the crematorium.

The warmth in the air surprises them. A balmy breeze is coming off the lake.

Irène nods and explains that the gas chamber was next to the crematorium.

'And the awful camp you mentioned where they made them wait naked in the snow, where's that?'

'It's not part of the memorial museum. It's about two kilometres away.' She points to the woods to the south.

'Come on, let's go,' he replies.

*

They climb over a padlocked gate which leads to an overgrown path. As they move away from the fence, it narrows and begins to wind through the trees. Now out of view of the memorial, Irène and Rudi make their way to the abandoned buildings where Siemens set up workshops and dormitories for the workers that the SS rented to them for next to nothing. The women slaved for twelve hours a day and, if they didn't hit their targets, the foreman would smash their faces into the machines. When they were too exhausted to work, Siemens could just send them to the scrapheap and order more.

'Forced labour is a capitalist's dream,' says Rudi, staring at the tangled branches above the crumbling walls. I imagine these people got off scot-free after the war?'

'Entirely unscathed and without even a pang of guilt.'

She jumps when she sees something move in the darkness behind a broken window. It must be an animal. But she's glad she's not alone in this grim place.

Brambles are growing between the old railway tracks. Irène and Rudi walk deeper into the dense, dark forest, like something out of a fairy tale. The tops of the old beech and oak trees are bathed in sunlight, their branches filled with birds. The path is barely visible amid the under-brush. The grass reaches their knees, and they have to bend over in places to avoid branches. After a long while, Irène begins to suspect they're lost, but Rudi looks as though he knows where they're going.

'It can't be much further now,' he suddenly turns and says with a smile, as if he's just read her mind. 'Are you thirsty?'

He hands her his flask, and she takes a long gulp of water with a strong metallic aftertaste.

Ravensbrück feels like it's miles away now. She imagines the women who reached this point thought maybe they'd actually escaped it as they dreamed of Mittwerda. A safe haven where they could finally rest, free of roll calls and forced labour. But very soon the illusion would be shattered, exposing the macabre farce. A child out in the snow. The cold wind whipping at naked bodies. Where could they run or hide? The frozen forest offered no refuge.

Irène and Rudi find themselves on a cracked road, between stretches of bare heath on one side and pine thickets on the other. A rudimentary sign, in bright blue paint, marks the entrance to the camp. They've made it. The foundations of the old barracks peek through the sandy earth.

Between high grasses and poppies, a red sign marks the former *Lagerstrasse*. A bouquet of wilted flowers clings to a stone memorial. On a white cloth banner pinned to the trees, a German mother has written: *Nature is erasing what remains of them. All I've found is the dock on the Havel where Siemens loaded up its boats. And a few stones from the block where my daughter was murdered.*

Maybe nature is covering up all traces in order to protect these murdered women, thinks Irène. The sturdier trees bend to prop up the warped ones. Memories are etched into their bark, bleeding down to the roots.

Someone has placed the signs and excavated the site with the meticulous hand of an archaeologist. She wonders who is so discreetly tending to this open-air sanctuary.

Irène and Rudi stand motionless in the open space levelled by the wind. Neither feels the need to speak, though she's acutely aware of his presence and of the moment they're sharing.

The sun shifts, revealing figures on the edge of the woods. Irène shivers as she makes out sculptures of women crafted from metal fencing. They merge with the foliage, so poignant in their powerless grace. Ghosts of deported women.

Rudi clasps her arm and points to a warning nailed on a tree trunk. *Enter at your own risk.*

'What does that mean?' Irène wonders aloud.

'That the site isn't secured,' a female voice behind them responds.

They jump and spin round to see a young woman with short blue hair in denim shorts and a baggy T-shirt. Her bike is propped against the trunk of a pine tree. Hammer in hand, she sizes them up with her kohl-lined green eyes.

'It's all right, you two don't look much like the neo-Nazis who vandalise the memorial,' she jokes.

They apologise and introduce themselves. The woman with the elfin face is called Ursula. Her grandmother was interned here at the age of fifteen for being "antisocial". She didn't meet the Third Reich's criteria for femininity. After the war, she didn't receive any compensation. Just like the Roma, Sinti, and prisoners the SS labelled "homosexual", as well as deserters and prostitutes. She wasn't the right sort of victim. When the Russians left in the nineties, they burnt everything to the ground, Ursula explains. No one cared about this camp.

So an association of anti-fascist feminists decided to preserve the memory of these women – women they saw themselves in. They destroyed the old Soviet barracks and exposed the foundations of the original prisoner blocks. They cleared the site of the *Lagerstrasse* and erected a stone monument, where they take turns laying flowers. Every year, they invite survivors to visit. In the summer, they hold an annual convention to discuss their plans for the place. 'We absolutely don't want to make it a museum,' Ursula says. 'We want a living memorial.'

'What do you mean by that?' Irène asks.

'We don't want a museum where people come to cry, then leave thinking their conscience is clear,' Ursula says. 'We want to make people think about the ways history's repeating itself, about new forms of fascism. As we speak, people are burning migrant welcome centres and Roma camps. We exclude transgender people, queer people, Jews, anyone who's different. It's time we opened our eyes.'

They'd like to put on an exhibition, but they don't have enough money to secure the site. The federal and regional governments couldn't care less about this camp for "difficult", "crazy", or "useless" women. With a sparkle of pride in her eyes, Ursula explains that it's their responsibility to watch over the women who were held here.

'We're feminists and anti-fascists, the two go hand in hand.'

Then she nods goodbye and gets back on her bike. Irène and Rudi watch her disappear between the trees.

Irène imagines she'd get on well with Julka.

'If we don't hurry, we'll miss the last train,' Rudi murmurs in her ear.

He takes her hand, sending an electrical current through her body. She feels the heat spread through her arm as he guides her to the paved path, then on to the forest.

When he lets go, she misses the feel of his fingers in hers.

She walks quickly, dry vegetation whipping at her legs. She glimpses paths under the foliage and wonders if they ever served as escape routes. She wonders if little Léon saw them from the lorry on that dark winter night. This is the way he and Wita came on their final journey.

Once they make it out of the woods, Irène and Rudi walk along the old railway line. In the fading light, the ruins of the workshops look even more macabre. Irène can feel a sticky sort of sadness clinging to her throat. She wants to run away, to rip herself from this place and its shadows.

Rudi waits for her and registers her broken expression when she catches up.

'This place,' he says, 'it's so powerful . . .'

'I've never seen anything like it.'

'I'd like to make a film about what those women are trying to do here.'

*

On the train back to Berlin, Rudi announces he'll take the DNA test. He wants to know the truth.

'I always thought my father was unfair to my grandparents. I used to hate the way he raged at them. I never imagined he could have been a victim without even knowing it. But maybe he did know, deep down. Maybe a broken childhood leaves an indelible mark on a body. When he wasn't in the throes of anger, he was the ultimate idealist. Always defending pariahs and underdogs.'

'And now you make films about migrants,' Irène observes, coaxing a smile from him.

'Now you've got what you want, are you going to disappear back to the far reaches of Hesse?' he asks.

'Wouldn't you like me to?' she replies, holding his gaze.

'No,' he whispers.

He doesn't elaborate on what changed between them today, what she opened up in him.

But this *no*, though almost inaudible over the noise of the carriage, is enough to disarm her.

Elvire

THE LETTER ARRIVES one July morning, when the team have grains of sand in their sandals, beach towels sticking out of their bags, restless legs, and reflections of the lake in their eyes. Their holidays start tomorrow, and they're distracted. They've already partially checked out of work mode at their last meeting.

Now that he's sleeping again, Henning looks ten years younger, and the team are all impressed by how efficient he's become. With a sort of measured joy, he announces that his wife is pregnant again.

Before they break up for the summer, the director comes to congratulate them. They've returned an impressive number of objects, thanks in part to invaluable help from volunteers. She's even planning to set up a travelling exhibition, to raise awareness of the *Stolen Memory* project. The first step would be a tour of major European cities. After that, why not the world? Irène's team politely clear their throats. *Hmm, what an excellent idea. Why don't we let the idea stew and discuss it more when we're back?* Then everyone finds an excuse to slip away: a dental emergency or a case that has to be closed today. Even Henning sneaks off, leaving Irène to the loneliness that comes with power.

'You found that little boy who was kidnapped by the Nazis,' Charlotte Rousseau says. 'I honestly didn't think you could do it. Your stubbornness really paid off.'

The DNA results confirmed Karl was indeed Agata's brother. Rudi has asked Irène to set up a meeting in Berlin.

'Reuniting families is the best part of our job,' Rousseau adds.

'True,' Irène says. 'I hope their reunion will go well. They've waited so long . . .'

She's worried about Karl, especially since Rudi introduced them a few weeks ago. They took him for a walk in the clinic gardens, where she watched his blue eyes alight on cherry tree flowers, processionary caterpillars, and a goldfinch chirruping on a high branch. She could really see the filmmaker in his studied gaze. This man whose childhood had been ripped from him found peace in paying careful attention to the world and its tiniest creatures. She knew right away that she'd like him, and now she feels protective of him. Up until then, she'd thought only of Agata and dreamt of rewarding her for holding out hope. But now she realises just how fragile Karl is. He's so disoriented by his fading memory. How will he respond to a stranger he was separated from as a toddler?

Charlotte Rousseau says Irène is looking very well, even though she hasn't had much time to rest of late. 'Is it the glow of summer?' she asks.

'I'm looking forward to the holidays,' Irène replies a little too quickly.

She fears being unmasked, as if she's breaking a professional code of conduct. It's been two months since Rudi Winter entered her life. They split their time between Arolsen and Berlin, but she doesn't feel comfortable with him here in town yet. She clings to the walls, hoping they won't bump into anyone she knows at the bakery.

'I understand, I'm counting the days until I'm back home on the Montagne Noire. I'll look forward to hearing all about Berlin though. Actually, the network is spotty in my backward little town. My daughters are already dreading it. I'll see if I can find a spot with a strong signal nearby. Or maybe I'll just call when I go to the market.'

A letter is waiting on Irène's desk, in the middle of the mess she needs to clear up. It's got even worse since she started seeing Rudi, her life overflowing in overwhelming piles of admin, forms, letters, open cases, invoices for Hanno's university fees, a lease renewal for his place, a quote for the repair of her terrace, which was damaged by spring rains. Finding the time to love someone is a real challenge, and now the rest of her life is in disarray. It feels as though a single breath could send everything tumbling.

Irène's heart skips a beat when she sees Elvire's address on the back of the blue envelope. She opens the window wide and starts to read.

Dear Irène,

I often think of you and all you've done for me.

When we said goodbye, I didn't have the words to thank you properly. It had all happened so fast. I wasn't sure I could even keep the puppet in this flat where I grew up, where my children come to visit me. It exudes death. I put it away in the back of a closet. But even then I couldn't sleep. Still, I can't throw it away. That would be like throwing him *away. My father. You see, I've managed to write it.*

For a few days after you left, I thought I'd rather not have known. Then I hated myself for thinking that. I'm going to be completely honest with you: I don't know how to live with this new information. I'm a big girl but I'm still afraid of ghosts.

When my children were little, I couldn't bear to be away from them. When they left the house for a weekend, I was always terrified something would happen. My husband didn't understand, and I couldn't explain it properly.

Now Raphaël is a father and Mathilde has just got married. Still, that old fear comes back every time they leave me. I hug them so tightly, I find it so difficult to let them go. They know how I feel and call me as soon as they get home. We even joke about it.

After that jihadist killed those children at a Jewish school in Toulouse four years ago, I couldn't sleep. Then again, just a few months ago, when a woman who kept to herself was beaten and thrown from her own window in Belleville, not far from me. Just because she was Jewish. When I get anxious, I struggle to cope. I repaint the walls and fill my house with music and friends. But now I feel as though I have a live-in ghost.

Like in a story I used to read to my children, where a witch lived in the wardrobe. It's awful.

My mother rejected sadness. And now that I've been put in her position, I understand. I hope my children will be cautious, but I don't want them to be plagued by fear. That's no way to live.

So I give them my love. I still remember the terms of endearment my mother, Uncle Rafo, and their friends gave me. Pasharika. Hanoumika. Kokonika de mandel. *Tia Lisa taught me how to play bridge. Tia Eugénie sang love songs in Ladino that enthralled me, even though they always ended badly. Tia Dolly would turn up with her arms full of desserts. I still dream of her rosewater* malabi. *Tio Sento was full of stories. His words alone could carry you from the streets of Cairo to the banks of the Bosporus. I admired the way they could all switch between languages, like jugglers. I believed they only had happy memories. I played with their grandchildren, we grew up together.*

So now we cook to relive those moments. We test twelve recipes for borekitas de muez, *we bicker endlessly about how best to cook meatballs and how to prepare* filas (*if you've never tried them, I'd be delighted to make them for you*). *We never manage to recreate the exact flavour of our memories, but we try.*

I'm learning Ladino, and I'm proud to be able to read my mother's letter in the original.

The story reminds us of our kantigas, *where love is a wave which washes over you, then returns to the sea. But when it retreats, what is left?*

My mother always saved a seat at the table for those we'd lost. Just in case. And that's what she did with him. I've been rereading the postcards you sent me, the ones he sent to his Israeli friend. I'm so glad to see he still talked about her. Maybe they really did love each other until the very end, from opposite sides of the world.

Irène, I don't know if I'll ever get used to this puppet. But I wish I had been given a chance to know Lazar. To watch him repair the hulls of boats and travel with him.

Thanks to you, he really exists. I'm planning to take my children to Prague to look for Kaprova Street, and to visit Thessaloniki with them by my side.

I'll show them the city where Lazar and Allegra fell in love. I'll tell them their grandparents chose life, even if, sometimes, it's the hardest thing to do.

So, to thank you for all that, I'm sending una abrasada, *as we say.*

Elvire

Irène feels Elvire embrace her. The way you hug someone on the dock before they sail out to sea. She imagines Elvire at the beginning of a long journey which will take her to Lazar.

Karl

THEY'RE SITTING SIDE BY SIDE beneath leafy branches in the park. It's that time of day when the sun is softening, giving the skin a golden sheen. It's blurring the dry lines on Eva's face, which is no longer drawn from illness. Her hair is tied back in a grey bun and she's wearing a dark skirt and her usual tired loafers. The fire in her eyes doesn't intimidate Irène any more. Her chest inflates with the joy of seeing her friend again, but she doesn't dare hug her. She knows Eva hates public displays of affection.

Eva's rolled up her white shirt sleeves.

This time, Irène doesn't avert her gaze.

'Tell me,' she says. 'Tell me all about Auschwitz.'

Eva's piercing green eyes seem to measure Irène's resolve.

'Please.'

'Are you sure?' Eva asks, revealing her bad teeth.

'Absolutely.'

Eva leads her to the other side of the barbed-wire fence. Irène clings to the sound of her voice, but fear intrudes on her feelings of tenderness. It feels as though she's walking a tightrope over an abyss. Gradually, she finds a path towards peace, through the horror and loneliness. Irène accepts the pain conveyed in Eva's words, like the passing of a baton. She knows she must protect it. The words keep tumbling from Eva's mouth, and Irène gathers them all, relieved to know it isn't too late. Time speeds and slows. The two women have never been so close. When she's finished, Eva's features fade, and Irène catches a glimpse of her teenage self – naked, trembling from the freezing cold. Irène reaches out to warm her, but the moment she touches her old friend, she wakes to the familiar surroundings of her bedroom.

For a few seconds, her mind floats, trying to cling to the dream. She tries to remember everything Eva told her, but it's gone, not a single word remains. Sadness grips her heart when she realises this moment, which she still feels so keenly, was only a mirage.

*

'You little sneak!' Antoine exclaims. 'How long has this been going on for?'

She's calling him from her car on the way to Berlin.

'Two months. I didn't tell you because it's complicated. He's a descendant, you know. He's linked to one of my investigations.'

'Are you afraid of being excommunicated from the Order of Archivists?' he jokes.

She can't help but smile. 'No, but—'

'Do you often get the urge to sleep with descendants? Because if it's becoming a habit, I think you should get help.'

'It's never happened before!' she protests with a laugh.

Their relationship is so easy that Irène wonders if she may have ignored signs that were there from the beginning. She and Rudi are both naturally obsessive, so they understand one another, and their respective dysfunctions somehow coexist in harmony. Her past lovers would be drawn to her independence, then set about eroding it. But now, for the first time, she doesn't feel like she's under siege in a relationship. She and Rudi know how to be alone when they're together, and how to be together when they're miles apart. Neither of them sleeps well, so they're delighted to spend time together in the middle of the night, making love and chatting on Rudi's balcony at four in the morning. It overlooks the rooftops, gardens, and shadowy courtyards of Kreuzberg: the jewel in his dusty old apartment's crown. They snuggle under a blanket and get lost in the sky as they watch for shooting stars and blinking satellites. They listen for warbles, trills, and rustling from winged or four-legged neighbours.

'He can be a bit brusque, a bit clumsy,' she concedes. 'And he's a worrier. He feeds off society's problems. Then he doesn't know how to step back and take a breath.'

'Well, you have more in common than I expected,' Antoine replies playfully. 'But so far you've only told me about his mind. I hope you're doing more than talking!'

Irène keeps quiet. She'd forgotten about the sensual woman hiding just beneath her skin. But her desire is still there, beneath her deceptive reserve. In his big, strong arms her body has simultaneously softened and reasserted its presence, demanding to feel his weight on top of her, overpowering her, inside her. Only then does her mind surrender to the flow of endorphins. The ghosts vanish.

'So when are you going to introduce us?' asks Antoine.

'Not just yet. He's got to meet his Polish family first.'

'When's the big day?'

'They're all coming to Berlin for lunch today. We have no idea how his father will react. We're all a bit on edge.'

'And how is Hanno taking everything?'

'He's happy I've met someone. Well, you know what he's like, he's very cautious, very wait-and-see. But he and Hermine are also in Berlin at the moment, trying to exorcise bad memories from Christmas. Anyway, it's far too early for them to meet Rudi.'

'If you say so . . . Sometimes I feel as though you have a Victorian chaperone living inside of you, just waiting for you to step over the line so she can smack you on the wrist with her ruler,' he teases before hanging up.

*

Irène spots Agata first, thanks to her height and shock of white hair. She's chosen a pretty flowery blouse, cream trousers, and sandals with silver straps. This investment in her appearance melts Irène's heart. As she takes Rudi's hand, she feels how nervous he is, and gives his fingers one last squeeze.

Roman notices Irène before his mother does, and waves joyfully from behind the customs desk. Julka is talking to her grandmother as the two of them scan the crowd for the Frenchwoman who changed their lives. Irène wonders if they're feeling nervous too. If their trembling legs feel as if they might give out. As they come closer, both parties walk with stiff, solemn steps, though they're trying to look relaxed. In the first minutes of uncertainty, Rudi and Roman shake hands. Irène hugs Agata and Julka. Then the old woman goes up to Rudi and takes his face in her hands.

'I'm so happy I finally get to meet you,' she says in English. 'My brother's son. Aren't you handsome!'

Agata's emotion takes Rudi by surprise. With her pale eyes and lilting accent, a Polish aunt is slipping into the space left by his adoptive grandmother. He bends down, and she takes him in her arms.

Rudi's booked a table for lunch on a terrace overlooking Schlachtensee. His guests are delighted by the idea of dining in such idyllic surroundings, just a few yards from the pale green water, with its swimmers and paddle-boarders. But Rudi struggles to relax. He gets up several times to make calls, and steals a cigarette from Irène, even though he quit years ago.

'I'm sorry,' he says when he sits back down. 'A nurse from the clinic just called. My father isn't doing well. I don't think we'll be able to visit him today.'

Agata's hands tremble so badly she drops her fork.

'What's happened?' she asks in English.

'He's finding it increasingly difficult to speak. The whole thing tires him out and makes him feel isolated. He goes through phases where he's so sad he cuts himself off completely. Sometimes he even gets hostile.'

'How long has he been unwell?' Roman asks.

Rudi replies that it's difficult to know exactly, but about a decade. At first the symptoms were mild, and he put them down to tiredness. Rudi's son was the one who eventually raised the alarm when he noticed his grandfather was forgetting a lot. Two years ago, Karl started getting lost in the street, so they decided it was best to put him in a memory care facility.

'Tell me about him,' Agata says.

'He taught me the virtue of patience,' Rudi replies. 'When you're filming, you have to wait for something to happen. Something you weren't expecting, something that gives meaning and shape to your story. When I was a boy, he'd take me to shoots. I found it fascinating to watch him work. He was constantly on the lookout. That hasn't changed, actually, though he can't hold a camera these days.'

Agata is overcome by emotion at this description. She apologises for speaking Polish and asks Roman to translate.

'When my brother was little, he was always glued to our mother's side. He'd get upset if she left him just for a moment. I had to come up with tricks to distract him. Since Irena told me he was kidnapped, I can't stop thinking about what he must have gone through when they ripped him from her arms.'

They sit in a silence punctuated only by the buzzing of insects, and the distant shouts of divers on the opposite bank. Irène thinks of Bull, the seeker of stolen children, who didn't think it was possible to grow up tall and strong in poisoned soil. Karl built a family and a life, but the poison may still be running quietly through his veins.

'Look,' Rudi says. 'Let's try it. We'll go and assess the situation when we get there.'

Irène is so relieved for Agata she wants to kiss him.

*

The clinic is on a calm green avenue in Zehlendorf. Though the facility is fully secured, the patients live in relative freedom inside, to the extent their condition allows. Since moving here, Karl has seemed less anxious. The staff run afternoon workshops: gardening, singing, or reading aloud. Karl's favourite thing is wandering through the grounds.

They're halfway up a gravel path lined with boxwood and hornbeam hedges when the imposing building comes into view in the centre of a park modelled on an English garden. Rudi points to Karl's window on the second floor. His room looks out over a stone pond full of water lilies. Flower beds are overflowing everywhere they look. Roses, agapanthus, lilacs, echinacea, lupins, and daisies. An explosion of colours and fragrances.

'It's lovely here,' Agata says in English. 'You chose well.'

Ever since they left the car, she's been surprisingly calm. She was so terrified she wouldn't get to see him.

The group sit down under a trellis of purple wisteria while Rudi goes into the building alone. He returns half an hour later, supporting his father and his halting gait.

Irène is moved as she watches his slow, careful steps. She thinks of the radiant young man who ran through the streets of Berlin waving his red flag.

They stand up, but Rudi motions for them to sit back down. There are too many of them, he doesn't want to startle Karl. He leads his father to the next bench and sits down with him there. Then Rudi leans in and talks to his father for a long time. Looking weary, the old man wipes sweat from his brow. His pale eyes have taken on the milky hue of a seashell and his face is scrunched in torment. His son's words slide off him, as if intended for someone else.

Rudi motions for Agata to join them. Before she stands up, she places Irène's hand on her pounding chest. Irène watches Agata's back as she walks away, tall and brave in her Sunday best.

Rudi stands to let Agata sit but keeps his hand on his father's shoulder to reassure him. From where she's sitting, Irène can't tell what he's whispering. She sees Karl turn towards his sister, and Agata smiles, her eyes welling with tears. But her love for her brother, and all those years of waiting, meet nothing but sadness in Karl. A man deprived of words and his own memories. He glances at her, but the light in his eyes has gone dim. He turns away.

Irène's stomach flips. She feels so bad for Agata, for all of them.

'It's crazy how much they look alike,' Julka whispers.

They're all mesmerised as they look from Karl to Agata, taking in their blue eyes, prominent cheekbones, white hair, and tall foreheads. Age has eroded their differences.

Wita's orphans are both right here in front of Irène – so similar, and yet total strangers.

Rudi tries to guide Karl's attention back to Agata, but he doesn't respond well. He shuts down completely and pushes his son's hand away.

This isn't going to work, Irène thinks. *What a disaster.*

Just then, Agata starts to sing. At first, it's just a quiet hum, but it grows as it travels through the air, carried by her deep, trembling voice. Then the melody emerges, like a river finding its true course. Its rhythm is a perfect match to the pace of a mother rocking her infant. And as it soothes Karl, it instils in him a uniquely Slavic melancholy – the same melancholy he drank with his mother's milk, without knowing it would never leave him.

Karl's been stock-still since the first bars. Agata carries on singing and gently takes his hand. He doesn't push her away. A range of emotions cross his face as he stares at Agata, listening with all his soul.

Julka quietly hums the words beside Irène. Roman is silent. Both of them drink in the fleeting grace of the moment.

Karl joins in at the third verse. His hoarse voice stumbles on consonants he hasn't heard in years, sounds he's brought up from the farthest depths of his memory. Gradually his voice grows stronger and he sings along, remembering the words that used to lull him to sleep. His eyes brim with tears.

Agata clasps his hand tightly in hers, uncertain whether she's singing or crying now. There's not a dry eye among them.

You can't fix people, Irène thinks as she wipes her eyes, *but if you can give back just a sliver of what was stolen from them – even if you're not quite sure what that is – then nothing is truly lost.*

Julka, Niclas, Hanno, Hermine, and Lilly

THEY STAYED A LITTLE LONGER with Karl before Rudi took him back to his room, exhausted by the intensity of the experience. As the others walked towards the car park, Rudi told Irène that a part of him hadn't quite believed it was true until he heard his father sing in Polish. Sometimes reality is so strange that it seems more like something straight out of a deranged writer's head. The brain tolerates it without buying in.

'What did you say to him earlier?' Irène asks.

Rudi explains that he had no idea how to go about it, so the truth just came out. He heard himself saying words which could have devastated his father. *Your mother died in a concentration camp, you have a sister in Poland, she's come a long way to see you.* Once the words were out, they floated in the air like bubbles so fragile they'd burst at the slightest touch. Maybe because he didn't believe them himself. But Agata's voice gave them substance. Her voice rekindled the love his mother put into the lullaby when he was a boy. No one will ever know precisely what doors she opened in Karl's heart. An indecipherable transformation.

'It's all thanks to you,' he concluded, holding her close.

Irène felt her legs wobble from the intensity of it all, her red eyes blinking in the light.

'Given everything that's happened, should we invite everyone over to mine?' he asks.

'Everyone?'

'The Warsaw contingent . . . and our children,' he replies with a smile.

*

They've switched on the coloured lanterns on his balcony, unwound the extension cables, and covered the table with white paper which was immediately baptised with a few drops of Prosecco. The guests take in the fiery-red dusk sky. Agata is enamoured of this city where nature is on every corner: on balconies, in courtyards, and in the acres of parks and forests where oval lakes gleam. All the green makes her feel she can breathe easier.

With her ballerina bun and strappy dress, Julka lithely slips from conversation to conversation. Hanno and Hermine are filling glasses, delighted by the impromptu party. Out of the corner of their eyes, they study the documentary filmmaker who's just entered their lives. He welcomed them warmly, then introduced his son Niclas, who looks a bit like a Viking, and his daughter, Niclas's younger sister, Lilly, a short brunette in thick glasses who casually throws out biting comments about the state of the world. The children are all roughly the same age, apart from Julka, whose position as a teacher impresses them.

Irène hears them chatting in a Globish that artfully blends English, German, and Polish. She wants to capture the moment. When she was younger, she used to imagine that a camera was nestled right inside her pupils. All she needed to do was blink to snap a photo.

Rudi clinks a spoon against his glass.

'When Irène first contacted me, I somehow knew she was going to upend my quiet life. And I reacted like a bear – as I often do. I spend my time proving that the stories that reassure us are too simple to be true. But when it comes to me, well, that's a different story. So it's a good thing Irène insisted, because otherwise I would never have known my father could sing in Polish. And you all wouldn't be here. When I look at you, I see a Frenchwoman, Poles, Germans, and several generations reunited – a microcosm of Europe. The war devastated Wita's life, my father's life, and Agata's too, but it's peace that's brought us together tonight. So I'd like us to drink to Europe, which Václav Havel aptly called the "homeland of our homelands". I'm going to forget how often it disappoints me and remember instead that it was established to preserve peace. So here's to Europe and to peace!'

The children raise their glasses.

'To a humanitarian Europe,' Hanno says.

'To a feminist Europe,' Julka chimes in.

'To an inclusive Europe,' Lilly adds.

'Go explain all that to Kaczyński and Orbán,' Roman says, laughing.

Night has fallen, enveloping the city in a muted light, as if millions of fireflies are sparkling in the sky. Rudi is getting to know his cousin Roman in German. Out on the terrace, the kids are chatting as they take in the Kreuzberg skyline.

Irène goes to sit with Agata and Julka, trying to decipher the reverie in the old woman's eyes.

'You've given my *babcia* a wonderful gift,' Julka says. 'And not just for her, for all of us.'

It's also a gift for Irène. To have got to their story just in time.

She asks the name of the lullaby.

'"In Wotjus's Ashtray",' Julka replies. 'Babcia would sing it to me when I was little.'

'What's it about?'

'A spark leaps out of an ashtray and promises a boy it'll tell him a long, beautiful story. But every time, the story stops when the spark dies out. By the end, Wotjus doesn't believe it any more. He knows the story will only last until the spark goes out.'

'About as cheerful as "The Little Match Girl," Irène remarks.

'That's true,' Julka says. 'But I've actually never found it sad.'

'Who wants to go dancing?' Lilly asks the room.

Hanno, Hermine, Niclas and Julka go along, kissing their parents goodbye before disappearing into the Berlin night.

Agata wants to go back to her hotel to rest so she can visit her brother again in the morning.

'I have so many years of love to give him,' she tells Irène, her eyes welling up again.

Before she leaves, Irène finally shows her the locket. Agata is deeply moved when she sees the drawing of her brother hidden inside.

'That's how old he was when I last saw him. Who drew this?'

'I think it was your mother.'

'I don't remember ever seeing her draw,' Agata replies, puzzled.

A new mystery, Irène thinks.

'I have a treasure to show you too,' Agata says as she exhumes from her bag a few lines written in pencil on a piece of worn cardboard. She's too tired to translate them, so Roman takes over.

My dearest sister, I'm writing from a cattle truck. They say we're going to a labour camp. Take care of Adzia. Don't worry, I'll be back soon. All my love.

Above the note, Wita has scribbled Maria's name and address.

'She wrote it on the train to Auschwitz and dropped the message on the track. A railway worker brought it to my aunt,' Agata explains.

Irène stares at the scrap of cardboard in stunned silence.

Jean

WHEN IRÈNE READ WITA'S MESSAGE, memories she'd stored in the farthest reaches of her mind suddenly resurfaced. She was so shaken she struggled to hide it. Back in Treblinka, looking at the railway line, she'd felt something similar, something she couldn't quite pinpoint, a beacon in the fog.

She told Rudi she had to make a quick trip to Bad Arolsen and back, just twenty-four hours.

'Is it something serious?' he asked, concerned.

'I need to visit my grandfather.'

Not in the literal sense, of course. Jean had been laid to rest in a small cemetery in the eastern suburbs of Paris with his parents, wife, and elder brother, who died during the Battle of Sedan in 1940 – one of the soldiers that the French government had preferred to forget about. Their sacrifice seemed to heighten the shame the country felt at its rapid defeat.

The day Jean was buried was perhaps the only day the shy man had ever shone, through homages delivered by his grieving friends. Irène remembers his distant smile and the cap that was always glued to his balding head. She remembers his smell too: grease, tobacco, and sweat. Railways were his world. Along with his evening card game or a corner table at the local bistro, Chez Paulette. Men of his generation understood one another. They kept each other company on the bad days.

As a child, Irène spent most of her time with her nose in a book. Jean only read the Sunday sports pages, but he loved it when she would tell him about *The Count of Monte Cristo* or *The Knight of Maison-Rouge*.

Then, one morning he didn't wake up. The discreet departure was just like him – he'd never liked to cause a fuss. His rail worker friends came in a steady flow to the small suburban house to drink ratafia and shed a tear. At twelve, Irène was bored in her black dress. She wished she could just read alone in a corner, so she eventually slipped into her grandfather's workshop. She still remembers the smell of damp wood, the old bronze lamps rusting on shelves alongside obsolete railway signs, and a yellowing blanket featuring a train engine puffing smoke out its stack beneath the words PARIS-EST.

She opened the desk drawers and found a notebook. She flipped through it, but didn't understand the significance of the difficult names or messages, which all seemed to be the echo of a single cry. It's strange, how attuned children are. Irène immediately knew that these messages were secrets – secrets that now belonged to her.

For the first several months, she hid it behind her books. She reread it so often that she learned some of the messages by heart. But after a while she lost interest and stored the notebook in the back of a wardrobe. When she left France, she carefully placed the notebook in a folder which bore her grandfather's name: Jean Deslorieux. It's travelled with her everywhere she's gone, from her university dormitory in Tübingen to the attic of the house she lived in with Wilhelm, and now her current home. She's rather surprised she kept it.

Maybe because it was the only thing that connected her to the grandfather she'd barely known.

*

'There you are,' she whispers when she finds the folder at the bottom of a box.

The ink has faded and the pages are fusty. Jean's handwriting is meticulous.

Though he didn't attend secondary school, he carefully transcribed these names full of consonants. Some of them, like Marcel or Fernande, had been familiar to Irène as a child. But the ones she'd never heard before fascinated her: Jankiel, Pinkus, Rivka, and so on.

Now she's reading them again.

Some of the messages urge friends or relatives to enquire about children the authors were separated from after their arrest. They make sure to remind the reader that the children are French. Others ask their concierge or a female neighbour to take their children in, appealing to their kind hearts and the grace of God. They apologise for having no money left to give. Sometimes they mention hiding places in flats they were forced to leave: *take whatever you'd like.*

Most of the authors are trying to reassure their correspondent: *I'm well, please don't worry. I'll be back soon. I'm made of stern stuff.*

One expression pops up again and again: *unknown destination.*

It runs through the letters like a terrible thread. Looms over the reassuring words and optimistic conjectures.

I'm headed to an unknown destination.

We're on our way to an unknown destination.

I'm travelling to an unknown destination in a cattle truck.

Maybe we're going to Poland, or somewhere else.

They send their love to their children and beloved husbands. They give final instructions. *Be good, be brave. Work hard. Be patient.*

Jean transcribed these messages dutifully, leaving blanks where the handwriting was illegible or crossed out.

One message breaks her heart. It's written by a boy who begins, *From Titi to Mummy dearest: I know I'll servive and that I'll see you agin! I don't know how I groo up so fast. I'm a man now.*

Irène wonders for a moment about the spelling mistakes and decides Jean was so meticulous he copied them as they were from the original.

Like when she was a girl, she can't tear herself from these words of love and distress.

When she was twelve, she didn't understand why her grandfather had taken the time to record these messages, or where all these people taken from their loved ones were going.

Now she knows all too well.

It's taken thirty-eight years.

Years of exile and growing up. It's taken decades of tying back together the threads of unravelled lives. Meeting people like Jean. Humble people full of secrets.

How many times has she heard about these messages dropped onto train tracks without realising the connection?

Rail workers would collect them and try to send them on. To Poland, Czechoslovakia, or France.

In 1942, Jean was nineteen. He did maintenance on the Paris-Est network, between the Bobigny and Le Bourget stations, where the deportation convoys began their journey east.

She imagines how awful it must have been to see the children reaching through the barbed wire. To hear the moans and screams rise from the carriages. She imagines how powerless he felt.

He could gather the scraps of folded paper that fell from the wagons. That much he could do.

Maybe he was afraid their messages would get lost. Sometimes there was no address, other times no one was there.

It must have taken him so long to copy the messages, one by one. And yet he didn't tell a soul.

Irène sees herself in his painstaking devotion.

She's spent most of her life in the archives, but she forgot she had one of her very own. It's taken her so long to realise how valuable it is.

Did this notebook somehow steer her towards her calling?

She thought she'd reinvented herself. That she'd come to the ITS by chance, forged her own path.

But all these years, Irène has been looking for the people Jean saw leave. Trying to find out what lay at the end of the journey and collect any traces left behind for their descendants. It's incredible to realise that she and Jean share the same life's work.

Who knows? Maybe she's been walking to meet him all this time.

Acknowledgements

The investigations and characters in this novel are all fictional. Though I include elements of the Arolsen Archives' true history, I took certain necessary liberties to develop the plot and narrative structure.

The story behind this novel began on a winter's day in 2020, when my friend Aurélie Serfaty-Bercoff told me that the Arolsen Archives held administrative documents from Robert Desnos's imprisonment in various concentration camps. I wondered why I'd never heard of the archives before, particularly since they were founded immediately after the war. Fuelled by curiosity, I began conducting research and happened upon an article by Élise Karlin about the process of returning objects found in the camps to victims' descendants. I'd like to thank her here, because the idea for this novel took shape as I read her text.

That said, I think it had been brewing inside me for some time. At the age of twelve, World War II and the Holocaust entered my life through books and films—and they've been with me ever since. So I think it fair to say that this novel is the product of a deep-seated need to write about these terrible events.

This book is based on significant historical research. I am deeply grateful to the witnesses, historians, journalists, sociologists, and artists whose books, work, and films inspired the fictional material in the novel. I'd like to extend special thanks to Laurent Joly for his invaluable and attentive reading.

Thank you to Nathalie Letierce-Liebig, Coordinator of the Arolsen Archives Research Department, for so warmly welcoming my project and for tirelessly answering my many questions. The details she shared about her work and her commitment to the cause helped me to embody Irène, my fictional archivist.

Many thanks to Renata Masna and Beata Petkiewicz as well as to the staffs of the Pod Zegarem Museum, the Teatr NN in Lublin, and the Jewish Historical Institute in Warsaw. Thank you to Katarzyna Kubicius, head of information and research at the Polish Red Cross, and to the director of the Warsaw Rising Museum for their time and kindness.

Thank you to François Azar and Abraham Bengio for their precious knowledge of Ladino and the Jewish community of Salonica.

To Georges Sougné for allowing me to join him during a deeply moving meeting with a Holocaust victim's descendant.

To Véronique Dubois, who told me her story and shared the poignant fates of many members of her father's family.

To my editor, Juliette Joste, for our long conversations about the characters and investigations, for her high standards and eagle eye, and for believing in the novel from day one.

To my agent, Susanna Lea, for her enthusiastic support, her intelligence, and her sense of humour.

Thank you to Olivier Nora for placing his trust in me, and to the entire Grasset team.

I'd also like to thank my "beta-readers" who brought me joy in moments of doubt: Bénédicte Bagot, Jacques Fraenkel, Sarah Gastel, Marguerite Martin, and Marion Riva. And most especially Tatiana de Rosnay, Alexia Stresi, and Julie Printzac, talented novelists and excellent readers, for their invaluable advice.

Thank you to Maren Baudet-Lackner for the talent and literary and historical rigor she brought to the English-language editions of the text.

And to Zoe Yang for her enthusiasm and for placing this story in British readers' hands.

Thank you to my family and to Ninnog.